QL 4

A NOVEL

James Garrison

TouchPoint
Press

QL 4 by James Garrison
Published by TouchPoint Press
Jonesboro, Arkansas
www.touchpointpress.com

ISBN 10: 1-946920-00-2
ISBN 13: 978-1-946920-00-3

First Edition.

Editor: Kimberly Coghlan
Front Cover Design: Geoffrey Garrison

Visit the author at https://jamesgarrison-author.com/

Printed in the United States of America.

QL 4 was a highway in South Vietnam. In 1969, anyone going south from Saigon into the Mekong Delta would follow this national route, traversing an expanse of green rice paddies, passing through busy towns and quiet villages, and crossing wide fingers of the Mekong River by ferry. Squat red-and-white concrete posts marked the highway as "QL 4." These concrete markers—old and battered and faded—mimicked those on the country roads of France.

"He saw the Jungle of his life and the lurking Beast; then, while he looked, perceived it, as by a stir of the air, rise huge and hideous, for the leap that was to settle him." —The Beast in the Jungle *by Henry James*

QL 4 has followed a long and steep road from 1970 to the present. Along the way I had help from many, both family and friends. I want especially to thank my wife June, who both suffered with and sustained me through much of this journey, and my son Geoff, who suggested I write the book and then found himself contributing his editing skills to the text and artist's eye to the cover. My daughter, Kathryn, who can be a meticulous writing critic, served mainly as advisor, super mom, and crime fighter in the wings. Also, I'm thankful for the suggestions of my editors and readers, especially Eric McIntyre and Jack Yeoman, and others who have helped me channel my writing over the years, including Susy Kramer, Alison Young, and Johnnie Bernhard, who as my agent went above and beyond the call of duty.

PROLOGUE

SERGEANT JOHNSON SHOVED THE DOOR OPEN. Tepid air redolent of fish sauce and incense washed out over them. Staring into the gloom, all Bell could make out was a dark corridor lit by a single, naked bulb in a distant stairwell.

"Move, move," ran through his mind, but "ah, fuck!" short-circuited the signal. Johnson was almost to the stairs before the message reached his feet. His first day on patrol and here he was following some Black Panther, who probably despised his newbie white ass, into a dark building looking for a fucking fugitive or something.

Long shadows cast by the bulb danced along the floor and the walls as Johnson bounded up the stairs. Bell gripped the butt of his .45, then pressing the billy club to his thigh, finally moved. He hustled to catch up, but when he reached the stairs, he slowed and searched out each step in the shadows.

A scurrying noise below startled him. Jerking his head around, he struggled with his .45, then dropped it back in the holster. Two steps down was an old mama-san, her wrinkled face a pale mask.

"*Di di, di di*," he said, "go, go," about the only Vietnamese words he knew. He motioned her back. The sweat trickled in long streams down his sides. His back and arms felt like he'd stepped into a warm shower.

Glancing up, he caught the flicker of Johnson's shadow at the bend in the stairwell. *I need to stay with him*, he thought, and charged up the steps two at a time. The flop-flop of the woman's steps behind him sounded as loud as the thud of their jungle boots.

In the upstairs corridor, he stumbled to a halt inches behind Johnson and stared up at the faded fatigue collar and the furrows in Johnson's neck, glistening with perspiration below the helmet liner. The tall MP's shadow to the front filled the corridor and darkened a row of closed doors.

Johnson pounded on the first door and called out, "Roberts?"

From inside came a stream of Vietnamese, but the door remained closed.

From behind, a shrill voice echoed in the corridor: "MP, who you want?"

"Roberts," said Johnson without looking around.

"There," the old mama-san said, shoving past Bell. Steadying herself with one hand on the wall, she hobbled by Johnson and stretched out a thin arm toward the last door. "There." The door was set back in a recessed frame, solid and forbidding within the shadows.

Slipping past her, Johnson hammered on it. As he pounded a second time, Bell edged around the mama-san and stopped across the hall.

He didn't want to be here. Anywhere but here. Well, almost anywhere. Back in Chapel Hill would be good.

No one answered Johnson's pounding.

"He no leave." The old woman's voice lashed out at them. "There!" She jabbed a skeletal finger toward the door.

Johnson grabbed the doorknob and gave it a twist. The smell was the first thing to hit Bell.

CHAPTER ONE
Road to the Delta

HE SHOULD'VE GONE TO CANADA, taught high school, any number of things other than graduate school. He should've followed up on the slot in the reserves a friendly dean had found for him. Now look where he was.

The deuce-and-a-half lurched through a pothole and then jolted down an embankment and across a pontoon bridge over a narrow river. Above them loomed a jumbled span of concrete collapsed into a jagged "V." On the other side, a bridge guard, his M-16 slung upside down on one shoulder, slouched against a mud bunker as if he were holding it up.

From the bed of the truck, Private First Class Justin Bell stared back at the montage of bunker, ruined bridge, highway, and rice paddies receding in the distance and merging with the bright green-meeting-blue line of the horizon. A bicycle bearing a wizened old man hunched over the handlebars disappeared in a swirling cloud of dust only to reappear far behind the truck as a gaunt wraith borne along by the wind. Beside the road, a woman in black pajama pants, a white shirt, and a conical *lan* trudged head down, seeming in the shimmery heat to jog in place, framed by a yoke with bouncing baskets at each end.

Early on, they talked and tried a few hands of poker, but by the outskirts of Saigon, the potholes and broken asphalt forced them to fall silent and move apart, each into his own reverie. Braced against crates of fresh food and supplies, they hunkered down on their duffel bags to gawk at the scenery.

"Where we going?" yelled Hodge from beside him. Bell had met Charles Hamilton Hodges the fourth, or just plain "Hodge," only a few days ago in Long Binh, within a week of each arriving in country.

"Van Loc," Bell yelled back. "Other side of the river on QL 4."

The truck crossed another temporary bridge and bounced past a crew of U.S. Army Engineers, then bumped and swayed onto freshly laid pavement. As the truck picked up speed, the tires sang on the new asphalt, and the rhythm became to Bell's ears a marching cadence from MP training, the one when the lifers had gone. He sat up and jabbed Hodge's arm.

"Hey, Hodge," he yelled. "Your platoon ever march to this?"

Hodge blinked up at him from the truck bed where he had slid down against his duffel bag. Bell rendered the cadence, off-key and monotone, to the tune of "When Johnny Comes Marching Home."

They issued us some jungle boots,

Hurrah, hurrah,

They issued us some jungle boots,

Hurrah, hurrah,

They issued us some jungle boots,

So we could run when Charlie shoots,

And we'll all be dead in the winter of '69.

Hodge echoed the last refrain, and then they both fell silent. Ignoring them, the others dozed or stared through the side slats at the countryside.

Hodge gave a long sigh. "God, I miss Glenda." A theme, Bell had learned in the short time he'd known the man, as regular as the click of the rock caught in the truck's rear wheel. Shaking his head, Hodge leaned back and closed his eyes, his sun-bleached hair a wind-blown pompadour above a tan face.

Bell slumped down, elbows on his knees, and stared at the grit-covered bed of the truck. He listened to the sound of the tires, unable to lose the tune and the words that kept repeating themselves.

Dead in the winter of '69, dead in the winter of '69, dead, dead, dead.

The deuce-and-a-half left the road in a clatter of gravel and skidded to a halt, throwing bodies, duffel bags, and crates forward against the cab. Dust and diesel fumes enveloped them all.

Pulling himself up by the side slats, Bell stared through the haze at a pagoda pocked with holes. At the base was a recessed doorway, boarded up. At the apex, an ARVN sentry, M-16 resting aslant on a sandbag, stared down at them, a cloud of cigarette smoke wreathing his face. Next to the pagoda was a cinder-block structure surrounded by coils of concertina wire.

"Okay, you FNGs, get your sorry asses outta there."

The hoarse yell came from the driver's side. Within minutes after exiting the plane at Bien Hoa, *they* were the "fucking new guys," entitled only to scorn and abuse from the veterans like Sergeant Hayes.

Walking past, Hayes banged on the wooden slats. "*Di di, di di!*"

Hayes' fatigues were starched, tailored, and tapered at the ankles, not rumpled and bloused like theirs. His cap, with its raised front displaying his staff-sergeant's rank, reminded Bell of a photo he'd seen of a German field marshal.

They clambered to their feet as Hayes lowered the rear gate and pointed to two soldiers.

"Andrews, Higgins, you two are stayin' here in My Tho. Get your shit outta the truck."

Andrews and Higgins grabbed their duffel bags and hopped down.

"What's this place like, Sarge?" Higgins asked, dropping his duffel bag to the ground. "I mean, is it okay?" Bell watched sweat trickle down sallow valleys on Higgins' neck. Glad it wasn't him being left here, next to this battle-scarred pagoda.

"Sure, it's okay. Never been overrun." Hayes, squinting, stopped to scratch his crotch. "Well, not since Tet in '68. 'Course, Charlie took every district capital down here." He chuckled. "Little fuckers left quicker'n shit through a goose when we came back."

That didn't sound comforting to Bell. Tet was just around the corner, January, or was it February? He started to ask, but remembered his rule. Never draw the attention of a lifer, much less irritate him. Or show your ignorance.

"What's that over there, that smoke?" Higgins pointed to a column of black smoke rising above the rice paddy on the other side of the road. In the distance was a raised area surrounded by sandbag walls and rolls of concertina wire. Bunkers guarded each corner, and a lopsided two-story structure—a large bunker topped by a tower—stood in the center.

"That smoke?" Hayes snorted. "Burnin' shit. Firebase Schroeder. Used to be Ninth Division, but they're fucking gone. Viet-damnation or some shit like that." He spat in the dirt.

The door on the passenger's side of the truck swung open, and a lumbering bear of a sergeant eased out of the cab. Turning, he came toward them, arms swaying out to his sides like a sumo wrestler.

"What d'ya say!" Hayes threw one hand up, as if in greeting. "Sergeant Beadle!" He turned back to Higgins. "Sarge here can tell you all about this place. He's gonna be your new operations sergeant for the whole fucking delta."

Sergeant Beadle placed his hands on his hips and stretched. Unlike Hayes, Beadle's fatigues were unpressed and sagged around his shoulders and legs, even though as a master sergeant, he outranked Hayes.

Beadle grinned at Hayes. "Carry on, Sarge. You're doing a fine job." He turned his grin on Higgins and added, "I'll let the expert tell it."

Bell had been surprised—shocked to his Southern roots—the first time he'd heard that voice and the clear, precise words coming from this huge, black army sergeant. Better English than Bell had ever spoken, even with studied practice in his university days.

A convoy of ARVN trucks roared past, kicking up eddies of dust. As it settled on their new jungle fatigues and boots, Higgins and Andrews hefted duffel bags onto shoulders and headed toward the block building. Hayes followed but paused at the entrance to point to a gravel path between the pagoda and the main building.

"Latrine's back there. Or you can piss out here like the gooks." He pointed up at the sentry.

Bell and Hodge were the only ones to take the path to the back.

The latrine was a wooden shack on cinder blocks with chicken wire around the top, a tin roof, and a thousand flies. Shunning their welcome, Bell backed down the steps and let Hodge go past.

"Be my guest," he said. Hodge grabbed the door, gasped, and then plunged inside, letting the door slam shut behind him.

Bell found a dusty patch of weeds next to the pagoda and spent a long minute studying its walls. The upper levels had been demolished, leaving three stories of pitted and faded red brick. Here and there, scraggly vines had struggled out of cracks and in the dry season withered like knotted hair. Several holes had been punched in the rear wall, and a jagged opening at the bottom was big enough for a ten-year-old to scramble through.

Waiting for Hodge, Bell strolled over to the opening. As he bent to look inside, Hodge reappeared, fastening his belt and slamming the latrine door.

"Come on," Hodge called, his voice low. "Let's get the hell back." He started toward the path between the buildings.

"Hey, man, wait." Bell motioned to him. "I want to see what's in here."

"What the hell for? What if we offend somebody's ancestors?"

"Oh, for Christ's sake, the place's been trashed. Nobody gives a shit."

Hodge waved his hand toward the top of the pagoda. "This mother could fall down anytime, right smack on my sweet ass."

Bell rapped his knuckles on the wall. "Solid as a rock."

He stooped low and slipped through the opening—and promptly stumbled and fell to his knees on a pile of loose bricks. The first thing he noticed as he got up was the musty smell of damp decay and dust.

"Ah, fuck," said Hodge outside. But after a moment, he followed.

They were in a small room. Light seeped through the holes in the walls and broken ceiling, but the corners were dark, and most of the room was in twilight. A single ray of sun lit up one wall as if focused there by a projector.

A lizard scuttered across the rubble toward a dark corner, then another and another. Moving forward, Bell swept a spider web away from his face, and something crawled along his neck. He smacked it off. In one corner, he could see a black mass that seemed to pulsate and move as one.

Not only spiders and bugs and lizards, but snakes and other poisonous things crept into Bell's mind. Followed by thoughts of booby traps, what they kept talking about in training: Bouncing Betties, Pungie sticks, grenades with trip wires. He shook off the feeling. *Not likely, not next to an MP compound.*

Once his eyes adjusted to the light, he could make out on the far wall a closed door covered with lusterless yellow lacquer, and to his right, a broken altar. In front of the altar lay a loose bouquet of crumbling flowers. The sunlit wall held faded images of a pagoda, rice paddies, palm trees, and water buffalo.

Bell heard a screen door slam. Footsteps sounded along the gravel path, and someone swore in a rising voice.

"Told you the cocksucker'd fuck us over, didn't I? Huh? Didn't I? Goddamn it!"

Bell and Hodge both stood still next to the sunlit wall. It was Hayes.

"That's the last shit I'm moving for you people, by God." A hoarse two-packs-a-day growl, not Hayes. "They're watching you. Roberts is scared shitless, says the CID has eyes down there,"

"Avery. We'll take care of him." Hayes again. The steps were approaching the pagoda.

"That nigger captain—"

"Gone before the monsoons. Count on it."

"What about that black turd out there?" The growl had become a snarl.

"Beadle? Man, they tagged that mother for a load of booze missing out of the port. Sent the fucker down here to keep him on ice."

"He's not with us. He's an unknown."

"He can't..." Hayes' voice faded, as if he had turned away.

Bell could hear boots crunching in the gravel, back toward the main building or the latrine. Moving carefully, he picked his way across the rubble to the opening and crouched down on a pile of bricks to peer out. Hodge followed but stayed back from the opening.

The second voice belonged to a short, bantam-rooster of a sergeant wearing camouflage fatigues and a green beret and carrying a thin briefcase. Taking a last drag on a cigarette, the Green Beret flipped it toward the pagoda, then he and Hayes moved away. Their voices became indistinct.

"Let's go," whispered Hodge.

Bell waved him back. "Wait, wait," he hissed. "Let 'em leave." He wanted to see what this was about; more importantly, he didn't want to be seen.

The two outside continued arguing in low, angry voices. Then the Green Beret held out the briefcase but pulled it back before Hayes could take it. In one swift motion, Hayes grabbed the smaller man by the throat, lifted him off the ground, and jerked the briefcase away from him.

The Green Beret broke free and raised his empty hands, palms out, his voice rising. "That gook major's fucking crazy. You're all fucking crazy. I'm goin' back to the World, and you motherfuckers are—"

In a muffled clatter, Bell slid sideways off the pile of loose bricks.

"What the...!" said Hodge, grabbing Bell's arm.

Outside, the two men fell silent. There was a soft scrunch of gravel in the path, coming toward the pagoda. Then it stopped.

After a long moment, Bell heard a hoarse whisper, then a pair of boots hurrying away, scattering gravel as they went. A few seconds later, the second pair followed, going back toward the main building.

The screen door closed with a dull thud.

Bell remained stretched out, leaning back on his elbows amid the brick debris, while Hodge crawled forward and squatted to one side of the opening.

"No one in sight," he whispered.

"Let's get outta here," Bell said, twisting over onto his hands and knees. He scrambled off the brick pile, past Hodge, and outside. One hand on the pagoda wall, he blinked in the sunlight and looked around. Nothing moved, not even a breeze in the dead weeds. Only a few muffled sounds came from the adjacent building. Side-by-side, they slipped across the yard to the path. As they turned the corner of the main building, a creaking noise caused Bell to glance back. Someone had opened the screen door and was watching them from the shadows. Then the door gently closed.

"What was that about?" Hodge asked once they were out front, weaving their way through the razor wire.

"No fucking idea," Bell said. He stopped and gave a furtive look toward the entrance to the low block building, then brushed dirt off the back of his fatigues. *We weren't supposed to hear that. Hayes figures out we did, we're fucked.*

All he said aloud was, "We better watch it, Hodge. The bastard saw us."

They joined Beadle and the two other FNGs in the shade of the truck. Not long after, Hayes—carrying the contested briefcase—came out of the sandbag entrance to the MP compound. Approaching them, he motioned with his free hand toward the deuce-and-a-half.

"Let's go, scumbags." His eyes fixed on Bell's, lingered a few seconds, and then shifted to Beadle. "Not talking to you, of course, Sergeant Beadle." A forced smile crossed Hayes' face.

Beadle returned a hard look. "No, I am sure you *were* not, and I am *quite* sure that these gentlemen do not qualify as scumbags either."

Hayes ignored this and pointed across the road to Firebase Schroeder and the column of black smoke. "Guess that's not shit burning. They got hit last night." He pressed his lips together and slowly shook his head, still staring across the highway. "Lots of fucking VC around here. You boys oughta be glad you're going on south with us." He spat in the dirt by the rear tire, turned on his heel, and stalked away, toward the cab of the deuce-and-a-half.

CHAPTER TWO
A French Villa

IT WAS AN OLD COLONIAL BUILDING, two stories high with an offset third story at the rear, a hotel or villa or something like that. Or a movie-set fortress on the Spanish Main. At the very top was a wooden guard tower covered by a slanted tin roof and surrounded by a truncated pyramid of green sandbags. But the stucco sides of this villa looked freshly whitewashed and clean.

A billboard at the gate greeted them:

Welcome

Headquarters and 1st Platoon

118th Military Police Company

Van Loc, RVN

Beyond the sign, the gravel road they had taken off QL 4 continued on for a hundred yards or so through a grove of palms and banana trees and ended where the trees framed a bright landscape of green rice paddies and blue sky.

The truck rolled through the gate, past a sandbag bunker with a narrow window shielded by chicken wire. The guard inside gave a flaccid wave of his hand and then looked back down at whatever he was reading.

To the right of the villa were more stucco buildings, mildewy and decrepit, separated from the MP compound by a tall, wire fence and twenty yards of packed dirt. As soon as the deuce-and-a-half skidded to a halt, the dirt area filled three or four deep with children, a few waving and shouting, the smaller ones thrusting upturned hands through the holes in the fence—but most just staring in silence.

Slamming the driver's door shut, Sergeant Hayes, still clutching his briefcase, came around to the back. He pounded on the sides.

"Bell, Hodges! Get your butts outta there. This is your new

home."

Bell grunted, "Fuck you," under his breath and stumbled to help Hodge undo the rear gate. Grabbing their duffel bags, they climbed down as Hayes ejected a stream of tobacco juice onto the metal runway at their feet.

"Get your shit inside." Hayes jerked his thumb toward the entrance at the corner of the building, a screen door protected by a row of 55-gallon drums and a waist-high wall of sandbags. "You gotta sign in. Sergeant Beadle here's taking your friends on down to Can Tho."

On the vehicle's passenger side, Beadle ambled toward them, taking his time and surveying his new surroundings.

"Unload those fucking crates," Hayes barked at the two GIs still in the truck. "And get Beadle's shit outta there." He pointed to a duffel bag and two large suitcases, then gave the black sergeant a sly smirk. "Unless the man wants to stay down there."

"I shall return," said Beadle, giving a benign smile and dipping his head.

Turning abruptly, Hayes waved a hand over his shoulder for Bell and Hodge to follow him.

"Hey, Sarge," said Hodge, bending under the weight of his duffel bag, "how long you been here?"

"Long enough," Hayes said. He held the screen door open for them.

"This place ever been hit?" Bell asked, thinking of My Tho.

Hayes didn't answer. He shoved past them and led the way down a narrow corridor that ran the length of the building. The exterior wall was solid and stuccoed about waist high, then topped by thick columns and latticework covered with screens and protected from the elements by an overhanging roof. The walls and air held a slight vibration that intensified as they advanced. From the rear of the building came the dull hum of a diesel generator.

Halting at a door on their left, Hayes said, "Orderly room. Leave your shit out here."

Inside was a large, open area brightly lit by fluorescent lights like a schoolroom or office back in the World. Bell glanced around, taking it all in: gray concrete floor, bare white walls, high ceiling. Two gray interior doors, one closed, one open. On the closed door was a stenciled sign: "First Sergeant Quarters" and "First Sergeant Ronald Dietz." Several yards away was a partly open door with another stenciled sign: "Commanding Officer," and beneath it on a slide-in panel, "Capt. Reginald Templeton."

The only furnishings were some gray filing cabinets, a couple of chairs, and two gray metal desks. As they entered, a Spec. 4 clerk behind one gave them a smile and quick nod; then he resumed his typing.

At the second desk sat the first sergeant, or what Bell could see of him: pressed uniform shirt and an elliptical crew cut. He didn't look up when they entered but continued staring at a small stack of papers in front of him.

Bell and Hodge waited stiffly until the head came up, revealing a gaunt, red face, hooked nose, and bloodshot eyes.

When the first sergeant didn't speak, Bell said, "PFC Justin Bell, sir, re—"

"Don't call me sir, you friggin moron. It's First Sergeant or Top." His fingers crimped the edges of the paper he was holding, and his face grew redder.

"I wasn't thinking—"

"Get your head out of your ass, *if* you want to stay here."

The room was silent except for the keys striking the typewriter. The fluorescent lights pulsed, dimmed, and then returned to their original brightness.

"Yes, First Sergeant."

"Get your shit together, and we'll all go home healthy and happy." Dietz showed his teeth as if he were trying to smile. His eyes shifted to Hodge.

"PFC Hodges, Charles Hamilton Hodges, the fourth, First Sergeant."

Now click your heels together, Bell thought.

"The fourth? Where the hell did you get a name like that?"

Hodge opened his mouth to answer, but the first sergeant waved him off.

"Okay, you two give your orders to Specialist Bowman." He nodded toward the clerk, who kept typing without looking up.

"He'll take care of your paperwork. You'll get your MP assignments—"

"Top!" A voice, strong and resonant as a bass fiddle, called from inside the C.O.'s office. "I need those requisitions. I'm leaving in *five* minutes."

"Yes sir!" Top's response rang out, loud and crisp, but his eyes rolled upward before returning to glare at Bell. With a grating noise, he pushed the chair back and snatched the papers off his desk.

From behind Bell came a low hiss, "Captain Midnight calls."

Bell looked around. Sergeant Hayes, leaning against the wall, flashed him a mirthless grin. His hat was off, and what little hair he had was red stubble, his face leathery, almost immobile. The mystery briefcase stood upright at his feet.

Orders in one hand, Bell sidled over to the company clerk's desk, on the way craning to see through the open door. A head of closely cropped black hair was bent over papers the first sergeant held out.

The officer said something and looked up, showing a deep, ebony color and sharp features, a square jaw and high forehead—a handsome movie star face carved in black marble. A hard-edged version of Sidney Poitier.

***

Hayes conducted them up to the second floor and left them in one of the two bays that served as the enlisted barracks. They talked little, and then in hushed tones as they emptied their duffel bags and arranged articles in their new wall lockers and footlockers.

Impervious to their presence, a GI clad only in boxer shorts dozed on a bottom bunk nearby. On top of a footlocker, a fan rotated with a gentle whirr.

Later, lying on his new bunk, Bell was engulfed by a sense of overwhelming gloom. He had eaten, met some of the other inmates, and finished unpacking. Now he tried to sleep. The green nylon poncho liner that Poteet, on the next bunk, had loaned him kept off the mosquitoes and blocked the glare of the fluorescent lights, but it didn't block the sound of the tape deck on Poteet's wall locker: "Number nine, number nine, number nine..."

He lay awake and tossed. In basic training, his mind had been scrubbed, his identity erased. Now he wore the same clothes and spoke the same vernacular as every other scrap of cannon fodder in this place. There was no future beyond this: a draftee in the lowest sub-basement of the army, subject to the whims and stupidity of petty tyrants like Hayes and Dietz. He had been waylaid, sidetracked, kicked into this dung heap by... By whom? Whom could he blame? Nixon? Himself? Or just fate?

Now it was all gone: the school honors, the scholarships, his escape from the furniture factory where his father had toiled out his life and the shirt mill where his mother still worked for minimum wage and no benefits. His Phi Beta Kappa key and learning to talk like a Yankee were worthless here.

And what was that business in My Tho between Hayes and the Green Beret? Avery? Captain Midnight? The briefcase. Forget it; stay out of it. Lifer bullshit.

Dozing, he awoke with a start when the tape player clicked off. In a half stupor, his mind tumbled through a troubled wave of libido, conjuring her once again, coming through the door after her shower. A white towel around her waist, drying her black hair with a second white towel.

He's gritty with sand and salt. She's clean-scrubbed, red-tinged white, the hint of a tan line starting to appear above her small out-

turned breasts.

"Will you put some baby oil on me?" she asks. "My skin's dry."

Someone extinguished the fluorescent lights. The barracks area was dark except for a few shadows cast by the perimeter lights and quiet except for a last gasp of artillery and the desultory croaking of frogs, and beneath it all, the low growl of the diesel generator.

CHAPTER THREE
Life's a Beach

A RAUCOUS CHORUS STARTLED HIM AWAKE, blue jays scolding in the maple tree outside his bedroom window. Opening one eye, instead of his matador poster, he saw the battleship gray of a wall locker, and smelled cigarette smoke.

Sliding up in his bunk, he peered out at the corridor, already sun-checkered by the latticework. The racket emanated from an elfish old woman, wagging her finger at a young woman in black silk pajama pants. A little papa-san with a shock of white hair paced around them, waving a cigarette and adding his voice to theirs. With the arrival of a teenage boy in faded fatigues, all four moved off down the corridor.

Bell groaned and swung his feet onto the cement floor. Then he dropped his face into his hands. A sergeant had come by at six and banged on the metal frames of the bunks and yelled for them to get up, but he'd fallen back into an uneasy sleep. Except for two guys on night patrol, the other bunks were empty. Even Hodge was gone.

The shuffling of boots caused him to raise his head. A stocky soldier leaned around the end of the bunk and stared at him from behind black-rimmed glasses.

"Ira Meyer," the soldier said. "Ira back home, just Meyer here." He slipped between the bunks and held out his hand. "Some call me Mad-dog."

Bell could see why. Meyer's round cheeks held a smudge of beard, and his curly black hair defied both gravity and army regulations.

"Justin Bell." They shook hands. Meyer's were soft, uncalloused.

"You must have just arrived in our lovely establishment," Meyer said. "Do you have work detail this morning?"

"Yeah, shi-it." Bell looked at his watch. "God-damn, I'm late!"

"Not to worry. Been here two weeks; if Hayes says seven, he won't be out there 'til eight." Meyer had a soft, educated accent, slightly nasal.

"Guess I should've got up when the sergeant came through."

"That was Avery. He'll leave you alone unless you have patrol."

"That's good. Where you from?"

"Chicago. Finished my first year in grad school and bang—draft board said I needed to *ser-r-ve my country.*"

"Yeah, me too. English lit." Bell nodded toward the corridor. "What was that about?"

"You mean the majordomo? Mama-san in charge." Meyer pointed to a pair of polished boots under the next bunk. "Our lovely tropical resort has a staff of servants to do our domestic chores. The old papa-san's our handyman, keeps the generator running for lights and other amenities when the local power company's on the blink. Which is most of the time." Meyer grinned at him. "For all this, you pay twenty dollars each month, military funny money of course."

"I'd pay that to avoid KP."

"All taken care of. Also pays two lovely young women who tend bar in our delightful cabaret down the hall," he pointed to the corridor, "and it covers the wash we send out every Thursday—just like home. Maybe better, depending how home was."

"I knew the Vietnamese did a lot of the shit work, but—"

"Only the best for Uncle Sam's warriors." Meyer chuckled as he turned to leave. "See you at the beach. Lots of sand to play in."

Meyer departed with the same shuffling gait with which he'd entered.

Bell remained on his bunk, staring into space. In the last week, he'd met a lot of people. Most he'd never see again, or only in passing. In his short five months of army life, that's how things seemed to work. People come, people go; you knew them only a brief time—measured in weeks or even days. This place would be different. Meyer, he had a feeling, he'd get to know, and know well.

And Hodge, also. The lifers he'd just as soon drop out of his life now and forever. Like Dietz and Hayes and Beadle. And Captain Midnight.

* * *

After a breakfast of greasy bacon, pan-singed eggs, and limp toast, he joined Meyer, Hodge, and a fourth GI named Jerry Keller near the entrance to the compound, where they waited in the morning sun until Hayes drifted out carrying a cup of coffee. He led them over to a pile of sand by the fence and instructed them on the finer points of filling plastic bags with the sand and hauling the bags over to the villa's fortifications.

To prepare for Tet, they were building new corner bunkers and adding a low sandbag wall a few yards inside the razor wire and chain-link fence already there. The plan was to embed claymore mines in concrete all along the wall on the east side facing the canal. The VC had attacked from there in Tet of '68. On the other three sides were ARVN Ranger and artillery units and the road.

They worked in pairs, Hodge and Bell, Meyer and Keller, whom Meyer called, "Killer"—to Keller's obvious irritation. In the half hour before Hayes' showed up, Keller had revealed only that he was married and from Mississippi.

The sun was hot on their backs. Once they stripped off their fatigue shirts, their green undershirts were soon soaked in sweat.

From the other side of the building came the high, sing-song voices of children playing in the ARVN compound. A few military trucks and jeeps rattled by on the gravel road to the canal, then a couple of motor scooters and a rickshaw-like contraption that Meyer said was a *xich-lo*. Every now and then, ARVN soldiers or civilians—men, women, children—appeared, carrying parcels or just walking alone or in groups, or riding bicycles.

As they shoveled and filled, they talked about how they had ended up here—except Keller, who had little to say. The talk eased Bell's depression a little. Hodge and Meyer, like him, had been drafted out of graduate schools: Hodge was working on a PhD in history, Meyer on a Masters in chemistry. And they talked about how much they wished they'd avoided the draft.

"My draft board ran out of blacks, delinquents, and college drop outs," Meyer said with a chuckle. Lifting sand toward the bag Keller held, he spilled half of it. Straightening, he added, "My parents run a deli. Only connections I had was working in my uncle's hardware store."

"Huh?" Bell said. "Connections?"

Meyer pushed his cap back and leaned on his shovel. "Plumbing, electrical. You name it." He grinned.

"Ah, shit!" Hodge snorted and pitched a shovel full of sand onto Meyer's boots.

"Hey, watch it," Meyer said, jumping back. "I learned some real skills there. If we ever want to break out of this place, I can do the locks." He gestured at the front gate that stayed open during the day but was padlocked at night. "Even have my own picks."

"Right," said Hodge. "Then we all swim home." He took a deep breath and let it out slowly. "My old man," he paused and shook his head. "He said the experience would be *good* for me. *I* should've flunked the physical. Heard you can raise your blood pressure with uppers and cough syrup."

"Does it work?" asked Meyer.

"Guy told me it worked for him." Hodge pulled off his cap and ran his fingers through hair that had been bleached blond by the California sun while he was home on leave. "My cousin managed to get a perforated eardrum," he said, replacing his hat. "All it cost him was a week at the beach."

"Smart," Bell said. He turned to Keller, sitting on a stack of empty bags, staring up at him. "So, Killer, how'd you get here?"

"Enlisted when I was nineteen." Keller had sandy hair and a sinewy appearance that Bell recognized from the regulars at George's Pool Hall back home. Keller spoke with a slow drawl.

"Y'all talk like y'all are somethin' special, but ev'ry damn one of you dodged the draft in college. Me? I was the top ground gainer in my conference, but it didn't get me any money to play college ball. So's all I got was a fuckin' construction job, haulin' bricks."

"Why do they call you 'Killer'?" Bell asked.

Keller shrugged. "Everybody's got a handle. 'Cept Johnson. He's a fuckin' panther, and he don't have no truck with nobody but his own kind."

Bell wanted to know more about "Killer" and about Johnson, but the screen door at the front entrance to the villa banged open, and he turned to look. A big man shaped like a bowling pin had charged out of the building. Close behind him was Hayes. As the two cleared the row of sandbags, Hayes grabbed the first man's arm, and the man spun around. He was a good head taller than Hayes and fifty pounds heavier.

"Goddamn you, you bastard!" Hayes shouted.

"Avery," said Keller. "Looks like he and Hayes are havin' a little disagreement."

Hayes moved closer to Avery and shook a finger in his face but lowered his voice so that Bell couldn't understand what he was saying. Avery didn't answer, or budge.

Another man came out of the entrance and joined Hayes, facing Avery but off to one side. He appeared to interject his own barbs, while Hayes continued to crowd Avery, who stood like a bottom-heavy boulder. Avery didn't say anything, or if he did, it was so clipped and quiet that the words didn't carry.

"That's Foley," Keller said. "Motor pool sergeant. Hayes' asshole buddy."

"What are they fighting about?" Bell asked.

"Who knows," Keller said. "I'm waiting for one of 'em to take a swing at Avery. He'll cold-cock the both of 'em."

"Nice to see camaraderie among our leaders," said Hodge, leaning on his shovel.

Now Top and Sergeant Beadle burst through the screen door. Top halted near the sandbags, well short of the melee, while Beadle tried to wedge between Avery and Hayes.

Hayes was shaking his fist in Avery's face, but he didn't touch him. Avery's feet remained firmly planted; his hands hung loosely by his side.

"Them three's all E-6's," Keller said. Meaning the same rank. "Avery kept Hayes from gettin' promoted, so I hear. Kept him from bein' head of operations. Now he just does shit 'round here for Top."

Beadle placed a hand on Hayes' arm and, using his bulk, shoved between the two men. Hayes twisted away and moved back toward Avery.

Trailing a cloud of dust, a jeep rolled through the gate and skidded to a stop a few yards from the non-coms. Captain Templeton climbed out of the driver's seat. Starched fatigues, mirrored aviator sunglasses, and a stiff cap like Hayes' but with captain's bars on the front.

"Likes to drive himself," Keller said. "Don't trust us white boys."

Hayes and Beadle had fallen silent, and now Avery took a couple of steps back from his hardened position. As the captain approached, Top pivoted and strolled inside as if nothing had happened. The captain started to follow, but Beadle said something to him, and he turned toward the men.

Avery, Foley, and Beadle saluted him. Hayes didn't at first, then he did. Walking up to the group, the captain returned their salutes.

There was a lot of talking, mostly by Hayes and Beadle, but it was unintelligible out at the sand pile. The captain finally pointed toward the four of them, then to his jeep. Then he turned and went into the building. Beadle, Avery, and Hayes followed him inside as Foley climbed into the jeep and drove it around to the back of the building.

"Avery must be buttin' into Hayes' business," Keller said. He picked up a sandbag that he and Meyer had been filling and began tying off the end.

"Looks like a lifer cluster fuck to me," Hodge said. "Getting the C.O. involved like that."

"Ah, he won't do a thing," said Keller, tossing the filled sandbag on top of several others.

"I heard Hayes call him Captain Midnight," Bell said.

"NCOs hate his black ass." At the look Bell gave him, Keller added with a shrug. "Guess he's not a bad sort, but he's reg'lar army, and he don't have no friends here."

They went back to filling sandbags. After a few minutes, Avery appeared through the front entrance and came over to them. He greeted Keller and Meyer by name, then introduced himself to Hodge and Bell and asked their names, where they were from, and what they had done before the army.

"Always glad to have new people here," he said once Bell and Hodge had finished their brief bios. "This won't be like your civilian lives..." He paused and looked from one to the other, skipping Keller, and an amiable grin crossed his round face. "I know you hate being here, but you'll learn a few things you'd never learn in grad school."

Staring down at the sand, Bell rolled his eyes. *Yeah,* he thought, *I've learned I damn well don't like being here, and I don't like doing this shit.*

Avery went on to tell them a little about the place. It was an old French plantation house the Navy Seabees had fixed up, and then Charlie chased them off during the Tet offensive. After the VC moved out, the MPs had taken it over and built the club and an outside deck. The real porcelain toilets and urinals and inside showers, though, were all compliments of the Seabees.

There were about thirty-five GIs here now, he explained, not all MPs. Headquarters staff—motor pool, supply room, cooks, a company clerk—and two officers: Captain Templeton and the Ex.O, Lt Floyd. Each day, two jeep patrols worked the town and the airfield in two shifts, and two road patrols in V-100 armored cars guarded convoys and looked out for mines on QL 4. Most days, a single MP spent the day at the My Linh ferry crossing on the Mekong, and one or two others went out on a combined patrol with the National Police.

After he had finished, Bell asked, "Do we get some training or something, before we go out?"

"OJT. But you start with an experienced partner, and I'll be on the desk." He turned to Keller. "Keller, you're back on duty Friday."

"Thanks, Sarge." Keller's face lit up. "It was—"

"Just don't let it happen again."

As he started toward the gate, Avery waved over his shoulder and shouted, "Don't work too hard, boys. Life's a beach."

Beyond the gate was a *xich-lo*, the motorbike muttering softly. Watching him leave, Bell thought, *this guy I could get to like, even if he is a lifer.*

"OJ fuckin' T," Keller said as Avery climbed into the back of the *xich-lo*. Keller took off his sunglasses and wiped his eyes. "He's right. You go out with a short-timer, and *they'll* show you the ropes. Show you the best whorehouses to get a free piece of ass or a beer, how to change a little money and do a little business with the gooks." Behind them, a jeep rattled by on the metal runway and sped out the gate without slowing.

"There goes Hayes," Keller said. "Sergeant Foley's with 'im. Prob'ly headed into town."

"Coke time for us," Meyer said and threw down his shovel.

Retrieving their fatigue shirts, they headed for the building. As they crossed the parking lot, Bell held Hodge back.

"Hey, what do you reckon that little altercation was about? Have anything to do with Hayes and his briefcase from My Tho?"

"No fucking idea." Hodge stopped and stared at Bell in an odd way. "Doubt it had anything to do with that at all."

"But Avery, Captain Midnight, they're the ones Hayes and the Green—"

"Don't fucking care what that bunch of lifers is fighting about."

"Well, it was *fuck-ing* bizarre."

A quarter-ton truck ground past the compound, going toward the canal, and they both watched it out of sight.

"Shouldn't we tell somebody?" Bell asked when the noise had faded. "Like maybe Avery? His name—"

"Fuck no!" Hodge started forward, then stopped. "Look, Bell, we need to keep that to ourselves. You and me. Okay? Like one of your rules, man. Okay?"

"I don't know—"

"You... we don't know shit about these people." He started off again toward the villa's entrance. "All I want to do is *ease* on through this and get the hell out of here. That means," he glanced back at Bell, "*not* pissing anybody off."

"Well, maybe you're right," Bell said, catching up with Hodge. "But I don't like it. I. Just. Don't. Like it."

CHAPTER FOUR
Day Patrol

SERGEANT AVERY LINED THEM UP in the dim light near the building and barked out the orders for each. Meyer, droopy faced and rumpled, would be the lone MP at the My Linh ferry crossing. Hodge, fidgeting and muttering wisecracks, was going out with the road patrol in a V-100. Bell, decked out in starched fatigues, a shiny MP helmet liner and armband, was on town patrol.

He was armed and ready for action, gun belt festooned with handcuffs, a billy club, two ammo clips, and a black leather holster with a loaded .45. His partner was Alonzo Johnson, who was decked out the same way, except Sergeant Johnson looked like it all belonged on his tall, gangly form.

Leaving the lineup, they headed for a jeep parked in front of the villa.

"I'll drive," Johnson said in a deep drawl. "You need to learn the roads."

"No-o-o problem," Bell said. Before MP school, he had never driven a stick shift, and there, he'd driven only in convoys on dirt roads.

Sliding into the passenger seat, he snagged his billy club under his leg. The gear was still alien, despite eight weeks of training, the .45 nearly worthless since the stationary target usually evaded his aim.

As they made the three-mile trip into Van Loc, the sky turned a pale pink, then light blue spackled with red-tinted clouds. Far across the rice fields, a jagged line of Hueys rose at an angle from the Air Cavalry staging area at the airfield and turned away from the sunrise toward the Cambodian border.

The morning air had not yet succumbed to the reek of diesel

fumes and gas exhausts, but there were other odors: ones that he related to driving through the Great Dismal Swamp at night on the way to the beach, or riding behind a garbage truck at home. And the smell of lime in his father's garden in the swamp behind their house—when his father was still alive.

At Van Loc, QL 4 continued on around a traffic circle, toward the airfield and the ferry, while the town's main street jaunted off to the right. Spinning the steering wheel in that direction, Johnson pointed to a low, two-story building.

"Where they make bread," he said, his first words since leaving the compound. A sign above the entrance to the building said "Boulangerie."

He waved his hand to the front. "Le Thai-to Street, where we do most of our business. Over there," he nodded to his left, "bars, restaurants. Some shops. People live above 'em." He pointed to the buildings on their right. "Lots of folks live back in there. Hooches on the canals. Only dumb-ass GI's go there." He paused, then added, "And us."

Most of the buildings had two or three stories of crumbling, off-white stucco topped by red tile roofs. At street level, retractable metal gates, painted green or red or blue, protected the storefronts. Lush plantings concealed roof patios, flower-filled boxes clung to second-floor railings, and bougainvillea spread fuchsia and pink across beige walls or draped a balcony in front of partially closed shutters and doors. Below this pastiche of colonial architecture, plants, and colors, the street was lined on both sides by broken sidewalks and ditches half full of black water and trash.

People were beginning to emerge from the bars and shops and pull back the metal gates. Pedestrians materialized from the alleys and scurried along the sidewalks. In the blink of an eye, the street was filled with gasoline fumes and the staccato of motor scooters and xich-los.

Coming out of a two-story building next to one of the alleys, a GI in fatigues stepped into the street and hailed a xich-lo. It shuddered to a stop, and he climbed into the tin carriage. As it turned in front of the MP jeep and putted off toward the airfield, the GI waved to them.

"He's out early," Bell said.

"Probably spent the night with his girlfriend. So long as they stay inside after curfew, we don't mess with 'em."

The MP station was located in a one-story stucco building on a side street lined with tall eucalyptus trees. In front, there was a concrete porch covered by a tin roof and enclosed with chicken wire. To keep out stray grenades and satchel charges, Johnson said. The MP's shared the building with the Vietnamese military police, or Quan Canh, and the civilian National Police.

As they went up the concrete steps, Johnson nodded to a khaki-clad officer standing in a doorway on the left side and said, "Chao ong, Lieutenant Nguyen."

Bell only nodded, wondering what the greeting meant. The lieutenant was taller than most Vietnamese—not that Bell had actually met many—and he had neatly parted black hair and high cheekbones that, along with his smile, gave him a genial appearance.

He replied to Johnson in slightly accented English. "Hello, Johnson. Fresh meat?"

"Uh huh," Johnson grunted, or maybe it was a chuckle. Bell wasn't sure.

As Johnson introduced them, explaining that Nguyen commanded the local Vietnamese military police unit, two other Vietnamese came through the door behind the lieutenant. One wore the khaki uniform of the Quan Canh, like the lieutenant, and the other the white shirt of a civilian policeman. Both said their names and something else, none of which Bell understood.

The civilian policeman held out a small hand. The silver tag above his left pocket gave his name as Phan. Vigorously shaking hands, Phan gave a wide grin that didn't quite fit with his unblinking eyes. Phan the frog, Bell thought, and decided he didn't like this guy.

Once inside the MP station, Johnson leaned across the chest-high desk and addressed the desk clerk. "Night patrol leave us anything, Singleton?"

Before Singleton could answer, Sergeant Avery, who was leafing through a binder on a table by the window, spoke. "GI in a truck ran over a xich-lo. Killed the friggin passenger. Old mama-san." He undid the binder, pulled out some forms, and placed them in a stack next to the base station radio. "And one of them damned engineers got drunk and stole a twenty-ton crane. Son of a bitch flattened a storage building. You need to get statements on both."

"Uh, Sergeant Avery," Singleton said, looking over at the desk sergeant, "how about the civilian—"

"Oh yeah. Nguyen had a call about an American civilian. Downtown. He's one of ours, so you need to check on him."

"What's the problem?" Johnson asked.

"No friggin idea. All Nguyen said, he had a call. Guy's probably drunk, making a ruckus." The folding chair creaked under Avery as he closed the binder and turned toward them. "Name's Roberts. He's a contractor, works for MACV, could be CIA for all I know.... Flies Air America out of the airfield sometimes."

"What are MACV and Air America?" Bell asked, his elbows on the counter.

"Military Assistance Command, Vietnam," Johnson said. "They work with the Vietnamese—lot of stuff I don't understand, but they live in nice digs at a hotel on the way to the airfield. Air America is the secret CIA air force that runs drugs out of Laos."

Avery laughed. "As if you had any friggin idea what they do."

He stood and handed two sheets of paper across the front desk to Johnson. Avery was as tall as Johnson, but as big in the butt as Beadle, and he had a florid, baby face. Give him a red suit and a white beard, Bell thought, he'd make a decent Santa Claus. One that sounds like an Irish cop.

"Here are the write-ups," Avery said. "Witness names and

locations at the bottom. Most at the airfield. Check on Roberts on your way."

Roberts. Bell knitted his brow, thinking hard. Why does that sound familiar?

Turning back to his table, Avery added, "Apartment's on Le Thai-to Street. Near that new bar, one run by Walker's honey."

***

Johnson stopped the jeep at a two-story building, next to an open ditch with a plank across it. A sign on the building said "Kikki's Bar." Although the bar was closed, the blue metal gate in front stood half open. Inside the bar, a thin woman wearing black pants and a blue blouse matching the color of the gate was wiping off tables and arranging chairs on the floor around them. Between the ditch and the entrance was a sidewalk and a tile patio enclosed by a waist-high metal railing, also blue.

As they crossed the patio, the woman's face lit up in a broad grin, displaying white teeth that would have delighted an orthodontist back in the World. She wore feline, sequin glasses that were a tad too wide, and her thin, black hair fell only to her shoulders. But she had a soft pleasant look. Mid to late thirties, Bell guessed. Not that he could tell how old any of the Vietnamese were.

"So, Johnson," the woman said, "you come see Kikki's place. How 'bout a Coke for you and your han'som pa'ner." She gave Johnson's arm a pat and Bell a smile.

"Nothing now, Kikki. This is Bell." Before Bell could say anything, Johnson continued, "I'm looking for an American who lives around here... Roberts."

"Oh, Mista Roberts. He stay next door. No see him today."

"Somebody called the QC's. Said we need to check on him. He cause any trouble?"

"No. No trouble. He live alone. No girlfriend. No party. Sometime he drink too much, friends carry him there." She pointed to the second floor of the stucco building next to the bar.

"Okay, let's go see him," Johnson said. Not waiting for Bell, he strode out of the bar and across the patio to the sidewalk.

"Please to meet you, Kikki," Bell said, then rushed to catch up with his partner, while wondering what the hell was going on with this Roberts. And why anybody cared.

CHAPTER FIVE
Roberts

"HE NO LEAVE." The old woman's voice lashed out at them. "There!" She jabbed a skeletal finger toward a door at the end of the second floor corridor.

Johnson grabbed the loose knob and gave it a twist. The door swung open, and stagnant air bearing a sharp, sweet smell engulfed them. Bell almost gagged, and he put his hand over his mouth and nose.

The room was small and dark, with what little light there was seeping past closed curtains on the far wall. Bell could just make out a still figure stretched across a bed in the center of the room.

Johnson bounded around the bed and jerked open the curtains, exposing French windows. He pulled the windows inward and shoved the outside shutters open. Sunlight streamed in.

A man, naked from the waist up, lay across the bare mattress. His legs were sprawled out toward the windows, his balding head thrown back over the edge of the bed, toward the door. The left side of his head was black with dried blood, and a pool of congealed blood, a small flat mound, lustrous like black obsidian in the light, covered the floor beneath his head. His right hand had fallen across his chest— pallid and covered with black hair—and rested there on the butt of a long-barrel revolver.

Bell braced himself against the wooden doorframe. He had started shaking as soon as he saw the blood, and he felt bacon grease from breakfast rise in his throat. Hoping that Johnson wouldn't turn and see his reaction, he slunk backward. From behind him, the old woman touched his arm with a bony finger, and he lunged forward into the room.

"Looks like suicide," Johnson said. Keeping his eyes on the

corpse, he began working his way back around the bed. At the man's head, he stepped gingerly over the black pool of blood, and then stopped, still looking down.

Bell, just inside the doorway, stood rooted, his eyes fixed on his partner. He let out the breath he'd been holding in a wheezing gasp. Johnson looked up.

"Bell, why don't you go out to the jeep and call the station. Tell Singleton to raise the medics at the airfield. Tell 'em to bring a body bag."

"Okay," was all Bell could manage. But he still couldn't move. His eyes stayed on Johnson, who was retracing his steps to the window side of the bed.

"I'll look around here and try to find the bullet," Johnson said. "Looks like...," he paused and squinted at the wall above the headboard. "Like it came out the left side. Angle may tell us somethin'."

Bell stumbled past the old woman, now joined by two of Roberts' neighbors, and hurried down the corridor to the stairs and finally outside. Still shaking, he gave the station's call sign and conveyed the message, he hoped without betraying his frayed emotions. Once he had signed off and replaced the handset, he took several deep breaths. He held the last one to calm his nerves and stared down at the black water in the gutter beside the jeep. He remained there for several minutes, measuring each breath, oblivious to the *xich-los*, scooters, and three-wheel Lambrettas that clattered by him in the street.

When he arrived back in the room, Johnson was standing on a chair by the wall on the far side of the bed, his head bent down at an angle, his hair scraping the ceiling. Using a pocketknife, he dug furiously at a growing hole in the stucco-covered wall.

Bell slipped inside and leaned back against the doorjamb to watch.

"Got it," Johnson grunted. His boots thudded to the floor.

Standing in a rectangle of sunlight by the window, he held up a small oblong object between his fingers, while Bell concentrated on taking shallow breaths through his mouth to avoid the sickeningly sweet smell.

Johnson tapped the side of his head. "He must've put the gun below his right temple, fired at an upward angle." With a bent index finger still tapping his head, he shifted around to the foot of the bed.

"Yeah," Bell said and started to add something about how the gun had fallen across the man's chest. He stopped when a fresh tremor coursed through his arms and his gut.

"Bell, you wait here for the medics... start on our report."

"I got Singleton."

"Good, good." Johnson nodded absently, bouncing the bullet in his palm. Bell stared at the object, thinking how it had passed through bone and brains and discharged much of a man's blood onto the floor.

"I want to talk to the old woman," Johnson said. "See if anyone 'round here heard anything. Kikki can translate."

Without looking at Bell, Johnson went out, closing the door and shutting out the old woman and her friends in the hallway. Leaving Bell alone with the corpse and the stench of drying blood. And silence. Outside, there were sounds of traffic and people on the street; here there was nothing but silence.

Focusing his eyes on a bright patch of sunlight under the window, he made his way around the bed and eased down in the straight-back chair on which Johnson had been standing. He resisted looking at the body, but he couldn't ward off the smell. Then he caught the low buzz of a fly, maybe two. Homing in.

How was he going to get through this? He knew about the horror of blood mostly from Macbeth, or movies. He'd never seen it—or so much of it—not like this; smelled it, drained from a corpse. Congealed and black and lustrous in the lambent morning light.

Why had Johnson closed the door and left him alone like this? To keep the neighbors out? Fuck with whitey and laugh about it later with the homeboys? Or maybe some sort of initiation? A baptism in violence? Or did leaving him here mean nothing? Two soldiers with a job to do.

He had to do his job—as best he could. That would help him cope. Not completely lose it. He'd read about war nerves, shell shock, shirkers, cowards. He wasn't going to be one of them.

Taking a small spiral notepad out of the side pocket of his fatigue pants, he started to write down what he knew: name and description of deceased, location of body, time discovered. His hand shook, and the pen moved in squiggly lines across the page, making illegible words. Unable to control his shaking, he returned the pen and notepad to his pocket.

Willing himself to rise from the chair, he looked around the room—still trying to avoid the body. But his eyes wandered down to it, jerked away, and then back down.

He edged along the wall to a vanity across from the foot of the bed, opposite the wall splattered with blood—where Johnson found the bullet. A mirror hung on the wall above the bureau, and he saw his reflection in it.

"What the hell am I doing here?" he asked the reflection.

He took off his MP helmet liner and stared at himself. Gray army glasses, regulation moustache, and stooped shoulders from too many nights in the library. Not a real MP. Not tall and steady like Johnson. He sighed and plopped the helmet liner back on his head, the white "MP" in front.

Shifting his eyes to the bottom of the mirror, he settled his gaze on the reflected head of the dead man hanging over the edge of the bed. Mostly bald with a fringe of hair visible on the right side, the side not covered with blood. For the first time, he noticed that the man's eyes were not quite closed. And for the first time, he thought about this person, this human—and not just a corpse. Who was this man? Roberts.

Roberts.

The Green Beret at My Tho had referred to a Roberts. "Scared shitless," or something like that. If it was the same Roberts, what was he, Roberts, scared of? And why had he done this?

His gaze dropped to the top of the bureau—to a color photograph in a gold frame. A woman in a plain, straight dress, her hands in the pockets, smiled shyly toward the camera. On either side of her stood two small girls, evidently twins, each with pink ribbons in their blond hair. A dogwood tree covered with white flowers filled the picture behind them.

The tremors and his revulsion at death and the gore were gone, replaced by a deep sadness. Pushing it aside, and his own feelings of grief and loneliness, he resumed his survey of the bureau's surface.

A few inches to the right of the photograph was a stack of papers held down by a 105-howitzer shell casing. The top paper was flecked with brown spots. Moving the casing, he picked up the paper.

Were the spots blood? How could blood get over here when the gun had been on *this* side pointed toward the opposite wall? Sprayed backward from the blast?

He looked from the paper to the man on the bed and back. It must be ten, fifteen feet. And the bullet's entry point was so small.

Holding the paper, a blank U.S. Army requisition form, in one hand, he leafed through the other papers. Completed requisitions for vehicles and parts, lists of munitions and equipment, and something that made him pause again: a typed schedule showing dates and times, all at night, 2300 to 0600 hours.

At the bottom of the schedule, written in a smudged scrawl, was "Major Binh? Ask Hayes."

He shook his head. Sergeant Hayes? What would an MP Sergeant have to do with this dead civilian? In My Tho, one of them, Hayes or the Green Beret, had said something about the CID, the MPs' Criminal Investigation Division. "Eyes down here." Something about Avery.

He replaced the papers as he had found them, the one with the brown flecks on top, then the shell casing, and then he opened the top drawer of the bureau. It contained a few loose pictures along with the usual detritus of a single man in a foreign country: pill bottles, a broken pair of sunglasses, opened letters, writing paper, pencil stubs with well-worn erasers, and two plastic Hong Kong Holiday Hotel ballpoint pens.

Leafing through the letters, he found nothing that looked like a suicide note. He closed the drawer with a bang, jumped, then glanced around as if he expected the dead man to rouse. Nothing moved except a slight billowing of the curtains beside the French windows.

Chagrined at being so jittery, he opened the other drawers in quick succession. All they held were clean clothes: slacks, shirts, socks, and underwear. And a pair of swim trunks.

As he carefully closed the bottom drawer, someone knocked and yelled, "Anybody home?" The door opened before he could answer.

Two GI's, both with the pallid skin of FNG's, came through the doorway—the first shoving a folded stretcher in front of him, the second with a plastic body bag folded over his arms. Both wore fresh green fatigues that hadn't yet seen a laundry. The one in the lead, his paleness highlighted by carrot red hair and freckles that covered his face and ran down his neck, stopped short when he saw the figure on the bed. He gave a disgusted grunt, followed by a low whistle. He looked over at Bell, still standing by the bureau.

"What happened here?"

"Looks like a suicide," Bell said, imitating Johnson's confident tone. But the shakes were starting again. With an effort, he gritted his teeth and tried to sound flip. "Guess you guys get to wrap him up and haul him off."

"Yep," freckle face said, "he's our first." He gave Bell a wan smile and dropped the stretcher on the floor.

The second medic, who said nothing and looked like Bell felt, unzipped the body bag, and the two started to work. Eager to escape, Bell edged toward the door as the freckled-faced medic grabbed the corpse's feet and gave a quick jerk, bumping the bloody head onto the mattress. With another jerk, he twisted the body all the way around.

Eyes averted, Bell slipped outside to guard the door.

CHAPTER SIX

Unknowns

THEY SPENT THE REST OF THEIR DAY interviewing witnesses to the *xich-lo* accident and the crane theft and then filling out reports. At the end of their shift, Singleton sent them to retrieve Meyer at the My Linh ferry, since the V-100 crew that was supposed to pick him up had gone off to investigate a road mine near My Tho. Bell drove on the way back, carefully steering around *xich-los*, three-wheel Lambrettas, and bicycles while jeeps, trucks, and motor scooters careened around him, the scooters often bearing two or three people clinging to each other and the machine.

When they reached an open section and a lull in the traffic, he glanced at Johnson and asked, "Did you get anything out of the neighbors? On Roberts?"

"Nothing worth much." Johnson was so tall he hunched forward in the passenger seat to make room for his legs. "The old mama-san heard him around suppertime last night, talking to somebody outside. American, she said. Then she didn't hear anything else. No one knew anything... Damn, we could use a real interpreter." He shifted to one side so that his right leg almost hung out of the jeep. "Gunshots around here ain't that unusual," he paused, and then added, "and the walls are thick."

Bell told him what he had found on Roberts' bureau. "One list looked like a typed schedule of some sort. It had a note to ask Hayes about Major Binh."

"Umm," Johnson said and shifted his legs again. "Anything else?"

"No." He didn't mention the brown flecks on the paper. If they were blood, they had probably come from the gun blast.

"Who's Major Binh?" he asked.

"Only Major Binh I know about is the district military chief."

"That our Hayes?" asked Meyer, leaning forward from the back seat.

"I wouldn't know," said Johnson. "I... " He stopped as Bell swerved around a *xich-lo*, then back into their own lane to avoid an oncoming jeep.

"Why would Roberts have lists of equipment?" Bell asked. "On army forms? And what's with the schedule?"

"Well, if he really was CIA, that could be supplies for his people up river, over the border," Johnson said. "Schedule could be flight times, boat schedules, who knows what. Lot goes on here we don't know about, out on the river and on all those fucking canals. Both the CIA and Charlie move shit all over the delta, even on into Cambodia and Laos."

"But why would—"

"When we went by the station, Avery told me MACV'd already called. Told him to give 'em the report and they'd handle it. Not your problem, the man said."

"So where does Hayes come into all this?" It had to be their Hayes, Bell decided, and Johnson must think so as well, but wouldn't say it.

He braked for a three-wheel Lambretta loaded to the top with old boards. As the mini-truck wobbled back and forth in front of them, he tried to go around, then swerved onto the shoulder to avoid a deuce-and-a-half that sliced by them from the opposite direction.

"Hey! Watch what you're doing," yelled Meyer from the rear seat.

Johnson seemed unfazed by the sudden deceleration and swaying of the jeep.

"That Hayes gets around," he said. "Wouldn't be at all surprised if he knew Roberts." He took off his helmet liner and scratched his head. "But I doubt he has any connection with the CIA."

"How about the CID?" Meyer asked. "Could the man have been

undercover? Working with Hayes?

"Hayes? No way. He's only out for himself. Been here longer'n just about anybody in the compound." Johnson spoke in a slow measured voice while holding his helmet liner in his lap and readjusting his backbone to the seat. "He's tight with a couple of Air Cav Officers out at the airfield, and he knows all the local honchos, so I've heard." He drew in a breath and let it out in a sigh. "Glad I'm going home." After a long pause, he looked over at Bell. "You need to know something. A few months back, there was a sergeant here... he crossed the bastard and got shipped out to the Highlands."

"What did he do?" Bell asked.

"Guess he didn't play by the rules. I stay out of it."

No one said anything as they drove past the entrance to the airfield, and a few minutes later, past the vine-covered wall and metal gate in front of Madame Phoung's house of pleasure. After they came to the intersection with Le Thai-to Street and Bell turned south toward the MP villa, Meyer leaned forward again.

"What's the story with the new Ops Sergeant?" he asked. "We heard he was sent down here because a truckload of booze disappeared while he was watching it. Are he and Hayes, what do you call it... tight?"

Johnson gave a hollow laugh, the first time Bell had heard him exhibit any humor. "That's a good one. Georgia cracker and a Yankee Nee-gro who speaks like an English lord." He laughed again, then grew somber. "Yeah, I heard that shit, but I don't know a thing about Sergeant Beadle. Always some don't like to see a black man get ahead."

CHAPTER SEVEN
Waiting for Godot

SITTING ON THE EDGE OF HIS BUNK, Bell stared down at a paperback he was trying to read. But his mind kept rewinding the scene: the head thrown back, the pool of blood, the photograph on the bureau.

The sound of Poteet's tape recorder pounded in his head, "number nine, number nine, number nine..." Poteet, unfazed by the noise and fluorescent lights, snored away on top of the adjacent bunk.

The only other person in the barracks was Steve Walker, the company courier, propped up on the lower bunk to the other side of Bell. Walker was writing letters and placing them in a small stack beside his leg.

"So, Bell," said Walker as he finished a letter and folded it over, "you started patrol this week? Who with?"

"Johnson." Bell twisted around to face Walker. "Day patrol first; then the ferry. After that I'm with Cole on nights."

"Cream of the crop." Walker licked and closed the envelope and began writing the address on the outside.

"I've met Johnson. What about Cole?"

"Both are weird. Johnson stays to himself, but he's not a bad cop... Cole's another matter. Cocky bastard. Frankly, I think the fucker's crazy."

"Thanks, that makes my gut feel better."

"Got the runs?"

"Yeah. And a pain all the time, here under my ribs." He rubbed his abdomen.

"Gook water. Stick with Cokes and beer." Walker finished the address and held up the envelope. "And always take your malaria tablets."

"I heard they're no good."

"Take mine every day." Walker swung his legs over the edge of his bunk and leaned toward Bell. "You know where heaven is?... The real world. And I'm going back in one piece."

"I hear the first month's the worst."

"Well, this ain't a grunt unit," Walker said. "Only one dead since I been here. Poor ol' Biggers. Jeep flipped over, and he landed under it."

"It was an accident?"

"A fucking accident." Walker slapped his leg. "On patrol, Bell—hell, anytime in this place—watch what you're doing. Keep your eyes open. But duck first, look later. Don't volunteer for nuthin." He shook his pen in the air. "Find you a good, safe job. But anything's better than humping the boonies. Been there, done that." Leaning back, Walker resumed checking the addresses on his envelopes.

"Makes sense," Bell said, rolling his eyes then looking away. All this he already knew. He noticed a thin briefcase sitting between Walker's bunk and wall locker.

"That yours?" he asked, pointing to the briefcase. A briefcase like the one Hayes had taken from the Green Beret.

Walker glanced over at the brown case. "Yeah, the army's. All the couriers have 'em. Handcuffs and a chain to lock it on my wrist."

"You get around a lot, don't you, Walker? Saigon, Can Tho. Sounds like a good job. Carrying the mail and stuff."

"Shi-it! Ride in C-123's that shimmy like pole dancers? Chopper pilots who think they can fly upside down? Then somebody'll take a pot shot at you. But the good part is," he wagged his finger, "nobody fucks with you. I even got a house and girlfriend downtown."

"How did you manage that? I mean, with the curfew and all. We're supposed to—"

"Bullshit! Most of the officers and NCOs stay down there all the time. Just don't go wandering around after curfew. You married?"

"No. Not even a girlfriend. You?

"Divorced. Girlfriend here owns a little bar—Kikki's."

"Right. I met her."

Walker stretched with his head down to avoid hitting the upper bunk. He was about Bell's height, but broader, heavier, and more muscular, with a round face and short hair combed forward like in paintings of Napoleon.

"Stop by there when you get a day off. She has a younger sister, Mai." Sitting back up, he grinned at Bell. "Ripe for the picking."

"Not sure I want to get mixed up with anyone in this place."

"You're here for twelve months, pardner, and a steady piece in town sure beats the hell out of getting the clap at Madame Phoung's." He looked at his watch. "Well, gotta go see if Top has anything for me, 'fore he gets soused. Be cool." Walker stood and placed the letters in the top of his wall locker.

While they talked, Poteet's tape player had clicked off, and several other soldiers had come in, turned on their fans, and wrapped themselves in poncho liners on their bunks. As Walker left, Bell folded down the corner of the page he was reading and tossed the book into his open locker.

A beer in the club would be better than staying here and dwelling on the dead man.

CHAPTER EIGHT
The Club

THE CLUB HAD A REAL BAR with a long mirror behind it and a low stage for Filipino bands when they showed up. A few square tables with straight-back chairs joined a ragged couch that faced a small television set mounted on the wall in one corner. A Star Trek rerun was playing, but no one was watching. Outside on the deck, a short-timer was strumming a guitar and singing a country song. He was joined in the refrain by several of his buddies: "Oh-h-h, how I wan-n-ta go home."

Bell purchased a Pabst Blue Ribbon beer from Thuy at the bar and went to join Hodge and Meyer at an inside table. As he approached, Hodge hit the tabletop with his hand, rattling the plastic cups and beer cans in front of him and causing the four soldiers at the next table to look in his direction.

"Goldwater was fucking right!" His words were slurred. "Should've bombed the hell out of the North."

"Yeah, bring the Chinese right down to join them," Meyer said slowly and shook the ice in his cup. He poured more Coke into it from a can on the table.

"You really wanna go north? Go see Ho?" Bell asked as he sat down.

"Ho's dead," Hodge said. Hodge's trim moustache had grown into a thick brush, a brown contrast to his sun-bleached hair. He knocked over an empty can, causing two others to topple with it. "Fucking gooks don't even want to fight this war. So why should we? All they want to do is go to the fucking PX."

"You see how they live?" Bell asked. "Not just mud huts with thatched roofs." Now it was his turn to slap the table. "Whole damn families in mud bunkers, shanties made of flattened beer cans." He held up his PBR. "Living off our garbage, shit we throw out. You see the trash heap outside the airfield? Mama-sans, kids, pigs, all rootin' around in there, lookin' for something to eat... or sell. Guys," he leaned forward, hands extended, "they eat our fucking garbage. Our garbage! The whole stinkin' mess covered with flies."

Bending across the table, Hodge pushed aside the empty cups and cans. "And here we are," he said, his voice close to a whisper, "fifty years of education, filling sandbags for imbeciles." Then he gave a choked snort. "Can you *imagine* anything more subversive—three graduate students who are PF-fucking-C's?"

"Subversive? Oh, come on, Hodge." Meyer's usually calm demeanor disappeared. "What have you been smoking? We're the ones filling the sandbags. If we're so smart, why are we here?"

"Yeah," said Bell, "wannabe PhD's playing military cops." He shook his head. "After that guy today..." His voice trailed off, and then he added with determination, "I'm here, and I'll do what I have to, but not one goddamn thing *more* than I have to."

"Yeah, yeah. So now you're an observer, not a participant," said Hodge. "That your plan?"

"Yeah, that's right, just like I was back home in front of the fuckin' TV."

"Could be worse," said Meyer. "We could be out wading through rice paddies. Having people we've got no quarrel with shooting at us."

"God! Like the song says, I want to go home, back to Glenda." Hodge closed his eyes and pantomimed hugging. "My sweet, adorable wife and her sweet... unhh." He groaned and gritted his teeth.

While the three talked, the club had emptied except for the next table, where Keller, Sammy Sanderson, the armorer, and Alan Markovic, a motor pool mechanic, sat playing poker. As Hodge demonstrated his affection for his wife, Sanderson pounded on the table and gave a yell, flinging down his cards.

"Three fucking Jacks! Beat that."

He reached out and raked in a pile of MPCs in the center of the table, then shoved his chair back and stood while Keller swore at him and Markovic gathered up the cards. Tucking his winnings into a pocket, Sanderson strutted over to the erstwhile grad students' table. Without waiting for an invitation, he plopped down in the empty chair and looked around at the solemn faces.

"Man, you FNGs are taking this shit too damn serious," he said, shaking his head. "You need to lighten up."

Behind Sanderson, Keller and Markovic were just filing out of the club. Markovic, chuckling, reached over and gave Sanderson's hair a vigorous rub.

Sanderson jerked his head sideways. "Hey, motherfucker, cut that out."

"For luck," Markovic said and scooted away from Sanderson' backhanded swipe. "Get you back tomorrow night."

Sanderson waved a hand in Markovic's direction, like a cat batting a leaf. "Don't be messin' up the perm, white boy."

As the armorer, Sanderson bunked downstairs in the armory, among the racks of M-16's and .45's. He was short, wiry, and moved like he had springs in his shoes. His moustache was neatly trimmed and his hair shorter than that of the other black soldiers.

"Yeah, man, we been talking about what a great vacation spot this is," Hodge said, "fucking club mad." Hodge's clarity was fading again. "Just enjoying the ambience of this lovely *boite*." He swept his arm toward the bar.

Thuy, turning around from locking up the liquor bottles in a cabinet, beamed back at Hodge. She had dark eyes, red-lipstick lips, and rouge-tinged cheeks framed by straight black hair.

"Hey, don't knock it," said Sanderson. "You have free food, new clothes, and a clean place to sleep. Somebody else makes your bunk, shines your boots, and does your laundry. And your mama ain't here to nag you about it." He scrunched up his face in a broad grin. "Life is good, man."

"How about if papa-san fills the sandbags and pulls guard duty for me tonight," said Meyer. "In fact, he can do everything I do, and I'll go home."

Laughing, Sanderson leaned back in the chair and hooked one arm over the corner post. "You'll be glad you filled those sandbags come Tet. Hayes even got us a .50 caliber from the airfield and a rocket launcher. We - are - fucking ready for a regiment of mother-fucking NVA."

"Sounds like Custer's last stand to me," Hodge said. He took a long swallow from his plastic cup.

Bell was only half listening, still thinking about the morning. He stared past Sanderson at the deck. The guitar player and his companions had gone. Dull flashes illuminated the horizon, and then faded as artillery rumbled like low thunder off to the east.

Thuy came over and cleared the table of empty cans and plastic cups, eyeing the ones they still held but not saying anything. They watched as she made a final pass at the bar with a damp cloth and collected a yellow purse from under the counter. With a wave, she said, "*Chao ong*," and gave them a parting smile as she left with the night patrol for home.

"No use trying to get into those black pajamas," Sanderson said, rocking back on the rear legs of his chair.

"You know that for a fact, personal like?" asked Bell.

"Yeah, you might say that." He grinned. "She don't speak much English, but she sure let me know she was married."

In a loud thumping roar, a Huey passed low over the perimeter and the trees beyond, then crossed the canal to the rice paddies. Its spotlight swept back and forth, creating white patches on the ground like a stage waiting for its players.

Sanderson dropped his chair to the floor. "You guys check out the whorehouses yet?"

They all shook their heads.

"Lots of pussy downtown," he said. "Careful, though. They're like leeches. Whole damn place lives off us, just like we live off them."

"Some of the kids look pathetic," said Meyer. "I've been giving gum to the ones who hang on the fence out back."

"Ah man, don't give them gooks nuthin. There's never enough. After you been here a while, you'll swat 'em off. Just wait'll one of 'em points a finger at you and says, 'G.I., tomorrow you die.' And watch out for the white shirts—the National fucking Police. Get you to buy 'em beer and cigarettes at the PX, then they sell it all over town." He rocked back in the chair again. "Course some of the folks out at the airfield do their own business selling stuff."

"You mean, like... on the black market?" Bell asked, cocking one eyebrow.

"I've heard it happens." Sanderson shrugged, hands out. "No personal knowledge, of course." He looked around and lowered his voice. "Rumor has it we're getting new MPCs, and the locals are scrambling like rabbits to convert their GI funny money before it's worthless." Military Payment Certificates were the currency Americans used on U.S. bases. "Some of the officers at the airfield have ways they can exchange beaucoup MPCs for the gooks and take a cut."

"No one here would do that, right?" Bell asked, giving Sanderson a sideways look.

Sanderson returned a fake laugh. "Who better to make a profit?" He grinned at them, started to say something, then stopped. The others were silent.

"What about Hayes?" Bell asked and glanced over at Hodge.

"Ah, don't start that again." Hodge sat up from where he'd slumped down in the chair. "Thought your great plan was not to get involved. Just watch, like it was on TV."

"Hey, I'm curious," Bell said. Then to Sanderson, "We saw him get a briefcase from some Green Beret on the trip down here. Like the one Walker has. I've been wondering what was in it."

"Hayes? Man, I don't know nuthin about Hayes and what he does." Sanderson looked around the table, his eyes wide.

"A case like that could hold quite a bit of money," Bell said.

"Come on, you guys, finish your brews." Calling out to them and rattling a set of keys, Bowman entered the club from the corridor. "Top wants a Coke, and I need to lock up when I get back."

The thought struck Bell that the company clerk was the perfect flunky: pudgy and rosy-cheeked with well-trimmed blond hair, gray army-issue glasses, and starched fatigues. Always kowtowing to his masters.

"Top needs a chaser," Sanderson snickered, after making sure Bowman had gone.

Looking at Sanderson, Hodge tapped his empty cup on the table. "I heard Beadle was sent down here 'cause he's suspected of hijacking a liquor truck."

Sanderson gave his snort-snicker again. "Just one? Whatever the fuck they think he did, he's the head nigger in charge of the MP-fucking-operations in the whole fucking delta. No one's gonna pin anything on him."

"How about drugs?" asked Meyer.

"No one said Beadle was involved in that."

"No, no. I mean is there much of that going on around here?"

"There's some." Sanderson's manner became more serious. "Mostly marijuana." He shook his head and leaned back in the chair again. "Just don't get caught. That's the fastest way for an MP to end up eleven bravo, if you stay out of LBJ. You know, Long Binh jail. You want a joint, go to the Yankee Bar on Le Thai-to Street. Personally, I stick with bourbon."

Bowman came back and told them to get out. He was locking the door. As they threw their empty cups and beer cans in the garbage bin next to the bar, Sanderson kept up his travelogue.

"You want pussy, Madame Phoung's the best whorehouse in

town. Worst thing you'll get there's the clap."

"That from experience?" Bell asked.

"Hell no. I just jack off five times a day." Sanderson made a motion with his hand, and the other three started laughing. "Maybe check out the 'steam-n-creams' at the airfield sometimes." He chuckled and did a side shuffle down the corridor as Bell and Hodge turned into their bay.

CHAPTER NINE
Guard Duty

HE CLIMBED THE WOODEN LADDER TO THE WATCHTOWER, M-16 slung over one shoulder and his new tape recorder under his arm. Poking his head through the trapdoor, he mumbled a greeting to Keller and received a grunt and yawn in return.

"Nuthin goin' on," Keller said, collecting his gear. He started down the ladder as Bell settled onto a folding metal chair and shoved a magazine into the M-16.

With a long sigh, he leaned the rifle against the plywood wall and gazed out over the trees and canal and the open rice paddies to the east. Coming through a somnolent haze, the night's sights and sounds gave him a detached-from-reality movie sensation.

His eyes drifted down to the perimeter.

Spotlights, darkness, stillness. To his left, the compound's entrance and the gravel road led to the canal. On the other side of the road was a soccer field, trampled down by ARVN soldiers to hard dirt and patches of grass, and beyond that, the ARVN artillery compound with its sprinkling of lights. To his right lay the ARVN ranger base and the housing for the rangers and their families, whose children regularly lined the wire-mesh fence next to the villa.

He twisted around, toward the airfield. Several choppers were patrolling along its perimeter and the open fields around it. A flare lit the sky. A Cobra banked low, sweeping a spotlight across the paddies. He waited for a rocket or mini-gun to lash out. But nothing happened, to his disappointment, and then relief.

Turning again toward the canal, he focused on the fence line. Spotlights in each corner illuminated the empty ground outside, leaving the compound in shadows and giving the nearby grove of palms a ghost-like hue. Nothing moved except a night breeze caressing the palms and stirring the tops of bamboo near the canal. A single light on a building at the end of the gravel road winked as palm fronds danced gently in front of it.

He tilted his head and listened. Amid the croaking of frogs came the low drumbeat of artillery. *Who's firing those howitzers,* he wondered, *and what are they firing at? Enemy soldiers creeping along a jungle path? Or are they only trying to ward off demons in the night?*

A deep rumbling, different from the artillery, sent a shiver through the building and the chair beneath him. *B-52s?* He held his breath and listened, but the rumbling had stopped. *Thunder?* Stars shown in a moonless sky, but a low bank of clouds clung to the horizon off to the east. *A fogbank rolling in from the South China Sea? The flashes below it most likely aren't lightning.*

He refocused on the canal and the thick grove of palms and a smattering of banana trees along the road. While the sandbags provided cover and the perimeter lights didn't silhouette the tower, he would be an easy mark for an RPG or a sharpshooter of even moderate ability.

A light moved down the canal toward the building at the end of the road. He looked at his watch but couldn't see its face. Finding the flashlight, he illuminated the dial—0242 hours.

Shit. Shouldn't have done that.

He switched off the flashlight and looked up. The small dot of light on the canal had stopped near the light on the building.

He tensed, then relaxed.

Probably a fisherman. They fish for carp in the canals, and in the morning the mama-sans sell it in the market.

He checked the magazine in his M-16 and the safety. It was on.

He looked around the perimeter again and stopped to stare out at the canal and rice paddies. The light hadn't moved from the spot near the building. He strained to see if anything stirred on the ground around it.

People lived in hooches along the canal, and they might go out there at night. But why that warehouse? If that's what it is?

He understood almost nothing about this place.

Mesmerized, he watched the two lights blinking through the palm fronds. Then, taking up the binoculars, he tried to examine them. The entire area was shrouded in shadows. Next he tried the starlight scope—nothing beyond an opaque gloom among the trees near the perimeter.

Maybe I should set off a flare? Smack it against the wooden shelf, send it rocketing over the trees to light the area above the warehouse? That'd bring the NCOs running, and piss them off. If the sorry fucks aren't all downtown.

The lights remained where they were, blinking at him through the swaying palms. He took a deep breath, held it, and counted to sixty. He let the air out with a gasp. Then he counted all the trees he could see outside the perimeter toward the canal. He rubbed his neck and wished time would pass faster—tonight, tomorrow, the day after, until he could go home.

He shook his head to stay awake. Not long after, his chin hit his chest. He stood, heedless of snipers and RPGs, and stretched, then took another look around. A Cobra patrolling along QL 4 banked sharply and retraced its path in the wake of a dancing searchlight.

Sinking down on the folding chair, he stared in the direction of the canal. The light was moving away from the building, back toward the town.

"Oh, what the hell," he said aloud. He picked up the flashlight and checked his watch again: 3:10am. He listened for the noise of a motor on the canal, but heard only the choppers near the airfield and a few frogs. Then a deep-throated, distant rumble of artillery.

Was the sampan too far away to hear the motor? Maybe they were poling it? He let out a long breath. Fifty minutes left. He placed the tape recorder on his lap, picked up the mike attached to it, and pushed the button to record.

"Hello, Mother. Everything's fine here in the sunny Republic of Vietnam. I'm on guard duty. Nothing much going on."

He would always start this way. No problems, no danger. A nice place to visit with not much to do.

CHAPTER TEN
Dead Boys

DURING BELL'S FIRST DAYS ON PATROL, Johnson took him to the principal bars in town and showed him how to edge along the wall like a lawman in the old west while Johnson covered him from the entrance. The threats to life and limb inside these smoky interiors, Johnson explained, usually came from inebriated patrons. Outside lurked the other enemy, the boy-san who'd race up on a motor scooter so that a satchel bomber in back could swing a packet of explosives through the open gate.

Driving down a street close to the station, Johnson pointed to a jagged hole in the side of a building and the broken sign above it. At the edge of the street lay a lone sandal among the loose bricks and shards of wood.

On their fourth morning together, Johnson stopped at the side of the road in a spot that appeared devoid of any mark or object of interest.

"This is where two kids blew themselves up," Johnson said from the driver's seat. "Cole and I stopped right here. Parts of the scooter still smoking... a kid's head next to that pole." Johnson pointed to a concrete light pole that tilted away from the road. "That fucking Cole, you know what he did? He kicked it. Kicked the head. Must've gone ten yards, blood and stuff flying out."

Bell made a choking noise.

Johnson shook his head and pulled the jeep back onto the pavement. "That sorry fucking Cole." He rammed the gearshift into third. "They were just kids. Probably high school, no older than my little brother."

"Are there many problems with the gooks?" Bell asked.

"Don't call 'em 'gooks,'" Johnson said, his voice rising. "Not around me. I don't like the word. No more'n I like 'nigger.'"

"Well, I hear blacks calling them gooks."

"Those are some dumb-ass brothers. Calling somebody a name like that, it takes something away from 'em." He paused, his tall form slouched down in the seat. "Bein' human, maybe. Makes 'em easier to kill."

Bell kept silent, unwilling to risk offending Johnson again.

"Our biggest problem, Bell, ain't the VC. It's the shitface GI's. Potheads are easy enough, but the booze, it sends people out of their heads. Then you add guns and the shit people been through here." He shook his head and glanced over at Bell. "Like that friggin engineer with the crane." Johnson slowed down after the turn onto Le Thai-to Street. "Another thing's the ARVN rangers. Can't have weapons in town, so they carry grenades. Any of 'em, anywhere, they may have one under their shirt, or in a pocket."

Bell stared at two ARVN soldiers walking together, holding hands, on the opposite side of the street. No evidence of any grenades.

The jeep rolled to a stop near an open gate. A sign said, "Duc To Tailors. Fast Service." Johnson slid out of his seat. "Have to pick up some pants. Takin' 'em home with me."

Alone in the jeep, Bell stared down the main street toward a cathedral-scale church with clean white sides. Next to it, surrounded by a high white wall, was a one-story building. This appeared to be the destination of a stream of children of all sizes: the boys in blue slacks and crisp white shirts, the girls in white "*ao dais*," a dress-like top reaching from the neck to below the knees, with a slit beginning at the waist on each side to reveal black silk pants.

Watching them pass, he felt like a time traveler who had discovered a race of beautiful Eloi. The older girls were especially pretty, long black hair draped over white *ao dais*, slender forms, olive skin, and dark eyes. Some held hands and chatted, heedless of him. Others walked alone and silent, seeming to glide along the sidewalk in their billowing *ao dais.*

A teenage girl near the jeep turned and looked at him. One of her arms was foreshortened and shriveled, her face scarred on one side. Her single eye stared directly at him.

He quickly looked away and found a different sight. Coming out of the Hoa Binh Bar, between the jeep and the school, were three bar girls in brightly colored mini-skirts and tank tops.

Johnson returned with his new trousers folded over one arm. As he got into the jeep, the radio squawked their call sign, and Singleton sent them to investigate an accident on QL 4 near the airfield.

***

Giving short blasts on the siren, Johnson threaded their way through a jam of idling trucks, *xich-lo*s, and jeeps to an American deuce-and-a-half standing by itself in the middle of the road. A GI sat on the running board, his elbows on his knees and his face in his hands. No Vietnamese police were in sight, and the only sign of an accident was a large brown stain under the truck's left rear wheel.

"Stay here and direct traffic," Johnson said, then hurried off to talk to the GI. Around them, horns blared while people shouted and waved fists, and motor scooters careened through the narrow passages.

Left standing in the road, Bell shook his head and said, "Fuck!" How was he, a lone American, going to stop all the scooters and get the other traffic moving? To his relief, the Combined Patrol jeep appeared on the opposite side of the traffic jam, its siren blaring and red light flashing. Two civilian policemen, white shirts, got out, followed by an American MP. It was Johnson's bugbear, Bobby Cole.

Ceding traffic control to the Vietnamese, Bell went to meet Cole at the deuce-and-a-half. They arrived as the GI was telling Johnson that a motorbike had cut in front of his truck after passing it. The bike skidded and flipped over.

The soldier sobbed, "I must've dragged 'em thirty yards... Just kids... I knowed they were dead. Oh God.... One almost tore in two—guts a hangin' out. Layin' out there like chitlins... God-d-damn! Goddamn it all!"

Bell turned and looked down the road, but all he saw were jeeps and trucks filling the roadway, covering up any other sign of the accident.

"That's not all," Cole said. He had been listening along with Bell. "One of our guys was in front of this joker and tried to do a U-turn and come back. Fucking jeep flipped."

"One of ours? Who was it?" Johnson asked.

"Dunno, not for sure." Cole removed his MP helmet and wiped his forehead with the back of his hand. He had a dark, handsome face, black eyebrows, black moustache, and straight black hair neatly trimmed within military regulations. "But from what this sailor, Coast Guard, told me," Cole added, "it sounds like Sergeant Avery."

"Shit!" said Johnson.

"Well, his timin' was good. Some medics were coming this way and pulled him—"

"Just him? By himself?" Johnson asked.

"HQ pool vehicle. I checked it out, but I couldn't find a trip ticket."

"Let's go look."

Telling the GI to stay put, Johnson took off at a trot past the jeeps and trucks stopped along the shoulder. Bell and Cole trailed a short distance behind him. Two lines of traffic were now crawling in opposite directions down the center of the asphalt surface.

They found the MP jeep across the road in a ditch. Dodging into the passing traffic, Johnson raised his hand and brought a Lambretta sputtering to a halt. A deuce-and-a-half braked and blew its horn before swerving past behind them.

The jeep, open, without a top, was now back in an upright position, the driver's side covered with dirt, the windscreen bent into a V, and the front seats broken loose from their anchors. The drive shaft rested at an angle on the ground, and the front wheels slanted outward. Below the dirt-covered side next to the driver's seat, a black stain covered a square yard or so of the gray sandy soil.

Bell whistled. "How'd he survive that?"

"If he did," Johnson said.

"Well, he was alive," Cole said. "Sailor told me he was over at Madame Phoung's when all hell broke loose. Comin' out the gate when he saw the medics put a guy in the ambulance. Big fellow." Cole nodded, as if he had convinced himself. "Bet it was Avery. Day off, too."

Johnson looked down the road. "Be just like him to come back to help."

"Probably turned too quick," said Bell.

"Yeah." Johnson rubbed his neck. "But he was a good driver."

"Least old blubber butt had plenty of cushion." Cole chuckled.

Johnson grimaced. "We need to go to the hospital and find out about the boy-sans. I'll check with Singleton, see what he knows about Avery, if it was Avery." He hesitated. "Cole, get a statement from the driver and have him sign it. And call someone to come get this jeep and take it back to the compound."

Cole's eyes squinted into narrow slits, and his thin black moustache jerked up in one corner.

"Yassuh, boss." He gave a limp salute.

The two glared at each other. Cole was clinching his right fist as his muscles rippled under his rolled up sleeve. Finally turning away, Johnson motioned to Bell and strode off.

Following him, Bell glanced back at the jeep and frowned. *It may be way too late to tell Avery anything, even if I wanted to.*

CHAPTER ELEVEN
Major Binh

THE HOSPITAL WAS A ONE-STORY STUCCO BUILDING not unlike the others along QL 4, except larger and set back from the road, inside a low concrete wall bordered by eucalyptus trees. Johnson parked the jeep next to one of the trees, then led the way down a gravel path through a dirt courtyard unmarred by plants or undergrowth. The path ended at a raised veranda of faded blue-and-white tiles and a ballroom-size hall filled with beds.

They entered the hall through an opening wide enough for double French Doors, but there were no doors, and on the tall windows on the sides, there were no screens. The only protection from the elements was an overhanging roof.

Arranged in parallel rows, the beds were covered with woven brown mats. No sheets. The occupants were all men, most dressed in shorts and green t-shirts and many with white bandages or casts. Still more men lay on mats on the floor or sat with their backs against the walls. Some were motionless, an arm covering a face or hanging over the side of the bed, while others talked and swatted at mosquitoes or waved away flies. Whatever disinfectants or scouring powder the hospital applied failed to mask a pungent odor of lime like that emanating from the canals along QL 4.

A pole fan thrummed uneasily above the murmur of voices. Then a long keening moan rose and fell like a distant siren.

A nurse in a crisp white uniform like a nun's habit stepped in front of them. Using a mix of Vietnamese, English, and gestures, Johnson tried to tell her that they were looking for information on the boy-sans hit by an American truck. She responded with a pained look and a sharp retort in Vietnamese, then turned and marched down the nearest row of beds.

"She want us to go with her?" Bell asked.

"Damned if I know what she wants," Johnson said and started after her.

They followed her out of the hall and across a courtyard to a smaller building that had a closed door and screens on the windows. From inside came a high-pitched wail and cries in Vietnamese. The nurse held the door open and stood to one side, letting them peer in.

Against the far wall was a gurney holding a still form covered by a sheet, a valley in the middle between the thicker upper end and the thinner lower part. A bare foot, twisted at an odd angle to one side, extended beyond the edge of the sheet. The wailing came from a woman in a light blue *ao dai* and white silk pants. She sat rocking back and forth in a metal chair by the gurney, her hands moving up and down across her face. Her fingers tore spasmodically at what must have been a stylish coiffure.

At the other end of the gurney stood an ARVN soldier facing away from the door. His back and thick shoulders shook, and he clutched at the arm of a much shorter, almost bald man in a long white coat.

Seeing the MPs, the doctor pried himself away from the ARVN soldier and walked over to the door. He motioned for the two to follow him outside.

"Both dead, boy in there ripped apart," the doctor said in French-accented English, his mouth a grimace beneath a neatly trimmed moustache. "Father is very powerful man. Major Binh. *Une mauvaise affaire*, this."

Johnson nodded. "I'm sorry," he said. "Do you have a report on the injuries and a death certificate with the names of the victims?"

"*Merde*. Not yet. This afternoon." From behind his gold-rimmed glasses, the doctor fixed his eyes first on Johnson then on Bell, who shifted from one foot to the other. "GI drive crazy, shoot your guns. Beaucoup Vietnamese die. You Americans, you don't care you kill Vietnamese. Two times. Two times this week." He held up two fingers and waved them at the MPs.

On the way back to the jeep, Bell tried to shake off what he had seen on the gurney—and inside the hospital. The suffering and lack of decent facilities would only haunt him for a while. The image of the grief-stricken parents with the dead boy was seared in his brain forever.

Major Binh, the doctor called the man. "A powerful man."

I've heard the name, seen it. On the schedule in Robert's room. The district military chief Johnson called him. And in My Tho the Green Beret said something about... what was it? A "crazy gook major." Major Binh?

CHAPTER TWELVE
The Real Johnson

AT THE AIRFIELD DISPENSARY, a clerk confirmed that Sergeant Avery was the driver of the wrecked jeep, and its only occupant. An Air Cav doctor, a tall, blond contrast to the short, bald physician at the hospital, said Avery had a concussion and severe injuries to his leg and hip. Once he was stabilized, the doctor had placed him on a Medevac chopper to Saigon. From there, he'd go on to Tokyo.

Riding in the usual dead silence with Johnson, Bell's thoughts shifted from the dead boy to Avery. What was it *one of them, Hayes or the Green Beret, said outside the pagoda? "Eyes down here?" Was it Avery? "We'll take care of him?"*

What if this wasn't an accident? But it had to be. Avery just happened along and turned too sharply to go back. He should have told Avery about it. Fuck Hodge and the rule.

They ate chow at the compound and then returned to town by a back road that ran along a narrow canal. On either side, a thick canopy of palms shrouded stretches of marshland speckled with sunlight, and lush vegetation crowded into small streams that disappeared among the trees.

Johnson drove, while Bell took in the sights.

Within one thick grove, he caught a glimpse of two ornate buildings surrounded by a raised lawn of green grass. Each building had carved dragons on its roof and a porch with spiral columns and huge red doors. Two ancient cannons guarded a path leading to a dirt piazza in front of the buildings, and terraced steps led from the piazza up to the porches and the red doors.

"What were those?" Bell asked, pointing back over his shoulder.

"Some sort of government thing," Johnson said, "maybe French, maybe before."

They were crossing a stone bridge arched barely high enough above the water for a sampan to go under it. Johnson waved a hand at the dark tunnel of branches and leaves concealing the canal.

"This place is full of things we don't see, a whole different world." He paused as they approached a brightly painted blue-and-white, four-story pagoda on the other side. "We barely see what's in front of our face. And *we* talk about *the real world*. Been here eleven months, and I still don't understand this place, or the people. Still a mystery to me."

"Sort of like Alabama to the rest of the world." When Johnson didn't react, Bell looked out at the passing trees, dappled by the sun, and tried to think of a more serious response. "Know what you mean," he said after a moment. "The world we live in here—it's the one this morning on QL 4—trucks, GI's, *xich-lo*s. It's the blown bridges and bunkers where a bridge guard and his whole damn family live."

He stopped as they went past a small market. A mama-san squatted next to the road, the heads and tails of fish draped over the edges of a flat wicker basket in front of her.

"I watched the children going to school," Bell continued. "We aren't in their world. Just look at 'em like fish in a bowl. Or maybe we're the fish."

"Yeah," said Johnson, steering with his left hand and resting his right on the gearshift. "Interesting damn place... most of the men in the army—those who aren't too old or too young. It's the mama-sans who do all the work. Out in the rice paddies, sell the fish, even dig the ditches, and fill the potholes in the roads. It's the damn women."

"Maybe the men prefer the macho stuff. Playing soldier."

"Shi-it. They're like you, they don't have no damn choice." He shook his head. "Only place I ever been where men hold hands."

Johnson pulled off the road and stopped the jeep under a grove of palm trees next to a wood shack that served as a drink stand.

"Let's get a Coke. Singleton'll call if he needs us."

They bought their sodas and settled back in the MP jeep to drink them in the shade. From a pocket in his fatigue pants, Bell took out the book he had been reading, *The Hobbit,* while Johnson pulled out a folded tabloid newspaper. Glancing over, Bell saw that the cover contained a stylized print of a man with a large Afro and an assault rifle raised in one hand above his head.

"What you reading?" he asked.

"Something you wouldn't be interested in." Johnson shook the pages loose and opened the paper to an inside page.

"You don't buy that... stuff, do you?" *Best not to say shit*, Bell told himself.

"Nothing to buy to it. The Panthers have a lot to say about the black man in America. You ain't black. You didn't grow up in Alabama being black. No white man will ever understand how it is with us in your white world."

"Whoa, I didn't mean to hit a sore spot."

"Listen," Johnson said, lowering his paper, "one of the first things I remember is my grandmother telling me to watch out for the Klan. She lived down a hill from the old cotton mill where the whites had good jobs and my mother cleaned the toilets. I stayed with Granny after school. There was times she'd tell me 'you can't leave. Klan's out tonight.' I'd see 'em in their stupid pointy hats and sheets, carrying torches, coming down the hill. Grown men, pillars of the community." Johnson waved one side of the paper at Bell. "Burned a cross in my uncle's yard. He led his church members out of the balcony at the movie theater downstairs to the white section... The Rabbit Town drunk—Rabbit Town's what they called where colored folks live—well, he was found dead one morning. Lynched. I don't know why, even if there was a reason. They left him against the tree, noose 'round his neck."

Johnson's face had a sullen, bitter look. He slapped the paper shut and put it across his knee.

"That was 1958, not the 1920's. The good, decent white folks all wore those white sheets—sheriff, banker, the feed-store owner. They'd speak to you, take your money during the day, just so you kept in your place. The black man ain't ever going to put up with that shit again. We're gonna fight back. My children ain't ever gonna have to be afraid of the Klan. Never."

Bell listened, not interrupting. He couldn't say he understood; he didn't. He'd grown up in the South, seen the segregated theaters and swimming pools, heard the white leaders talk against the evils of integration and mixed marriages and rail about ungrateful colored maids spitting in the food of decent white families. He'd lifeguarded at a swimming pool that was integrated in the end—after being closed for two years; but he'd known few black people outside an old woman who ironed clothes for his mother when he was five. He called her "Aunt Mary."

"I can see what you mean," he said, breaking the silence. "But I think the times are a-changin', like the song says."

"Ah, bullshit." Johnson raised his voice for the first time. "Times may change, but the white bigot always finds a way to keep black folks in their place." He folded his newspaper and smacked it against his leg. "And here I am fighting for freedom my people don't have in my own damn state."

He finished folding the paper and slipped it back into his pocket. "We need to make a run through town."

CHAPTER THIRTEEN
The Attack

EXPLOSIONS SHATTERED HIS SLEEP—each one closer than the one before, until the last two shook the building. The siren outside wailed. In the top bunk across from him, Jack Dupre sat bolt upright, screeching in sync with the siren:

"Mortars! Mortars! My God! There goes the parking lot."

Rolling out of his bunk, Bell hit the floor on his hands and knees and started clutching for his glasses inside a jungle boot where he had left them. Just beyond the latticework on the outside corridor, the siren continued its deafening wail, rising and falling and rising again.

He scrambled to his feet, jerked open his wall locker, and grabbed for a pair of fatigue pants, knocking them off the hook. Retrieving them, he sat down on the bunk and stuffed both legs in at the same time, then pushed his bare feet into his boots. He ran for the stairs, the untied strings flapping on the floor.

The steady rap of an M-60 machine gun and pop-pop of rifles came from the ARVN compound. With a whoosh, the tower guard set off a flare from the roof above.

"Shit!" he muttered as he reached the stairwell. Grabbing the doorframe, he spun around and ran back for the flak jacket and steel helmet under his bunk.

All about him was frantic motion. Dupre, tall and gangly in boxer shorts, steel pot on his head, flak jacket over his T-shirt, headed barefoot down the stairwell. On his heels, Poteet was pulling up his trousers with one hand and holding a flak vest in the other. Lunging down the stairs, they bounced off the wall and collided with each other, and with Keller in front them. Falling and recovering, Poteet yelled, "Move it, move it!" amid a chorus of curses.

When he reached the armory, Bell went down on one knee to tie his boots. His hands shook, and the laces wouldn't go through the holes. While he struggled with the bootlaces, his steel pot slipped down on his glasses.

In rapid succession, three sharp mortar blasts came from somewhere close by. The floor shuddered under him. In panicked resignation, he wrapped the laces twice around the boot top and tied a double knot to keep the loose ends from tripping him. As he finished, he looked up, and through the legs running past, he saw First Sergeant Dietz crouched in the shadows under the stairs, down on one knee like himself. Top's hands covered his face; his shoulders were shaking.

Sergeant Hayes appeared. Bending down beside the first sergeant, Hayes spoke to him in a low voice, then grabbed him by the arm and yanked him to his feet. He led the trembling man, whose hands were now clenched by his side, down the corridor toward the orderly room.

Bell stood and looked at his own hands. They, too, were trembling. His whole body was trembling, just like Top's.

The yelling and confusion faded from the hallway, shifting to the outer corridors and then outside. No more mortars fell, but the machine gun and rifle fire continued unabated and reached a crescendo.

I've got to move. Go the next step in this absurd nightmare.

He ran inside the armory and grabbed an M-16 off a rack on the back wall and two bandoliers of magazines out of a trunk on the floor. He paused to loop the bandoliers across his chest, then on the way out, seized six more magazines from a barrel by the door. Five of these he stuffed into the side pockets in his fatigues and the sixth he crammed into the M-16, chambering a round as he ran down the empty hall and through the supply room.

He pushed open the outside door and peered out. All the exterior lights were off, everything black. A wild cacophony of deadly noises resounded everywhere in front of him. A flare popped high above the perimeter, bathing vehicles, bunkers, fence line, and the trees beyond in an eerie white light.

He waited. The flare faded and then winked out.

He ran, scrunched over like a chimpanzee, across the parking lot, past the V-100s, and through the open entrance of the corner bunker next to the ARVN compound. Bouncing off the metal wall on the far side, he came to rest between an unmatched pair of bare arms, one soft and hairy, the other lean and hard.

Meyer and Keller. They stood close together, their M-16s pointed out two narrow gunslits toward the trees and canal. Beyond the canal, long red streaks laced the sky. The chatter of machine guns and the whump, whump of grenade launchers echoed from the rice paddies. Two Cobras circled, bright spotlights on the ground. After a final pass, they twisted sharply up, then dove, one after the other, swooping downward, rockets and mini-guns lashing out at unseen targets in the rice paddies.

The MP compound's defenders, reduced in number by those downtown, were scattered along the perimeter, on the roof, and in three bunkers. The corner bunker at the road abruptly spewed out an M-16 burst, then another, cutting into the trees in front of them. The second burst drew choked screams, followed by frantic movement among the trees, going deeper into the gloom.

"Stop shooting! Stop!" someone squawked. It sounded like Beadle.

To their right and to their left came a rising chorus of small arms and M-60's. And behind them, a long, loud chir-r-rp.

Bell, Meyer, and Keller spun around together to stare out the bunker's entrance. Coming from the ARVN compound next door, a line of tracers slashed in a long arc over the compound. The tall antenna on the guard tower slowly toppled and fell with a crash onto the roof of the villa.

"Ah, fuck!" yelled Keller as they hugged the corrugated metal walls. But only for a moment. They each took a gun slit and stared into the night, ready for what was out there, ready for what came next.

Bell started humming, "When Johnny Comes Marching Home," his mind brimming with the dark cadence: "They issued us some jungle boots, hurrah, hurrah..."

But they hadn't run. He looked down at his hands. They weren't shaking.

The firing stopped. The Cobras continued circling, now joined by two Hueys, flashing crisscrossed beams of light over the open fields beyond the canal.

Bell was still breathing hard. "Where'd the mortars hit?" he asked.

"Ranger area," said Meyer, turning his head. His glasses reflected a perimeter light that had come on, shining through the gun slit. "I was coming off duty. Thirteen. I counted. Last three were close."

"Who the fuck was shootin'?" Keller asked. "Wasn't nobody out there."

No one answered. They stood staring out the slits at the night, the circling helicopters, and a few flares that floated down over the canal. They waited for what seemed like hours until two short blasts on the siren sounded the all clear.

Keeping in the shadows of the V-100 revetments, the three slipped back inside the villa. Sergeant Beadle met them in the corridor with Cole and Poteet.

"Keller, you and Bell go with these two and see what Cole was firing at. Be careful. Stay close to the perimeter and watch for booby traps. We can't take a chance with sappers. There's an NVA unit in the area."

Bell glared at Cole, but he didn't say anything. He was scared shitless of going out there, outside the fence, into the trees, where God only knew what was waiting—especially going out there with Cole and Keller. But he wasn't shaking. He was just scared.

Kneeling in the corridor, he unwrapped the laces from around the uppers of his boots, carefully threaded them through the eyelets, and tied them in double knots. He made sure his flak jacket and steel pot were securely in place before following the other three out of the building. In the parking area, as the others waited for him, he checked his M-16: round chambered, safety off, semi-automatic. Then they filed through the front gate and down the road beside the compound, toward the canal, Cole in the lead.

They were back in half an hour. They had crept through the undergrowth beneath the palms in front of the corner bunker where Cole had fired the two bursts from his M-16. The track of shredded leaves and bark was easy to follow. It ended in a bloody mess.

Meyer greeted them as Bell and Keller trudged up the stairwell carrying their M-16s and battle gear.

"Find any bodies?" Meyer asked.

"Three," Keller said and kept going through the bay and out into the corridor where a group sat smoking and talking with the lights out. M-16's, steel pots, and bandoliers lay on the concrete floor beside them.

"Three!" Meyer exclaimed. Everyone was paying attention now.

"Yeah, three," Bell said. He dropped his gear on the floor and sank down beside it. "Rooster and two fucking chickens." He chuckled. "Stew for dinner, if Cookie can separate the guts and feathers and shit."

CHAPTER FOURTEEN
The My Linh Ferry

JOHNSON AND KELLER DROVE HIM to the Mekong ferry crossing west of town for his day's assignment. Except for GIs going north to Saigon or south to Can Tho, he would be the only American there. The civilian policemen directed traffic and maintained order; a company of ARVN troops on the north side of the river, the far side, provided security; and he, the lone American MP, served as the liaison between the Americans and their allies. He felt isolated and vulnerable, and he took little comfort from the arsenal he had brought with him.

"You got something to read?" asked Keller. "I use the time to write letters. Just have to ignore all the commotion."

"Yeah, some fantasy thing." Bell patted the side pocket of his fatigue pants and added to himself, *as far away from all this shit as I can possibly get.*

"You'll have plenty of time for it," Johnson said, looking over his shoulder. Bell was slouched down in the rear seat, a bandolier of ammunition looped across his chest and an M-16 beside him. "Not many of our people come through these days, but keep your eyes open. Anything's goin' down, the locals will be outta there like crows in a cornfield. Watch the shopkeepers; they'll close up and disappear. No sweat. You do same-same—*di di mau* the hell out of there."

"So where do I go when I *di di mau?*" Bell stared sourly out across the empty rice paddies beside the road.

"Anywhe-ah but the ferry," Keller said. He glanced back at Bell and chuckled. "Don't think you'll be needin' all that ammo, bub."

Now well up over the rice fields, the sun lit a brilliant blue sky stretching from horizon to horizon. It hadn't rained in weeks, and the monsoons were at least two months off. Winter here was a relative term; it was hot and humid, but the short-timers said it was less hot and less humid now than it would be in the summer. Christmas came and went as nothing more than another work day marked by a few cards and packages and the mess sergeant's canned turkey and dressing for chow.

He watched the tropical scenery sweep past. The canals along the road had filled with black water during the night, and the ebbing tide bore a few low sampans out to the Mekong. Once, trying to comprehend the immensity of the river, he had traced it on a map, back through Cambodia and Laos until it disappeared as a thin blue line in the Tibetan plateau.

Johnson steered into a wide parking area of red dirt with sections of old gravel and broken asphalt. On three sides were wooden buildings that looked like ruined farm sheds. Sparse traffic lined the road up to a dock where a ferry was maneuvering to tie up. Buses, trucks, motor scooters, and jeeps sat in rows along both sides of the ferry's rust-red pilothouse, and a crowd of people clustered against a chain at the front.

"Come on, I'll show you around," said Keller. He started across the parking area while Johnson wandered over to the docks.

Keller led him to a ramshackle building with waist-high walls on three sides, an enclosed section in back, and a dirt patio covered by a tin roof in front. Crossing the patio, they stepped through an opening and onto a rough plank floor.

"*Hai Moui Mot* restaurant—'21' in English," he said. "Wouldn't eat the food, but suit yourself."

Not eating the food suited him. He had a box of C-rations, a candy bar in his fatigue pocket, and a P-38 can opener for the C-rations on his key ring.

Keller pointed out a jumble of crude wooden tables and chairs. "From back heah, you can see the parking lot and market. Also the ramp to the ferry. Buildings give ya a little cover, an-n-d you're out of the fuckin' sun."

Next to the patio was a booth with an ancient machine fastened to a table. A papa-san took green stalks out of a large burlap sack on the ground and fed them one-by-one through an opening in the machine. Vibrating and sputtering, it spit out pulp on the far side and a cloudy liquid from a spout below. A boy about nine or ten years old caught the liquid in a glass.

"What's that stuff?" Bell asked.

"Never seen nobody press sugar cane?"

The boy added ice from a bucket and handed the glass to a woman.

"They squeeze out the juice and use it in lemonade," Keller said. "*Nuoc chanh*. Some drink it. I don't."

Johnson walked back toward them. "Hey, we gotta go," he yelled at Keller. Coming closer, he added, "Make yourself at home, Bell. Somebody's bound to come back and pick you up at the end of the day."

"Thanks, that gives me loads of comfort." He scooped up his box of C-rations from the back of the jeep but left the bandolier of ammo.

After they had gone, he meandered around the parking area, his M-16 over one shoulder and C-rations in his hand. Stopping to watch the ferry reloading, he asked a civilian cop how long it took to get across the river, but even his hand gestures and raised voice couldn't penetrate the language barrier. Giving a shrug and walking away, he vowed once again to study the Vietnamese phrase book he'd stuffed in his pocket.

Back in the shade of the "21" restaurant, he selected a table with a good view of the ferry and sank gingerly onto the rickety chair, leaning the M-16 against one leg and setting the box of C-rations in front of him. As the morning progressed and the traffic to and from the ferry increased—primarily military vehicles and motor scooters—he felt like a spectator at a three-ring circus. All around him were eclectic aromas: lime and incense, ancient earth and cooking oil, decay and fish sauce, diesel fumes and sharp spices.

Only a few civilian cars went past, a big black Mercedes, an old gray Citroen leaning to the driver's side, and now and then a three-wheel Lambretta or motorcycle. A haze of dust rose and floated across the parking lot, never quite settling before the next wave of vehicles replenished and amplified it.

A motorcycle coughed to a stop next to the patio, and a man wearing a trench coat, scarf, eye goggles, and a Yankees baseball cap, all coated with dust, got off. He took a table near Bell's, gave his order to the boy-san, and soon received a glass of lemonade and a baguette in butcher paper. From an inside coat pocket, he took a folded sheet of newspaper, unfolded it, and extracted two small chicks. No feathers and down, but otherwise complete. Breaking open the baguette, he placed the chicks end-to-end inside the bread.

Feeling his breakfast rise in his throat, Bell stood and pocketed his book. He slung his rifle over one shoulder and, leaving the C-rations on the table, strolled out to the docks and stared at the river. On the far side, a ferry pulled squiggly lines of white foam behind it, and diesel smoke from its stacks streaked a smudge of green jungle and the blue sky above it. On the near side, sampans with painted eyes on their bows floated down river or struggled upstream past each other. Tree branches, a black log, and pieces of two-by-fours swept by in the swirling water near the dock. Close to shore, a line of water buffalo, submerged except for their snouts, swam with the muddy current. Two teenage boys rode on the backs of the lead animals while the last buffalo towed a sampan with an old mama-san hunched forward between the gunwales. All around them sunlight sparkled on the riffs in the turbid water.

As he angled back across the parking lot, an arriving ferry debouched a convoy of ARVN trucks. The first, filled with soldiers leaning over the sides, roared past in a cloud of dust. After the first few, though, the trucks carried no soldiers—no live ones, but stacks of coffins covered with the yellow-and-red South Vietnamese flag, two coffins on the bottom and one on top.

Feeling more depressed than usual, he trudged back to the covered patio, where he reclaimed his table and box of C-rations. The chick-eater had departed.

Extracting the paperback from his side pocket, he signaled to the boy-san and asked for a *yuk john*, as Keller had called it. "*Nuoc chanh*," the boy responded and hurried off to get him a glass.

Now numb to the noise and dust and the stench of diesel and gasoline fumes, he settled back to drink his lemonade, the best he'd ever tasted, and to escape into his book. But not for long.

Hearing shouts and a woman's scream, he dropped the book and grabbed his M-16 by the stock. The chair crashed to the floor as he bolted out of it. Then he froze, mouth agape.

A passenger had fallen under the wheels of a bus and lay writhing in the road behind it. In response to the rising shouts, the driver threw the bus in reverse and backed it up. Bumping over the man's chest again in the opposite direction.

Driver and passengers poured out of the bus. A crowd gathered, and several of the men began berating the driver. Two civilian police appeared, collected the victim, no longer writhing, and hauled him away in the back of a police jeep.

By now, the ferry had finished loading. A long horn blast signaled its departure, and most of the crowd shifted in a wave back toward the docks. Within seconds, the bus coughed to life, and passengers rushed to climb back inside and on top, while others grabbed onto its windows on the outside. Thus invested, the bus lurched off toward QL 4.

The ferry gave another whistle blast as it left the dock and a worker pulled the chain across the back. A new line of buses, cars, trucks, and jeeps began to form along the entrance ramp, pedestrians and bicyclists flocking past them to mass at the front as if nothing had happened.

He bought a Coke and opened the box of C-rations. Glancing up from removing its contents, he saw the MP road patrol pull into the parking area. The V-100 stopped beside an American deuce-and-a-half, which was a little forward of an American flat-bed, lowboy truck on the side of the road. The three vehicles together blocked access to the ferry ramp.

Hodge, his head and shoulders above the V-100's gun turret, waved.

Replacing the C-rations in the box, Bell slung his rifle over his shoulder and hurried to the side of the armored car. Mounted on four huge tires, it looked like what the crew called it, a coffin on wheels.

"What's up?" Bell yelled above the noise of the idling engines.

"Mine blew up a jeep—20 klicks north." Hodge hoisted himself out of the turret and started down. "Going to check it out."

The door on the side of the V-100 popped open, and a second MP, George DeRosa, climbed out. An olive-green boonie hat, swarthy complexion, and thick black moustache gave him the look of a brigand.

"Let's get a Coke," he growled at Hodge. "Clark'll stay here with this goddamn thing." He jerked his thumb back toward the V-100 as a black MP with a round face and flattened afro appeared in the turret. Clark waved to Bell and shouted something unintelligible above the din of the idling trucks and the clatter of a motor scooter going around them to the front of the line.

DeRosa spoke with a Brooklyn accent. "How ya doin' Bell? Drinking da *yuck john* and getting the shits? Lovely fucking place, ain't it? Ya haven't found somewhere to sleep yet? Shoot any gooks with that fucking gun you luggin' around? And don't tell me it ain't a gun; it's a fucking gun." DeRosa, dark hair, dark complexion, and Roman nose, sported the preeminent faded fatigues in the unit, and he was scheduled to DEROS, the army acronym for leaving Vietnam, in a few weeks.

As they walked to the "21" restaurant, an ARVN jeep skidded to a halt behind the V-100. From the jeep's passenger seat, an officer shouted and began waving his hand, motioning for the vehicles in front to move. Turning at the shouts, the three MPs watched the officer stalk over to the armored car and pound on the side with his fist.

"Looks like he wants us to move," said Hodge.

"Yeah, so's the fucker can go to the front of the line," said DeRosa. "Sorry gook bastard. Hey, you!" he yelled at the officer. "You can fuckin' go to hell and wait in line to get there like everybody else."

Clark stuck his head out the side door of the V-100. The officer, who had the gold insignia of an ARVN major on his collar, let loose with what sounded to Bell like a stream of Vietnamese invective directed at them, their parentage, and especially their mothers.

Backing the jeep away from the V-100, the major's driver tried to go around the far side of the armored car but couldn't get past the trunk of a large palm tree. From their shady spot under an adjacent palm, the four GIs from the deuce-and-a-half and the lowboy were enjoying the vignette while calmly smoking cigarettes and not moving.

DeRosa advanced toward the ARVN major, holding his arms out and motioning with one hand for him to get back from the V-100. As DeRosa approached him, the officer pulled a .45 from his side holster and waved it in DeRosa's direction. He was no longer shouting but speaking quietly in Vietnamese and broken English.

"No, GI, you move," was all that Bell could make out from where he and Hodge were standing back near the "21" patio.

DeRosa stopped mid stride, his hands still extended. The crowd gathering to watch the spectacle scampered back and away from the two, but didn't leave.

"Uh oh," Bell said under his breath. "Gunfight at the OK Corral." He felt a rising panic. What could he do? He gripped the stock of the M-16 with his right hand, but left it suspended from his shoulder.

"Hey, DeRosa," yelled Hodge. "I think he has all the high cards. I wouldn't fuck with him."

"Okay, okay," said DeRosa, dropping his hands. "Be cool now." The crowd had gone silent, and DeRosa's voice carried above the idling of the engines.

"You GIs, you numba fucking ten," the officer said, louder now. "Make us do what you want, kill children, take women. This our road, our ferry." He punctuated his words with thrusts of the .45 toward DeRosa. "You move, now. Please." Holding the .45 up in one hand, he pulled the slide back with the other, making it clear that he was chambering a round.

DeRosa backed away, and the crowd moved back with him. "I don't need this shit, man. I'm short," he said. Then to Clark, he shouted, "Move over Clark. Let the fucker by."

Clark, however, had climbed into the V-100's turret and swung it around to point the twin .30 caliber machine guns at the Major.

"Back off, you cocksucker!" Clark yelled, raising his head just above the turret. The sweat glistened on his forehead and ran in lines down his face.

Ignoring Clark, the major stepped forward, lowering the .45 as he moved. He pointed it straight at DeRosa's Roman nose. The major's driver, still in the jeep, lifted an M-16 out of the backseat and held it across his legs.

"Clark, you can't hit him," yelled DeRosa, beginning to hyperventilate. "Not unless... you get me... and a bunch... of these fucking people.... Move that... goddamn thing... before he ruins my face."

Long seconds passed, and the major took another step forward and pushed the .45 closer to DeRosa's nose.

Bell and Hodge stood frozen at the back of the crowd. Bell's mind raced over what to do, but he remained immobilized and confused. The GIs under the palm tree next to their trucks had stopped smoking but still didn't move.

"Clark!" DeRosa yelled between short shallow breaths.

Then Clark's head disappeared from the turret. After more long seconds, the V-100's engine started with a roar. In a clash of gears, the armored car pulled over to the side of the road, at an angle between the two American trucks.

The major smiled and nodded. "Good."

He slipped his .45 back into the holster, spun around on one heel, and headed to his jeep. Behind him, DeRosa took several deep breaths and doubled over, grabbing his knees.

Once seated in the passenger's seat, looking straight ahead, the major motioned for his driver to go around the vehicles in front. As the jeep edged forward, the crowd melted away.

"Jesus fucking Christ," said DeRosa, letting out his breath in a gasp as he walked back to Hodge and Bell. "I think the bastard would've shot me."

Bell took a deep breath and blew it out in a whistle of relief. DeRosa looked at him.

"Hey, Bell, would you have shot the motherfucker if he'd blown my head off?" DeRosa pointed at the M-16 still slung by its strap over Bell's shoulder.

Bell gave a small shrug but didn't answer, watching a newly arrived ferry release its stream of vehicles, scooters, and people down the exit ramp.

Clark's head appeared at the V-100 door. "Let's go, you lazy fucks," he yelled. "You caused enough shit here, and we need to get on this ferry. Your friends are already there." He pointed to the major's jeep at the front of the line.

With a vague wave over his shoulder, DeRosa started back to the V-100. Hodge turned to look at Bell. His face was serious.

"Watch yourself with our ARVN friends."

"That major," Bell said. "Could you see his name tag?"

"Not really."

"I'm sure he's the one whose son got run over. On QL 4."

"Explains why he hates us so much. Gotta go."

"Keep your head down."

"Yeah, sure. Oh, we're supposed to pick you up." Hodge gave him a tight smile. "See you then."

He climbed into the V-100 through the side door, and the armored car rolled away toward the ferry.

Bell walked back to his table and bought another Coke to replace the one he had left there and was now gone. The box of C-rations, though, remained where he had placed it, untouched. As he sat down in the rickety chair and opened his rations, he felt his legs trembling and the sweat running down his neck and under his arms. The bright midday air, charged with dust, diesel fumes, and noise, hung over the ferry crossing like an aura of mocking evil.

CHAPTER FIFTEEN
At the Convent

THE SLEEPING BAY WAS PEACEFUL. Even Poteet's tape player and the fans on the wall lockers were silent. Morning sunlight filtered through the latticework and provided a pleasant half-light by which to read. Lost in a fantasy world, he barely heard a pair of Ho Chi Minh sandals clomping past.

"Hey, Bell, you want to go to the airfield?" Steve Walker's voice shattered his fantasies. "Gotta run some errands."

"Nah, I want to read."

He looked around at the empty bunks, then at Walker shaking off his sandals and reaching for his boots. His fantasy bubble burst; he felt lonely and homesick.

"Shit," he said to himself, then to Walker, "sure, why not," and folded down the corner of the page.

"We need to take the laundry in the three-quarter ton," Walker said as he finished tying his boots. He added on the stairs, "Oh, yeah, Hayes wants me to drop off some stuff at the Convent."

They met Meyer in the supply room, and with the help of Tranh Le Nguyen, the boy-san who worked in the motor pool, loaded sacks of laundry into the back of the truck. Hayes' "stuff" for the Convent was already there—cases of soft drinks, soap, and toilet paper from the airfield post exchange.

Bell and Meyer rode up front with Walker, while the boy-san reclined on the laundry bags in back. The bags they deposited at Tran's Laundry, a warehouse-size building echoing with the chatter of workers and twang of Vietnamese opera amid clanging machinery and hissing steam.

Farther down QL 4, a little beyond Madame Phoung's, they turned left onto a gravel drive leading to the Catholic convent and orphanage. The complex consisted of a chapel and a series of low stucco buildings built around a long courtyard. There was a scattering of tall palm trees, and along the walls, neatly trimmed bushes and beds of yellow and red flowers. In the center of the courtyard was a narrow piazza of blue tile bordered by white marble benches. At the far end, a grassy lawn led to a swimming pool full of clean, blue water. No one was in the pool or the courtyard, but in the outside corridor of the nearest building, there was a straggling procession of children of all ages dressed in blue-and-white uniforms.

Walker drove around the gravel drive to the front door of the chapel and stopped behind an all-white statue of Christ, standing with arms outstretched toward the swimming pool. Farther along the drive was an ARVN jeep. The driver was leaning back in the seat, seemingly asleep.

"The nuns run the orphanage," Walker said. "Some of us try to help 'em out, you know, give 'em shit they need," he gestured to the rear, "like in back."

They got out and started around the truck as Tranh hopped out of the back. A diminutive nun in a stiff white habit appeared from the building next to the chapel. Inclining toward elfin plumpness, she had fair skin and wisps of red hair showing from under her wimple.

"Well now, you came in the nick of time," she said in a strong Irish brogue. "We're about out of toilet paper."

Introductions were made. Sister Agnes and another Irish nun, along with several Vietnamese nuns, had operated the orphanage for years, fleeing when the Viet Cong overran the town in '68 and coming back with the Americans when the VC left. The stucco walls of the chapel and the buildings still bore the marks of bullets and shrapnel.

They were unloading the boxes, not a difficult task, when Bell noticed that Tranh was gone. Then, carrying a case of soft drinks over to the kitchen, he saw the boy standing by the Vietnamese jeep down the drive. Talking to him was an ARVN officer.

Bell stopped and stared. It was the major from the ferry, Major Binh. Tranh was handing a book-size package to the major, who was nodding and speaking to him in a low voice.

Tranh was a fixture in the compound. He was well-liked by the troops, who treated him like a member of the family and had taken to calling him "Tony." But they knew almost nothing about his outside life, whether he was in high school or where he lived, only that he was somehow related to the old mama-san in charge of the Vietnamese staff.

The major's eyes shifted from Tranh and met Bell's eyes. A scowl crossed the major's face. He quickly took the package and climbed into the passenger side of the jeep. Tranh, turning toward Bell, gave him a sheepish grin, and shrugged. Bell stared past him, at the jeep. It was speeding off, around the swimming pool and down the drive.

What the fuck was that all about, Bell wondered as he carried the case of drinks into the kitchen. Meyer and Walker were already inside, opening cold cans of Coke next to a shiny white Frigidaire. Adding the case of drinks to a stack by the refrigerator, he decided he didn't want to know. But he was curious. Maybe he'd ask Tranh, aka Tony—if he could get him to understand what he was asking. He opened the fridge and took out a Coke.

After they finished unloading the truck, Bell walked across the piazza to the swimming pool, which looked to be a standard twenty-five meters long. A slight breeze rippled the surface, and he knelt on one knee to touch the water. It was surprisingly cool. Sister Agnes came up beside him.

"You're welcome to come swim." Her voice was soft and gentle like the water. "Come any afternoon during the week, before three. The children only use the pool after school and on weekends."

"Thanks. I'd like that." The noise from QL 4 was muffled here and sounded almost like waves at the shore.

"Think nothing of it," Sister Agnes said. "Your Mr. Hayes has been a big help to us. We're always pleased to have MPs come visit."

CHAPTER SIXTEEN
New Friends

AT THE AIRFIELD, Walker drove through the First Air Cavalry area and around to the rear of the Air Cav Mess Hall, where he turned off the road and stopped.

"I have to find this mess sergeant friend of Beadle's. He's supposed to give us some frozen lobster tails and T-bones. Sounds too good to be true, but we'll see." He shrugged and opened the door. "Don't know how Beadle does it, and I don't ask."

"You want us to come with you?" Meyer asked.

"Nah. Don't want to scare the guy off. You wait here, and let me see what I can dig up."

Walker went inside the mess hall while Bell and Meyer ambled over to the edge of the gravel road, and Tranh snoozed in the back of the truck. A high ceiling of clouds had covered the sky and given the day a gray hue to match the color of the weathered wooden buildings around them.

On the opposite side of the street, two black soldiers with Air Cav patches on their shoulders stood talking in front of a barracks. One was a tall sergeant with three stripes, the other a Specialist Fourth Class, the same as Bell's and Meyer's recently acquired rank. Both men wore the faded green fatigues of soldiers who had been in-country for a long time. The Spec. 4 sported a short Afro, and his hat rested on it at a jaunty angle. Raising his arm, he exposed a black wristband called a "slave bracelet" by the black soldiers who wore it. Bell found himself in sympathy with them. The slave part.

Passing close to the two, both Bell and Meyer nodded and said, "Hello."

The Spec. 4 ignored them, but the sergeant glanced their way and said, "'Lo, MP." Moving closer together, the soldiers continued their discussion in lowered voices.

Bell and Meyer drifted on down the road, Bell relating what he had seen Tranh giving Major Binh at the Convent, Meyer dismissing it all as meaningless. They turned at the corner to retrace their steps. From between the barracks came three more black soldiers with Army Engineers patches. All had incipient Afros, but none to the extent of the Air Cav Spec. 4.

"Yo, brother. How's my main man?" one of them called to the Air Cav sergeant. The speaker, who also wore sergeant stripes, had a rough ebony complexion and a scar above his left eye. "Give me some dap, bro," he said.

The other echoed the greeting, and the two slapped the palms of their hands together and went through an elaborate set of hand motions. The others performed the same ritual, laughing and talking loudly, ignoring Bell and Meyer.

For our benefit, Bell was thinking when the sergeant with the scar whirled around.

"Hey, white boys, you see something that interests you?"

"No," said Bell, startled and embarrassed. He turned away and headed across the road, to where the truck was parked.

"Actually, I do," Meyer said. "I was wondering what that means, and why you do it." Two of the soldiers laughed and one gave a disgusted snort, but the sergeant kept a serious expression.

"It means we're soul brothers," he said and took a step in Meyer's direction. "We're black," he paused; "and we're proud of it. What *the fuck* is it to you?"

The others, now silent, glared at Meyer.

"Hey, that's cool with me," Meyer said, raising his hands, palms up. "You mind if I watch how you do it?"

"Come on, Meyer, let's get out of here," said Bell. He had stopped dead and turned around at Meyer's first question. The tall sergeant with the scar glowered at the much shorter, somewhat stooped Meyer in his fresh green fatigues, his dark frame glasses sliding down his nose and curly black hair sticking out from under his cap.

The engineer sergeant laughed. "Ah hell. Come on, Red, give me some dap." He went through the hand motions again with the Air Cav sergeant. Then turning back to Meyer, he said, "Okay, you satisfied? Know any more'n you did before?"

"Well, it's an interesting manifestation of ethnic identity and pride."

The sergeant did a double take. "Ha, ha, ha, that's a good one. Where you from, white boy?"

"Chicago," said Meyer.

"Chicago? Hey, my man," he threw his hands up, "so am I. Now ain't that *too* fuckin' weird. Knew there was something funky about you."

While Bell and the others looked on, Meyer and the sergeant, who said to call him "Stick," bandied about the names of streets and jazz clubs they both knew in Chicago. Leaving Bell to roll his eyes. He couldn't believe Meyer had ever seen the inside of any of these places.

Across the road, the screen door of the mess hall slammed shut and Walker came around the truck carrying two freezer boxes. After handing them to Tranh in the back, he came to meet Bell at the edge of the road.

"What the hell's he doing?" Walker asked, nodding his head at Meyer.

"Jivin' bro." Bell grinned at Walker.

Walker scowled. "Well, let's jive the hell outta here." He jerked open the door of the truck and climbed inside. Finishing a clumsy effort to dap with his new acquaintance, Meyer hurried over to join them.

"Meyer, what's with that shit?" Walker asked, turning onto the main road. "Those guys do that crap just to irritate us. All they want is to make trouble."

"It doesn't hurt anything," said Meyer. "And that guy Stick's all right. You listen to people, you might learn something."

Walker grunted and then let out a string of epithets at a group of black GIs walking in the road, forcing him to drive around them. "Those black bastards all hang together. That hand shit and carrying on. Don't let Hayes, or any of the NCOs, see you doing that shit. They hate 'em all, 'specially the captain. Captain fucking Midnight!" Walker eased the truck through the airfield's main gate. He waved to the African-American guard standing by the bunker. "Bet your sweet ass they're gonna get rid of him."

"The captain? How can they do that?" asked Bell. "He's the C.O."

"NCOs have ways to make an officer look good or look bad."

"How about Beadle?" Meyer said and prodded Bell with his elbow. "He's black and he heads up operations. Won't he help the captain?"

"Hah! They're watching Beadle like a hawk. You know what the battalion clerk told me?" He glanced over at his passengers. "He told me the colonel wanted that lard ass out of Saigon. No secret the CID's after him. Still looking for a load of booze. Guess you heard about that?"

"Sort of," Bell answered.

Walker paused as he went around a Lambo. "Know what you can get for a pallet of Scotch down town?"

"I can imagine," said Meyer.

"Beaucoup bucks. More'n you'll see in your sorry year over here."

Bell thought a minute, then cleared his throat and asked, "What about Hayes? I hear he's into a lot of shit."

Walker craned his neck to look around Meyer, at Bell, who was squeezed against the door. "Hah! That fucker's been around forever. Connected to more people than a spider web to a tree... Engineers, First Air Cav. Gook honchos in town. I even heard the VC wouldn't hit us 'cause they have a deal with Hayes. Why..."

Walker stopped what he was saying when he saw an MP patrol jeep starting out onto the pavement from the worn dirt area in front of Madame Phoung's. He blew the horn and waved to the driver, Bobby Cole, to pull over.

"Let's give those freezer boxes to Cole. He'll take 'em back for us, even if I have to break his arm." He gestured over his shoulder. "And he can take Tony, too." Walker grinned at his passengers. "We can go downtown for a beer."

***

Bell remembered Kikki's Bar from the day he and Johnson found the dead American in the room next door. As soon as they got out of the truck, Kikki, smiling and talking in Vietnamese, came out of the bar to greet them, or to greet Walker. He hugged her, and she kissed him on the cheek.

"Long time, no see, MP," she said, her eyes fixed on Walker's.

"Not since last night." He put his arm around her waist as they started inside.

"Come in, come in," she said to Bell and Meyer, "and have some..." then she lapsed into food terms Bell didn't understand.

"That's Vietnamese for soup and egg rolls," Walker translated. "The old mama-san makes the best damn egg rolls you'll ever taste." He touched his thumb and first two fingers of his free hand to his mouth and made a kissing noise.

The object of his culinary praise appeared with a shuffling gait, bent at the waist, her gray hair in a bun. She was the same old woman who followed Bell up to Roberts' room.

The inside of the bar was long and narrow, holding only four square tables with pitted aluminum legs and red Formica tops with four cast iron chairs at each table. The "bar" was a raised counter with a faded blue top that appeared to have been salvaged from another era. A fan with translucent blue plastic blades, like the ones in the barracks, sat high on a ledge behind the counter and oscillated in slow half circles.

It was not quite noon, and the only other person in the bar was a girl in her late teens or early twenties.

"Mai, my sister," Kikki said, waving a hand at the girl.

Mai was pretty in the same fashion as the other Vietnamese girls he had seen—shimmering black hair, dark eyes, olive skin, and thin with a slight figure. Her face and nose were broader than Kikki's and her skin darker, yet she seemed more attractive to Bell, and he wondered if they were really sisters. Mai spoke broken English, and not as well as Kikki.

"What your name," Mai asked Bell, ignoring Meyer.

"Justin," he said.

"Justin?" She looked him directly in the eyes without blinking.

"Justin Bell."

"I'm Ira Meyer," Meyer said while she continued to look at Bell.

"You come here first time?" she asked Bell.

"No, I came here with another MP, Johnson, when the man died over there." Bell gestured with his hand in the direction of the house next door.

"Roberts," she paused as Meyer gave up and walked around the tables, feigning interest in the décor. "He kill self." She stopped. "Why he kill self?"

"I don't know," Bell said. "Did you know him?"

"He seem nice. Give me 'mercan dollas."

"He got to no good," said Kikki, who had been talking with Walker. "He work—no, no, how you say? Deal too much with Vietnamese and Americans who numba ten. Last time he come here, he very sad."

"When did he come last?" Bell asked.

"Maybe one, two day before he die."

"Do you know why he was sad?"

"Oh, I don't know," Kikki said. "Vietnamese major come see him. Bad man. Not good know too much."

"Who was the major?"

"Majors all same-same." She laughed and shook her head. Walker gave a shrug and looked away as the old woman hobbled in with a tray holding blue-and-white plastic bowls of clear hot soup with wontons and a few green vegetables. She placed the tray on a table and went out again through a bead curtain at the rear of the bar.

"How about a beer?" Walker asked, steering away from Kikki's hand on his arm and going behind the bar. He opened a small refrigerator and brought out three cans of Schlitz, then found three glasses under the counter.

The mama-san reappeared, this time carrying a platter stacked with finger-size egg rolls, almost black in color, still sizzling and redolent of cooking oil and spices. Mai followed her with a tray holding plates of lettuce leaves and fresh mint and a bowl of dark, putrid-smelling brown liquid. Urging them to sit and eat, Kikki explained that they should wrap the egg rolls in the mint and lettuce leaves and dip them in the *nuoc mam,* a Vietnamese fish sauce. She sat at a table with the Americans, but only nibbled at an egg roll, refusing anything more despite Walker's urging. When they were finished eating, Mai cleared the table. As she worked, she smiled often at Bell, and in passing behind him, placed her hand on his shoulder. Watching her remove the bowls and glasses, he asked how much he owed.

Kikki laughed. "MPs friends. You come with Walker, you no pay."

Walker patted her on the arm and reached into his pocket.

"Look, sweetheart, if you're going to run a business," he pulled out a wad of piasters, "you have to make money." He leaned forward and placed several of the notes in Kikki's hand, squeezing it gently shut around the folded bills. "Everybody pays."

Kikki grinned. "You good man, Walker." Then a wistful smile crossed her thin face. "You numba one." Walker smiled back, and the hard, sarcastic smirk that usually graced his face evaporated. He was older, and he had signed up, but he wasn't a lifer. He'd be out in another year, and he had two teenage kids back home and an ex-wife who still wrote to him, and him to her. That was the reason for all the letters, so he'd told Bell.

As they left, Mai walked beside Bell between the tables and under the awning outside the bar.

"You come back, see Mai?" she said.

He looked down at her, her head close by his shoulder. She smiled up at him, lips slightly parted, eyes dark and unblinking.

"Sure," he said, "I'd like to come see you again." Returning her smile, he thought, *maybe the days left in this place won't seem so long after all.*

CHAPTER SEVENTEEN
Night Patrol with Cole

BOBBY COLE STOOD ON THE PASSENGER SIDE OF THE JEEP. The same height as Bell, Cole worked out with barbells in the supply room. Not something Bell wasted time on. But Cole had the physique to show for it, and show off, strutting like a rooster, chest out, shoulders back.

"You drive first, peckerwood," Cole said, adjusting his MP helmet as he swung into the seat. "I'll call the station, see what's up."

He grabbed the handset, gave the station's call sign, and told the desk clerk they were on the road without waiting for a response. Singleton's voice came back through the crackling static.

"Roger, unit one, meet Victor one zero zero coming from Quan Loc 4 south at Vietnamese morgue on Le Thanh Street. They have a body, elderly Vietnamese male with head wound. Over."

"Unit one, here. Copy that," Cole said. "What are we supposed to do with body? Over."

"Body goes to the morgue. You fill out the report and investigate. Victor one zero zero info is that papa-san was shot by engineers on new road. He was riding a bicycle on the old road next to the canal. Over."

"Roger, will do. Unit one out." Cole reached behind him and placed the handset back on the radio. "Shit," he said. "We're wasting our fucking time for nothing but a dead gook."

The morgue was on a tree-lined side street between Le Thai-to Street and the river, three blocks west of the MP station. A strong smell of incense and lime came through large open doors leading into a low brick building. Several wooden coffins, all empty, were lined up on the sidewalk outside the doors—waiting for their occupants.

As they stopped near the entrance, the V-100 came around the opposite street corner. A scarecrow-like figure hung half way out of the turret, head and shoulders jerking and thumping against the metal side. Below it, a long stain darkened the dust-covered vehicle.

Once the V-100 had ground to a halt, Hodge climbed out the side door. "Yo, Bell, he yelled, "you doing the autopsy?"

He started toward the MP jeep while Clark, the crew leader, squeezed past the dead papa-san and hoisted himself out of the turret. He headed inside the building, followed by Cole. Isaac Peoples, the third crewmember, emerged from the side door after Hodge and plopped his large frame down on one end of a coffin. Lighting a cigarette, he let out a stream of smoke, then leaned forward with his elbows on his knees and stared up at the frail body hanging out of the turret. The smoke drifted above Peoples' sweaty face and formed a wreath around his short Afro.

From his post by the jeep, Bell also stared at the corpse. It looked almost like a child, except for the iron gray hair around the back of the head and on top where it was not covered by a plaster of dried blood.

Hodge lit a cigarette.

"They must have plugged the old guy from a mile away," he said. "We were coming up from Can Tho when a crowd stopped us. QC, he was the only one who spoke English, told us the papa-san was riding along on his bike; then he just seemed to fall over."

"Where'd they hit him?"

"Well, there's a small hole in one side of his head." Hodge caught his breath and wiped his forehead with his sleeve. His head was bare, and his sun-dyed hair looked oiled to his scalp from sweating inside the armored car. "Exit wound's a lot bigger. QC claims GIs on the new road fired at him. Two roads must be a mile apart, nothing but rice paddies between them."

"So how do we investigate? We don't have a clue who did this."

"Had to be engineers. New road's closed to other traffic, and they're still working on it. Probably a bunch of them got bored and started screwing around." He paused. "Had to be an accident. Take a damn good shot to plug someone in the head a mile away, especially on a bicycle."

"Yeah, a lucky shot," said Cole, who had come up behind Bell.

The others gave him disgusted looks.

"Hey, what's one gook more or less." Cole finished lighting a cigarette and tossed the empty pack next to one of the new coffins. "No one's going to miss the bastard."

"Crowd on the road sure did," Hodge said.

Clark came back from inside, followed by two men, civilians in white shirts, baggy pants, and flip-flops. He stood listening to the discussion on the other side of the patrol jeep, and then interrupted them.

"Cole, you and Bell go out to the airfield and talk to the engineer's duty officer, find out who the hell was out there today." He looked toward the V-100, and they all turned to watch the two civilians pull the papa-san's body out of the turret and lower him to the ground.

"The Vietnamese expect us to do something about this," Clark added.

Cole grunted and took a drag on his cigarette, then tossed it in the gutter behind the jeep. None of them spoke while the Vietnamese carried the papa-san inside the morgue, one holding his feet, the other his shoulders.

Once they were gone, Peoples hoisted himself off the coffin and went over to the V-100. Glancing up at the empty turret, he traced the stain down the side, his fingers just above it.

"Gawd-damn," he whistled, "all that fuggin' blood." He shook his head. "Have to wash this motha good tonight."

"Yeah," said Clark, "they wouldn't let us leave him. Said we had to do something." He grimaced and glanced over at Bell almost as if he were apologizing. "We couldn't let him bounce around inside, bleed all over the fucking place."

The visit to the engineers' duty officer provided no leads to the papa-san's killer. The officer maintained his work crew was north of the kilometer marker Clark had given them, but said he "would ask around." He was more interested in talking about his missing equipment, in particular a three-quarter-ton truck he couldn't locate.

"I reported this to your operations sergeant two weeks ago. What's his name? Beadle?"

The officer was a rosy-cheeked first lieutenant with carefully combed blond hair. *He's just arrived in country,* thought Bell, looking at the new green fatigues. *Probably ROTC, just graduated last spring from some state college. What was on his nametag, Fitzhugh or something like that? Need to get my glasses checked,* he thought, while the officer continued his grousing.

"We haven't been assigned to look for a lost truck," Cole answered him. "Sergeant Beadle probably turned it over to CID," adding "sir" after the lieutenant narrowed his eyes. "How could you lose a three-quarter-ton truck, anyhow—sir?"

"We're supposed to have five, according to the books." The lieutenant leaned back in his chair. "I did an inventory, and there are only four in the motor pool. One's gone."

"It could have been gone for months or your books could be wrong," Bell said. *Telling Beadle is like asking the fox to go look for the chickens.*

"Don't think so," the officer responded. "The motor pool clerk says there were five before Christmas. That's when the motor pool sergeant and a couple of others went home." Now the lieutenant raised his eyebrows, his most mobile feature.

"Well," said Cole, "I suspect an ARVN captain got himself a nice, freshly painted truck."

The officer's eyebrows jerked upward. "Well, that's dandy, just dandy." He turned back to the papers on his desk and started flipping through them. Glancing up, he added, "I'll call you if anything turns up... on that shooting." He dismissed them with a wave of his hand.

***

They ate dinner in the engineers' mess hall, the only benefit of their visit to the lieutenant. While they ate, Cole expounded on his ambitions after the army. He wanted to join a big city police force back in the World, maybe in Los Angeles or New York. He loved police work, had read a lot about it. Best police force ever was the Gestapo. No problem there with law and order, crime, hippies, queers, or riots. They weren't hamstrung by all the dumb-ass restrictions the courts placed on American law enforcement.

"So you're saying that criminals should just be tried and shot on the spot once you arrest them?" asked Bell.

"Oh, hell no! I'm not saying that, and you fucking know it. You're just giving me more of your pinko college shit." Cole balled his napkin up and threw it on the table. "I'm saying you shouldn't have to do crap like reading a criminal his bullshit rights. And we even do it here. What a fucking joke!"

The mess hall was almost empty since it was after 1900 hours. He was weary of Cole's harangue and ready to leave, but Cole wasn't.

"Let's get some coffee," Cole said and headed over to a silver urn on a table by the wall. Bell followed, trying to tune out Cole's rant.

"The motherfuckers should be encouraged to cooperate. Tell it straight, like it happened. You know, we need to solve crimes, not coddle the bastards." He turned and took a sip of his coffee. "Look, you're a bright guy. Surely, you agree the system can work better than it does?"

"Maybe," said Bell, "but just because someone's a cop or judge doesn't mean you can always trust them to do the right thing. That's why we tell people their rights so that there are limits on what the cops can do—make sure somebody's watching." He took a swallow of the bitter coffee and left it on the table.

"Goddamn it, Bell, criminals have more fucking rights than the victims. System's fucked up. Fucked up! My mother and your mother shouldn't have to wait to get raped before someone protects 'em from some fucking nigger."

CHAPTER EIGHTEEN
Following Cole

BY THE TIME THEY HAD STOPPED AT THE PX and started back toward town, it was after curfew. As they left the airfield, Cole gave a malevolent cackle.

"Let's check out Madame Phoung's. See if we can catch some dumb-shit GIs."

Bell raised an eyebrow. Johnson had told him that they didn't bother with curfew violators—if they stayed off the streets. But Cole was the senior man, and besides, he was driving.

Madame Phoung's was located on QL 4 between the airfield and the town, next door to the Catholic convent. A white stucco house, it was set back from the road in a grove of palm trees, surrounded by a high white stucco wall. In the center of the front wall was an equally high, green-metal gate, solid at the bottom with close-set metal bars in the top half. The two sides were always fastened together with a chain and lock. During the afternoons and evenings, a young girl sat on a stool near the gate and opened it for GIs to come in, four or five at a time. When the girl was not there, the soldiers would grab the bars, rattle the gate, and yell until one of the girls came out of the house to let them in. The green paint had been knocked off the metal in spots, the bars at top had been bent, and the bottom had been dented by kicks from numerous jungle boots.

As Cole stopped the jeep on the dirt shoulder between the road and the wall, Madame Phoung came out through the gate. She had a broad face and flat upturned nose. On her left cheek was a dark scabrous spot the size of a quarter—a mole or a sore. Bell tried not to stare, but he was constantly drawn back to it.

"Hello, MP," she said. "You come see girls? New cherry just for you."

"We're just looking around," Cole said, reaching around her to push open the unlocked gate. "Any GIs in there?"

"No, no. All go home. You go see."

She bobbed her head and stood back to hold one side open as a small girl, no more than ten years old, hurried out of the house to take them inside. Leaving them with the waiflike child, Madame Phoung padded up the sloped gravel shoulder and waved down a passing *xich-lo*, sliding into the seat as soon as it stopped. She turned to look back at the MPs and grinned, showing a jagged line of dark teeth.

"I go airfield. Bidness." Then she called "*di di, di di,*" to the driver and urged him forward with an imperious wave of her hand.

The girl locked the gate behind them and led the way down a gravel path to the door. As the two followed, Bell looked at Cole.

"Business? What kind of business can she have at the airfield? And at this time of night?"

"Hey, the woman has beaucoup friends. Big currency exchange coming up. Probably working on a deal to unload her old MPCs."

"That's not legal."

"So?"

They went inside. Five Vietnamese women sat in a semi-circle watching a color television set. They were all completely naked, their brown bodies thin and lithe with small breasts and slim legs. Most were sitting on straight chairs in different positions, some with legs and arms akimbo, but one sat on the floor in a lotus position exposing a scant mass of pubic hair. When the two MPs came in behind the small girl, the women made no move to cover themselves or to shift to less revealing positions. There was a cloying scent of perfume and perspiration.

Bell stared at them in the low light from the television set, ignoring the Indian actors on the screen. Two were young girls, the youngest perhaps fourteen or fifteen. The oldest of the five was heavier and harder in appearance, but of indeterminate age.

"Hey, MP, you come for short time?" asked the oldest one. "No charge."

Cole walked over to the youngest girl and placed his arm over her shoulder and his hand on one of her small breasts. "Not tonight. But I'll be back tomorrow. How about a beer, baby-san?" he asked, addressing the one he was fondling. She lifted his hand off her breast and padded across the tile floor to a small refrigerator in the corner. A fan on top of the refrigerator rotated back and forth, moving the warm air around the closed room.

While Bell watched Cole and the young girl, a seasoned harlot in a chair near him reached over and rubbed the front of his pants with her fingertips. He didn't move. Feeling his tumescence, she grabbed him through the fabric.

"How 'bout you, MP? Kim show you good time."

After first swelling, he shrank from her rough clutch. He felt attraction, desire, and revulsion all at the same time. Stumbling backward, he bumped into another girl's chair—and out of Kim's reach.

"Uh, no thanks," he said.

"Maybe next time." She smiled at him over her bare shoulder. "You come back soon, go boom-boom. No charge for MP."

"You want something to drink?" Cole asked, taking his beer from the girl.

"A Coke's fine."

Without looking at him, the baby-san brought Bell a Coke from the refrigerator and then walked back to her chair in front of the TV. The only other furniture in the room was a polished mahogany table, where she placed her feet when she sat back down, and a dark green loveseat next to the refrigerator. Heavy red drapes concealed the wall opposite the TV, while the front wall next to the road was covered with green sandbags stacked to the ceiling. Any windows were shuttered or blocked by the sandbags and drapes. Two doorways covered by thin flowery curtains led to interior rooms.

"Let's take a look around," said Cole.

Pulling aside a silky curtain to one side of the TV, he revealed a room lit only by the yellow globe of a Chinese lantern sitting on a nightstand. Bell hesitated, but once Cole let the curtain fall back in place, he followed, holding out his can of Coke like a talisman for protection.

Two low beds occupied most of the space in the small room. They were pushed up against opposite walls, leaving only a narrow gap between them for the nightstand and a small passage at their foot. Both held white sheets, the sheet on one twisted and bunched into a ridge against the wall, exposing a stained gray mattress. Stacked halfway to the ceiling at the head of the beds were the ubiquitous green sandbags.

While Bell hung back and stared, titillated and repulsed by what the beds suggested, Cole made his way back into the room of assembled whores and through the second doorway. Hurrying after him, Bell entered a larger room containing a king-size bed covered with a rumpled yellow sheet. A second sheet hanging from a rope stretched between hooks on opposite walls divided the bed into two work areas. No one was in either room, but an odor of human bodies and fluids lingered throughout both.

Slipping through a bead curtain to one side of the double bed, they entered a tiled alcove where a woman wielding a short hose squatted next to two footpads. With a flash of understanding, Bell stared deliberately ahead. The woman ignored them. Beyond the alcove, they entered a room that held a large refrigerator and a modern stovetop and oven like the ones at the compound.

Surveying the smart-looking kitchen, Cole said, "Madame Phoung's doing well for herself." He tossed his empty beer can into a shiny metal sink. "No one here. Let's go."

On the way out, Kim, the one who had invited Bell to come back, grabbed his hand and said, "MP, you change money for me?"

"No can do. Big trouble." He pulled away.

"Only little money." She held up her hand with her thumb and index finger slightly apart. "Boss lady change big time." She tried to grab his sleeve and then reached her hand toward the front of his fatigue pants.

"No way," said Bell and moved toward the door.

"You numba ten," she yelled. "No have girlfriend. No fucky-fuck." She turned back to the other girls around the television set and started talking rapidly in Vietnamese.

Cole was laughing as the little girl unlocked the gate and let them out.

"You're not gonna get any pussy that way, Bell. These girls are the best in town. Change a little money for 'em, bring 'em cigarettes or beer and you can have all the nookie you want."

Outside Madame Phoung's, the road was quieter and darker than before, and on their way into town, they passed only a few scooters and Lambrettas. There was no moon, and the halogen street lamps gave off little light beyond a pale cone at the foot of their concrete poles. Along QL 4, none of the shops were open; their folding gates were pulled tight and the little vending carts stored out of sight. Even the town was quiet, with only an occasional yellow light flickering in the window of a house or a bar frequented by locals. Outside one still-opened gate, silhouetted men sat smoking and talking.

After passing the church, Cole stopped in front of a brightly lit shop, the only one they had seen open. The sign above it was in Vietnamese, no English.

"Gonna eat ice cream," Cole said, bounding out of the jeep.

A young girl, not unlike Cole's baby-san at Madame Phoung's, but fully dressed in black slacks and a white blouse, fished two small cups of ice cream, like the Dixie cups in Bell's grade school, out of a deep freezer and exchanged them for a couple of 20 dong coins.

Standing under a streetlight, Bell pulled off the top. Although the frozen custard was white, he had no idea what flavor they had bought.

"Umm," he said, taking a bite with the small wooden spoon.

"Don't know how they make this stuff," Cole said, digging into his. "You reckon it's sanitized or whatever?"

Bell hadn't thought about that. "God, I hope so. I've..." He didn't finish with "had the shits for weeks." He looked at the ice cream. "Probably the *nuoc chanh* at the ferry."

"Ever seen where they wash the glasses?" Cole snickered. "In the goddamn river. They wash the fucking glasses in the river."

Bell almost choked. His gut gurgled, and the cramps at the base of his ribs came back for the first time all day. He dropped his half-eaten cup of ice cream into the open gutter.

"Let's go to the station," he said. He really needed to get to the station.

Cole finished his with a flourish, as Bell hurried around to the driver's side of the jeep. He was lifting his foot to get in when Cole froze on the sidewalk.

"Wait a minute!" Cole stood like a cat on the hunt, peering into the gloom. "What was that?" He pointed down the shadowy street.

"What was what?"

Bell looked in the direction Cole was pointing, but he didn't see anything unusual. The only noises came from a distant scooter and muffled conversation in the bar next door, not much louder than the subdued rumble of artillery and the steady thump-thump of helicopter rotors at the airfield.

"Saw a GI come outta that house and go down the alley," said Cole. "Let's get the motherfucker."

Cole didn't wait for Bell to answer. He took off down the sidewalk, one hand holding his billy club against his leg and the other on his .45. Trailing far behind, Bell followed at a walk, cursing Cole and holding his ribs, wishing the cramping would stop.

Cole turned the corner into the alley and disappeared. By the time Bell entered the narrow passageway, he could hear the sound of Cole's running feet, but he couldn't see him. After a few steps, he was in complete darkness. He placed his hand on one wall and followed the rough surface. Once his eyes had adjusted to the dark, he saw that the alley ended at the edge of a small canal. Beyond the canal was a dense grove of trees and tropical plants.

Bell heard a shot echo well in front of him, then Cole's voice. "Stop, you motherfucker! MPs! Stop!"

Bell took off at a trot, feeling the cramps at each step. At the end of the alley, he stopped and peered across the canal. All he saw was dark foliage and a few shadowy huts. Gritting his teeth, he crept along the bank until he found a section of prefab metal runway that served as a footbridge. He edged across it and started down a path on the other side. Then the thought struck him. *What if Cole doesn't know who I am in the dark?*

He slowed his pace and yelled, "Cole, where the fuck are you?"

No answer.

Faint lights twinkled in the hooches among the trees. He could hear someone running, boots on dirt, bushes or limbs slapping against a body, maybe 30 yards off. Toward him? Away from him?

An arm snaked around his neck, and a fist hit him in the lower back. His helmet liner flew off his head. Kicking with one foot and ramming his elbow into the man's abdomen, he struggled against the arm choking him and attempted to pull it away from his throat. They both stumbled forward.

"You fucking MPs," said a low voice in his ear.

He grabbed at his billy club, hesitated, and thought of his .45. The fucker might try to get it. He shifted his one hand to the .45, still pulling at the arm around his neck with the other. The fist hit his back again, harder, and he felt an excruciating pain.

Writhing in agony, he swung his elbows, twisting around and hitting at every part of the man's body he could reach. The arm released his neck, and the man shoved him down an embankment, into a ditch full of slimy water up to his knees. His boots sank in the muck, and he stumbled forward. One arm went down into the water almost to his shoulder. Only by grabbing the rough bark of a palm tree did he avoid falling flat on his face.

He scrambled to his feet and grabbed at his .45. Still there.

Feet were running down the path, back toward the alley.

Panting from the struggle and holding his back against the pain, he stared over the edge of the ditch. He saw nothing except the dark outline of bushes and the palms and banana trees along the narrow path.

He grabbed an overhanging bush and pulled himself up the sloped side of the ditch. Standing at the top, still in pain and gasping for air, he started to draw his .45.

I can't just shoot down the path. Then from MP school. *"Don't draw your weapon unless you intend to use it, and don't use it unless you intend to kill." But I don't want to kill anyone.... Or do I?*

His heart thumped against his chest, and he tried to catch his breath. He should go after his assailant. The footsteps hadn't faded; they had stopped.

Had the man gone into one of the buildings along the alley? Or a hooch?

Again, he started to draw his .45 and go down the path, back to the alley. No. He couldn't follow the sonovabitch into a Vietnamese house, or even one of the hooches. Not without a whole squad of MPs.

Shit! It's just me and Cole. That fucking Cole.

"Cole," he yelled. He listened for Cole, but all he heard was excited Vietnamese voices in a nearby hut.

He looked around for his helmet liner. They had a flashlight in the jeep. Why hadn't they brought it? *Cole should've known better. He's the pro. The real cop. That sorry fucking Cole.*

He finally spied the reflective white letters of the helmet liner. In the ditch, floating top down in the dirty water.

"Cole!" he yelled again.

Without waiting for an answer, he grabbed an overhanging bush and slid down the embankment to retrieve the helmet. Plopping it on his head, he said in a low voice, "Where the fuck are you Cole?"

Then it hit him—*maybe Cole's hurt. Or dead.*

He was back up on the bank when Cole came skulking out of the darkness on the path. His .45 was in his hand, down at his side.

"Bastard got away," Cole said. "Took a shot at me."

"Well, the sonovabitch, or somebody, jumped me while you were out there farting around," Bell said. He rubbed his neck, then his back.

"Why didn't you grab the fucker?"

"He got me from behind. Pushed me in there." Bell pointed to the ditch.

"You pussy." Cole shoved his .45 back into the holster.

"We don't know what the fuck's back here." Bell took a deep breath. "We're easy-ass targets. Walk into an ambush, set off a mine. We might even shoot each other."

"Eh!" Cole gave a dismissive grunt and flicked his hand in the air.

Bell bent over, holding his stomach. "Let's go," he said with a groan. His boots and fatigues were soaked, his helmet covered with scum, and his hands scraped and bleeding.

"You're no fucking good as a cop," Cole said. "How'd you ever get in this outfit?"

"Got drafted," he muttered, more to himself than to Cole.

"We'll leave all this off the report," Cole said. "No use lettin' everybody know how you got jumped back here."

"Me! Where the fuck were you?"

But Cole had already started down the path at a jog. He bounded across the footbridge and into the alley.

Bell followed, lagging behind and wanting to move faster but held back by the cramping in his gut. He watched Cole in front of him and wondered if Cole was lying about being shot at.

Bell grimaced. *Maybe Cole fired the shot himself. If he did, he sure as hell wouldn't want that in any damn report.*

CHAPTER NINETEEN
Avery's Jeep

THE NEXT TWO DAYS HE SPENT IN HIS BUNK. The third morning, he went to the dispensary where the medic laughed at his questions about tropical diseases and told him to stop drinking "gook" lemonade.

When Bell returned to the villa, Hayes was standing at the front entrance, coffee cup in one hand, eyes on the work detail chipping away at the hollowed-out volcano of sand near the fence. There was a hint of bourbon when the sergeant stuck his leathery face close to his and quizzed him on where he had been. Answering, Bell glanced down at a woven black cross on a lanyard around Hayes' neck. *Probably explains the gifts to the Convent,* Bell thought, as Hayes called him a faggot and told him to check in, then get his ass over to the work detail.

On his way to the sand pile, Bell drifted past the entrance to the motor pool. Inside was Alan Markovic, struggling to remove a rear wheel from a jeep. The smooth-faced mechanic, just turned nineteen, claimed to love tinkering with the military vehicles and worked long hours in the motor pool without complaint.

Bell detoured inside and asked him what he was doing with the jeep; the rear was suspended in the air by a block and tackle. Behind Markovic, his helper Tranh sorted through an array of tools on the workbench. All around were the comforting smells of a full-service garage: grease, dirt, and used motor oil, with a hint of solvent.

"Sergeant Avery's," Markovic said, between grunts as he tugged on the wheel. "Been setting out by the fence. Thought I'd see if I could fix it."

"Looks in pretty bad shape."

"Oh, these babies are tough. Mostly the windscreen and the rear axle," he gave the wheel a jerk, "that's bent. I can scrounge those, and the drive shaft and insides, I can put back together." He waved to his helper. "Come here, Tony. Help me pull this mother off." As the boy-san hurried over and grabbed one side of the tire, Markovic added to Bell, "Something's funky about the front end, though. Steering's gone. That could take some work."

Together the mechanic and his helper tugged on the tire. As the two strained, kneeling on the floor, the wheel popped off, and they both tumbled backward. Markovic jumped up as the wheel wobbled like a top on the grease-stained floor. Tranh remained on his rump, laughing and looking up at the two GIs. Markovic pointed to the boy.

"Boy-san here's been drafted. He turned eighteen and Uncle ARVN wants him."

Tranh, aka Tony, was a member of the Nguyen clan that made up almost a quarter of the population. Almost as tall as Bell, Tony had thick black hair, olive skin, and a thin, pleasant face given to wrinkled smiles and laughter when the Americans teased him. Bell considered, with a little jealousy, that the girls back home would've found the boy handsome in a fresh, unspoiled way. He always wore faded khaki fatigues, evidently inherited from an ARVN relative.

Hopping up, Tony grinned and said, "Go fight Ho Chi Minh. Win beaucoup medals."

"Yeah, right," Markovic said. "We go home, Ho Chi Minh come here. *Finit* ARVN. You in *big* bucket of shit. No DEROS, no go real world."

"Ho's been dead six months," Bell said.

Markovic chuckled, "He's got plenty of friends left."

Tranh continued grinning.

Listening to this, Bell recalled Tranh going with them—Walker, Meyer and him—on their day off, to deliver some PX goods to the Convent, stuff provided by Hayes. Studying Tranh, Bell thought, *Tranh also made a delivery, to Major Binh. A package. What was in it? Was that from Hayes, too?*

"Any chance the Vietnamese will let Tony stay here and learn..." Bell jerked his thumb at the jeep, "whatever it is you do with these things?"

"Doubt it," Markovic said. He picked up a rag from the workbench and started wiping his hands on it. "Maybe Beadle could help him. He's taken a real shine to the kid. Teaching him English. Even took him to the PX."

"How about Major Binh?" Bell asked, addressing Tranh, who was sorting through wrenches next to Markovic. "You know him, don't you, Tony? Can't he help you? Stay here, learn a trade?"

Tranh slowly turned his head and looked at Bell. His face was blank, and he wasn't grinning.

Khom bic," he said. Meaning, he didn't understand.

Markovic laughed. "They understand what they want to understand." He tossed the rag into the sink. "Now Hayes, he's the one who's got the pull with the locals. Maybe he could delay it a while."

"What the hell is he, King Rat?" Bell asked, thinking of the book.

Markovic gestured toward a tarp-covered object in the corner; it was obviously a motorbike, and not army issue.

"That's a Honda he got somewhere. One of these nights... poof, it'll just disappear." He pointed to Tranh. "Boy-san here makes deliveries for him. But he won't say who or where."

"Doesn't anyone report this crap? Someone come down here from brigade to see what the hell's going on?"

"Who are you going to report it to? Besides, I'm sure there's a story to cover how he got the bike. What I'd like to know is what he's got stashed outside the compound."

Markovic went to the other side of the jeep and bent down to remove the lugs from the second raised wheel. Bell paced around the back as the mechanic continued talking.

"One time Foley was drunk, he said tires are big items downtown. Like, would you believe, deuce-and-a-half tires? Make some real money on those."

"Foley's your boss. Wouldn't he know if any tires are leaving here?"

"Foley's a good ol' boy who does what he's told and doesn't make waves."

As they talked, they ignored Tranh, who was helping with the wheel. He gave no indication he understood what they were saying.

"So why do you think Hayes is selling tires downtown?" Bell asked.

"Didn't say Hayes was selling tires. Foley was drunk, pissed off about not getting the parts he wanted. See, he doesn't control what's ordered from Long Binh... or who picks it up. Anyone here who can sign a requisition form—"

"Or forge a signature on one."

"Yeah, or forge one. They can bring down *whole* fucking jeeps and trucks from Saigon and no one would know squat about it." He glanced over his shoulder as he removed the final lug nut. "Bell, there are four locations where we have stuff in the Delta." He tugged the remaining wheel off the rear axle with far more ease than the first and let it drop to the floor with a dull thunk. "We don't keep the records on the other locations. Hell, we don't even have decent records on what's in this place."

"Aren't there records somewhere? Wouldn't the C.O. know if something goes missing?"

"Hey, this is Vietnam. Who knows where all the shit being sent over here ends up? And Captain Midnight? What does he know about anything here?"

Markovic stood up from the rear of the jeep and came around to where Bell was leaning against the workbench. He pointed across the motor pool to a desk against one wall. "Look at those things on Foley's desk." Markovic chuckled. "Like I said, he's a good ol' boy. From Alabama."

Bell walked over to the desk and bent down to stare at two

shotgun shells standing upright near the front edge. "Captain Midnight" was printed in neat little letters on one and "Beadle" on the other. Bell looked back at Markovic.

"Surely they'll see these shells. Or somebody'll tell 'em."

"You have to get close to see it." He shook his head. "They never come back here, unless it's an inspection, and then Foley slips those into his desk. And, who the hell's going to tell?" Markovic tossed his wrench onto the workbench and stretched while Tranh rolled the wheel across the floor and leaned it against the wall. "Foley and his buddies would kick the shit out of them and say they fell down the stairs." He shrugged. "You know how that works."

Markovic picked up a flashlight from among the tools and went to the front of the jeep. He lifted the hood.

Drifting back to the workbench, Bell idly surveyed the neat rows of shiny wrenches on the wall above it and the contrasting dirty rags, open cans of oil, and greasy rags underneath it. He really needed to get outside and get to work, but it was cool in here, like a cave or musty basement, a pleasant seclusion away from the sun and Hayes.

"Hey, this is strange," said Markovic, talking to himself now. Backing out from under the hood, he dropped down on one knee in front of the jeep and pointed the flashlight at the frame next to the front tire.

As Bell started forward, the mechanic stood up and turned. He stopped, his mouth open to speak, and sucked in his breath. Twisting around, Bell followed Markovic's stare. Silhouetted against the outside light at the entrance was Hayes. Tranh took two quick steps and knelt down beside the jeep, as if examining the front tire.

"I thought I put you on detail, *Bell*," Hayes said, his voice rising with "Bell." "Get your ass out there and get to work." He stalked inside, his unblinking eyes focused on Bell, until they shifted to the jeep.

"Goddamit, Markovic. I told you to leave that Goddamn jeep alone. We're turning it in." His voice dropped, and it became almost wheedling. "That's the only way we can get a replacement."

"But Sarge—"

"You heard me! Put the damn thing back together and get it *down* from there." He gestured with his thumb over his shoulder. "And take it the hell outside." Pausing, he glanced at Bell, then back at Markovic, who still held the lit flashlight next to his leg. "Go ahead and hook it up to the three-quarter ton, so we can tow it down to Can Tho."

Giving the silent Markovic a consoling wave, Bell limped past Hayes and then slowly and deliberately across the parking lot. He could feel the angry sergeant's eyes burning holes in his fatigue shirt.

CHAPTER TWENTY
Hayes and the Prisoners

THE WORK DETAILS HAD FINISHED THE WALL on the canal side of the compound, topping it off, waist-high, with cement and leaving four shrine-like openings for fixed claymore mines. The two steel shipping containers at the corners, with gun slits facing the perimeter and the road, were close to being completely covered with sandbags.

Keller, Hodge, and Peter Landrieu, a new arrival, were filling bags from the edge of the sand pile. Working in a depression in the center were two small Vietnamese men with chains stretched between their ankles. Bent over, their heads down, they kept working and did not look up at Bell.

"Where'd those guys come from?" he asked, pointing to the Vietnamese.

"VC prisoners from the Ranger Company next door," said Hodge. "Hayes brought them over this morning."

The prisoners wore shabby, light-blue shirts and shorts. They were not young, and one had gray hair. Both had dark, weathered faces and spindly arms and legs.

"Poor bastards look half starved," Bell said. He helped Hodge finish a sandbag, tied off its top, and tossed it aside. "Why don't we get 'em a Coke?"

Hodge straightened up and kneaded his back with one hand. "Hell, why don't we take them to the mess hall for lunch?"

"You're joshing me, right?" Bell picked up an empty bag.

"Hell no." Hodge swung his arms from side to side to loosen his muscles. "Let 'em have a real meal. Kill 'em with kindness."

"Hayes won't like it," said Keller. "They b'long to him. All of 'em."

"What's with Hayes?" asked Landrieu, returning from throwing sandbags on the bunker. Landrieu had a thick neck, muscular arms, and a pitted forehead and face below his short-cropped, brown hair. He sported neither moustache nor sideburns below the tops of his ears.

"He's the head motha-fucker in charge of the fuckin' delta," said Keller.

"Doubt Hayes would appreciate your compliment, Killer," Bell said, then to Landrieu, "Hayes seems to run things around here. C.O. may think he does. First sergeant may think he does. But it's really Hayes." Bell found himself repeating what he had heard as if it were his own personal knowledge.

"Why do you think that? Doesn't the C.O. know what goes on in his own unit?" Landrieu pursed his lips in disapproval. "Why's he letting a sergeant bring in those people," he nodded at the prisoners, "to fill sandbags? That's not SOP for damn sure."

"Ya sure ask a lotta questions," Keller said. "How long ya been in country?"

"Six weeks." Landrieu grunted as he tossed a full sandbag on the growing stack next to the sand pile. "But I was in Long Binh 'til you guys needed a replacement down here."

"Well, worryin' about what lifers are up to won't do you no good," said Keller. "Crazy Ahr-vins—biggest problem ya have. That and accidents."

"Like leaving a round in your .45," said Hodge. They'd learned from Sanderson that Killer had once left a round chambered and plugged a pole fan in the armory when he was checking in his .45 after patrol. Thus the moniker, "Killer."

Keller stared at Hodge, his mouth open, like a smile but not a smile.

"Heard last week, down in Can Tho," Keller said in a low voice, "man threw a grenade at that sorry-ass Lieutenant Floyd ri-ight theah in the compound. Missed 'im, but he didn't miss the wa-tah truck driver. Opened up with an M-60, sliced the poor sonovabitch's legs off at the knees."

"Ugh. He live?" asked Landrieu.

Keller shrugged, and they were quiet as they finished filling the bags.

While the others carried sandbags to the bunker, Bell watched the prisoners. They squatted in the sand like two wizened crickets, smoking the cigarettes Hodge had given them down to the filters.

Minus Landrieu, who refused to go along with their plan, the work detail adjourned to the mess hall—with the two prisoners shambling along between Hodge and Bell, their chains clinking on the cement floor like the villa's ghosts. Hodge directed them to a table: red-and-white-checked tablecloth, salt and peppershakers, utensils already in place. Killer veered off to go sit with Dupre at the next table, while Hodge and Bell retrieved plates of food for themselves and their guests; then Bell went back to fish cans of Coke out of the cooler. By the time he returned, the prisoners were shoveling steaming-hot, cream-chicken-on-rice into their mouths like someone was going to take it away from them.

They had almost cleaned their plates when Hayes materialized in the doorway and started across the mess hall, Foley and Sanchez, the supply sergeant, right behind him. Spying the prisoners, Hayes came to an abrupt halt and let out a yell.

"What the hell is this? Those motherfuckers can't come in here!"

His face livid, he raised his arm, hand and index finger stretched toward the door. "Get 'em out!" he bellowed. "Get 'em the fuck out of here!" His arm remained rigid, pointing toward the door. The veins on his temples pulsed in anger.

Foley and Sanchez moved to one side. They were laughing.

"Bell, Hodges," Hayes continued yelling, "You two've done it now. You're confined to quarters 'till... 'till I decide what the fuck I'm gonna do with you. Now get them gook bastards outta my sight."

Bell and Hodge had jumped to their feet as soon as Hayes started screaming at them, but they made no move to evict their guests. The two prisoners remained seated, staring blankly up at the sergeant.

Then Keller leaped up from the next table. "I got 'em Sarge," he yelled.

He grabbed the younger prisoner by the arm and gave it a jerk. The man lurched up and out of his seat, catching the chains around his ankles on the chair leg. He stumbled forward, knocking the chair onto the floor with a clatter. Somehow he managed to hold onto his Coke can, even as Keller shoved him toward the door.

The older, gray-haired prisoner finished a last bite of bread and got up slowly, carefully pushing his chair back, all the time eying Hayes. He glanced at his two benefactors, smiled, and dipped his head in a quick bow before reaching behind him and pulling his chair out of the way. Then he edged sideways along the wall, chains scraping the floor, until Keller grabbed him by a thin shoulder and jerked him out the door.

Keller prodded the two along, leg chains clinking, down the corridor and out the entrance to the building. Going in the opposite direction, Bell and Hodge trudged down the hallway to the stairs.

They had been in their bunks less than an hour when Bowman came to get them. Top required their presence, ASAP.

After chewing them out and threatening them with a transfer to Eleven Bravo, infantry, he gave the nearest thing to a laugh Bell had ever heard from him.

"God-*damn*, that's a good one." A series of cough-like chuckles followed. "Hayes should never had those gooks in here." Then a snort. "How the hell he got the ARVN's to give him prisoners..." He gave another dry chuckle and picked up his coffee cup. He looked over it, his face almost pleasant. "They sure were pathetic lookin' little bastards. And God knows," he shook his head slowly, lowering the cup, "they needed a good meal."

Bell, standing at attention next to Hodge, was starting to feel relieved. Then Top scowled and banged the cup down on the desk, sloshing a stream of brown liquid out over his hand.

"You Goddamn peaceniks, you can't go coddling these gooks. You hear me?" Not waiting for an answer, he added, "Get your dumb asses outta here and don't go stepping on your dicks again, or I'll grind you up like hamburger."

"Yes sir," they both said at the same time. What fear Bell had come in with was gone, after he understood the first sergeant's reaction.

"Don't..." Top stopped and glared at them. "Goddamn your worthless hides. Get the hell out of here." He snatched up a stack of forms from the desk.

On the way out of the orderly room, they passed Hayes in the hallway, headed inside. The hard, squinting eyes glared at them, and he spoke in a quiet, measured voice.

"You shits mess with me again, and you'll be out of here quicker'n shit through a goose."

Eyes straight ahead, they didn't say anything—and kept moving.

CHAPTER TWENTY-ONE
Sergeant Sanchez

THE CHASTENED "PEACENIKS" spent the rest of their work detail in the supply room, helping Poteet the supply clerk, stack boots, sort bedding, and place office supplies on shelves, while listening to Sergeant Sanchez expound on his plan to escape Vietnam. The supply sergeant was short and garrulous, telling everyone who entered his domain, "Just call me Enrique." A twenty-year army veteran, he had seen action in Korea and signed up for a second tour in Vietnam despite having "seen beaucoup shit" during his first tour near the DMZ.

Today he sat at his gray metal desk, going over forms and passing a few to Poteet to retype. Occasionally he paused to check his reflection in a small convex mirror on a file cabinet near him. Rather than being irritated at his helpers' escapade with the VC prisoners, he was chuckling about it.

"That Hayes," Sanchez said, shaking his head, "what a nice racket he's got. Hard work somebody wants done and don't want to do it themselves, he give 'em those little bastards."

"You mean he hires out prisoners?" Hodge asked.

"Hey, *amigo*, Vietnamese work cheap, but they don't work for free."

"So how's he get 'em?" Bell asked from where he knelt on one knee, lining up boots on a bottom shelf.

"Better you stay away from his business," Sanchez said. He reached over and fondled a gold-tasseled Puerto Rican flag at the front of his desk. "*Madre de Dios*, do I need to get home."

"The prisoners are a new line," Poteet said, looking up from his typewriter. "All it costs is a small contribution to the local ARVN relief fund."

"*Basta, basta*! You don't know that," said Sanchez, waving a hand to shush his clerk. "He's a businessman; I'm a lover. I signed up to come back here before I met my Isabella." He touched a gold-framed picture close by his hand. "We married when I was on leave." He sighed, throwing his hands in the air. "Leave, leave? Leave my beautiful island and Isabella. For what? To come to this accurs-sed place and shuffle forms."

Sanchez took a comb out of his pocket and pulled it through his hair, patting the sides with his other hand. All the women, he said, told him he looked like Desi Arnez.

Out of this discourse, Bell finally determined that Sanchez suspected his young wife of cheating on him and wanted to go home to San Juan to straighten things out, as he put it. What he did not want to talk about was Hayes' business endeavors.

Sanchez droned on, filling in numbers on forms while Poteet typed and the other two unpacked supplies. At last Sanchez revealed his perfect plan: a medical leave to go back to the States for a hemorrhoid operation. When Hodge and Bell laughed at the scheme, he jumped out of his chair.

"You fuckers don't believe me? You do not believe the pain Enrique Sanchez endures for love?"

Turning around, in one swift motion, he undid his belt, jerked down his fatigue pants, and bent over to display a raw pink mass of piles protruding out of his anus. Bell made a choking noise and swallowed his wad of Juicy Fruit gum.

"Ah... God!" said Hodge, then grabbed a box of fatigue shirts to go on a shelf by the far wall. Bell hurried to follow him.

Behind them, Poteet laughed while he kept typing on a form. "You just got the speedy Sanchez show. He keeps working on those things, but the doctor at the airfield won't send him any farther east than Saigon. A nice hospital... good asshole doctors there. But old Enrique, he keeps hangin' on for a trip to the States and the best care his ugly old asshole can get." Poteet chuckled and shook his head.

The supply clerk claimed to be a Tuscarora Indian, and after a few rounds in the club, he demanded to be called Little Hawk. To Bell, he looked more black than Indian, and he'd told Poteet that. Poteet laughed, said there were black Indians just like half the white people in the South were part black.

"Hey, *amigo*, you laugh," said Sanchez, his pants back in place. He shook a finger at Poteet. "I'm gonna be outta here by Tet. You watch, motherfucker."

Poteet continued laughing as he jerked a form free of the typewriter. From outside came the noise of trucks unloading asphalt and the engineers' heavy road equipment pressing it into a new blacktop parking lot.

"How'd we get them to pave the lot?" Bell asked, gesturing toward the supply room exit.

"They owe Top a favor," Sanchez said, gingerly easing down into his chair. "Or maybe they owe Hayes a favor. Who the hell cares? We got it, that's what counts."

Grinning, he winked at Bell and held up his right hand, rubbing the thumb and first two fingers together. "Know the right person, you get most anything in this fucking place."

CHAPTER TWENTY-TWO
Something Rotten

ON HIS WAY THROUGH THE BARRACKS, Bell passed by Johnson, who was sitting on his bunk, his tall frame hunched over his footlocker. He was pulling papers and letters out, some going into a suitcase and others in a jumbled pile by his foot. Bell sat down on the empty bunk across from him.

"Packing already?" he asked. Johnson's DEROS was still more than two weeks off.

"Yeah, can't wait to get out of here."

"Yeah, me too."

Johnson's only response was a low, "Uh-huh." They both were silent as he arranged letters and papers in the bottom of the suitcase. It occurred to Bell that Johnson wanted to be left alone, but he was thinking of his patrols with the man. Johnson was a good partner, one he could trust. And he was thinking about his first patrol.

"You remember the suicide, the one—?"

"Yeah," Johnson said, checking his locker. "Roberts."

"Didn't you follow up with MACV?"

"Yeah, he worked for MACV, but they didn't need our help. Said they'd take care of it." Johnson continued pulling articles out of his footlocker and examining them as he talked. "Pretty clear what happened." He paused. "Nothing to investigate."

"Was there a suicide note or anything like that?"

"You saw what was in the room."

"Any idea why he killed himself?"

"Nope. Just got tired of living, I guess." Johnson seemed distracted as he shifted through papers he had thrown onto the floor next to his locker.

"Wasn't he working with the locals? Maybe with a Major Binh?"

"Could be." Johnson suddenly seemed to focus on Bell's questions. "Do *I* have any idea why he killed himself? Now that's a dumb-ass question. Why are you interested in this guy?"

"I was wondering if there might be a connection between Roberts and Major Binh. He seems to pop up everywhere we go."

Johnson patted down the clothes in the top of the suitcase and looked at him. "The major's a district military chief, and Roberts moved all over the delta, maybe even over the border for all I know. Roberts could've dealt with most of the muckety-mucks around here."

"Any reason he would've been dealing with Sergeant Hayes?

"Huh? Roberts? Dealing with Hayes? What gives you that idea?" Johnson looked hard at Bell. "Oh. Yeah. Didn't you—?"

"There was something about Binh and Hayes in the papers I saw there, in Roberts' room. On a schedule or something."

Johnson grunted and didn't answer. He picked up the pile of discarded items on the floor and placed them in a metal trash basket next to his bunk. Hesitating, he pulled a newspaper back out and tossed it to Bell. The letterhead said *The Black Panther,* the paper Johnson had been reading on one of their patrols.

"Here's something for your education," Johnson said, giving him a sly smile.

The conversation about Binh was over. As Johnson snapped the suitcase closed and slipped it under his bed, Bell leafed through the newspaper. Coming to a page with images of AK-47's around the margins, he stopped and started skimming an article on "Organizing Self Defense Groups." It contained pictures and descriptions of various rifles and handguns.

Johnson stood up. "Something else you want, Bell?"

"Umm," Bell said, staying seated on the adjacent bunk. "Nothing here about Martin Luther King—like, you know, non-violence."

"Look where it got him," Johnson replied. But he sat back down and leaned forward to keep his head from hitting the frame above him.

"These things won't get any better results." Bell pointed to the page on firearms. "You see how the people in this place suffer."

"What do you know about suffering, Bell? What do you know about me?"

"Not much, I guess."

"You said you wanted to learn more about how black people feel. Well, here it is. I'm not saying I agree with everything the Panthers say, but the white man needs to understand our anger. See what he's done over the last three hundred years." Johnson thumped the back of the newspaper with his finger. "I hope it don't go like that."

"I hope it don't either. You're probably the best cop here, Johnson, and they know it. Even made you a sergeant. Maybe you should join the state police when you get back to Alabama."

Johnson threw his head back, almost hitting the upper bunk, and gave a loud guffaw. "You think they're gonna hire a black man? Defender of white society?" He stopped laughing and rubbed his forehead. "That's a good one," he said, shaking his head. Then he gave Bell a rueful smile. "I guess you're all right, bro, even if you do live in a make-believe world."

When he got back to his bunk, Bell found a letter and a package lying on it. The package was from his brother, the letter from his mother. Nothing from Terri, his ex-girlfriend, and he didn't expect anything, not now, not ever.

The package contained a box of Coronella cigars, chocolate chip cookies, a civilian shirt and pants, and a note telling him family news and more importantly, that he wouldn't receive any more *Playboy* magazines since his sister-in-law deemed them bad for the morale of soldiers without women.

The letter from his mother consisted of one page torn from a grade-school tablet she'd probably bought at a local dime store. The writing was shaky block letters, incomplete sentences, and misspelled words.

"Hop yu ar fin. I am fin."

If she had gotten beyond the first grade, she never admitted it. The letters always said the same thing, and he knew that this one had been written like all the others, with painstaking concentration at the kitchen table, the single light bulb reflecting off the yellow Formica surface.

After dinner, he sat by himself at a table in the club and wrote letters to his mother, brother, and an eleven-year-old cousin who had adopted him as her pen pal. Aside from Terri, the girls he'd known before the army had stopped writing him when he was in basic training. He was out of their lives and forgotten, or *perhaps*, he thought, *they got tired of my bitching about the army and how miserable I am.* Now that he was in Vietnam, he vented his frustrations on his brother.

Dear Brother,

There's a war around here somewhere. Dunno where yet. There was a battle between ARVN's and NVA (North Viets) about 2 miles from here. We could hear dull thuds of rocket and artillery explosions. An MP who just came in from patrol said they brought in 50 ARVN bodies at the base hospital. The South Vietnamese lost. We're on alert here tonight.

I'm convinced the war is lost. The Americans hate the Vietnamese and they feel likewise toward us.

He continued in the same vein, telling his brother about the whorehouses and the bar girls, about all of the poverty, and about life in the compound. He ended by asking his brother to send bathing trunks for him to use at the Convent pool.

He stopped writing and listened to the low buzz of conversation and the television in the bar, the hum of the generator and the distant rumble of artillery. Staring vacantly out the open doorway to the deck, watching the nimbi of two flares drifting downward over the paddies, he thought about the prisoners and the conversation with Sanchez.

What was going on here? First the business with Hayes and the Green Beret in My Tho, then Roberts' suicide. And Avery's jeep today. Markovic had seen something odd, and Hayes stopped him from fixing the jeep.

All of it's unsettling. Something rotten Denmark. But like they say, mind your own business.

He looked around. Markovic wasn't in the club, and he hadn't seen him since the motor pool in the afternoon.

I'll talk to him tomorrow, find out what was bothering him about the jeep. Why Hayes didn't want him to fix it.

A hand patted him on the shoulder, and Hodge swung past and into a chair catty-cornered to Bell's. Their other drinking buddies weren't around: Meyer out on patrol and Sanderson probably downtown.

"Hey, good buddy," Hodge said, leaning close to Bell's face and whispering, "how about going up to the roof for a little party?"

"Nah, gotta write some letters." And he wanted the time to himself. "Why are you whispering?"

"Shhh," said Hodge. He clearly had had enough to drink already. "Ernie's got some good shit, and he's sharing it with friends."

Ernie the cook. Everybody's friend, Meyer said, like the guy with the rollout watch display who happens to run into you on the city street. When Ernie emerged from the kitchen, he shuffled around the building like he was stoned half the time.

"No thanks," Bell said. He pursed his lips and gave Hodge a hard look. "Better watch yourself, bro." *Hodge has changed*, Bell was thinking, *more reckless and careless of what he says. More drunk every night.* But he still pined for his wife all the time, and when he received a letter from her—pink or lavender envelopes, x's and o's all over them and redolent of perfume—he'd kiss the letter, inhale the scent, and give an exaggerated sigh.

"Ah, shit, man," Hodge said, "we're up on the fucking roof. None of the lifers are here."

"Top's here. Hayes and Foley may be."

"All gone, airfield or downtown. Ernie scoped it out." He shook his head and got up. "Don't know what you're missing."

"Not my thing."

Hodge shrugged and patted him on the shoulder again as he went behind him and out the door.

Finishing the letter to his brother, Bell sealed and addressed it, placing his APO address in the upper left corner and writing "Free" in the other corner.

Next he wrote to his mother: the usual banalities. He asked her about her work and the weather at home—whether it had snowed, and he told her to be careful driving if it was icy. He lifted his pen from the paper and tried to visualize her driving his car. A yellow Mustang with a big engine and an American flag sticker upside-down in the rear window. She only drove it to work at the mill and downtown for her newspaper, but he cringed at the thought of her gunning the engine and sailing through a red light. Then there were the people who berated her about the flag, which she refused to remove.

He sighed and finished the letter. Then he marked off another day on his Julian calendar, fifty in all, each day thoroughly colored in with blue or black or red ink.

The next morning, before going outside to join the work detail, he slipped into the motor pool to see Markovic. But Markovic wasn't there. He and Poteet had left for Can Tho at first light, Foley said. Driving the three-quarter ton and towing a jeep. To turn it in for salvage. From Can Tho, Markovic and Poteet would be going up to Saigon to get a replacement.

CHAPTER TWENTY-THREE
Cole Again

THE REST OF THE WEEK Bell spent on work detail or as the guard on the front gate, where his only accomplishment was to finish the first book of *The Lord of the Ring.* Then back on patrol. When he saw Bobby Cole was his partner, the rumbling in his gut started again.

Bell drove, and Cole rode shotgun—and toted one. As Tet drew near, the night patrols started carrying M-16s, but tonight Cole wanted to try something new. He patted the barrel of the 16-gauge lying across his lap.

"A sweet piece," he said, more to himself than to Bell.

"That's gotta be useless against the VC." Bell jerked the gearshift into reverse to back away from the building.

"We're in town, dickhead. One shot from this baby will blow any motherfucker who messes with me into next week. Fucking perfect for the alleys."

"I'm not going down any more alleys with you, Cole." Bell shook his head. "No fucking way. We'll stay on the street tonight."

"You're chickenshit. Chickenshit, chickenshit."

Bell didn't respond, just clamped his mouth shut and gritted his teeth as they drove out the gate and onto the gravel road. Across from the compound, the bright sunlight shimmered on the dusty soccer field. *How much longer until it rains,* he wondered, *until the monsoons will come?*

"What were you doing up in Long Binh?" Bell asked once they were on QL 4. While he was on the front gate, Cole had made a trip north with Sergeant Beadle and Wesley Akers, Lt Floyd's driver. Bell had waved the trio through the gate, Akers driving a deuce-and-a-half, Beadle and Cole beside him.

"Beadle had stuff to pick up," Cole said.

"I didn't see anything in the truck this morning."

"Already unloaded it. Last night."

"What did you get?"

"Tires and stuff."

"Didn't see any new tires in the motor pool." Before leaving on patrol, he had stopped by to see Markovic, who was back from Saigon. But Foley was there, and he didn't want to get into any discussion about Avery's jeep with one of Sergeant Hayes' entourage listening in.

"Bell, you ask too damn many questions," Cole said. "Beadle was getting tires and shit for some other folks. You know, My Tho and the engineers." He laughed. "How the fuck do you think we got the parking lot paved?"

Bell didn't say anything. Trucks, jeeps, and motorbikes raced around them as he drove slowly toward town. Ignoring Cole, he studied the now-familiar tableau of rice fields, palms, and banana trees on either side of the road, and the canals lined with higgledy-piggledy rows of hooches, sampans moored along the steep banks below many of them.

"You know," said Cole, "that fat ass Beadle is as queer as a three dollar bill." He paused, as if he were waiting for Bell to take the bait. When no query came, he continued. "Caught him fucking the lieutenant's driver. Up in Long Binh. Fucking him in the ass." He snickered. "Opened the door to his room and there they were. Him and that bow-legged Texas sheep boy."

"Who? Beadle and the wiseacre?" Bell tried to suppress any sign of shock that might gratify Cole's intention.

"Yeah, bigger'n shit. That black mother was really goin' at it."

"I don't need to know this, Cole." He clenched his teeth, then added, "What they do is their business."

"Old Beadle just stared at me, all glassy eyed and sweaty. Over Akers's shiny white back. I—"

"All right, Cole. I said no more." He shook his head to rid his mind of the image. "Enough!"

Cole's laugh dissolved into a long, exaggerated snicker.

The radio crackled. "Unit one, unit one this is base. Come in. Over."

Cole picked up the handset and answered the call.

Sergeant Carter, the desk sergeant, came back on, "Victor one zero zero alpha patrol spotted somethin' that looked like a body, off in a field near Quan Loc 4 south of compound. Same side, half a klick. Go investigate. Over."

Cole pushed down the button on the handset. "Roger. Why don't they take a look themselves? Over."

"Unit one... do like I fucking tell you to." Carter's words always stretched out and dropped off at their endings, like he'd practiced elocution using John Wayne as a model. "Victor one hundred has a mine report forty klicks south. Now get your asses on down the road. Over and out." Sergeant Carter was not a patient man.

"Roger," said Cole to the dead set. "Will do. Unit One out." Then to Bell, "You heard what the man said. Get your ass on down there."

Cole leaned back in the seat and cradled his shotgun in both arms as Bell did a U-turn and headed back down QL 4.

Several hundred yards past the gravel road to the compound, he slowed the jeep to a crawl and edged toward the side of the highway.

"I don't see anything," he said.

Cole stood up and held onto the windscreen to look over the top of the jeep. Bell continued to coast with Cole hanging onto the top.

"There," said Cole after scanning the field a few minutes. He pointed off to their left. "Back in the tall grass, past the ditch."

Bell made a U-turn. Before the jeep came to a stop, Cole jumped out and started off through the chest-high grass, pushing it aside with his shotgun. Pulling onto the dirt shoulder, Bell cut the engine and followed Cole through the swaying grass.

Not more than twenty yards off the road, a body dressed in coarse khaki fatigues lay stretched out in a flattened area of matted grass, a broad-brimmed boonie hat covering the face as if the person were asleep in the hot afternoon sun. The body was still and lifeless, but there was no sign of any blood or injury.

Cole knelt down and lifted the hat. Two eyes stared at them, and above the left eye, a hole the size of a half dollar revealed a red-tinged white mass beneath the shattered skull.

Cole whistled. "Holy shit! Just like scrambled eggs."

Unable to detach his gaze, Bell stared at the open eyes and missing piece of skull. A wave of thick black hair curved down to just above the jagged hole. His gut churned; he wanted to be sick. The trembling started. He had to refocus, try to stop it. *Be clinical, be objective, detached*, he urged himself, gritting his teeth.

"You know who it is, don't you?" Cole asked.

"Yeah," was all he could choke out between clenched teeth.

After a contemplative moment, Cole replaced the hat and carefully adjusted it to cover the eyes and the hole in the skull. A length of white cord lay beside the body, and a similar piece of cord still bound the boy's legs a little below the knees.

"Tony," Bell said, his muscles and his teeth finally under control. "Looks like he was executed."

Cole gave a non-committal grunt and stood, but he continued to stare at the body.

"Guess we better call the National Police," Bell added. To himself, he kept repeating, *I have to do this; I can't let Cole see; I have to do this.* Looking around the circle of crushed grass, he spotted an indented path leading to the road. "Bet he was dragged through there."

"Yeah, the pretty boy in the motor pool." Cole was still staring down at the body. "Beadle's friend."

Already moving along the path, he almost turned to yell at Cole, but decided better of it. What good would it do? The kid was dead.

Cole followed him through the tall grass, both of them stepping gingerly, watching for booby traps.

At the road, Bell searched the shoulder for tracks while Cole walked along the ditch. Bell's mantra had steeled him to the task, especially now that he was away from the body. "Nothing here," he called out, raking dirt and loose stone to one side with his hand. Then in a low voice, "A shit-load of people could've stomped through here, and you'd never know it. Ground's hard. No rain in weeks."

"Wait a minute," Cole shouted behind him. "Here's a shell casing." Cole hurried over to him, holding out an object he had picked up next to the ditch. He handed it to Bell. "5.62 millimeter. M-16."

While Cole shifted sideways along the ditch, head down, Bell examined the casing. He felt another shiver—before he caught himself.

"Blood on the bank over there," Cole called out and jabbed his finger toward the ground not far from where they had come out of the grass and crossed the ditch to get back to the road. "Lots of it down in the ditch. Probably shot him right there—right there in the fucking ditch—barrel against his head. Bang!" Grinning at Bell, Cole crooked his finger like he was pulling a trigger and said "bang" with an enthusiasm that discomfited Bell even more.

He looked down at his hands; they were steady, not shaking like they had when he saw the body. Or with the suicide. His anger at Cole had overcome—whatever it was.

"I'll call the station and get the white shirts out here," Cole said. "Their problem, not ours." He shifted the shotgun strap to his other shoulder.

"Yeah. Go ahead."

Cole started for the jeep. Bell didn't move. The sun was still high in the late afternoon sky and hot on his neck and shoulders and back. He stared vacantly across the ditch at the verdant grass fields and the bright blue sky. A few cotton candy clouds floated low on the horizon.

When he finally looked around, Cole was occupied with the radio.

Taking a series of deep breaths, he sifted back through the bent grass until he reached the dead boy's feet. He stared down at the still form. A slight breeze riffled the grass around the trampled area, startling him and drawing his eyes away. A stronger gust pushed the tall stalks down in a wave before releasing them to spring back up, swaying in the heat.

Looking down again, he studied the body. Wondering what had happened. And why. Thinking, *there aren't any flies. Too hot, too dry? Not here long enough.* Then he saw one crawl out from under the brim of the hat and down the dead boy's neck. Then a second one.

He turned, intending to go back to the road, when a glimpse of something white stopped him. Something peeking out of the top of Tranh's right boot—where the bottom of the trousers was hiked up to expose a bare leg. A thick wad of paper wedged between the boot and the ankle.

He reached down, and touching the leg, smooth and cold against his fingers, pulled out a folded piece of thin paper. He unfolded it and crumpled MPC notes separated like dried leaves and floated to the ground. He gathered them up and saw $20 bills, five of them.

Holding the five bills in one hand, he finished opening the crinkly paper. On it was Vietnamese writing and what looked like numbers.

As he studied the paper, he heard Cole shout and a jeep's tires skidding along the road, followed by angry voices. He quickly rewrapped the money and replaced the paper in the top of the boot. Then he hesitated and started to remove it again to show Cole but changed his mind. *Vietnamese case, their evidence*, he thought. *Leave it alone.*

He stood as Cole and two white-shirted National Police came thrashing through the grass. The lead one, who had a dark, sloping forehead and an odd face, looked familiar.

"Flagged these jokers down," Cole said. "Had to jump out in front of their fucking jeep."

"You know, I wonder if we shouldn't—"

"Look, Bell," Cole interrupted him. "I know where the fuck you're headed, but this is *not* our problem. He's Vietnamese, and he's way out here at the road."

Bell sighed. "Okay. I guess you're right." He took off his MP helmet liner and wiped his forehead. "Yeah, these guys can handle it."

What he really wanted was to get away from here. Just forget what the boy's face looked like when Cole took off the hat.

"Damn straight they can," Cole said.

But Cole made no move to leave, and Bell couldn't, or wouldn't, leave without Cole going too.

While Cole poked around in the trampled grass and along the makeshift path, Bell watched the civilian policemen. One lifted the boy's hat and replaced it, just as Cole had, then walked around the body talking and gesturing with the second. Finally, the one who seemed familiar pointed to the folded paper sticking out of the boot and bent down beside Tranh's foot.

Bell caught a glimpse of a silver nametag. Phan. *That was it. At the station, my first day on patrol with Johnson. The frog-faced white shirt with something slimy about him.*

As Phan removed the paper and started to open it, Bell heard a vehicle grind to a stop on the highway. Looking around, he saw Meyer and two Quan Canh disembark from a jeep on the other side of the road. Weary of watching the white shirts and not understanding what they were saying, he made his way past Cole—now exploring the path as if he might find something—and through the grass to the edge of the ditch. Ambling across the road, Meyer paused to adjust his MP helmet on his thick hair, then straightened his gun belt around his thick middle.

"Take your time," Bell said. "We've got all day."

"Yes, that's right, my friend. Fact is, we got all war." He chuckled.

"Meyer, Tranh's out there. He's dead."

"Tranh? Our Tony? From the motor pool?"

"Tony from the motor pool. Looks like..." Bell took a breath and let it out, "like he was shot at close range. In the head."

"Oh, good God! Why would anyone do that?"

Wending their way slowly back through the tall grass, he told Meyer about discovering the body and Cole's comment about "scrambled eggs."

In the trampled clearing, the civilian policemen were wrapping the dead boy-san up in a poncho. Once done, the two carried the bundle between them as if they were lugging a sack of rice, through the grass and across the ditch to their jeep, where they tossed it into the back seat. Standing stiffly to one side, the two QCs who had arrived with Meyer said little to their civilian counterparts.

After the body was in the jeep, Phan turned to the three MPs.

"Okay, okay. We take care. No sweat. Go. Go." He waved his hand for them to leave, then grunted something to one of the QC's, evidently serving as their dismissal, as well.

"Case closed," Meyer said, giving a shrug.

"For us it is," Cole said with a snort. "Let's *di di* the hell out of here."

The QCs headed back to their jeep, and Meyer turned to follow them. "Hey, hebe," Cole called after him. "Too bad. You gotta stay with our gook friends. All-a fu-cking day. Have *rots* of fun."

"Better a day with them than with you." Meyer waved his middle finger over his shoulder as he walked away.

Bell snarled, "Asshole," under his breath at Cole and started back to the MP jeep. He was passing between the roadside ditch and the National Police jeep—with its poncho-wrapped body in the back seat—when he almost stepped on a balled-up piece of white paper lying on the ground near the vehicle's rear wheel. Doing a little two-step to avoid the paper, he stooped and picked it up.

It looked like the paper from Tranh's boot—same size, same crinkly texture, same color, and Vietnamese writing—but not folded, just wadded up and discarded. And no money.

The National Police jeep roared to life and scratched off past his leg. It accelerated up QL 4 toward town—leaving him standing with the crumpled white paper dangling from his fingers.

Still staring at it, he slipped past Cole and installed himself in the passenger seat of the MP jeep. He grinned up at Cole. "*Xin loi.* Your turn to drive, partner."

"Fuck you," Cole grunted, but he placed the shotgun in the backseat along with the bandolier of shells and went around to the driver's side.

Bell smoothed out the crumpled paper on his knee and examined the Vietnamese characters and numbers. After realizing that he didn't understand anything on it, he refolded the paper along its creases.

"Cole, this paper was in the top of Tranh's boot," he said, holding up the folded paper as Cole started the jeep. "There was money in it. Five MPC notes, $20 notes. I pulled the paper out when you went to call the station."

"Well, well, lost MPCs. I'm sure they have a new home now."

"Where would Tranh get money like that?"

"Who knows. Probably from the old mama-san." He turned the ignition, then leered over at Bell. "Maybe from Beadle or maybe he just fucking stole it." He gave a sarcastic laugh. "But it's the white shirts' now. More'n those jokers see in a month, I bet."

He did a U-turn across the highway behind an ARVN convoy that had roared past, shaking the jeep and covering them with dust and diesel fumes.

"Shouldn't we report this?" Bell asked.

"Who the hell to? Ain't our case."

"Yeah, but the money…" then Bell was silent, tapping the edge of the folded paper on his palm. "Look, let's go to the station, see what Sergeant Carter thinks. I don't want this shit on the radio."

"If you say so, pardner." Cole shrugged and speeded up, swinging the jeep out to pass a three-wheel Lambretta. He cut back in front of it just before a deuce-and-a-half swept over them from the opposite direction.

***

Bell told the desk sergeant about Tranh and the missing MPCs, then showed him the folded piece of crumpled paper, smoothing it out on the desk. Sergeant Carter's reaction was similar to Cole's.

"That's really too bad about the boy." Carter nodded, tightlipped. "He was a nice kid. But shit, Bell, this is a fucking gook case, and I don't have time to fuck with it. If it's buggin' ya, go tell Nguyen," which he pronounced "goo-yen."

"He's our liaison with the locals."

Carter brushed the paper aside and waved him away in the same motion. Seeing no advantage in arguing, Bell picked up the paper and headed next door to the Quan Canh station.

Peering inside before stepping through the open doorway, he saw no one. The station was similar to the MPs', but larger, with a Vietnamese calendar and colorful travel posters on the walls.

He jumped when a voice snapped at him in Vietnamese, and then added in English, "What you want?" A QC, his face wrinkled in a frown, sat hunched over and almost hidden behind the chest-high desk.

"Is Lt Nguyen here?"

Without speaking, the desk clerk jerked his thumb toward a door at the end of a short corridor, then returned to whatever he had been reading.

He found the lieutenant in a windowless office, seated behind a metal desk, and leaning forward on his elbows to talk to an ARVN officer in a chair across from him. Bell stood in the doorway until Nguyen stopped talking and stared over at him.

"What is it?" he asked.

"Specialist Bell, sir. Sorry to bother you. If you're busy—"

"No sweat. What can I do for you?"

Bell eased around the ARVN officer's chair to get closer to the desk—and launched into his story, avoiding the usual Pidgin English. Nguyen nodded a couple of times and grimaced when Bell told him that Tranh had worked at the MP compound and again when Bell got to the missing MPCs. He made no response to Phan's name. Sitting to one side, the ARVN officer stared straight ahead, ignoring Bell, and gave no sign he understood anything the MP was saying.

When Bell finished, Lt Nguyen slowly shook his head. "The boy was probably shot by thieves. They missed the money if it was hidden in his boot. He should not have MPCs." He gave a tight smile. "Thanks for telling me. I will pass this on to the National Police for them to look into."

"But he was tied up," said Bell. "Why would robbers tie him up?"

The lieutenant shrugged. "That sort of thing is not in my—how do you call it?—control. It is civilian problem. Like you, we're military police."

Not satisfied with this response, Bell added, "The money was wrapped in this paper." He unfolded the paper and held the crumpled page out to the lieutenant. "Whoever took the money, threw the paper away. It had to be one of the white shirts."

Nguyen glanced at the paper but made no move to take it. "That paper," he said, shaking his head, "old piece of rice paper for kites." He pushed the paper back toward Bell. "This means nothing to me."

No one spoke while Bell carefully refolded the paper and replaced it in the side pocket of his fatigue pants, next to his paperback copy of *The Fellowship of the Ring*. He looked from Nguyen to the ARVN officer, who stared at the wall above Nguyen's head. Nguyen smiled benignly at Bell and said nothing.

"Thanks for your time," Bell said in a low voice. "Sorry to bother you." He dipped his head in a slight bow, then edged sideways out the office door.

Back on patrol, Cole asked if he had any luck with his mission and snickered when Bell told him what had happened with Carter and Nguyen.

"Told you," Cole said. "Bet they all just forget about the kid. And Nguyen won't mention the money—"

"I don't believe that, Cole."

"Except maybe to get his share."

"We can't just forget about Tranh." Bell hesitated. "Well, at least we... I tried."

"Ah, fuck it, Bell. Leave it alone."

CHAPTER TWENTY-FOUR
The Whore Patrol

CRUISING THE TOWN WITH NO DISTRACTIONS, Cole started complaining about his wife. No letter from her in weeks, and he was convinced she was cheating on him, spending all the money he sent home. If he divorced her, he'd have to pay, so someone had told him, but he wasn't sure what that meant.

"Goddamn it, Bell. I've been good to that woman. She's a bitch, but she's a beautiful bitch. Showed you her picture, didn't I?"

He had. Blond, pale white skin, movie hairstyle, fake smile if he ever saw one. A thoroughly haughty visage. Cole said her family had money, but they wouldn't give her any, so she spent his.

After Cole's venting for several circuits around the town, Bell wearied of the subject and told Cole to drop it. But Cole said he had a solution. A friend from Philly knew this guy who'd take care of it for him.

Bell was interested. *Where was this going?* Cole looked at him out of the corner of his eye and gave one of his snickers.

"I'm not going to pay that bitch a dime. And she's not going to fuck me over and get away with it. Not me."

"So what are you going to do about it?"

"That guy my friend knows. Well, he's a..." Cole smirked, "you know—a hit man." With that, Bell had heard enough.

"Cole, why don't you shut the fuck up and drive. You aren't going to do jack shit, and you know it."

"Oh yeah. You watch, Bell. No one fucks with Bobby Cole and gets away with it. You watch."

Bell sighed and slumped down in the seat. It was almost time to pick up Doc for the whore patrol. *But what if Cole's serious? Should I tell somebody? People I know don't go around killing each other, not where I'm from. Okay, I've read about the Mafia and seen gangster movies, but this shit doesn't happen with real people. Cole's just pissed off. Just talks a bunch of shit all the time. Besides, how could he hire someone to kill his wife—send a letter? Get a money order?* He chuckled at the thought.

"What's so damned funny?" Cole asked pulling up to the station.

"Nothing," Bell said, but thinking, *Cole's full of shit.*

Doc was a warrant officer who wasn't a doctor, but who had some vague function at the airfield dispensary. MP night patrols sometimes ferried him around town, visiting whorehouses and stopping prostitutes on the street to offer checkups for VD and to dispense penicillin. While the small owlish man had a name above his fatigue pocket, he preferred what he called his *nom de guerre*— "Doc," like almost every other army medic. The girls at Madame Phoung's called him "penicillin man."

After many years in the army and his second tour in Vietnam, Doc knew both his VD and his whores. He pointed out which houses had the fewest cases of gonorrhea—including Madame Phoung's— and the house off a back street where one of the girls had syphilis and had passed the gift along to at least two GIs.

Doc rode in back, Bell drove, and Cole sat in the passenger seat cradling his shotgun. When they passed a prostitute he knew, Doc would call to her by name, sometimes telling Bell to stop so that he could ask if she'd had a checkup this month or needed any penicillin.

"That's Sandy," he yelled in Bell's ear from the backseat.

They were driving along the docks near where the U.S. riverine patrol boats tied up and a Coast Guard tug lay at anchor. Doc pointed to one of the prettiest Vietnamese women Bell had seen—gorgeous enough for any slick magazine cover back in the World.

She walked along the sidewalk between the street and the river. *No,* he thought, *it's more like she promenades.* Shoulder-length black hair, full breasts accentuated by a sheer, low-cut blouse, and shapely legs amply exposed by a red mini-skirt. A small white plastic purse hung from a long strap over her right shoulder.

"She's part French, you know," Doc said.

"She looks it," said Bell, "like, out of a French movie."

"Lovely to look at, but don't touch. She's had everything in the goddamn book. Believe me—every goddamn venereal disease known to man."

"And she's one of Binh's babes," said Cole.

"Binh's babes? What do you mean?" Bell asked.

"Fuckin' gook has his own string of high-class hookers." Cole snickered. "Wouldn't be surprised if the Queen Bee herself don't work for him."

"Queen Bee?"

"Yeah, yeah, Madame Phoung. The old hooker-in-chief."

"Well this one's pretty, but I wouldn't call her high class," Doc said.

Bell pulled the jeep up beside Sandy, who stopped walking and stared sullenly at them.

"MP numba 10," she hissed. "Sailor no come talk if MP here." Even the dark red lipstick and excess rouge she wore failed to mar her cover-girl complexion and features, as much French as Vietnamese.

"Had your checkup, Sandy?" Doc leaned out the back of the jeep. "Taking your penicillin?" He reached toward her. "Here, let me see your arms."

She stepped away from the jeep and gave her hair a flip. "Sandy no need no-thing." Placing one hand on her hip, she swung the small white purse against her red mini-skirt.

"Sandy," Doc sounded gentle in the way he said her name. "You've had some bad stuff. You need to stay away from the GIs and the sailors."

"Fuck you," she said. "GIs, sailors, my friends." She smiled for the first time, showing dazzling white teeth. "Give me beaucoup dolla."

The lights along the docks sparkled in the black rippling river behind her. On the other side of the river, a series of flares sparkled in the black sky.

Cole laughed, trailing once more into a snicker. "Hey Sandy, we - all - love - you.... You one beau-ti-ful fuck-ing whore."

Grabbing her purse by the strap and shaking it at Cole, Sandy emitted a stream of harsh-sounding words in Vietnamese. Then she switched to English, "You basta'd, you no love me. You love body. No love me. Nobody love me."

She spun around and flounced off toward the Coast Guard tug anchored by the dock, her shoulders back, her white pocketbook swinging next to her short red skirt, and her hips swaying to the soft soughing and lapping of the river, a mocking caricature of a runway model on a half-lit concrete stage. Far across the river the flares winked out one after the other like falling stars.

***

After Doc finished with his rounds at Madame Phoung's, they headed back to the airfield. The yellow twilight in which they had started out had long passed into the sharp darkness of the tropics. The night air was still overheated from the day, oppressive and heavy with the damp odors from the canals.

They fell in behind a jeep full of Americans, two of whom were hanging out the sides over the back wheels. When the jeep sped around an empty *xich-lo*, one of the GIs leaned out and launched a beer can at it. The old papa-san on the motorbike ducked under a spray of liquid as the can sailed over his head and crashed into the tin passenger carriage.

"You motherfuckers," growled Bell and flipped on the siren. He accelerated close behind the jeep.

"What are you doing?" yelled Cole.

"Those assholes can't do that. He's not hurting them."

"Ah shit, Bell!" Cole said. "He's just an old fucking gook—and they didn't even hit him. Give it a rest."

"Yahoo! Go get 'em!" yelled Doc from the backseat.

The American jeep skidded over to the side of the road and stopped. Pulling his jeep in behind it, Bell hopped out and strode forward without waiting for Cole. The jeep's driver was a first lieutenant with blond hair and no hat. Bell saluted him. The lieutenant kept his hands on the steering wheel.

"Somebody in the back of your jeep threw a beer can at that papa-san you passed," Bell said, staring hard at the lieutenant. "I'm not going to write you up... *sir.*" His tone was mocking. "But that sort of thing makes our job harder." He noticed the engineers patch on the lieutenant's shoulder. "Yours and mine both."

The lieutenant, who appeared to be the most sober of the group, turned around and glared at the three men in back. The one sitting over the right wheel leaned over the side and retched. The others sat slacked face and clearly intoxicated, staring at Bell with dumb incomprehension and hostility.

The lieutenant turned back toward Bell. "I understand, Specialist. It won't happen again."

His eyebrows jumped up and down, and Bell remembered where he had seen him before. The engineers' duty officer they had interviewed about the old papa-san killed, shot in the head with an M-16, on QL 4.

"You're absolutely right," the lieutenant said, slightly slurring his words. "Thanks." He gave a wave with his right hand that might have been a salute.

"Yes, sir. Let's hope it doesn't happen again." Bell saluted and then waved the lieutenant back onto the road.

Returning to his own jeep, he found Cole slumped down in the passenger seat, the shotgun between his legs. "What a waste of fucking time," he said as Bell got in. "Those fuckers don't give a shit about any goddamn gook or anything a low-ass Spec 4 like you says to 'em."

"No, no," said Doc from the back seat. "You did the right thing.

We can't close our eyes to that kind of stuff."

Bell started the jeep, but he didn't take his foot off the clutch. Doc was leaning forward, his head and shoulders almost between the front seats. His voice had an urgent, lecturing tone, which didn't bother Bell, but Bell hoped would bother Cole.

"Nixon wants to Vietnamize the war," Doc was saying, "and get us out, but we won't succeed if we don't show respect for the people. Mistreat them, beat them down, we prime them for defeat. We act like racists or like the colonialists—white man's burden and all that— we end up losing."

Which sounded about right to Bell. They were losing, whether anybody else recognized it or not.

"Doc, you spout this shit like you're a goddamn left-wing commie," said Cole, turning sideways toward Doc. "Nuthin but *pu- ure* bullshit."

"I don't know what Nixon's doing," said Bell. "But I do know what's not right." He jerked the jeep into gear. "Throwing a beer can at that old guy wasn't right—gook or no gook." He popped the clutch, sending Doc back into his seat and prompting Cole to yell at him.

As he pulled onto the empty road, though, he wasn't listening to Cole. *That must be the same fucking bunch of engineers who shot the papa-san on the road to Can Tho.*

CHAPTER TWENTY-FIVE
Markovic

IT WAS MIDNIGHT WHEN BELL WENT to turn in the patrol jeep, but a light was still on in the motor pool. Markovic was standing in front of the deep sink by the wall, cleaning tools under the bright light above the sink. Bell threw the trip ticket into a wire basket by the entrance and headed to join the mechanic.

"You're working late," he said, then stopped when Markovic turned toward him. The young soldier's face was drawn, his eyes bloodshot, and his cheeks red from where he must have rubbed away tears.

"Yeah," Markovic said in a surprisingly normal voice. "Had to fix the transmission for the other patrol jeep—for tomorrow."

"You heard about Tony?"

"Yeah, sure." A strangled noise came from deep in Markovic's throat, but he remained outwardly composed. "I knew something was wrong when he didn't show up this morning..." He cleared his throat as if to add something, but stopped. He intently examined the wrench he was holding, then returned to rubbing it with a dirty cloth. Bell watched him work and remained quiet. Finally, the mechanic finished, "... never thought it would be anything like that."

"No.... It was terrible."

Bell kept to himself what he had seen: the hole in Tranh's forehead and the brains beneath the skull. Markovic probably had heard about it anyway. Cole liked to talk about shit like that. So he said softly, "It was worse than anything I expected—"

"Any idea who did it?"

"None."

"The gook cops say anything?"

"Nope. Doubt they'll ever figure out what happened."

Markovic turned back to the sink and quickly finished cleaning the wrench and laid it on a dry rag by the sink. He picked up another, cleaner rag and started drying his hands. Watching Markovic fold the cloth over and around each hand, Bell remembered the note in his side pocket, next to the paperback novel. He took it out.

"Ever see this before?" He unfolded the note and held it out to Markovic. "Found it stuck down in Tony's boot, with a hundred in MPCs inside it."

Markovic whistled. "A hundred MPCs. He never had that kind of money." He paused and tossed the rag onto the sink. "Unless someone gave it to him to give to someone else. Maybe the old mama-san—or one of his relatives."

"Or maybe he stole it?"

"Never happen, Bell. I'd trust him...," a choking noise came from Markovic's chest. "I would've trusted him... with my last dollar."

"Yeah, that's what I thought."

Taking the note, Markovic asked, "What is this anyway?"

"No idea."

After holding the note up under the light and quickly glancing at it, Markovic handed it back to Bell with a dispirited shrug. "All gook to me."

Bell refolded the paper and put it back in his side pocket. He had almost forgotten about Avery's jeep and what he had wanted to ask Markovic that morning. It came back to him as Markovic reached to turn out the light. "Oh yeah, I meant to ask you—what was wrong with that jeep?"

"The one wrecked? Avery's?" Markovic flipped the switch, leaving them in a dull half-light from the single bulb at the entrance. "Looked like the tie rod broke and someone soldered it back together again."

They walked slowly toward the open garage-door entrance. Bell didn't speak as Markovic continued talking.

"Sort of sloppy looking weld, but I didn't get a good look at it.

Broke in two where it had been soldered. Not something I did, or would do. Least bit of stress, it'd break again."

At the door, Markovic switched off the last inside light. The ammunition bunker and V-100 revetments were dark shadows between them and the perimeter lights shining outward from the fence line.

"Could someone have, you know, done that intentionally?" Bell asked. "So it would break?"

"What?" Markovic stopped and turned toward him. "Set it up to fail? Is that what you're asking?" He shook his head, his mouth open in incredulity. "Goddamit, Bell, that's crazy! Why would anyone do that?"

"Well, could they?"

"I don't know," but he nodded slightly, a motion Bell could barely see in the darkness. "If they knew what they were doing, but it would be dicey." His dark face was pallid in the dim light. "Shit, Bell, that's a damn crazy idea. Where'd you come up with something like that?" He seemed to shudder. "I don't even want to think about it."

"Who drove that jeep? Usually?"

"Hmmm." Markovic rubbed his forehead with the side of his hand. "Well, Avery a lot. Beadle... The C.O. when his jeep was being worked on." He swept his hand over his hair, then brought the hand down in front of him in a cutting motion. "Ah, come on, it was a fucking accident."

"Can you tell when the tie rod was soldered back together?"

"No way—not now anyhow. Hayes told me to turn it in. You heard him." Markovic extended a hand out toward Bell. "Hey, man, don't do this to me. Don't drag me into..." Markovic shook his head and gave a muffled sound. Bell could see his face become distorted in grief that he had been suppressing. "I can't take this shit. Not after Tony." Markovic swallowed a sob in a deep intake of breath, visibly willing himself under control, but his cheek glistened when he turned his head. "Just let it be, will you? We're stuck here. Let it be!"

"It's okay, Alan." He couldn't remember the last time he had used someone's first name. "Don't worry about it." He placed his hand on Markovic's shoulder. "I just, you know, was wondering how it happened."

Markovic shrugged off his hand and moved away from him toward the open garage door entrance to the showers and latrine. "I don't know," Markovic said. "I don't know how it happened."

They walked together in silence, under the deck and past the entrance to the supply room. Inside the latrine, Markovic stopped at a sink to wash his face and hands, while Bell kept going out the inside door and into the hall.

CHAPTER TWENTY-SIX
Sickness in the Land

THE PERIMETER FACING THE CANAL and open country now had two new corner bunkers with layered defenses between them: low sandbag walls, claymore mines, coiled razor wire, and a high chain-link fence. Mounted on the roof and trained on the palms and banana trees beyond the fence line were a scavenged .50 caliber machine gun and a rocket launcher. The task of fortifying the villa was finally done. But not for long.

Tet came and went. There was no attack by the VC or any other untoward event—except for a visit by Colonel Witt from brigade headquarters. He arrived the week before Tet and ordered all the claymore mines removed from the sandbag wall and the .50 caliber machine gun and rocket launcher taken down from the roof. The compound was "too goddamn close to civilians," and he wasn't going to risk a "firefight with phantoms and kill a bunch of mama-sans and baby-sans." Under brigade SOPs, this unit wasn't authorized claymore mines, large caliber machine guns, or rocket launchers.

After the colonel's visit, the work details spent their days disassembling the fortifications they had sweated over—all the while cursing the colonel and the army in general. They left the corner bunkers and a row of sandbags, sans claymore mines, inside the concertina wire and fence facing the canal. And at happy hour, they sang a new tune.

> We build 'em up, we build 'em up,
> You fuckin' A, we build 'em up.
> We tear 'em down, we tear 'em down,
> You fuckin' A, we tear 'em down.

Bell had a day off and no work detail. Tonight there would be a celebration, a DEROS party for Johnson, Poteet, and DeRosa.

DeRosa had already gone on his last road patrol, and Johnson would finish his last patrol tonight. The three would be leaving for Long Binh and home the following week—their "DEROS," the army acronym for the date that a soldier's tour ended.

Out late the night before on patrol, Bell slept in and ate a breakfast of pancakes and sausage after everyone else had gone. He still couldn't face an egg without seeing the image of Tony's cratered skull and hearing Cole say, "Just like scrambled eggs."

When he finally came back to the sleeping bay, he found Walker still in his bunk and wrapped up in a poncho liner.

"Aren't you making a run today?" Bell asked.

"Not today," came the terse response. "Feel like shit. Got the shakes. Must be a fever." Walker propped himself up on his bunk. "Will you take me to the dispensary?"

Bell agreed. Walker did look like shit.

He checked a jeep out of the motor pool and dropped Walker at the entrance to the dispensary. With nothing else to occupy his time while he waited, he drove over to the engineers' unit on the chance he might find the duty officer. He had a few questions about the papa-san's shooting on QL 4.

Not only was he there, the officer remembered Bell, but from the beer-can-throwing incident, not the shooting investigation. He was polite, but not friendly. He was sitting at his desk in the engineer's orderly room like before, and flipping through a stack of forms, like before.

"No one here knows anything," the lieutenant said in response to Bell's questions, giving his eyebrows a workout. "Why do you care? You're off duty, aren't you?"

"I was over at the dispensary," Bell said, coming a little closer to the cluttered desk, "and thought I'd check back with you." He held his cap in his hands, but he didn't feel the least bit supplicant with this joker. "You ask your people about it? Where they were?"

"Sergeant in charge says they were ten klicks on down the road mid-afternoon. They didn't come back this way until 1800 hours."

"The shooting took place earlier than that," Bell said. He looked past the lieutenant at the maps and diagrams on the wall. "I'm not sure of the exact location. Could I talk to the sergeant?" He brought his eyes back to meet the lieutenant's.

"Sure, but he's in Can Tho this week."

"I'll come back. Will you let me know when he's here?"

"Yeah, I'll call you." The lieutenant wagged his eyebrows again and waved his hand in the air like he was shooing off a fly. Irritated at the brush-off, Bell mumbled his thanks and left.

When he got back to the clinic, he found Walker sitting on a metal chair in the hallway.

"Oh man," Walker groaned. "They're sending me to Long Binh. Don't understand it, Bell." He rubbed beads of sweat off his forehead and started shivering. "I always take the fucking tablets. Every goddamn day. Never missed a one." He looked up. "Check on Kikki for me, will you, sport? Tell her where I am."

"Sure." Not knowing what else to say, he added, "Good luck. You'll be back before you know it." He patted Walker on the shoulder.

On his way out, he picked up a copy of the Medevac order for the company clerk. The word "Malaria" was printed in large red letters at the top.

Parking the jeep next to the motor pool, he took the trip ticket inside. Foley, the big blond linebacker of a motor pool sergeant, was talking loudly to Hayes, seated in front of Foley's desk, coffee cup in hand.

"I don't care what the son of a bitch wants," Foley was saying. "I run this motor pool and..." Seeing Bell, he dropped his voice, and Hayes twisted around to see who had come in. Bell hurried to complete the return time on the form and dropped it into a wire basket by the door. As he left, he heard Foley's gruff Alabama accent, resume with, "that black-ass motherfucker."

Who did Foley mean? Beadle? The C.O.? Didn't matter. The words, the undisguised hatred, the whole damn place made Bell feel uneasy.

Late in the afternoon, he was lying on his bunk, reading *The Two Towers*, when Poteet called to him from the stairway.

"Yo, Bell, you have a visitor at the front gate. Nice looking piece of ass. Maybe I need to stay here." Chuckling, Poteet swept by him and into the corridor, headed to the club for an early start on his DEROS celebration.

Puzzled, and feeling a thrill of anticipation, Bell slipped on flip-flops and reached into the top of his wall locker for his wallet. When he found it, he also scooped up some loose MPCs and a folded paper—the note from Tranh's boot. He stuffed the lot into his pockets and, flip-flops slapping the concrete, hurried down the stairs and out to the front gate.

On the other side of the gate, standing next to a motor scooter, was Mai. Another girl, thinner and younger, with short black hair and a mottled complexion, stood beside her.

"Bell, you no come see me," Mai said as Bell drew near. She leaned forward, her fingers wrapped through the holes in the fence.

Landrieu, on gate guard, grinned at him from the bunker window. "So, Bell, got yourself a girlfriend? N-i-i-ce."

"Name's Mai," Bell said, barely glancing at Landrieu, but he shrugged and gave Mai a smile.

"What's her friend's name?" Landrieu walked outside and came over to the closed gate next to Bell. A good head taller than Bell, Landrieu's dress and appearance were regulation military. The epitome of a real MP.

"Her name Anh Thu," Mai said to Landrieu, her voice impatient. Then to Bell, "Kikki sick. Walker no come today, and he," pointing to Landrieu, "say Walker sick, too."

Landrieu smiled obligingly and turned his attentions to Anh Thu.

"We need help change money," Mai continued.

"Yeah, Walker sick," Bell said. "What's wrong with Kikki?"

"She hurt bad. Here." She patted her stomach. "Go hospital yesterday." Mai did not wait for Bell to speak. "You change money? Please?" She held up a wad of MPCs. "Hav'ta change this week. Next week, money no good."

The much-anticipated conversion to new Military Payment Certificates was now underway—the U.S. military command's effort to dry up the supply of currency fueling the black market. To have any value, the old MPCs had to be exchanged for new ones by the end of the week.

Mai shoved the money into a space between the closed gate and the gray metal fence post.

"No can do, Mai," Bell said, making no move to take the MPCs. "If it were only a few dollars, maybe. But you must have several hundred there."

He was thinking, *an amount that large would be suspect, unless you have connections with someone in Finance to juggle the paperwork.* And he didn't.

Pulling the wad of money back to her breast, Mai stomped her foot and spoke at him in rapid Vietnamese, then switched to English, "You no friend. You no like Vietnamese girl."

"No, no, Mai. You're nice, and I like you, but I'm not going to do something illegal."

Landrieu, who had been talking to Anh Thu in a mix of English and Vietnamese, stopped and turned to listen.

"Okay," said Mai. "I find someone who help Vietnamese girl, maybe engineer."

"Fine," said Bell. "That's fine with me."

Many, probably most GIs would exchange money for the Vietnamese, some for girlfriends and some because they could take a hefty cut of the proceeds. But not him. Slipping his hand into his pocket, he touched the small wad of his own MPCs and with them, the folded rice paper he had picked up from the wall locker. He pulled it out of his pocket.

"Mai, will you translate something for me?" Unfolding the paper, he pushed it through the opening in the fence.

Mai gave a petulant snort of exasperation and slipped the MPCs into her small purse. Then she seized the rice paper through the fence. After scanning it quickly, she showed it to her friend. They chattered back and forth in Vietnamese, and Mai gestured down the gravel road. Anh Thu nodded.

Turning back to Bell, Mai said, "Tell how go rice place." Then shaking her head, "Don't know how you call it."

"Warehouse?"

"I don't know. Maybe." She placed the note next to the fence and pointed to two words. "This name, road here." Then she pointed toward the canal. "Go there." She paused. "This... don't know words in 'merican." She pointed toward a jeep in front of the compound. "Jeep go on. And numbas, I think maybe, five oh."

"Jeep go on? You mean tires?"

"Yeah, think maybe so... and people names... I don't know." She shook her head again.

He looked at the names through the wire fence. One looked like Binh.

"This name here," he pointed, "Binh?"

"Maybe. I don't know." She motioned with one hand to her friend. "I go airfield now." She looked up at him with a faint smile. "You come see me, hokay?"

"Okay," said Bell, surprised she'd still have anything to do with him after he wouldn't exchange the MPCs.

She folded the paper and shoved it back through the fence. Taking it, Bell put it into his fatigue pocket.

"Where did that come from?" asked Landrieu. They stood together at the gate watching Mai and her friend ride off down the gravel road, a trail of dust kicking up behind the rear wheel of the motor scooter.

"The paper? Off Tony—from the motor pool. We... Cole and I were the ones who found him. It's a long story."

"So what's with the paper?"

Bell sighed. "He had it in his boot. Maybe something to do with that building down there." He pointed down the road. "Mai called it a rice place—warehouse of some sort." Pausing, he became thoughtful, then grimaced. "Ain't our case. Tranh's Vietnamese, so the civilian police have it."

A V-100 clattered off the road and skidded to a stop opposite them. Giving him a puzzled look, Landrieu shrugged, then went to open the gate.

As he walked back to the villa, Bell saw that the usual audience had gathered next door. Clustering along the ten-foot-high fence, they stood barefoot on the hard-packed dirt. Several called out to get his attention: "Hey MP, hey MP." Two smaller ones, no more than three or four years old, scaled the wire like a ladder until they were at eye level with him as he went past. They stuck small dirty hands through the wire, palms up, opening and closing their fingers.

Ignoring them, he kept going, straight ahead and into the building.

CHAPTER TWENTY-SEVEN
DEROS Party

FOR THE BIG DEROS PARTY, Hayes hired a Filipino band with two female singers: glittering mini-skirts, low-cut tank tops, and painted-on makeup. A couple of floodlights at the front of the stage were rigged to add a strobe effect for the more intense music. The beer and liquor flowed freely. The soldiers clapped, yelled, and whistled, singing the words to the songs they knew and pantomime dancing with the singers.

Toasted repeatedly with raised cups and cans, Poteet and DeRosa had an aura about them that went beyond the alcohol haze. Johnson, the third honoree, hadn't arrived. He was still out on his last town patrol.

When the band took a break, the short-timers and some of the GIs who had been with them the longest gathered in a circle on the makeshift stage, stomping their feet, and singing, "We gotta get outta this place..."

Then in a chorus at the top of their lungs, over and over: "Hey, hey, go-o-od bye."

Finally, they broke into their own theme:
We build 'em up, we build 'em up,
You fuckin' A, we build 'em up.
We tear 'em down, we tear 'em down,
You fuckin' A, we tear 'em down.
Cause we're fuckin' ar-my
ALL THE WAY,
Always do what
THE LIFERS SAY.

The first sergeant listened impassively to the complaints about building and then tearing down the defenses, and probably agreed with them. He turned redder and redder, though, as the lyrics became more vicious toward the military in general and more personal toward the lifers, ending in "Fuck the lifers, every one." He leaped to his feet.

Waving his arms, he yelled, "You men, you don't appreciate what we've done for you. I spend every waking hour trying to make sure you're safe. That you have everything you need here."

The chanting had stopped; even the talking at the tables had ceased, and everyone stared at Top. He continued with only a slight slurring of his words.

"You don't understand shit about this man's army... what it stands for, what it's done for you and your country. You people... you have a dry place to sleep, running water, gooks to cook for you, shine your fuckin' boots." He waved his hand toward the door. "There are men out there dyin' while you sing your silly songs and carry on. People gettin' killed... I been there. I've seen it right in front of my eyes." He lowered his voice. "You pea-brains better get your head out of your ass and thank God you got it so good."

He turned and stormed out the door. The club was quiet a moment, and then there was low muttering. DeRosa brought his right fist up, catching the crook of his arm with his left hand and yelled, "Up yours!" toward the open door through which the first sergeant had exited. "You were shaking in your *fuck*-ing boots when we got hit, you lifer cocksucker."

The band started playing again, drowning out the last of DeRosa's statement, except to the ears of those who stood near him.

Once the general merriment resumed, Bell drifted over to the bar for a Coke, no beer this time; he had guard duty at 1100 hours. Standing next to him as he ordered was an army major, his back to the bandstand, nursing a drink in a plastic cup.

"You men don't seem to like the army."

Bell looked to make sure the major was talking to him. He was. Odd for an officer to be in the club, even more that he deigned to speak to a lowly Spec 4.

"It's all right," Bell said. At the major's skeptical smile, he added, "A lot of us were drafted, and we don't like being here."

"Can't say I blame you. It's a lousy war." The major held out his hand. Another surprise. "Name's Dobbs."

Major Dobbs explained that he had been in Vietnam for three tours, and he had just come out of the field as an advisor to the ARVN Ranger unit next door. He had to stay with his unit only a few more days before going up to Long Binh for out-processing, and then home.

"Thought I'd stop by to see Sergeant Avery," he said. "Then your C.O. told me he was hurt in a jeep accident."

"Yeah," Bell said. "Medevaced him to Saigon. Heard he ended up in Tokyo for a while."

"He's not doing so well. He's in a coma."

"What?" Bell felt a cold chill run down his spine. He gripped his Coke can tighter. "I... we didn't know—"

"I called your brigade headquarters."

The major raised his hand and asked Thuy for another Scotch and water. There were several plastic cups on the bar in front of him, empty except for the melting ice.

Turning slightly, Bell took a closer look at the major. He was no taller than the average Vietnamese. High forehead, dark complexion, and curly black hair streaked with gray. He wore a crooked pair of gray-frame army glasses. His fatigues were worn, rumpled, and covered with dust.

"Avery was in the highlands with me last year," the major said as he waited for his drink.

Bell nodded and hearing clapping and hoots behind him, looked around at the bandstand. DeRosa was shimmying in front of one of the singers.

"I didn't see the accident," Bell said after the major's drink had arrived. The band had paused, probably to get DeRosa off the stage, and the noise level dropped so that they could speak in a normal tone of voice.

"Or Avery," he added. "But I saw the jeep—it was in bad shape."

"That's why I'm up here. I want to talk to a Sergeant Johnson. He investigated the accident, didn't he? That's what they told me."

"I was with Johnson." Bell shook his head. "Wasn't much to investigate. Deuce-and-a-half hit a motorbike, and Avery did a U-turn to go back and help. His jeep flipped over."

"Avery drove for me all the time. He was a damn good driver."

"Well, it was a pretty bad situation, two boy-sans killed, one split almost in half." Bell started to mention the soldered tie rod, but the major interrupted him.

"I understand Johnson will be coming back for the party."

"Yeah, he's on night patrol, but they should be in early. By eleven."

"Great party," the major said. He finished his drink and looked around. He wasn't slurring his words, but he was hanging onto the bar with one hand to steady himself. "I'm sick of this place. This fucking war... going home. For good."

The band had resumed playing, and after a melancholy rendition of "Norwegian Wood," it was revving up with The Doors.

Bell finished his Coke and looked at his watch. Almost time to go change for guard duty. Maybe write a letter first.

The major cleared his throat. "Ah, would you give me a lift to the orphanage tomorrow? I want to tell the nuns goodbye."

"Sure," Bell said without considering whether he could get a jeep.

"I adopted a little girl," the major said. "She had polio. She's six now... back in the World. See her in a week, God willing."

The speakers were blaring out, "Baby, come on and light my fire," and Bell could barely hear the last few words.

"Alright, listen up!" From the doorway to the barracks area, Sergeant Carter's voice rang out above the music.

"Shut that fuckin' thing off!" he yelled. "Got something... I said shut that fuckin' thing off!"

The music stopped, and the room grew quiet except for a few desultory shouts and laughs.

"Listen up," Carter said again in a lower voice. "I got some bad news."

Carter paused and looked around. Even the last yelps of laughter stopped.

"Sergeant Johnson's been shot."

There was a shout of, "No, no!" and another voice, "You shittin' me!"

Bell felt the pit of his stomach drop through the floor. He didn't say anything; he just stared at the backs of the heads of the people between him and Carter. He felt sweat running down his neck and in huge globules from his armpits, soaking his t-shirt. He was shivering.

CHAPTER TWENTY-EIGHT
Meyer and Sanderson

THE BAND PACKED UP AND DEPARTED not long after Carter came in. Johnson hadn't just been shot. He was dead.

Carter didn't know the details. Only that Johnson and Cole had been looking for curfew violators off the main street, behind the town. Down an alley.

That's when Bell hurried out. He was starting to shake. It could've been him with Cole. He told the major he had guard duty and left before anyone could notice him shaking. He hurried across the deck and down the outside stairs. Stopping in the latrine, he hid in a stall until the shaking was under control.

His first thought had been of himself. Not Johnson. Not Johnson's little brother back home in Alabama, or his mother who cleaned toilets at the cotton mill.

Who would tell her? Who would tell my own mother if I were shot dead in an alley? When Uncle Jim's ship went down, my grandma got a telegram. Now they send soldiers in uniform, don't they? Would they send two white soldiers, lifers, to tell Johnson's mother?

He picked up his M-16 in the armory, then went up the inside stairs to get his flak jacket and helmet from his locker.

Poteet was passed out on his bunk, his tape player still on. "Number nine, number nine, number nine..." Bell reached over and turned off the tape. Across the aisle, Hodge's bunk was empty. He had gone to Can Tho with Sergeant Sanchez to pick up supplies. The airfield in Can Tho had the only phone in the Delta that could call stateside, and Hodge was desperate to talk to his wife.

Bell felt terribly alone, and he felt even more alone in the tower.

Leaning his M-16 against the railing, he placed his flak jacket and helmet on the floor and stared vacantly toward the canal and the rice paddies beyond. Just above the horizon, a single flare formed a pale halo. Artillery rumbled softly, then stopped, then rumbled again. Near the airfield, two choppers were making long sweeps, swinging their spotlights back and forth across the fields. Above them, a crescent moon hung low in the sky.

The collective voices of the celebrants in the club had faded into subdued muttering with only a few shouts now and then. And no laughter.

The steps leading to the tower rattled, and Meyer's wild hair popped through the opening for the trap door, followed by his shoulders and a hand holding a Schlitz can. A rarity for Meyer.

"Peace, bro. Thought I'd come up and keep my main man company. Bowman told me you were on guard when I got in."

"Were you on the desk?"

"With Sergeant Beadle."

Beadle had started working as desk sergeant from time to time. So that he could learn the area and the people, he said.

"How did it happen?" Bell asked as Meyer slid down in the corner, his back against the plywood wall.

"Sergeant Carter called us. He and Dupre had the other patrol. Said some Vietnamese flagged them down, told them an MP was hurt. They were a little leery of going anywhere with them, but a QC patrol came along, and they went back there with the QCs. Dupre told me Johnson was next to a path going down to hooches on the canal. He was already dead."

"Fuck!" said Bell, hitting the wooden ledge with his fist. "Where was Cole?"

"He showed up about the same time, so Dupre said. Cole told them he was chasing the shooter and didn't know Johnson was down."

"You don't believe that, do you? Johnson must've yelled out... or something." Bell was staring at Meyer's face, almost hidden in the shadows.

"I don't know." He sighed. "Beadle closed up soon as we got the call, and we went out there ourselves." Meyer took a swallow of his beer. "It was only a few blocks down Le Thai-to Street." He took a deep breath. "Beadle quizzed Cole pretty good while we were waiting for the medics to come."

"Cole let him know someone had taken a shot at him, at us... before?

"Not while I was there."

Meyer and Hodge were the only ones Bell had told. None of that had gone into any report.

"Anybody check Cole's .45?" Bell asked.

"No." There was a scraping of cloth on wood as Meyer shifted position. "You don't think—"

"I don't think anything." But he was thinking, *I need to tell someone about what happened back there with Cole. But who can I tell?*

He asked Meyer more about where Johnson was found and decided it was a different place, but not too far away from where he and Cole had gone. All the while, his mind was working. *Maybe there's a way to tell someone, even if we get in trouble for not making a report.*

"Will there be a formal investigation?" Bell asked.

"Don't know what—"

The ladder rattled below, and they both looked around at the trap door. Sanderson almost leaped out of the opening and staggered against the railing at the front of the tower. He was waving a bottle.

"Yo, my brothers," Sanderson said in a loud voice. "Killed any fucking VC?" He sloshed the liquid in the bottle, about half full.

"Hold it down," said Bell. "You'll have the lifers—"

"Fuck the lifers." Holding the bottle out in front of him, Sanderson sank to the tower floor next to Meyer. "They fucking chased us off. Wouldn't let us... *find* the moth-er-fuckers."

"We had a lot of reinforcements," Meyer said, shifting away from

Sanderson. "Hayes, Landrieu—even the captain showed up."

"And the three musketeers were there," said Sanderson, waving his bottle like he was going to make a toast.

"Sh-h-h," said Bell. "Wake the ARVNs, and they may start shooting."

Sanderson only laughed, even louder, and took a swig from the bottle.

"Yeah, bro here was there, too" said Meyer, "along with Moe and Markovic." Moe was a jovial, red-hair, red-faced Irishman who often joined Sanderson and Markovic in raising hell.

"God-*damn* if anybody's gonna shoot one of us and get away with it," said Sanderson. He was taking long, deep breaths like he was ready to pass out.

"They were all drunk," said Meyer. "Beadle hustled them out of there before Hayes—"

"Told us to get our asses back to the compound," Sanderson said with an indignant snort.

"Beadle told me to drive—"

"Sonovabitch chewed me out in front of my compadres," Sanderson said. "Said he'd bust my *black* ass to private if I ever let a bunch of drunks into the armory again."

"They were armed to the teeth," Meyer said.

"I asked what if we got hit—"

"Grenade launchers, M-16s. Even had an M-60—"

"And he called me a drunk-ass nigger and told me I knew what he meant."

"I bet you did," Bell said.

"Motherfucker had no business talking to me like that." Sanderson sat up. "All them *fucking* lifers have keys to the *fucking* armory, and most of 'em are drunk half the *fucking* time. Only reason they don't leave it open is 'cause they're afraid some private's gonna pop their asses."

"Well, there are Vietnamese in here all the time," Meyer said.

"It happens, man. How about down in Can Tho?" Sanderson paused to lift the bottle to his mouth. "You think the old papa-san's VC? Ah fuck." He staggered to his feet. "I think I'm gonna be sick." He twisted around toward the canal and puked over the side of the tower, down the sandbags in front.

"Shit!" yelled Bell, forgetting the lifers. "I gotta stay up here—"

"Wait," said Meyer, "let me help you down."

Sanderson was stumbling toward the trap door, leaving his bottle tottering on the sandbags beyond the railing. Bell grabbed it before it went over the side. Meyer took Sanderson by the arm and held on. Sanderson, swearing all the way, reached a foot for the first rung of the ladder, missed, and almost dragged Meyer with him as he slipped down to the next rung.

"Whoa, whoa, whoa," said Meyer. "One foot at a time."

"Come back for his fucking bottle," Bell hissed, his voice low now. "And your fucking can. Carter... any of the lifers, come up here, I'm screwed."

"I gotta pee," said Sanderson. "Po-o-or Johnson." He sounded like he was starting to cry. "Poor, po-or... black-ass Johnson."

"I'll get him down," Meyer said. He was bent double, holding onto Sanderson's arm, then his wrist, as Sanderson slid down the ladder. Meyer clambered down after him.

Once the noise below ceased, Bell placed Sanderson's bottle, Jack Daniels and three-quarter's empty, in the darkest corner of the tower, next to Meyer's Schlitz can. Leaning against the railing, he looked out over the perimeter. Quiet. He sniffed the air. Puke. Now how was he going to explain that?

A jeep rolled slowly past the compound, going down the road to the canal. Not long after, two more jeeps came to a stop at the front gate. An MP got out and opened the gate, and both jeeps drove through and parked near the villa entrance. *While Sanderson and Meyer were up here*, Bell thought, *a whole regiment of NVA could've marched by in formation and we wouldn't have noticed.*

After ten minutes, the ladder rattled again. Meyer climbed through the opening holding out a bundle of white towels—and a bottle of Lysol. Together, they wiped the puke off the sandbags as far down as they could reach without hanging by their toes.

"Meyer, we've landed in a bucket of shit," Bell said as he tossed a wet towel into the corner. "Tony, now Johnson. It's getting to me."

"Yeah, me too." Meyer finished wiping off the last sandbag and stood up next to Bell, who was staring out over the compound to the east. A series of flares popped, one after another, over the rice paddies.

"All this bizarre shit..." Bell hesitated and shook his head. "Hayes is up to his neck in the black market... him and Beadle both."

"They're an unlikely pair." Meyer absentmindedly rubbed a sandbag with the towel. "Almost everyone's into something. Sell a few cases of beer, few cartons of cigarettes." He lowered his voice. "Hodge told me they sold thirty gallons of gas out of their V-100, up near My Tho. Some of the crews fill up at the airfield, sell the gas, and park in the shade the rest of the day."

"How about the odometer?"

"Markovic fixes it for them."

"Markovic!"

"Our good little boy scout."

Bell grunted. "Shit! That's small potatoes. Beadle and Hayes are big time. Truckloads of shit—maybe even the truck."

He twisted to look over his shoulder, then down at the road. Nothing moved there except three dogs loping down one side toward the canal.

Turning back to Meyer, he added, "C.O.'s never here, and Top stays soused." Bell shook his head. "He covers for Hayes... I'm sure of it, and Hayes looks after him." *Like the night of the mortar attack*, Bell was thinking. "And I bet they're all making beaucoup bucks out of this war."

"They might as well. Look at all the choppers, the trucks and jeeps, the beer and cigarettes. Who do you think owns all the contractors? Buy a few politicians, and send us over here to keep the big green machine going. War—the rich make the money, and we get the shaft."

A chopper flying low over the canal caused Bell to wait before replying until the noise of the rotors faded.

"Hayes ain't in Washington, my friend, and he's making money right here. Right fucking here! With the new MPCs, he can skim hundreds, maybe thousands of dollars off the Vietnamese."

"So where do the locals get all those MPCs he going to change for them?"

"Prostitution, drugs, the black market. You remember that suicide Johnson and I found? I've been wondering if he was part of it. Killing himself like that—if he did. It gave me the creeps."

Meyer didn't respond. A gentle breeze rustled the palms and whispered through the open tower, billowing the sleeves of their shirts and drying the sweat on their faces and necks, before leaving them becalmed in the clammy night air.

Finally, Meyer said in a low voice, his head down, "They leave us alone, bro, we leave them alone. Isn't that what you said right after we got here? What you were going to do? Just opt out of the war?"

Bell sighed and shook his head. "Never in my life saw so many crazy people. Hayes, Cole. He loves the Gestapo, wants to place a hit on his wife. Foley and his shotgun shells. Then Keller was sharpening a bayonet in the stairwell last night. Why'd he be sharpening a bayonet? And up there?"

Meyer didn't answer. Instead he started gathering up the dirty towels, wrapping them around Sanderson's Jack Daniels bottle and then bundling the lot into a clean towel. Bell grabbed him by the sleeve as he was stuffing the empty beer can and Lysol bottle in the side pockets of his fatigue pants.

"Hey look at that." Bell pointed to two small lights, one behind the other, moving along the canal. "Ever notice that when you're up here?"

"Notice what?"

"Lights on the canal." The lights stopped near where the gravel road ended. "Why do ya reckon sampans go down there at night? It's a warehouse or something like that, but it's almost midnight, and I've seen 'em go down there at three in the morning."

"Probably people picking up stuff for the market in the morning or bringing in rice they harvested."

"Yeah, and maybe they're VC," Bell said, turning toward Meyer. "Planning to attack a bunch of dumb-fuck MPs." He gave a skeptical snort. "Don't think it's time for the rice harvest."

"Start thinking that way, you'll never get any sleep."

"There *are* VC around here, you know."

"I haven't seen any," Meyer said.

"You saw Hayes' prisoners."

"Those guys? They probably didn't pay off the local mandarin. They're nothing but peasants."

"Who do you think the VC are?" Bell picked up the binoculars to get a better view of the lights. All he could see was the dark outline of a sampan. "Did you hear? QC's caught a couple of old mama-sans planting dynamite on the road around town. You ever been down that road to take Thuy home?"

"For all we know, Thuy could be VC."

"Ah, bullshit. Look!" Bell pointed toward the canal. A single light moved away from the building, past the end of the road, and out of sight behind the trees. Watching it through the binoculars, Bell thought he could make out a figure standing in the back of the sampan. There was no noise of a motor.

Lowering the binoculars, he remembered the rice paper note from Tranh's boot. He told Meyer about Mai's translation, or the little she had told him.

"Wonder if Tony had something to do with that?" Bell pointed at the remaining lights. "Maybe his getting shot—"

"You're just a draftee playing cop. Don't start playing detective, too."

"One of these days, I'm gonna go check that place out." Bell gestured with the binoculars toward the building on the canal.

"Ah, look at the time. Got to go. Duty tomorrow." He patted Bell on the shoulder. "Keep your eyes open, bro, and follow your own advice. We'll be having our party before you know it."

As Meyer clambered down the ladder, Bell looked back toward the canal. Two lights, one on the side of the building and the other nearby on the canal, winked at him through the palms.

CHAPTER TWENTY-NINE
Major Dobbs

THE NEXT MORNING HE FINAGLED a jeep from Foley and picked up Major Dobbs in front of the villa. The major was toting a good-size box, which he said held a movie projector for the kids at the Convent.

"It's a beautiful day, and I'm in no hurry," the major said after he placed the box on the back seat. "If you don't mind, I'd like to drive around a bit."

"What if we start out down the road here?" Bell waved his trip ticket at Keller as the jeep coasted through the front gate.

"Fine by me. But why do you care what's down there? Road ends at the canal."

"I keep seein' a lot of sampans going to a building down there," Bell said, turning onto the gravel road. Then glancing at the major, he added, "While I'm on guard duty."

"Probably not VC, if that's what you're worried about. Too close to all these military posts—you folks, ARVN Rangers, the artillery group over there." The major pointed to their left across the ragged soccer field. "More important, it's too exposed, and the VC have better places to hide than this."

"Well, I don't understand why the sampans go there at night. Just curious, since it's so close to us."

He drove down the road to where it ended at the canal. To the right was a hanger-size metal building with a thinly graveled parking area extending from the road up to a large garage door in the front of the building. In the front corner, next to the grove of trees, there was a separate, people-sized entrance.

The doors were all closed, and Bell could make out a bar and padlock on the side door. Even though the sun had been up for hours, a single light bulb burned inside a wire cage above the door.

He idled the jeep where they could see the canal side of the building. A large sliding door, also shut tight, faced a cement dock extending out over the water. Nothing stirred anywhere around the building.

The major was looking out across the canal. "If you ever get hit," he said, "they'll come from over there." He sighted down his finger toward the open fields. "Have to cross the canal, but that won't slow them down. Or they could come along the canal, in sampans." He shrugged. "You never know." He turned to peer over his shoulder at the MP villa, the guard tower visible above the trees.

"You got some mortars a while back, didn't you?" Major Dobbs asked, turning back to face Bell.

"A few. But they all hit in the Rangers' area, three inside their fence line. The others were short."

"My bunch was in the field." He gave a low laugh. "I heard about the chickens."

"Cole's an idiot," Bell said and jerked the gearshift into reverse, harder than he intended. He drove to the far side of the parking area and stopped in the shade of some low palm trees.

They sat in silence, contemplating the canal and the rice fields. A sampan, a lone man hunched in the back steering it, glided past the warehouse, in the direction of the small river that emptied into the Mekong below the town. The putt-putt of the motor was the only sound, except for a few confused frogs and whirring insects. No artillery or choppers. The only thing disturbing the tranquil scene was the turmoil in Bell's mind over Johnson's death.

"Why have you stayed here so long?" he asked, attempting to bury it.

"It's a beautiful country... I love the people, and I used to believe we were helping them." He sighed. "We're only helping ourselves and ruining them." He paused, staring across the canal. "We just replaced the French—same song, different verse."

He shook a cigarette out of a pack of Winston's and offered one to Bell, who declined it with a shake of his head. Snapping open a silver lighter, the major applied a long flame to the tip, highlighting the lines in his weathered face. When he exhaled, a stream of smoke swirled upward in the light breeze.

Bell sniffed the air. "Well, the country *is* pretty, once you get past the filth and the smell." He waved his hand toward the blue sky and watery, dark green squares across the canal. "Maybe if I could just see it in a *National Geographic*. Now the girls, in their *ao dais, they* are beautiful."

"Specialist, you're enamored with the women and missing the reality. You see them like you wish you could see the country, filtered through the lens of a camera without any other senses or knowledge to intervene."

"Maybe so, but I like my images better than all the garbage dumps and havoc." He stared at the dark checkerboard expanse reflecting the white clouds. "But I don't understand the culture," he muttered and shook his head. "I wonder how it's changed because of us."

"Don't be fooled. These people are tough. They take from us what they can use, but they want their own country without us in it, even those who kiss our ass to get inside the PX."

Dobbs stubbed out his cigarette on the sole of his boot and shredded the filter. As the shreds floated to the ground, Bell started the jeep and turned the wheels back toward the road past the compound.

At the Convent, Major Dobbs was greeted by Sister Agnes, whom Bell remembered from his first visit, and an older nun with a wrinkled face, white hair, and glasses. She ran to the major as soon as she saw him, then held out a liver-spotted white hand to Bell.

"I'm Sister Margaret," she said in a strong Irish brogue and gave his hand a firm shake. "I've been here forever, but I go back to Eire next month, first time in twenty-five years."

As the major placed the box with the projector on a table in the dining hall, Sister Margaret asked about Ana, the little girl the major had adopted, and the major told her Ana was doing well. She had learned English and would start first grade in the fall.

Sister Margaret looked at Bell, "Major Dobbs is a good man. We thought she was going to die, and he took her to a hospital in the Philippines."

"I'm looking forward to seeing her, Sister. Next week," the major said. "My wife sent me a picture." He pulled out his wallet and showed them a snapshot of a smiling, dark-eyed Vietnamese girl in a pink dress with ruffles. She had braces on both legs.

"How many kids are here?" asked Bell.

"Sixty-five now," said Sister Agnes. "They keep coming. Some, mixed children no one wants. We have trouble getting enough clothes and money, and the longer the war goes on, the more children we get." Her frown turned to a broad smile. "Your Mr. Hayes is a big help. He and some officers at the airfield make sure we get all the food we need. A little money, too."

Sister Margaret coughed and gave a choking sound. "Money from the devil, I say."

Sister Agnes gave her a pained look.

"But I won't look a gift horse in the mouth," Sister Margaret added, raising her hands in defense. "It's for a good cause."

As they went out the iron gates to the Convent, the major picked up on the nuns' comments about Hayes.

"I don't know what's going on at your place, but I'd be careful who you get involved with. Sergeant Hayes may help nuns and orphans, but don't get too cozy with him." He dusted an imaginary speck off his knee.

On QL 4, the traffic had slowed to a crawl, and Bell took time to digest the major's statement as he drove along the shoulder and tried to work his way into the main lane.

"I try to stay clear of him," Bell said once they were wedged between a deuce-and-a-half and a three-wheel Lambretta, "but I seem to stay in his sights." When the major didn't react, Bell launched into a rapid account of Hayes and the Green Beret's exchange in My Tho and Markovic's comments about Hayes and the motorbike and the local black market. As quickly as he said it, he realized how garbled and innocuous it all seemed.

The major listened without responding.

Not far past Madame Phoung's high wall, a Combined Patrol jeep blocked one lane, and two white-shirted policemen directed traffic around an accident between an American jeep and a mangled Lambretta. Next to the Lambretta lay a still form stretched out under a poncho, and beside the jeep Meyer stood talking to a GI whose eyes were fixed on the ground.

"Doesn't anyone at MACV or up in Saigon know what's going on down here?" Bell asked once they were beyond the wrecked Lambretta and picking up speed. "I see all this shit that... that just seems to lead to him, to Hayes."

"Maybe somebody's protecting him." The major looked away, toward the shops along the street, and gave a sharp laugh. "Hell, I know it." He paused, then added, "There's also a local... a Major Binh."

"Yeah, I know who that is." Bell said, downshifting to turn onto QL 4.

"When I was in MACV, we suspected he was into some heavy shit—and the MPs were helping him."

Bell started to say something about Roberts, Tranh, and the note, but he already felt like a fool.

"Keep this to yourself, Specialist, but Avery was working with the CID on something, then he had his accident."

"You think maybe it wasn't an accident?" Bell glanced at him. "Our mechanic, Markovic, said there was something funny with the steering."

"I don't know about that," the major said slowly, "but watch yourself."

"Hayes stopped Markovic from repairing the jeep. Sent it down to Can Tho for scrap."

"That's interesting." The major sighed and looked off toward the hooches along the road. After a moment, he turned back toward Bell. "When I get to Saigon I'm going to see a friend in the Provost office. I'll give him your name." He reached over and placed his hand on Bell's shoulder as Bell downshifted the jeep for a turn. "You need to tell him—his name's Samson, Major Samson—you tell him what you know when he calls you."

CHAPTER THIRTY
Combined Patrol

THE DUTY ROSTER HAD HIM ON "COMBINED PATROL" with two Vietnamese National Policemen—in their jeep. To join his partners, he rode to the station with Cole and Landrieu. A brief rain had fallen in the night, a tease of the monsoon. The morning air was fresher and cooler than it had been for weeks. As they turned onto QL 4, he took a deep breath, inhaling the smell of wet earth and lime.

Sitting high on the backseat, he looked around and emptied his mind of thought, blocking out the banter between Cole and Landrieu and taking in the beautiful morning. The sun cast a soft yellow light on the tops of the palms, and people hurried along the side of the road: children, a boy and a girl, a wooden crate of soft drinks swinging between them; a mama-san, a yoke across her shoulders; the ubiquitous old papa-san on a bicycle. Already under assault by *xich-lo*s, three-wheel Lambrettas, and motor scooters, his reverie began dissolving and was finally shattered by a pair of deuce-and-a-half's roaring past.

He couldn't get Johnson out of his mind. Sergeant Beadle had organized a sweep of the area where Johnson was killed, using two MP patrols and a squad of QCs under Lt Nguyen—two sweeps in fact—one the next morning and one last night. Bell had gone with that one. Searched hooches and rooms in the buildings along the alley, the QCs playing the heavies. Beadle's theory was that the joker who'd shot Johnson, if he was an American, would come back to see his girlfriend or to get his town stuff. They found nothing, and Lt Nguyen said that no one in the place knew anything.

The C.O. had convened a board of inquiry. The bad part: the board was made up of Top, Hayes, and Lt Floyd. The first two Bell didn't trust to tell about his own foray down an alley with Cole, and

Floyd, he didn't know. What he'd heard about the lieutenant wasn't good and what he'd seen, he didn't like. "Floyd always has that toad Wesley Akers drive him," Keller had said not long after Bell arrived. "Both of 'em decked out in full MP gear: cuffs, billy clubs, the whole bit. Slickest two shits you ever seen. Floyd's R-O-T-C, looks like the Pillsbury Doughboy."

So he'd decided he wouldn't say boo. They had no reason to interview him anyway, since he wasn't on duty that night, and he and Cole hadn't included *their* incident behind the town in any report. Maybe someone would come from Saigon to join the inquiry, someone like Major Dobbs' friend.

At the station, he nodded at Carter and waved to Meyer, who had assumed the role of desk clerk while Singleton was on R&R. Carter was talking on a landline with the compound. He hung up as Bell leaned across the desk to look at the previous night's incident log. Shaking his head, Carter gave Bell an odd look.

"Only thing last night was a shooting over at the Ranger outfit. Advisor tried to stop a fight and caught a .45 round in the chest. That major, what's his name, the one who was goin' home."

"Not Major Dobbs?" Bell gripped the desktop.

"Yeah, that's him."

"But he was going to Saigon with DeRosa and our guys."

"Had to wait for his replacement. Stayed one too many nights with the gooks." Carter looked down at the logbook. "Poor bastard... made it three years here, but couldn't make it one more fuckin' day."

Now overwhelmed by gloom, Bell adjusted his MP helmet on his head as he walked down the station's steps to the Vietnamese patrol jeep. How was he going to get anyone from Saigon interested in this place? He had a name, Major Samson, but no way to contact the man, and the only person who could vouch for him was dead.

Poor bastard is right. What a nice guy for something like that to happen, to him and Johnson both. Bell gave a shiver. *The worst times to get killed are right after you get here and right before you leave.*

He rolled his eyes toward heaven. *And all the days in between.*

Already in the front seats of the green-and-white patrol jeep were two civilian policemen. Starched white shirts, black pants, and white high-peaked hats with short black bills and silver National Police emblems. The two carried .38 caliber revolvers in shiny white holsters on shiny white belts—but no rifles.

He shook hands with each and climbed into the back seat, which faced to the rear. Phan, stocky with a dark round face, he knew from his first day on patrol and from Phan's investigation of Tony's death—and the missing MPCs. The other he knew only from his nametag: Nhu, thin with a lurid birthmark running down his neck from under his left ear. Both were a head shorter than Bell, himself only average in height for Americans. The two white shirts spoke no more English than he did Vietnamese. The phrase book in his side pocket was no help.

No sooner had they reached Le Thai-to Street than he got a sample of the English the two policemen did know. Phan, sitting on the passenger side in front, turned and gave Bell a wide frogmouth smile.

"MP, you go PX. Buy soap, cigarettes. Yes?" The policeman held out a new twenty dollar Military Payment Certificate. The currency exchange had proved no more than an expensive inconvenience to the local entrepreneurs, though it provided a nice windfall to the GIs, who commanded 10 to 20% "fees" for exchanging the old contraband notes for new ones.

Bell twisted around in the back seat and offered Phan a big smile in return. "I no think so," he said.

Phan's smile disappeared. "Other MPs help."

"Not me. I'm not getting involved in that shit."

Phan curled his lip in disgust and whipped back around in his seat.

Bell had no control over where they went or what they did. He was there only to deal with any Americans they encountered.

"Today," Nhu said, "we go Sa Dec," a town farther up the Mekong toward the Cambodian border.

Even facing backward, the ride through the open countryside, with its newly green rice paddies and bright blue sky, relieved his gloom somewhat. There were few signs of the war, a firebase in the middle of a rice paddy or a bunker next to a bridge, and most of the bridges were still intact. Rice farmers worked the fields, their black pajama pants rolled up above the knees, their conical straw hats pointed toward the horizon. A boy-san was perched high on the gray hump of a water buffalo plodding across a rice paddy dike.

Sa Dec proved to be a pretty town with neat stucco houses and paved streets lined with leafy green trees. There were no open ditches and no fetid, black water. The raised tile sidewalks were clean and unbroken. But there was the usual malodorous town traffic of *xich-lo*s, scooters, and Lambrettas that reduced their progress to a crawl when they reached an arched stone bridge spanning a wide canal. Down below was a hodgepodge of houses on stilts extending out over the water and down the canal to a bend, where houses and canal disappeared behind a copse of trees.

From the opposite side of the bridge, an old man in a beige sport coat strolled toward them, moving at a faster pace than the traffic. He carried a folded easel under one arm and rolled canvases under the other. On his head was a flat cap, more suited to County Cork than the tropics, with thin wisps of white hair protruding from each side. Bell had a fleeting impression of what this place had been and could be, and he was saddened by what it was.

The police jeep stopped at a low building on a side street away from the canal. Without preamble, the white shirts disembarked and headed inside. Unbidden, Bell tagged along behind them.

It was a hospital. Just like in Van Loc, people were everywhere—on beds, on chairs, and on the floor.

Threading their way among the sick and injured, the well and unwell, the civilian policemen stopped at a bed and engaged an old papa-san squatting on the floor in an animated conversation. Standing next to him was a second man, younger, but weather-beaten and wearing the black pajamas of a peasant.

The bed's occupant paid them no attention, lying on his back like a corpse, eyes closed and breathing, but silent and unmoving. He was covered by a sheet pulled up to his waist and sloping down to meet the thin pad where his knees should have been.

Phan produced a wallet, from which he removed several notes—new MPCs. These he handed to the old papa-san while continuing to talk.

Bell watched from an adjacent aisle. Shifting from one foot to the other, he tried not to look at the drawn faces or the missing arms and legs—and wondered what the hell this was all about.

With a quick jerk, the papa-san took the money, interrupting Phan with a short burst of "dups" and "daps." Phan paused, extracted more bills, and shoved them at the old man, who snatched them in silence. Pocketing his wallet, Phan pivoted and walked out, while Nhu scrambled to catch up. Bell belatedly lurched after them, feeling all eyes—the open ones—focused on his back.

When they were well out of Sa Dec, Nhu swerved off the road and onto a dirt area in front of a rickety wooden shack set back in a clump of palm trees. Turning to Bell, Phan motioned with his fingers to his mouth and said, "We eat."

"Fine with me." He had been obsessing about food ever since Sa Dec and wondering where they could find any.

He followed Phan and Nhu to a plank table under a canted palm tree not far from the shack. As they sat down on sagging benches, two androgynous children, four or five years old, eyed them through a hole between the boards in the stand's broken wall. Almost immediately an old woman scurried from inside and came over, bobbing her head to the two civilian policemen.

Phan gave her an order in Vietnamese, and then patted Bell on the arm. "We buy," he said, displaying his frog grin.

The woman brought them a large plate piled high with meat that looked like chopped-up chicken with broken bones in it, a bowl of black fish sauce, a small dish of salt, and a platter of steaming white rice. She set blue-glazed plates and ivory chop sticks in front of each of them, followed by warm bottles of "33" beer, and three tall glasses containing a few pieces of ice.

Phan and Nhu set to work with their chopsticks, picking up bits of chicken, dipping them in the fish sauce and then in the salt. Bell followed suit. It was amazingly tasty, even with the putrid fish sauce.

While they ate, he tried to ask why they had gone to the hospital. At first, the two seemed not to understand. Then, with a snort, Phan said, "Money for family. Man hurt." This made sense. The MPCs Phan had given the papa-san would be worth a few months' wages to an ARVN soldier. "Major Binh help friends." Phan scowled. "Not like you."

"You run errands for Major Binh?" asked Bell, sitting up straighter on the bench and staring at Phan. He waited, but Phan only shrugged and maneuvered a piece of chicken from fish sauce to salt and into his mouth.

"I mean, you help Major Binh—"

"Major Binh number one," Phan said.

Nhu said nothing and continued devouring the chicken.

"Did you know an American named Roberts? He died, killed himself."

Phan dropped his chopsticks and made a sound like "*e-a.*" He started fiddling with something at his side.

"He help Major Binh, too?" Bell asked. Then he was staring into the shiny silver barrel of Phan's service revolver. Inches from his face.

Phan's mouth was stretched wide, in a frog smile. "How you say—"

"Hold on!" Bell leaned away, sweat popping out all over his body.

"Nose, nose."

As fast as the revolver had appeared, it was gone.

"Ha, ha," Phan laughed and poked his partner in the arm. "Big joke, yes? Ha, ha, ha!"

Nhu laughed, too, just as false.

They finished eating—or Phan and Nhu did—in silence, then Phan barked a command at the old woman, who quickly cleared away the plates. No money appeared to pay the bill, neither Phan's MPCs nor piaster. The children, no longer playing, watched through the cracks in the boards, and Bell struggled to understand what had just happened.

CHAPTER THIRTY-ONE
One Small Grenade

THE COMBINED PATROL WAS APPROACHING Van Loc's main street when the policemen received a call on their radio—their first since they had left the station. Nhu, who now rode in the passenger seat, listened as a rush of Vietnamese came through the static. After a break, he replied, exhibiting more animation than Bell had seen from him all day. Still holding the handset, Nhu flapped his free hand toward the street and released a jumble of words at Phan that sent a new wave of panic through Bell.

"What's going on?" he demanded.

The only response was another stream of Vietnamese.

Finally, as the jeep slowed, Phan told him, "Drunk soldier have grenade. Hoa Binh bar. We go." He wagged his finger in the general direction of the bar.

"Oh, shit!" Bell said and craned to see around the two in front.

Phan cruised past the bar, made a U-turn, and stopped across from the Catholic Church—taller, larger, and whiter than any other building along Le Thai-to Street. The bar was separated from the church and a low school building attached to it by a wide green lawn and a six-foot-high white stucco wall. The school day had ended, and students in their neat uniforms and *ao dais* were coming out the gate and walking in two's and three's along the broken sidewalk in front of the high wall.

The two white shirts hopped out of the jeep and without waiting for Bell angled across the street. Phan waved the students out of the way, yelling, "*Di di, di di,*" followed by words Bell didn't understand. The children stopped as a group. They hesitated a moment, then streamed across in front of the Combined Patrol jeep and continued on their way at a quicker pace, glancing back occasionally like synchronized dancers.

Bell scanned the area for Americans, and ARVNs bearing grenades. Except for the school children, the only people in sight were three bar girls in identical outfits—save for the color of their mini-skirts—standing on the open concrete patio in front of the Hoa Binh bar. They were gesturing and talking in excited voices. At Phan's approach, the one in a red mini-skirt grabbed him by the arm and jabbed a finger toward the bar's entrance, a narrow doorway covered with strings of beads.

Giving a staccato response, Phan unsnapped the cover on his white holster and moved toward the door. Nhu followed, and the two slipped through the beads. Bell hung back on the patio.

"What happen here?" he asked the bar girl in the red mini-skirt.

"Soldier, Vietnamese," she shrilled in his face. "Big fucking numba 10. Beaucoup drunk." She shook her head and bounced up and down, sending her long hair swaying. "He start fight. Have grenade." She raised her hand up over her head, waving her fist.

He was about to ask if any Americans were still inside when Nhu and Phan came barreling out the doorway. Slowing only to disentangle himself from the beads, Phan yelled at the bar girls. They turned and fled, into the street, their slender legs flying beneath their mini-skirts. One stumbled, lost a high-heel shoe, and left it behind on the pavement.

The white shirts didn't stop when they reached Bell. The only English he heard was, "grenade," but it was enough to send him close on their heels.

The white shirts stopped mid-street, but he kept going until he reached the Combined Patrol jeep on the other side. He ducked behind it; then still breathing hard, he peered over the hood. An ARVN soldier in tiger-striped fatigues was struggling with the bead curtain at the bar's entrance. His hands were in front of him. One held a grenade. The soldier stumbled against the doorframe, then shaking free of the beads, righted himself and stretched out his hands, showing an index finger hooked through the grenade pin.

If the soldier made any sound, Bell didn't hear it. He did hear a jeep— coming down the street from the direction of the MP station. Slowly rolling past Bell, the jeep stopped directly across from the bar, behind Phan and Nhu who were still standing in the middle of the street.

It was the town patrol. Cole hopped out of the driver's side, facing the bar, while Landrieu got out of the passenger side.

"It's an ARVN!" Bell yelled. "He's got a grenade!"

Landrieu quickly stooped down behind the right front wheel of the MP jeep. Cole stayed put not far behind the two white shirts.

Phan pulled his .38 from the holster and held it out at eye level toward the soldier swaying in the doorway. Then jabbing the air with the pistol and shouting in Vietnamese, he started forward.

The soldier slumped, head down, back against the doorframe. Nhu followed Phan as he advanced; behind them followed Cole. He had drawn his .45, and held it out in front of him with both hands.

Amid the mishmash of foreign words, Bell heard Cole shout, "Drop it, you motherfucker."

Perhaps not the best thing to say to the man, thought Bell.

The drunken soldier snapped to attention and raised his hands, this time high above his head—and married to the grenade. Then he pulled the pin.

Bell dropped to his hands and knees behind the jeep. Nothing happened, only more shouting. He peeked around the front fender.

The ARVN still held the grenade high above his head, neither releasing the lever nor throwing it, and Phan, Cole, and Nhu were scrambling backward. Revived and yelling at the retreating policemen, the soldier slid crablike, grenade above his head and back against the wall, toward the alley on the side of the building away from the church. When he reached the alley's entrance, he twisted sideways and ran.

To Bell's surprise, there was no explosion.

Cole quickly reversed course and careened across the street to the far sidewalk. At the entrance to the alley, he stopped, lifted his .45, and fired.

Phan, a few steps behind him, lunged forward and grabbed Cole by the shoulder.

"No! No!" The policeman yelled, shaking his head. "Beaucoup people." He moved in front of Cole and waved his hand toward the ground. "You stay here."

Phan turned and ran down the alley, followed by Nhu, while Cole stood alone at the entrance. His .45 dangled from one hand by his side.

Slipping out from the cover of the jeep, Bell sprinted toward Cole. "Are you crazy?" he yelled. "Why d'ya do that? He's not ours."

"Fucking gook deserved to die," Cole hissed through clenched teeth.

"Well, you fucking missed," snapped Landrieu, who had rushed to join them. "That was the dumbest goddamn thing I've ever seen."

They were still arguing when Phan and Nhu came ambling back down the alley toward them, talking and gesturing to each other. The passage behind them was empty all the way to a small canal and the green warren of hooches behind the town.

Phan looked at the MPs as he passed them and shrugged. "We go home. No more work today."

***

Bell turned the corner from leaving his .45 in the armory and saw Hodge in front of him. He was starting up the inside stairs.

"Hey, bro," Bell called, "how was Can Tho?"

Head down, Hodge continued up the stairs without answering. Bell followed, unsnapping his MP arm band and folding it.

"Ready to go drink a beer?" he asked, catching up with Hodge. Wanting to tell him about the grenade and Cole and then Phan and his revolver.

Hodge turned sideways and leaned against the wall. *Good God,*

Bell thought, *the man looks like hell.* His eyes were puffy with dark pouches under them and his hair uncombed. His uniform was disheveled. Not the usual Hodge with his finicky grooming.

"No," Hodge said, "I need to hit the sack."

"Rough time down there, huh? You guys tie one on?"

Hodge took a deep breath and let it out. "I got a problem, Bell."

"Don't we all, good buddy."

He wasn't feeling especially charitable at the moment, not toward Hodge. The guy had changed. He spent too much time drinking with his road crew and, Bell suspected, smoking dope with Ernie the cook up on the roof. Then there was the matter of selling gas out of the V-100.

"Reason I went to Can Tho," Hodge said as Bell went past him on the stairs, "I haven't had a letter from Glenda in over a week, almost two."

Bell continued up the stairs, unbuttoning his shirt as he went. He needed to get into something cooler than his duty uniform. Hodge followed, still talking, his voice low.

"I had to call her, make sure everything's okay."

"Was, wasn't it?" Bell said absently, stripping off his uniform shirt. The inside air felt cool and welcome on his sweaty green undershirt.

"She barely talked to me. Yes, no, mostly. She said she's pregnant."

"Hey, that's great," Bell said, turning around. But he didn't finish his thought that Hodge would soon be a papa. He was doing the math.

"She just found out," Hodge said. They were in the barracks now. "I need to go see her, find out what's going on. She said she'd written me a letter... I checked with Bowman, and there's nothing."

"Sometimes the mail gets hung up somewhere. Give it a few days." He stopped in front of his bunk and threw his armband and shirt down on it.

"You think I could get a leave? Sanchez says he's going to get *one...* to go see *his* wife. He thinks she's cheating on him."

"Sanchez? Don't listen to that damn lifer."

"I... I need to go see Glenda. I... I can't... I can't go on R&R..." He was shaking his head, his voice sounded like he was about to cry. "For three more months."

"Well, you can certainly try to get a leave." He could smell Hodge's breath now and see that he wasn't too steady on his feet. "Why don't you get some sleep, then you can get cleaned up and go see Top in the morning?" He patted Hodge on his arm, giving him a slight push toward his bunk. "Bowman probably has the forms. He'll type 'em up for you."

"Yeah," Hodge said. "I'll ask Bowman." Instead of going to his bunk, he stumbled back down the aisle, heading to the stairwell.

Bell eased down on his own bunk and took off his boots and socks. Slipping on a pair of flip-flops, he forced the images of Phan's revolver and the ARVN with the grenade out of his mind and decided to review his calculations. *How long had they been here? That was easy. Too long for Hodge's wife to just now figure out she was pregnant from fucking Hodge.*

CHAPTER THIRTY-TWO
Cats About Town

SANDERSON CAUGHT THE CLAP. Bell heard him moan at the next urinal.

"Oh, it burns.... Oh, oh, it hurts." Sanderson was leaning with one hand against the wall as he tried to urinate.

"You're joking," Bell said. "Thought you never went to the whorehouses."

"Ah-h-h shit! I let that fucking DeRosa talk me into going down to Madame Phoung's before he left. 'They're clean,' he said. 'The girls are safe,' he said. I'd like to kill that son of a bitch."

"Did your young Polack friend go with you?"

"Dummy follows along like a puppy."

"He get it too?"

Sanderson chuckled between groans. "Scared the shit out of him. Thought his pecker was going to fall off. You hear? He's been transferred to Long Binh."

"Markovic? No kiddin?" Markovic he liked and hated to see leave. "When's he going?"

"Today, the lucky shit. O-h-h god. I didn't know it could burn so bad."

He left Sanderson still moaning at the urinal like he was praying, one hand on the wall, his head leaning on his arm. Going past the showers, he exited through the garage door opening and headed for the motor pool to tell Markovic goodbye. But first he ran into Hodge.

Eyes on a letter he held in one hand, Hodge was striding toward the outside stairs to the deck. He was dressed for duty: full uniform, MP arm band, boonie hat the V-100 crew always wore.

"Ah-h-h-h," came an agonized groan as he hit his leg with the open letter, the envelope fluttering under it. "Ah-h-h-h, no, no, no."

He pounded the stairs' railing with his fist.

Forgetting about Markovic, Bell stopped at the stairs. "What's wrong?" he asked.

"Ah-h-h-h," came the sound of profound agony. "I've *got* to go home. I've *got* to get a leave."

The writing on the letter and envelope Hodge clutched in a hand pressed against the railing was plainly visible. It was from Hodge's wife, thinner than usual and with no hint of perfume.

Hodge hit the top of the railing with his other fist. He turned his head and looked at Bell. "G-o-d-damn it! Goddamn this fucking war! Goddamn this whole fucking place! I can't even talk to her."

"You put in for a leave, didn't you?"

"It'll take three weeks at least, Top says... *if* the captain approves it." He shook his head, his mouth in a tight line. "I need to go *now*, Bell. I can't wait. I can fix this thing if they let me go see her."

A V-100 roared in an arc from the front of the building and around the ammunition bunker. Clark, standing in the turret, yelled at Hodge.

"Hey, Hodge, we have a convoy taking fire... north of Can Tho. We need to get our butts down there."

Hodge stared at Bell a moment, then stuffing the letter back in the envelope, said, "She wants a divorce, and I can't wait on..." He shook his head but didn't finish. Turning abruptly, he sprinted to the idling V-100.

"Go talk to Top," Bell yelled after him, "Beadle, whoever. Fuck! Call HQ and ask for Colonel Witt." Hodge was closing the side door, when Bell added, "That's what I'd do."

When he finally reached the motor pool, Markovic had already left for Long Binh. He would never see the fresh-faced mechanic again.

Bell was scheduled for a work detail, then a day off. But the previous night, the C.O. had dropped the drive shaft out of his jeep while returning from a late-night trip to the airfield, requiring Bell and Landrieu on night patrol to retrieve him from an isolated spot on QL 4. After delivering their leader to the compound, they took Gus Begay, the new mechanic, back to fix the jeep and ended up towing it down the deserted highway at 3:00am. As compensation, Sergeant Beadle gave them a reprieve from the day's work detail.

Sitting on his bunk, he marked off another day. Four months, ten days. "Tomorrow, and tomorrow, and tomorrow." With a sigh, he pulled himself up by the bunk's metal frame and placed the calendar back in his locker.

The Board of Inquiry on Johnson's death had concluded without a finding of wrongdoing by anyone. He hadn't testified, and Cole had warned him to keep his mouth shut about their escapade down an alley. It would only embarrass them both, he said. They hadn't filed a report, and they'd both get in trouble.

Sergeant Carter had torn Cole a new asshole, though, over the incident at the *Hoa Binh* bar. The grenade was likely not a dud. Some ARVNs carried grenades with a little tape around them as insurance when they were off duty. Or maybe the man had put the pin back in it. But Carter said that Cole was a dumbass for getting involved in a Vietnamese problem and shooting at an ARVN with a grenade, whether it was a dud or not.

Bell started to tell Carter or Beadle about Phan holding a pistol under his nose. But he didn't. He'd have to explain how it had happened, and he couldn't trust any of the damn lifers. So he'd only told Meyer.

While he was tying his second boot, Meyer wandered into the bay and slumped down on the bunk opposite him.

"You hear about Walker?" Meyer asked.

"What about him?" Bell pulled a shirt out of his locker.

"Dupre saw him in Saigon. He's doing better, but he'll be in the hospital for a few more weeks."

"Lot of good those damn pills did him."

"I always take mine." Meyer walked around to Walker's bunk.

"Top said to leave his stuff here... He'll be back."

"You mean, he doesn't even get a ticket home?"

"That's right."

"Now *that's* shitty," Bell said. He finished buttoning his fatigue shirt. "You off today?"

"Yep. Beadle cancelled the detail. He's okay sometimes."

"Sometimes." He reached into his locker for his wallet. "Let's go downtown. We can stop at Kikki's, tell her about Walker."

"Time's a wastin', bro. Let's haul ass." Meyer pumped the air with his fist, then as Bell rolled his eyes, jumped up to go get his shirt and hat.

They hitched a ride with Ernie the cook. He was on his way to pick up fresh vegetables straight from the States—and probably a little local Mary Jane on the way back to the compound. When Ernie turned left at Le Thai-to Street for the airfield, they hopped out for the short walk to the main part of town.

Passing the bakery, they caught the smell of fresh bread and purchased a baguette for five dong, a few pennies, from a boy-san coming out the door with a flour sack full of baguettes. Chewing on the bread, they rambled along the broken sidewalk, dodging water puddles and shooing off the children who trailed behind them or danced in front begging for candy and money. Tearing off his second bite, Bell discovered a small curled-up ball.

"A goddamn weevil!" He started ripping the bread apart. "There's more of the little fuckers!"

"They won't hurt you." Meyer raised his bread up to the sunlight. "Pick them out, like this." He pulled a few small chunks out of the center and flicked them into the street. Then he broke off a piece of crust and popped it into his mouth, smiling as he chewed.

"Disgusting," said Bell. "Bet the little fuckers aren't kosher."

He threw what was left of his share of the baguette into the ditch where it came to rest next to a pool of putrid water. It stayed there only a moment before a small boy in short pants and a ragged white shirt grabbed it and ran off down the street. Meyer broke off the end of his half, put it into his mouth, and handed the rest of the bread to a smudged-faced little girl with her hand out.

"Can't have the little urchins eating dirty bread, can we?" he said, smiling and brushing his hands together.

"Ah, fuck!" said Bell. "I'm goin' to Kim Son's. You comin'?"

At Kim Son's restaurant and bar, the odds of getting real beef instead of rat meat or dog were better than anywhere else in Van Loc, maybe in the Delta. They each ordered hamburgers and Cokes from a polite, no-nonsense mama-san and paid with worn piasters. Eating slowly at a table near the front of the restaurant, they talked little until the hamburgers were half gone. Meyer, facing the street, seemed to watch the passing traffic, while Bell sat brooding over every bite, cogitating on things he wanted to forget. Swallowing a well-chewed morsel, he felt compelled to voice his thoughts.

"Meyer, I tried to ask the old mama-san about Tony." He paused to take another bite of hamburger.

"And?" Meyer answered absently, staring out the open gate.

The little girl to whom he had given the bread had reappeared not long after they'd arrived at Kim Son's. A small boy, a toddler in a ragged gray shirt and nothing else, stood behind her, clinging to her dress. The children's eyes moved back and forth between the remnants of the hamburgers. Whenever Bell or, more usually Meyer, looked in their direction, the girl held out a hand, palm up, and gave a mechanical wave of her fingers.

"He was her nephew—I think." Bell shook his head, chewing slowly. "It was like he never existed. She just clammed up."

The woman behind the counter wandered out to shoo the children away. They ran, but as soon as she returned to her post at the register, they reappeared.

"Well, she doesn't speak all that much English," Meyer said, watching the woman. A girl in a white blouse and black pants, pretty in the usual way, except for pockmarks on her face, began clearing cans and empty plates from an adjacent table. Meyer beckoned to her as Bell continued talking.

"Yeah, but she can communicate well enough when she wants to... especially when she wants something. But she didn't want to talk about Tony."

The girl came over to their table, and Meyer asked for another hamburger.

"You're surprised at that?" he asked, looking back at Bell.

"Yeah, a little," Bell muttered. "All I wanted to know was whether he ever ran errands for... well, anyone in the compound, or for Major Binh."

Meyer chuckled. "Peasants like us come and go. She, poor soul, she's here for good, and nowhere can she make the kind of money she and her clan make off us." He paused, sipping his Coke. "I thought you were opting out of this mess, bro."

"Humph," Bell grunted, studying his last bite of hamburger. Not looking at the children, he popped it into his mouth and chewed as the girl-san delivered Meyer's second one.

"You want another?" he asked Bell as he paid.

"Hell no. I don't need a paunch like you got."

"As you wish," Meyer said. "Some like beer, others like good old American burgers."

"Uh-huh, you know where it...?"

Bell stopped as his cohort picked up a knife and carefully carved the hamburger into four pieces. Pushing his chair back, Meyer walked with the plate to the entrance and placed two of the pieces in the outstretched hands of the little girl. Another he handed to the naked-bottom toddler. The fourth he stuffed whole into his own mouth. Grinning, his jaws puffed out like a chipmunk with a five o'clock shadow, he came back to the table and eased down onto the chair.

The children had disappeared.

"Fucking savior of the world, aren't you?" Bell asked. "Little bastards'll be back tomorrow, and they'll bring all their cousins."

Meyer continued grinning and chewing, reducing the size of the hoard in his cheeks. Bell nursed his Coke, moving the plastic cup in a circle on the table. He rattled the ice, sighed, and resumed dumping his morose thoughts on Meyer.

"Johnson's dead and I didn't say squat to anybody about what Cole did on our first patrol. Going down that alley... except to you and Hodge."

"Being true to your principles. Not getting involved."

"Well, I don't feel good about it." He rattled the ice harder, sloshing Coke onto the table. "And Markovic... getting transferred to Long Binh."

"He got lucky."

"You think so?" Bell shook his head. "I was thinking they were trying to make sure he stayed quiet."

"Oy! You still obsessing about Avery and that jeep?"

"Hell, just because I'm paranoid, you know..." Bell waved his hand in the air and took a deep breath, exhaled. "On the other hand, it could've been just another army fuck-up."

"So quit worrying about it. All this rehashing, it isn't going to get you anywhere, and you'd better keep quiet back at the compound."

"Keep quiet, huh?... Ah shit," he groaned. "You're right. Keep my mouth shut and ride out my time. Nobody gives a fuck about the crap that goes on around here anyway." He downed the rest of his Coke. "Let's go check out the *Hoa Binh*."

CHAPTER THIRTY-THREE
A Surprise Invitation

THE *HOA BINH* BAR WAS ALMOST EMPTY except for a few bar girls sitting together in the dark recesses at the back. In the gloom, Bell could make out the faces of two he remembered from the grenade incident. One came over to greet them with the usual bar girl mantra.

"Hey, GI, you buy me tea, ho-kay?"

Bell put his arm around her waist as he sat down at a table near the door. "Beaucoup GI buy you tea," he said. "How about you be my girlfriend?"

She twisted away from him. "No tea, no talk," she said and moved toward Meyer as a more likely mark.

Coming up behind Bell, another girl ran an arm over his shoulder and started stroking the back of his head and neck. Looking up, he recognized Sandy from the docks. She wore a flower-print mini-skirt and a tight pink tank top that curved down to reveal the tops of smooth white breasts. She slid around to stand beside him, and he slipped his hand around her waist, this time without resistance.

"Baby-san have to work," Sandy said, nodding toward the other girl and nudging Bell in the side with her hip. "No tea, no talk. No money, no honey."

From a tape player on the bar, Janis Joplin screeched, "Women is losers. Lord, Lord..."

"How did a nice girl like you end up in a place like this?" Meyer asked, affecting a Humphrey Bogart accent. The bar girl cozying up to him gave a puzzled look, then seeing another soldier come in, she turned away and drifted in his direction.

Sandy stayed. "I not know what you mean," she said to Meyer. "You make fun of Sandy?"

Bell patted her on the butt, letting his hand come to rest lightly on one side of the thin mini-skirt. Placing her hand on top of his, she lifted it off but held onto it with a gentle squeeze. She leaned over so that one breast almost pressed against his face. He could smell a sweet perfume.

"Be nice, GI. You feel, you buy."

"I no think so." He glanced over at Meyer, who was leaning back in his chair and grinning. "Hustle's too hot in this place, bro," he said to Meyer, then smiled back up at Sandy, "deadly to boot."

"I show you something, GI." With a yank of her hand, she pulled him half out of the chair.

"Whoa-a-a," Bell said, now on his feet. "Where d'ya think you're going?"

But he yielded to the small, thin fingers grasping his hand and followed her without trying to break free. She led him to the back of the bar, up a flight of stairs, and into a room at the end of a long corridor with closed doors. The corridor and then the room reminded him of going with Johnson, following him up the stairwell and down a similar corridor, to find Roberts. Roberts' blood-drained corpse.

But in this room, the French doors were already open wide onto an outside balcony, and when Sandy entered in front of him, the room pulsed with sunlight and shadows as a set of gauzy curtains billowed up, toward the ceiling. There was a low bed in the center of the room, a night table and lamp, and a straight-back chair in one corner. The bed was neatly made with white sheets, the top one folded back halfway.

Still holding him by the hand, Sandy pulled him inside and shoved the door closed with her foot. Turning, she released his hand and stood facing him, her back to the bed. She stared at him without expression.

Nonplussed, Bell bit his lower lip, trying to decide his next move and decipher hers. She cocked her head so that her black hair fell onto her shoulder. Then she smiled, and without speaking, whipped off her tank top, revealing a slender, smooth body and perfect, cream-tint breasts, brown nipples erect.

Letting out his breath, Bell whistled softly. "Jesus," was all he could say.

"You like, GI?"

Her hand was working loose a hook on the side of her mini-skirt. Before he could answer, she dropped the skirt to the floor, stepped out of it, and kicked it along with her sandals to one side.

She moved closer, but not touching him, her arms out, inviting him to stare at her body.

"I... I like," he stammered. He did like. A lot.

She was naked except for orange bikini panties—very much like the ones Terri had worn the last time—no, the next to the last time—he'd seen her.

He felt a rush of overwhelming desire that was being translated to his groin. But staring at this perfectly formed female synthesis of East and West, the breasts, the narrow waist and hips, tan thighs and legs, the beautiful face and hair, and being aroused by every inch of it, he couldn't purge the memory of what Doc had said: "every venereal disease known to mankind."

He scanned the beautiful, smooth surface, the gentle folds and creases, for any sign of lesions, sores, scabs, or welts. There was none. He saw nothing but the most beautiful female body he'd ever seen in the flesh, lovelier and more perfect than Terri's.

Smiling, confident of her witchcraft, Sandy stepped forward and pulled his face down to hers. He leaned into her, ran his hands around her bare sides to her back, and clasped her in a hard embrace. Her mouth was so moist and soft that kissing her was almost like intercourse itself, and it stimulated him to press his pelvis against her flat stomach. After a long moment, she drew her mouth away and stepped back—pulling his hands around in front of her and placing them on her breasts.

"You love Sandy, GI?" she asked staring intently into his eyes. She reached down and felt his erection through the fatigue pants and began undoing his belt with one hand. She was smiling at him in a way he hadn't seen before. Benign, almost pleading.

"I love Sandy," he said. His eyes drifted away from hers and down to where her small, delicate hand rested lightly on top of his on her left breast.

"You no love Sandy," she said.

He looked up. Her smile was gone, replaced by a scowl.

"You only love body."

What brought that on, he wondered. Had his insincerity shown in his face? Shown like a flashing neon sign. Staring into her unblinking eyes, he rallied what little honesty he could muster under her spell. "Sandy and body are one," he said.

"You want fuck numba one Sandy, GI?"

Her smile was back, but accompanied by a hard, ironic gleam in her eyes. Dark, knowing eyes, an exotic Asian contrast to her fair skin. Her voice was low, seductive. "One thousand piasters, GI. Three MPC, you fuck Sandy." Her smile grew broader, but the eyes stayed hard on his. She pressed his hand against her breast and tugged at the buttons on the fly of his trousers.

He stopped her. Thinking, *God is she beautiful, and I want to fuck her over and over.* But something was killing his desire.

"You want me to pay you?" he asked. "Me? I love you like nobody else."

She shook her head, still smiling up at him. "GI always pay. All man always pay. Maybe not dolla, man pay." She dropped her hand and started working in earnest on undoing his pants. "For you MP," she said, "we boom-boom alla day long. Ten dolla. Til sun go down."

Shaking his head, he grabbed her hands and pulled them away. "You are one beautiful woman." Quickly adjusting his privates, he began refastening his pants, remembering what Cole had called her— *one beautiful fucking whore.* "Nothing I'd rather do, but I can't, not this way." His belt fastened, he said, "Got to go," and reached for the door.

"What wrong with you!" Sandy shouted from behind him. "You no want Sandy?"

He was almost to the end of the corridor when he heard the door to the room slam shut. Sandy's voice, high and shrill, pursued him into the stairwell with a stream of Vietnamese invective interspersed with, "You numba fucking ten. No balls, no boom-boom." He glanced back and saw that she was dressed again in the pink tank top and flower-print mini-skirt. "You no can fuck, GI?" she yelled. "You got no balls? You queer?"

In the stairwell light, he could see deep, atavistic rage on Sandy's face. He hesitated, and out of a religious depth he no longer felt or believed in, he said to himself: "*Get thee behind me Satan.*" But he didn't answer her. He ran the rest of the way down the stairs and into the bar.

"Let's go," he said, slowing to a walk as he approached Meyer, still sitting at the same table, drinking a Coke by himself. The bar girls had all settled on more promising prey, a group of three engineers who had arrived during Bell's absence.

"That was quick," Meyer said, standing. "A real quickie, or short time, or whatever they call it."

"It wasn't anything they call it," Bell said.

The slap of sandals sounded across the barroom's cement floor, and Sandy appeared from the gloom at the back. She was moving at a tired walk, and her face was somber and set in a hard grimace.

"*Choi hoi,*" she said, coming up to them. "You numba ten cheap Charlie."

She stopped a few feet away and glared at Bell, her hands on her hips, pert chest out. But she didn't call him names, in Vietnamese or English. Instead, as Meyer pushed through the bead curtain over the exit, she said in a low, plaintive voice, "You no love Sandy. No one love Sandy."

Bell gave her an apologetic shrug.

She brusquely turned away from him and, smoothing her skirt

with small, delicate hands, targeted the engineers standing at the bar. From outside the bead curtain, he could hear her saying, "Hey, GI you buy me tea, ho-kay?"

Their next stop was Kikki's bar. The only people there were Mai, the old mama-san, and Sergeant Foley. Foley sat on a bar stool drinking a beer and talking with Mai across the faded blue counter.

Not pleased at Foley's presence, Bell asked Mai for a Budweiser and headed to a table. Instead of following, Meyer walked over to lean against the counter next to the motor pool sergeant.

"You aren't working on the C.O.'s jeep?" he asked Foley.

"Fuckin' nigger can walk far as I care," Foley growled. "His goddamn jeep ain't goin' nowhere for another week."

"Captain will get one of the others," Meyer said. "Probably yours."

"Never happen!" Foley rapped his beer can on the countertop and glared at Meyer, who grinned back at him. Foley treated the motor pool jeep like it was his own personal ride back home in Alabama.

Pushing away from the counter, Meyer asked Mai for a Coke and crossed the room to join Bell. Foley finished his beer, paid, and left.

"Where's Kikki? She better?" Bell asked when Mai brought their drinks and placed them on the table.

"She no here. Beaucoup sick. Go hospital." Mai waved her hand in the direction of the airfield.

As she spoke, she moved to one side of the table and stood in the light from the open front of the bar. Bell noticed how nice she looked—white silk pants and form-fitting blue shirt accentuating small breasts and the dark skin on her neck and arms, far darker than Sandy's European blend.

"Walker'll be back in a few weeks," he said. "You tell Kikki?"

"Okay, but I not know when I see her."

"Do you need anything?" he asked, without thinking what he meant.

First glancing around, she bent close to his ear and said in a whisper, "You come see me. Tonight."

Taken by surprise, he pulled his head back and stared at her—almond-shaped feline eyes, round cheekbones, dimpled smile. But he didn't reply.

She quickly wrote out an address on the back of a bar tab. "Okay?" she said, her eyes fixed on his.

He suffered a wave of conflicting emotions. His mind raced. Yes. No. Spending the night in town, breaking the curfew, being out of the compound alone, after dark, without permission. He didn't break rules. Yet, she was pretty—and female—and she wasn't Sandy or one of Madame Phoung's specialists. The clap was scarier than breaking army regs, plus being some girl's tenth trick in a row didn't appeal to him. But he'd found his strong attraction to Sandy unsettling.

Walker, Cole, Hayes, almost everyone broke curfew. Not even Cole would haul in another MP for violating curfew. Only Lt Floyd would do that, and he was on temporary duty in Can Tho. Maybe Hayes or Beadle would—if you were on their shit list.

Mai stood looking at him while Meyer stared out the open gate at the traffic on the street.

"Okay," Bell said finally.

Meyer smiled and said nothing.

CHAPTER THIRTY-FOUR
Bell's Night Out

A BRIEF SHOWER, ANOTHER TEASE OF THE MONSOON, met them at the front gate. Dashing inside, Bell almost collided with Jack Dupre in the hallway. The temporary courier, Dupre had just returned from Long Binh, and they begged him for mail. Meyer set off to read his stack of letters, while Bell, empty handed, roamed the villa, trying to kill the slow hours until dark and he could walk out the gate and flag down a *xich-lo*.

Still suffering from confused thoughts about Mai, he drifted up to his bunk where he tried to read. Stalled in the middle of *The Two Towers*, he swatted mosquitoes and daydreamed about Terri back in the World.

***

Brushing her shoulder length hair, she stands in front of the mirror, in orange bikini panties, one hand wielding the brush, the other smoothing her hair back, admiring her reflection. He watches. Her small breasts move in time with the brush strokes. Or was it Sandy he was seeing?

"Am I different from the others?" she asks.

"There haven't been that many. Only one really."

They never talked much. In the two short months he had known her, most of their interaction had been physical, which suited them both.

He walks up behind her, puts his arms around her waist, his bare chest against her warm back, and stares over her shoulder into the mirror.

"How about me? Am I different?" he asks.

She doesn't answer him. Instead, she puts the brush on the dresser, places her palms together in front of her, elbows raised, and flexes her arms. She laughs.

"I bet your other girlfriends couldn't do this." Her right breast jerks up, down. "Muscles," she says. "From swimming." Dark eyes in a pixie face look at him in the mirror. He kisses her neck, running his hands up her sides.

"I want to buy a bullfight poster," she says. She twists around against his chest and nods at the cheap painting on the wall beside the bed. "Like that one." In the painting, a bullfighter waves a bright red cape in front of a sepia bull silhouetted against a yellow background.

"Why that one?"

"I saw the bull... when we were making love. It was pulling the room in circles under the cape. I want it to remember this... to remember us."

But she hadn't remembered. Or if she did, he didn't know it.

***

After chow, he stopped in the club for a beer with Meyer and Sanderson, then climbed the stairs to the roof. Gazing out across the trees and the canal in the lowering twilight, he lit a cigar and ambled slowly along the wall that enclosed the flat roof. Edging around the corner beneath the guard tower, he almost fell over Hodge, who was sitting next to Dupre and Ernie-the-cook on the concrete floor, their backs against the wall.

Ernie released a stream of smoke from his mouth and staring dully at Bell, handed a thin cigarette to Hodge.

"What the...?" Bell sniffed twice.

"Bell, Bell," Hodge said slowly, "ring-a-ling, Bell. Have a puff on the magic weed. Make... your troubles... fly away."

"Yeah, Bell, join us," said Dupre.

"No thanks. I'll stick with Coronellas."

He held up his cigar and took a long draw on it. Looking out over the compound, he exhaled in a series of smoke rings.

The eastern sky turned rose as the sun broke through the clouds low on the horizon behind them. Hodge said something, but he wasn't listening. It was almost dark, time to go. He didn't want to get caught up here. He snuffed out his cigar on top of the wall and placed the stub between his teeth.

"Hodge, I'm headed downtown. Cover for me, will ya?"

"Sur-r-re, buddy." Hodge threw up his hand in a loose gesture. He would be doubtful cover for anyone tonight. "Just get some pu-s-sy for me, too."

A *xich-lo* was idling near the front gate, awaiting its nightly fare. Sliding onto the thinly padded seat, Bell handed Mai's address to the driver. After a quick glance, the driver returned the paper with a nod and a string of singsong words, then whipped the *xich-lo* around and onto the gravel road.

Out on QL 4, the traffic had subsided to a dying hubbub of small engines and the occasional roar of a deuce-and-a-half. An MP patrol jeep went past, and he ducked his head down in the tin carriage. A suspicious move, he was sure. But if they saw him in the shadows, they paid him no mind.

The *xich-lo* driver deposited him in front of a wooden door set back in a high wall overflowing with bougainvillea. As the *xich-lo* putted off, Bell gave the door a push. Locked. Stretching up, he peered through bars in a small window near the top. Inside the walls was a low stucco house set back in a courtyard. Dense vines draping a trellis separated the house's recessed entrance at one corner from a large single window in front. Through half-closed shutters, yellow light streaked the fronds of a date palm beside the window.

Rattling the gate, he called softly, "Mai." He waited. "Mai!" Louder now. What if she stood him up?

A figure appeared in the darkened doorway and, after he called a third time, stole across the narrow courtyard to the door in the wall and unlocked it.

"Bell, you did come," Mai said.

"Hey, I couldn't pass up the invitation."

As he entered the courtyard, she took him by the hand, and he pulled her close in a tight embrace and felt the silk of her blouse and the cool dampness of the skin on her arms. Her head against his chest fit easily under his chin. Bending and pressing his face against her neck, he caught a scent of dark earth and mysterious herbs.

She pushed him away. "No. No. Mama-san see." Taking his hand again, she led him inside.

Mama-san—he didn't know if she was mother, grandmother, or what—came up to them as they entered the house and spoke in Vietnamese, directed as much to him as to Mai. Mai answered, and the old woman—time-worn face, white hair in bun, shorter even than Mai—shuffled, like all the old mama-sans seemed to, toward the back of the house. Her loose sandals tapped the tile floor, her black pajama pants whispered in the silence. She was the same old woman who had fixed the soup and egg rolls at the bar. The same old mama-san who had led him and Johnson to Roberts' room.

"What was that all about?" he asked.

"I tell her bring you beer. You hungry?"

"No. I've eaten, thanks."

He examined her face and eyes. When she smiled, her high cheekbones gave her a warm glow that did not quite match the unblinking, feline eyes with which she observed his reactions. Her olive skin and black hair contrasted pleasantly with the pale blue of her blouse, which fit snugly across her breasts and hung loosely over the top of her white silk pants.

He looked around. They were in a small living area separated from the back part of the house by the bead-covered doorway through which the old mama-san had passed. The floor was clean and new, of slate-blue-and-white tiles. A short-legged, polished mahogany table, jade-green cushions along each side and at each end, filled the center of the room. A futon sat against the front wall, under the open window he had seen from the gate. Two miniature table lamps dimly lit the area and gave an eerie glow to a row of luminous blue tiles along the bottom of the walls. On a low table next to the far wall stood a shrine—a foot or more in height—containing the black-and-white photograph of a Vietnamese man in uniform. In narrow vases beside the shrine burned two sticks of incense, releasing thin wisps of smoke and an acrid, yet not unpleasant, odor.

Mai switched on a bright overhead light as the mama-san reappeared carrying a round bar tray with a can of Schlitz. Wordlessly, she handed him the can, then padded across the room to the shrine and sat down on a low stool next to it. She balanced the empty tray on her knees.

"Come," Mai said, taking him by the hand and leading him over to the mahogany table. "You sit, here." Releasing his hand, she slipped around to the other side of the table and eased down onto a pad across from him. She watched with a faint smile as he moved awkwardly to sit.

He grunted as one knee, then his butt hit the hard floor under the thin pad.

"You know Mah-jongg?" Mai asked.

"No." He rearranged his legs, trying to find a comfortable position.

"I show you."

She pulled a wooden box from underneath the table and began laying out Mah-jongg tiles, explaining the writing or symbols on each one as she did. Rather than place his beer on the polished table, he sat it down on the floor next to his knee. From across the room, the mama-san, shrouded in a haze of blue smoke from the incense sticks, watched in silence.

"Pretend you, me, same-same four winds, okay?" Mai said. She took out a pair of dice and rolled them across the table

He squirmed and smiled at her, nodding.

Explaining the game in broken English, she finished arranging the tiles and showed him how to look for matches among the strange symbols and Chinese characters. He only half listened, wondering what he was doing here and how people sat like this for so long.

"How's Kikki?" he asked.

"She very sick." Mai shook her head and looked down at the table. "Maybe she no live."

He thought surely she can't be serious. The last time he had seen Kikki in the bar she looked thin and wan, but not that sick.

"What's wrong with her?"

"Not know English word. Eat holes down here." She leaned away from the table and pointed toward her lower abdomen.

"Cancer?"

"No cancer. Tie something, I think."

Bell made a face and didn't say anything. Typhus, typhoid. He hoped it wasn't something you caught from a person who had it—or persons they lived with. His feeling of discomfort increased. He remembered the times he had eaten soup and eggrolls at Kikki's bar. He hoped the army had vaccinated them against whatever it was.

Mai jolted him out of his thoughts with a question about Walker. He answered, drank his beer, and watched her demonstrate the game to him. He understood little of what she was telling him, except that you matched up the symbols somehow. He listened to the click of the tiles as she moved them around, almost hypnotized by the procedure.

The sudden twangy noise of a Vietnamese soap opera made him jump. The old mama-san had slipped across the room and turned on a small black-and-white television. Staring at him, she squatted on a small stool beside it, then turned down the volume to a low drone.

Only slightly louder, Mai asked, "Bell, you help us get beer, whiskey? For bar. Kikki no can do." She arranged small stacks of tiles in front of her on the table. "Walker not here to help."

"I don't know," he said slowly. Thinking, *is this sickness of Kikki's exaggerated to get me to help them? Did she invite me here to use me to stock their damn bar with PX goods?*

"I might bring you a case or two of beer." He hesitated. "But I can't keep you supplied in enough stuff..." He shrugged and didn't finish. Maybe he should leave.

Mai didn't say anything. She continued to play her pretend game, and he watched until she finally came to some sort of impasse.

"You have girlfriend back home?" she asked.

"No girlfriend. I knew several girls before I..." He stopped and shook his head. "Most just friends, but they've all forgotten about me now. Out of sight, out of mind."

Mai placed the board and tiles in the box and slid it under the table.

"I want... I don't know how say... happy. I no like war, no like way GI do Vietnamese girl. Maybe have beaucoup money, someday go America."

"Maybe someday," he said. "But you have to marry a GI for that."

"I no think so. I no marry." She looked at him without saying anything for a few minutes.

While Bell weighed how to answer, a young Vietnamese boy, still in his blue-and-white school uniform, entered the front door and crossed the room in noisy flip-flops. He continued on through the bead curtain to the back section of the house without speaking and with no more than a glance at Mai and Bell. Rising from her perch, the old mama-san followed the boy out.

Mai and Bell sat looking at each other, then Mai reached across the table and placed her hand on top of his. "You stay here tonight."

Was this a question or a statement, he wondered. *Too late to go back to the compound—because of the hour, and because I'd look foolish.*

"Yes," was all he said. The night was looking up. Turning his hand over, he wrapped his fingers around hers.

She gave his hand a light squeeze before slowly withdrawing hers, caressing his palm with her fingers. With an easy grace, she stood up, yawned, and stretched her arms over her head, giving emphasis to her slim form and breasts. As he watched from his seat on the floor, she went over to the futon beneath the window.

"You sleep here," she said, bending down and patting one of the two long cushions. He hadn't noticed, but the cushions matched the slate-blue tiles in the floor. Reaching up, she pulled the shutters in slightly and lowered a bamboo curtain over the window.

As she came back across the room, he struggled up from the pad and reached out to her. She walked into his arms, and he embraced her tightly. Returning the embrace, she placed her arms around his neck and gave him a long kiss. But when he tried to slip his hand under her silk blouse, she pushed his arm down by her side and, after a few more seconds, edged back, not quite out of his embrace. She stood still, looking up at him with cat's eyes, then wrapped her hands behind his neck, while his arms remained around her waist.

"Won't you stay with me?" he asked, searching her eyes.

"I no think so," she said and twisted away. "You no help. You no like Vietnamese girl."

He caught her by the wrist, gripping it loosely. "I can't," he said. He started to add that it would be illegal and he was an MP. But that wasn't it. He wasn't going to pay her for sex, period.

She pulled her hand free—but slowly, brushing his palm with her fingertips. Turning, she walked over to the television and switched it off.

"G'night," she said over her shoulder.

"Don't go. Not yet."

She smiled at him, then slipped past just out of his reach in a rustle of silk. Without looking back, she disappeared through the bead-covered doorway, into the depths of the house.

Baffled, disappointed, and pissed, he studied the room—the tile flooring, the shiny table, the bamboo curtain over the window. He turned off the lamps and the overhead light; still in his fatigues and boots, he lay down on the futon.

After a few minutes, he sat up, took off his boots, and stretched out on his back with his arms under his head. On the ceiling and walls above him were distorted shadows cast by light filtering through the bamboo curtain. A Cobra came down QL 4 from the airfield. The thump of the rotors became louder and louder until the chopper's spotlight briefly lit the room; then the noise grew fainter and receded toward the river. As that sound faded, he strained to hear a far-off, kettledrum beat that seemed to make the air tremble. B-52s dropping hundreds of bombs on an empty patch of jungle near Cambodia? In Cambodia? Perhaps the jungle wasn't empty where the bombs fell— only dead. The deep rumble stopped, and he heard the comforting, familiar sound of artillery, higher-toned like a muffled snare drum, not atavistic and profound like the B-52s.

He lay awake and listened. More choppers came and went, but not as close. The rumble of the artillery rose and fell and stopped, then started again.

Maybe she'd come back after everyone was asleep. Maybe he would become her conduit for beer and booze from the PX. Walker had been. Almost anyone else in the compound would—except Meyer. That fucking Meyer.

He stared through the dim light toward the bead curtain covering the entrance to the back of the house. He lay awake and waited. But she didn't come. The futon was hard and uncomfortable, and he had to pee. He'd never felt so alone. Maybe he slept.

As the room grew lighter, he rolled off the futon and stood up. Feeling his way around in the half-light, he finally found an eastern-style bathroom with two footpads, just on the other side of the bead curtain. After returning to the futon, he sighed and began putting on his boots in the gloom. As he finished, the old mama-san emerged from the depths of the house. Using a series of gestures and bad Vietnamese from his phrase book, he persuaded her to unlock the front gate and let him out to the street.

The sky lightened to a pale gray as he trudged back toward QL 4, walking with his head down past closed shops and houses with faint lights showing through their open windows. When he reached the intersection with QL 4, he found the bakery already open, and he went inside and bought a baguette—which he ate without checking for weevils. Walking and chewing on the bread, he looked around at the awakening town, then lifted his eyes to see sunlight striking the tops of the palm trees along the road.

A *xich-lo* putt-putted toward him, an old papa-san crouched over the handlebars like a hunched-back gnome skulking through the shadows. Bell waved his free hand, palm down toward the ground, native-style. The rickshaw contraption came to a stop beside the road, and he climbed in and bid the driver to take him home, to the MP compound.

CHAPTER THIRTY-FIVE
Sergeant Carter

HE WAS BACK ON DAY PATROL. The stomach cramps and diarrhea subsided to an occasional inconvenience—now that he avoided the lemonade at the ferry and rarely ate the food downtown. With the weather growing even hotter and more humid, a random afternoon shower sometimes seemed to come out of nowhere to drench them at shift change. Whenever they stopped moving, the mosquitoes kept them company.

On rare occasions, Captain Templeton appeared, strolling to and from his jeep or coming outside to watch the desk sergeant line up the afternoon shift of four MPs and the desk clerk. Back straight, chest out, cap low over his mirror sunglasses, he'd walked slowly down the line, making only a few desultory comments about haircuts and uniforms.

Despite a spate of barracks inspections by the captain and harassment by the NCOs, the days had settled into an almost pleasant routine. By reading and more or less concentrating on his duties, Bell even managed to avoid dwelling on Johnson or Major Dobbs or Tony and all the other stuff. Except now and then.

All he could think about today was Sergeant Carter, who'd decided to go out on patrol with the day shift. He was going to make sure "their shit was tight," that they were doing their jobs. And today was Bell's turn.

Bell drove, and the sergeant sat beside him, giving instructions on what he called "good police technique." Of medium height and stocky build, the sergeant had a square red face and dark blond hair, well-oiled by hair tonic. From rural Kentucky, he'd joined the army after high school—his education, he said. He was nine years in uniform and five years as an MP, mostly in Germany and the States.

Bell considered Carter one of the dumbest human beings he had ever met.

After a trip to the airfield, they were riding back through town on Le Thai-to Street when Carter punched him on the arm.

"Bell, didn't you see that soldier? Sonovabitch was out of uniform." Carter pointed to a black soldier riding in a *xich-lo* going in the opposite direction, toward the airfield.

"Sarge, the guy just has his hat off and shirt unbuttoned. Give him a break—it's hot and his hat'll blow off."

"That's... what's wrong... with you... lazy shits." Carter punctuated the end of his words in a crude imitation of John Wayne. "You don't... fuckin'... enforce... the military code. Sloppy ass troops act like sloppy ass troops. Now turn your ass around and stop that nigger."

Bell did a U-turn, cutting off a jeep and a motor scooter coming toward them. As he straightened out, he flipped the switch for the siren and, after a short distance, pulled up beside the *xich-lo*. He motioned for the driver to stop.

Carter got out and began to berate the soldier, who wore an Air Cav patch on his shoulder, while Bell sat in the jeep and watched. Unlike most of the NCOs, Carter's fatigue pants weren't tailored or tapered at the ankle but were bloused in proper military fashion. Bell didn't tailor his fatigues in order to save money, Carter because it wasn't by the book.

As the GI buttoned his shirt and put his cap on, Carter finished the lecture, growling that he'd "write your black ass up" the next time. When Carter asked if he understood, the black soldier stared back, stone faced, and responded with a curt, "Right, Sergeant."

"See, Bell, you gotta keep 'em in line," Carter said as he climbed back into the jeep. "Stop the small stuff and you head off the bigger shit, like drugs and the black market."

"Sarge, we're in a fucking combat zone. Whether the man wears a hat in town or not doesn't matter." *And drugs and the black market are booming,* thought Bell, resisting the temptation to say it out loud.

Carter ignored the retort, and Bell whipped the jeep around to head back down Le Thai-to Street. They hadn't gone fifty yards when Carter hit the dashboard with his palm.

"Well now, let's go see what *those* fuckers are up to." He pointed at two American soldiers getting out of a jeep with engineers' markings.

It was mid-morning and most of the bars were still closed, but the soldiers had parked in front of one that had its gate partly open. Bell stopped behind the engineers' jeep, and Carter hopped out and did his John Wayne swagger up to one of the GIs standing on the sidewalk.

"Now, soldier," he said, "ain't you out a little early to be bar crawlin'?"

"It's okay, Sergeant," said the GI, holding his hands out to his side. "We only stopped by for a minute, to say hello to my girl." The GI, who had thick brown hair and a neatly trimmed brown moustache, was considerably taller and thinner than Carter.

"Well now, Specialist Albright," Carter said after dropping his eyes to the man's nametag, "are you off duty... and do you have a pass?"

"We're headed down to work on the new road. Just stopped by," Albright gestured toward the bar, "on the way."

The driver, a short, dark-haired soldier, stood in the street near the rear of the jeep. He was shifting from one foot to the other, not saying anything. Sidling up behind him, Bell peered into the back of the jeep.

"Who are these for?" he asked, looking across at Albright. Cases of soft drinks and beer were stacked on the back seat.

"I picked those up at the PX. They're mine." As he spoke, Albright waved his hands, as if to assert his innocence of any wrong.

"Let's have a look in that jeep," Carter said and gave Albright a slight push away from the side of the vehicle.

"You can't do that," Albright said.

Carter shoved past him. "It's military property, bub, and you're on duty—so you say. We're just checkin' ve-hicles for contraband." Carter jerked a drink case out of the back seat and placed it on the sidewalk.

Thinking he should make some effort to help—without prompting from Carter—Bell went to the front of the jeep and, leaning in past the steering wheel, examined the interior. Between the seats was a sheaf of papers. He leafed through them—nothing but requisition forms.

As Carter ripped open a case of beer, Bell checked the floorboard, then slid his hand under the driver's seat, and felt a small, rectangular package. He lifted the seat. A pack of Marlboros. Extracting it, he dropped the seat back in place and opened the loose top of the pack. Inside were rows of cigarettes with twisted ends.

"Hey, Sergeant Carter, look at this." He regretted it almost as soon as he said it.

Carter walked over, took one of the cigarettes out of the pack, and pulled the end off. Holding it under his nose, he sniffed.

"Okay, boys," he said, looking from one to the other of the GI's. He tossed the pack and broken cigarette onto the seat. "Up against the jeep and spread your feet."

Carter grabbed the driver, Gonzalez, according to his nametag, and shoved him toward the front of the jeep. Coming around to help, Bell put his hand on Albright's back and pushed him forward.

"Those joints aren't mine," Albright said, as he leaned against the hood.

"Shut up, shithead," barked Carter. "If they ain't yours, how d'ya know what they are?"

"But—"

"I said shut the fuck up. You gonna tell me the tooth fairy left 'em there?"

They frisked the two, finding only keys, money, wallets, and on the short one, a pocketknife, then handcuffed each man's hands behind his back. Bell pulled out a wallet card and in a slow monotone read them their *Miranda* rights.

"Oh shit, man, this can't be happening. It can't be," Gonzalez muttered over and over as Bell helped him into the back of the MP jeep.

On the other side, Carter prodded Albright into the front seat. Once seated, Albright turned sideways to plead with him.

"Look, I don't know how those got there. I... I checked the jeep out of the motor pool this morning. The cigarettes were already there. Just take 'em and let us go."

"That'll be up to your commanding officer, soldier," said Carter.

Bell drove the prisoners to the station while Carter followed in their jeep, the drink cases back in place. At the station, Carter stood the two in front of the MP desk and told Singleton to fill out the arrest forms and Bell to make an incident report. He was going to secure the evidence and call the engineers' duty officer. When Albright objected, Carter punched him in the stomach.

"Bell, take these fuckers into the back room," Carter said as Albright fell wheezing against the desk. "Do a cavity search."

"What the fuck are you doing?" Bell asked, loud but not yelling. *Rule: never yell at an NCO.* But he was shocked to see Carter hit the man, who hadn't done anything and was in cuffs.

"You heard me. Take 'em in the back room." Carter was on his way around behind the desk. Singleton, eyebrows raised, glanced at Bell, then handed Carter a plastic evidence bag, which they rarely used.

"Jesus Christ, Sarge," Bell said. "All these guys had was a few joints. This is crazy."

"Bell, goddamn it, you do what the hell I tell you." Carter glared at him, his face growing redder. "Get back there... now."

As Bell glared back at Carter, Singleton began dropping the prisoners' effects into property bags. Albright was upright again, holding his stomach.

"Can you... take the cuffs... off us," Albright said in gasps.

Bell took out his key and reached for Albright's hands.

"Leave 'em the fuck on, Bell."

Bell stopped. This was going all wrong—for him and the engineers. There had to be a better way. He was smart enough...

"Okay, you guys," he said, "you heard the man. Let's go."

He gave Albright a push toward the door to the back room. Then he grabbed Gonzalez by the arm and pulled him through the door behind Albright. As he kicked the door shut, he could hear the click of the typewriter keys. He gave the door another push, but it wouldn't close all the way, leaving a crack a few inches wide.

He turned the two around to face him under an overhead fluorescent light and told them to open their mouths wide, lift their tongues, and move their heads. He couldn't see anything and didn't know what he was looking for, but he was buying time to think.

He stepped back and peered through the crack in the door. Carter was picking up the phone.

Bell turned back to the prisoners, and inhaling sharply, said in a loud voice, "Turn around and drop your pants."

"Hard to do with handcuffs on," Albright said.

"Shh-h-h," Bell said, index finger to his lips. "Keep it down."

He undid Albright's handcuffs, then Gonzalez's. When Albright started to unbutton his pants, Bell shook his head and said, "no," in a whisper. He could hear Carter on the phone in the other room.

"Now bend over and spread your cheeks," he yelled. But he was shaking his head, vigorously. "Undo your belts, and pull out your shirts," he whispered. Body cavity searches hadn't been in his training, and he wasn't interested in learning the skill now.

Albright and Gonzalez were staring at him. "You sure..." Albright started, but Bell gave him a wave of the hand to keep quiet. He shuffled his boots across the cement floor as loudly as he could, moving around the two.

"I'm screwed," Albright said softly. "We're screwed." He nodded toward Gonzalez. "If you guys push this shit through."

"You can beat this," Bell said in a whisper. Then loudly, "Okay, stand up and button 'em." He shuffled his boots some more. "If the jeep wasn't assigned," he whispered, "and it's been in your motor pool over the last weeks."

"Yeah, that's true," Gonzalez said, tucking his shirt back into his pants. Bell shook his head, for no, leave it out.

"Ask for a court martial," Bell said. "They won't have the evidence—"

"Bell," Carter yelled from the other room, "get those fucks back in here."

"Better put the handcuffs back on or Carter will have a shit fit," Bell said as they finished fastening their pants.

"Your sergeant's a real hard-ass," said Albright, holding his hands out in front this time for Bell to snap the cuffs back on his wrists.

"He's a real cop... me, I just want to get out of this place in one piece." Gonzalez kept his head down and eyes on the floor while Bell replaced the cuffs on his limp hands.

"You and me both," said Albright.

Carter forced the two GIs down onto a bench against the front wall, across from the MP desk, where they sat hunched forward, their hands cuffed in front of them. If the sergeant noticed the change, he didn't say anything.

Bell paced back and forth in front of the two on the bench. Behind him, Singleton gave a clucking noise with his tongue, barely audible above the clicking of the typewriter keys.

The engineers' duty officer was the same blond first lieutenant Bell had interviewed about the dead papa-san on QL 4. On entering the station, he gave the men seated on the bench a hard stare.

"What the hell are you doing?" he spat at Bell, still pacing in front of the desk.

Bell grimaced and pointed at Carter.

Turning on the sergeant, the lieutenant yelled, "Get those goddamn cuffs off them. Now."

"Handcuffs are standard procedure, Lieutenant," Carter growled, coming from behind the desk.

"Standard my ass. I know these guys. Now get 'em off." Under his breath, he added, "What a crock of shit."

"Sign for 'em and they're yours," Carter said. He motioned to Bell. "Unlock 'em."

After Carter had signed over the prisoners, the lieutenant took them outside. Bell followed him out.

"You know the charges will never stick, don't you?" the lieutenant asked, as they went down the steps.

Bell grunted, "Dunno," and shrugged. Then he asked, "Has the sergeant gotten back? The one over the work detail? You didn't call me."

"What...?" The officer gave him a puzzled look that changed to sudden recognition. "Oh, that... He's been transferred. Up to Long Binh."

"Is there anyone else here who was with him... when the papa-san—"

"You mean the old man?" This came from Albright, standing at the driver's side of his jeep. "The one shot in the head? On the old road?"

"That's right," Bell said.

"You think it was one of our guys, right?" Albright paused, while Bell stared at him. Gonzalez was already in the jeep. "Well, you're wrong. We weren't there. We weren't that far south."

"They were yours, man." Gonzalez was hanging out the passenger side, looking back at Bell as he spoke. "I saw 'em go by us in an MP jeep—they were on the new road. Not supposed to be, but MPs go where the hell they want, don't they. One of 'em had an M-16... saw him pointing it out the side of the jeep." He faced forward, away from Bell.

Albright started to get into the driver's side, then stopped. "You need to check out your own people... and thanks for nothing."

Bell turned to the lieutenant. "You knew this already, didn't you?"

The lieutenant raised his hands and shrugged.

"Shit," said Bell. He pivoted around and stalked up the steps, back into the station.

CHAPTER THIRTY-SIX
Too Much Said

IN THE AFTERNOON, THEY PICKED UP three stumbling-drunk Air Cav soldiers who were breaking tea glasses and harassing the Vietnamese patrons and bar girls in Kim Son's. With the help of Meyer and Dupre on the second town patrol, they handcuffed the three and took them to the station. Shouting and staggering up the steps and through the door, two of the soldiers struggled fiercely against their captors until they all collided with the front desk.

Carter pushed the larger of the two, a dull-eyed man with a crooked nose and missing front tooth, backward onto a bench while Bell tried to reason with the shorter one, whose thin face and receding jaw reminded Bell of a rat. The third man staggered across the room and slumped to the floor in a fetal position against the wall.

"Take the cuffs off," Carter yelled, pointing at the rat-faced man.

Dupre pinioned the man's arms to his side while Bell fumbled with the cuffs. As they snapped off, Carter grabbed the front of the rat-faced man's shirt and jerked him forward.

"On the floor, asshole," Carter shouted, then jabbed the man in the ribs with a billy club

He screeched something sounding like, "Fuck you," and lurched forward. Carter stepped aside and punched him in the pit of the stomach. The rat-faced man doubled up with a sharp expulsion of air.

"I said... on the fucking floor." Then Carter hit him across the right shin with his club.

The man gave a strangled scream and fell heavily to the floor.

"On your back, feet and arms up in the air. Make like you're... a dyin'... fuckin'... cockroach."

When the rat-faced man continued lying on one side, moaning, Carter rapped him several times in quick succession, this time on both shins.

"Ow, ow, stop it, stop it!" he wailed, but rolled onto his back and elevated his arms and legs a few inches off the concrete.

"Higher, gawd-damn it," yelled Carter.

Still moaning, the rat-faced man raised his arms and legs higher.

"Now keep 'em there... till I tell you to drop 'em."

Carter's face was bright red. He took short rasping breaths as he turned to the bigger Air Cav soldier. Once his handcuffs were removed, the soldier had gotten up from the bench and was starting to struggle again with Meyer and Dupre. The third man remained curled up on the floor.

"Get on down there," Carter yelled at the big soldier.

The man stopped moving. He glared bug-eyed at Carter, then slowly eased down under the pressure of Dupre's hand on his shoulder, until Carter poked him in the stomach with the club.

"Ugh," the man grunted and doubled over, releasing a blast of foul air.

"Move your... fat ass! Move it," Carter yelled, breathing hard, almost panting. The man collapsed flat on the concrete floor, rolled over, and slowly raised his limbs. The third man stirred but only to turn his face to the wall.

Carter pointed his club at Bell and Meyer. "Use your fuckin' clubs... on their elbows... and legs... if they... start... to drop." He turned back to his victims. "Keep 'em up... motherfuckin'... roaches."

Meyer and Bell looked at each other, while Dupre leaned against the front desk. Singleton, on the other side, kept his head down as if he were working on something important.

"If they fight ya, hit the bastards in the gut... or the kidney," Carter said, scowling at them, still trying to catch his breath.

A minute, then two minutes passed, and the two men on the floor wheezed with the effort of keeping their arms and legs suspended in the air. The big soldier's feet settled to the concrete, and Carter rapped him across each shin.

"Get the fuck back up there!"

The man yelled out in pain, "Stop it! Can't do this... Goddamn! Stop!"

Next to him, the rat-faced man emitted a series of sobs, gasping for breath.

"We can't keep these guys like this," said Meyer, raising his voice. "And we're not supposed to hit—"

"I'm not using a club on a man on the ground," Bell said, glaring at Carter. His fists were clenched and his billy club was still on his belt. "We can throw 'em into the QC's cell until they sober up or someone comes to get 'em. But I'm not going to beat on somebody just for the hell of it."

Dupre nodded but didn't say anything.

"You pansy-ass pussies." Carter took a couple of deep breaths. "No wonder nuthin gets done when you're out there."

Carter paused to rap the little rat-faced man on the side of a leg sinking to the floor, but not as hard as he had hit the big soldier. The man lifted his legs higher with painful slowness.

"Okay, up you two," Carter said, his breathing back to normal. He slapped his club down on the top of the front desk.

The two soldiers collapsed, legs and arms hitting the concrete floor with a thud. They rolled over and stumbled to their feet.

"Handcuff those two cocksuckers together. Put all three of 'em in the back room and bar the fuckin' door."

As Sergeant Carter went behind the desk, Dupre and Meyer took hold of the men and began cuffing them.

"Back to back," said Carter.

Meyer and Dupre left on patrol, and Carter called the Air Cav unit to pick up their drunken soldiers. While the sergeant talked on the phone and did his paperwork, Bell paced, out the door onto the porch, and then back inside. Singleton went for a smoke and then next door to a street vendor for a Coke.

Alone with Carter, Bell stopped pacing and stood in front of the chest-high MP desk. He stared down at the sergeant on the other side, filling out forms on the Air Cav soldiers.

Carter looked up. "Bell, you better get your shit together if you wanna be an MP. You've got a job to do here."

He could feel the anger seethe through him and he rocked forward, elbows and forearms on top of the desk.

"Carter, you stupid bastard. Everything we did today was petty-ass harassment." He took a deep breath. "Pure bullshit. Blown out of all fucking proportion of... of anything." He gripped the back edge of the desk. "It serves absolutely *no* fucking purpose."

Carter's mouth fell open, but he didn't say anything. Instead, he tossed his pen on the table and glowered at him.

Bell backed away from the desk and raised his hands. "Why can't you leave the poor bastards alone? Air Cav guys spend a week in the field, go through hell, then we fuck with 'em, and we don't have to." The words were spilling out and he couldn't stop them. "You lifer S.O.B.'s, you play fucking games all the fucking time. You fuck with people 'cause you can do it—for no fucking reason at all."

He dropped his hands and stood stiffly in front of the desk, surprised at himself, at what he had said. Carter's stunned face turned even brighter red, then to an expression of cold rage.

"You could... go to... Long Binh jail... for... this kind of shit," Carter said in his John Wayne voice. "That's in-su-bord-in-a-tion." Like it was a word he'd practiced in front of the mirror and loved to say.

The two locked eyes as seconds ticked by on the clock above Carter's head. Bell was breathing hard and wishing he had kept his mouth shut.

"Look, I'm sorry," he said, trying to sound contrite. "But we shouldn't be hitting those guys." He had Carter there.

Carter shook his head and wagged a meaty finger at Bell. "Hayes has already talked to Top about you. You and your Jew buddy. You both could end up in the boonies... or out wadin' through the swamps. Same goes for that goofball Hodges."

Now it was Bell's turn to look stunned. Carter went on, his face still red, "I know y'all are college boys and don't wanna be here. But listen, you – are – here, and you don't understand shit about what's goin' on." He paused. "The army is my job, my life." He picked up the pen and shook it at Bell. "I do my job right—best way I know how. You need to do the same goddamn thing." No John Wayne voice now.

Carter looked down at his forms for a long minute, while Bell stood silently staring up at the clock. When the sergeant looked up again, his red face had returned to something close to its normal hue.

"Y'all could be good soldiers," he said, lips pursed, nodding his head slowly. "Good men—in your ways. But goddamn it, you gotta help me do my job, my way."

Bell spun around and rushed outside, past Singleton coming up the steps. Singleton glanced at him but didn't speak.

A three-wheel Lambretta hacked loudly down the lane in front of the station, drowning out the dull roar of traffic and murmur of voices from the town until it merged into the river of noise on Le Thai-to Street. The sky was overcast, an unchanging milky gray, but the air gave no hint of rain. Standing next to the MP jeep, Bell felt numb, his mind overcast and gray like the sky, his body weighed down by the oppressive air.

CHAPTER THIRTY-SEVEN
Captain Midnight

TWO DAYS ON PATROL WITH CARTER, and all Bell wanted to do now was relax with a drink and read his newspaper. First procuring a double gin and tonic from Thuy, he stopped at a table inside the club long enough to say hello to Sanderson and Meyer, then headed out to the deck through one of the open doorways.

Flip-flops smacking the planks, he crossed to the railing and stared out at the canal, and beyond it, the green rice paddies stretching to the horizon. The parking area below lay in a false twilight enshrouding the ammunition bunker and the sandbag revetments for the V-100's. It was quiet, no noise of engines or voices, no movement of tires or boots. The work details were done for the day, the night patrols were out on the road, and most of those off-duty were downtown.

Determined to forget his run-ins with Carter, he eased down on a bench only a few steps from the stairway to the tarmac. Turning sideways, he leaned his shoulder against the railing and, raising the plastic cup, gazed over it at the shadows creeping into the palms and banana trees, the green leaves above suffused with a deepening yellow hue. A solitary sampan putt-putted up the canal.

Feeling calmer and a little more distant from the day on patrol, he spread the *Stars and Stripes* out on his lap and took a long sip of the gin and tonic, savoring the taste. A mosquito buzzed around his head. He swatted at it and succeeded only in smacking himself on the ear.

Would the monsoons, when they actually arrived, be any better than this? He knew nothing about monsoons except what he had read in a novel somewhere.

A slight breeze rustled the tops of the trees and lifted the flag at the corner of the compound. His face and neck were wet with sweat, and the breeze cooled him like a gentle fan. The odors of rice paddies and canals, the scent of fetid water, loam, and lime barely reached him up here on the deck.

While he skimmed the headlines—General Abrams, Bob Hope, the currency exchange—he took a Coronella out of his shirt pocket and peeled off the wrapper. Shielding the match with a cupped hand, he lit the cigar, shook the match out, and tossed it over the railing. As he picked up his drink and exhaled, watching the first cloud of smoke drift upward, a yell came from inside the club.

"Hey, Hodges! What the fuck you think you're doin'? You can't have that thing up here!" It was the first sergeant yelling at the top of his voice.

There was a hurried clump-clump of boots, and Hodge stumbled onto the deck through the far doorway. He held an M-16 braced in the crook of one arm, barrel pointed at a low angle toward the sky. A cloth bandolier filled with M-16 magazines was draped across his sweat-stained, green t-shirt.

Bell froze, drink held up in one hand, cigar in the other. He stared at the rifle, then at Hodge's sweaty arms, then at Hodge's contorted face. There were long streaks down his cheeks. It wasn't sweat.

Before Bell could move or speak, First Sergeant Dietz plunged out of the doorway directly across from him. Stepping in front of Hodge, Top stood with his hands on his hips, legs apart, only a few feet from Hodge. Then he wavered and wobbled from one foot to the other, before righting himself.

Oh, shit, he's drunk, thought Bell, lowering his drink. *They're both drunk.*

"What the hell do you think you're doin'?" Top was fully dressed in neatly pressed and tailored fatigues. But his face and neck were bright red. "You can't have a friggin weapon up here," he yelled again, not moving from in front of Hodge.

Sanderson, Meyer, and Thuy appeared in the doorway behind the first sergeant.

"It's okay, Top, it ain't loaded," Hodge said. His voice was strained, higher pitched than normal. Huge beads of sweat ran down his tanned forehead from under his tangled sun-bleached hair. "Where's Captain Midnight? I need... I need to see him about my leave. I—"

"Gimme that," yelled Top, reaching for the raised rifle.

Before he could grab it, Hodge jerked the M-16 upward. It erupted in a short, loud "br-r-r-rp," sending the burst arcing over the ARVN Ranger compound next door.

Top jumped back, and Hodge brought the M-16 barrel down to belly level. He swung it back and forth between Top and Bell.

"Don't move," Hodge screamed, the words coming out in a long slur.

Even as he said, "don't," they were moving—Top diving through the door and rolling onto the floor of the club. Sanderson, Meyer, and Thuy lurching backward out of Top's way and bolting for the exit on the far side of the room.

Bell was off the bench even before Hodge's words penetrated the ringing in his ears. Newspaper and cigar in one hand, drink in the other, he spun around the end of the railing and, doubled over at the waist, lunged down the outside steps. No looking back at Hodge and the rifle.

He stumbled past the last two steps, flung himself under the deck, and fell to one knee, spilling his G&T. His cigar broke on the asphalt.

His heart pounded, and his breath came in gasps. He squeezed his eyes shut and willed himself not to start shaking.

He stayed crouched there, panting, listening to boots on the plank floor above, pacing, back and forth. The echo of people shouting and running through the building resonated in his head. This was a bad dream, and it was Hodge up there, not Cole or some crazy ARVN.

Staggering to his feet, he turned to go into the supply room—and there was Cole, standing opposite him in the open garage-door entrance to the showers. Cole, still in his MP gear, was staring up at the deck, one hand on the butt of his .45, the other stretched out in front of him. Pointing.

The pacing above stopped.

Cole yelled, "Hey, motherfucker..." Then he made a frantic sideways leap, back through the shower entrance.

A long burst of automatic fire followed him, and a line of bullet holes appeared in the door frame and down the shower wall behind where Cole had been standing. Stucco and concrete chips flew every which way.

Bell almost crashed into the closed screen door to the supply room before he could grab the handle and open it. He kept going past shelves of uniforms, boots, underwear, socks, and out the inside door into the hallway leading to the armory.

Then he stopped.

Coming toward him at a fast walk was Sergeant Carter, holding up a snub-nose .38 revolver at eye level, checking the open chambers. He slowed as he approached Bell.

"Top told me some fuck's upstairs shootin' at people," Carter said.

Bell didn't answer. Trying to stop the shakes, he stared blankly at Carter.

"I can take him out, if he don't see me," Carter said. As he passed Bell, he snapped the cylinder shut and stuck the revolver into his belt.

"You, Bell," he barked, "go find Sanderson and get an M-16. Fuckin' armory's locked up tight."

He kept going, on through the door into the supply room.

Bell stared after him. "What the fuck am I going to do with an M-16?" he asked between gulps of air. But Carter was gone—and he knew what Carter wanted him to do.

He continued on to the armory. Sanderson was just opening the door.

"See you got the hell outta there, too, man," Sanderson said, breathing hard from his run down the stairs. "Best let him alone 'till he sobers up."

"Don't think... they'll... do that." Bell leaned against the shelf on the lower half of the open Dutch door and caught his breath. Bracing himself to stop shaking. "Where'd he get the rifle? He wasn't on duty today."

"Sergeant Hayes took him and some others out for target practice this morning. He didn't turn it in when they came back."

"Carter told me to get an M-16. He wants to shoot him." Bell stared past Sanderson at the rows of M-16's and .45's lining the wall. "Carter has a .38, and Cole's out there with his .45."

"Ah shit, man." Sanderson shook his head and groaned. "He's just plain sick. Oh, man. He's sick over his wife, and he's had too much to drink. He'll calm down if they just let him be. They go up there with guns and shit, people are gonna get hurt."

Bell didn't say anything, but kept eying the M-16's. Another burst of rifle fire came in a muffled echo from somewhere above them.

Sanderson cringed, looking up at the ceiling. "Aw shit, what's he doin' now?"

Bell stepped across the room to the rack of M-16's and reached out for one. Then he stopped and willed the shaking to stop. "I can talk to him," he said, more to himself than to Sanderson. "I know him. He'll listen to me."

"He wants to see the captain," Sanderson said. "Don't think you're a—"

"Leave the firepower here." Bell was at the door, pushing Sanderson in front of him. "Come on," he said, tugging the door closed. "Lock it up."

"Shit, man, it don't look like he's in any mood to listen."

"One way to find out."

Shutting the armory door, Bell snapped the padlock back in place. Sanderson watched silently, then pocketed his keys as Bell took off down the hallway at a run. Sanderson followed.

As they rounded the corner going to the inside stairs, Keller appeared at the other end of the corridor. He wore a white towel wrapped around his waist and nothing else. His hair was plastered to his forehead.

"What the fuck's going on?" he yelled. "I was taking a shower, then all hell broke loose."

Keller padded down the corridor leaving wet sandy tracks on the floor.

Bell didn't answer and kept going.

"Grabbed this," Keller said, tugging at the towel. "Took off to the bunker. Who's—"

"Hodge," Sanderson yelled back at Keller. "He has an M-16 and wants to see the C.O."

"Where you goin'? Sounds like the C.O.'s problem."

"Bell thinks he can calm him down." They were on the steps now, taking two at a time.

Keller followed, but at the top, he turned back toward the barracks. "I'm gettin' dressed," he yelled, "and go find the fuckin' captain."

In the upstairs corridor, no one else was in sight. Not Top, not Carter, no one. Approaching the open door to the club, Bell edged along the wall and stopped just outside. He listened and heard the clink of a bottle.

He peered around the doorjamb. Hodge was holding the bottle, Jim Bean it looked like, in one hand, and facing the deck. The M-16 rested in the crook of his other arm, pointed where he was looking.

Bell saw no one outside, but he heard a voice from below, on the tarmac.

"Put down the rifle, you sonovabitch, or you're dead." *Carter.*

Hodge took a swig from the bottle and set it down on the table with a dull thud. He started toward the nearest doorway out to the deck.

Bell slipped inside the club.

"Give me the rifle, Hodge," he said as calmly as he could

manage. But he wasn't shaking. Sanderson stayed in the doorway, only a few feet behind him.

Hodge twirled around, the M-16 extended, barrel straight out. When he saw Bell, he quickly raised it across his chest.

Bell stretched his hands out, palms up. "Come on, bro. You're gonna get in worse trouble than you're already in. Just put it down."

Hodge slowly lowered the M-16 to waist level. His eyes moved from Bell to stare down at it.

"They tol' me... Cap'n's sending me to a grunt unit." The words were slurred. "Says I'm a fuck-up... won't give me a leave."

"Aw, man," said Bell, "you can't believe those fuckers. They don't—"

"I... I gotta... gotta go see Glenda." Hodge's words came out in a long hiccupping sob, "Only chance... fix things." He looked up and moved his head back and forth like he was in a daze. Sweat and tears ran down his face. "She'll come back... I know she will." His chest heaved. His hands holding the rifle were shaking.

"Come on now, just put it down, and everything will be all right." Bell kept his voice low, almost a whisper. He was fighting not to cry himself, and not to start shaking. He was afraid—not only for himself, but for Hodge.

They both stood still, Bell watching Hodge, and Hodge again staring down at the rifle, tears streaming down his cheeks. After a long half minute, Hodge crumpled to one side and fell into a chair. With a hard clunk, he thrust the M-16 onto the table beside him. Seated in the chair, he sobbed, chin on chest, rubbing his knees with his hands.

Bell crept forward, inching toward the table and the rifle.

Heavy footsteps echoed in the corridor, and Bell glanced back at the door. It was Captain Templeton. He shoved past Sanderson and stormed into the room, thrusting Bell aside and sending him stumbling backward over a chair. Bell and the chair hit the floor in a crash.

"Give me that rifle, soldier." The captain's voice boomed through the club as Bell untangled himself from the chair and rolled over to get to his feet.

Across from him, Hodge grabbed the M-16 off the table, and jerking it upward, fired into the ceiling tiles above the captain's head.

The captain froze mid-stride, less than ten feet from Hodge. A sprinkling of white fibers floated down onto the captain's black hair and his green fatigues and the floor around him.

But he didn't flinch or retreat. Bell, however, was scrambling sideways on hands and knees toward the door.

Hodge, the M-16 held across his chest, began backing up toward the doorways onto the deck. Then he fired another burst.

Still on hands and knees, Bell was out the door. Sanderson, already twenty yards down the corridor, stood with his back pasted against the wall.

Bell stopped and twisted around. Shaking violently, he struggled to make it stop, to look back inside. He stretched out flat on the floor and looked.

There was no blood, but everything was frozen, Hodge facing the captain, the captain not moving from under the snow settling on his head and shoulders from the shredded ceiling above him.

Bell started to slide sideways, away from the open door, but stopped when he saw Sergeant Carter step onto the deck from the outside stairs. From behind Bell came a loud whisper, "Bell, get the fuck out of there." It was Sanderson at the far end of the corridor. Meyer was with him.

Hands down in front of him, Carter began to slink toward Hodge. As he moved forward, he raised the .38 straight out in both hands, to eye level.

Where the hell has he been all this time? Bell wondered, his shaking subsiding as he watched Carter. *And where was Top? And the other non-coms?* Then a horrible vision of what was about to happen flashed through his mind. *They can't do this. They can't kill Hodge.*

With a quick motion of his hand, the captain waved Carter away. Hodge, his eyes directed at Bell on the floor at the exit, didn't appear to notice.

"Specialist, give me the rifle, and I'll try to make it as easy on you as I can," said the captain, his voice lower and softer than when he charged in.

Without aiming, Hodge fired a single round, hitting the window frame at the far end of the room and sending cement and wood splinters flying.

"I have to see Glenda," he screamed, his face taut and red, sweat and tears mingling and running off his cheeks.

Carter, almost through one of the doorways to the deck, lifted his .38 again, pointing it at the back of Hodge's head, only a few yards away.

The captain shook his head.

"I'll see what I can do," the captain said, and took a step closer to Hodge. "Give me the rifle."

Hodge was shaking all over, uttering guttural sounds. Then he stumbled backward and collapsed onto a chair by the open doorway. Jumping forward, Carter reached around him, grabbed the rifle by its stock, and lifted it away. He stepped back with the rifle in one hand and his .38 in the other.

Hodge stayed in the chair, his arms dangling by his side. Throwing his head back, he released a howl of anguish, followed by deep sobs.

The captain stared at him for a moment, then walked over and slapped him hard across his upraised face.

"You dumb bastard," he said. He wiped his palm back and forth on his fatigue pants. His quiet voice cut through the air like a steel blade. "I signed your emergency leave this afternoon."

He looked across at Top, who had appeared in the doorway behind Carter.

"Take this piece of shit over to the airfield and put him in a holding cell. I want him out of here and in LBJ by tomorrow."

"Yes, *sir!*" said the first sergeant, moving into the room past Carter. "Will do!"

Carter remained standing behind Hodge, the M-16 and .38 held up in his hands. His face was blank, unreadable.

The captain turned and stared at Bell, still on the floor. Then he nodded, almost imperceptibly, his lips drawn in a tight line. Bell glared back, his own jaw clenched. Without another word, the captain strode out of the club, carefully stepping around Bell at the exit.

Hodge continued to sob, his eyes down, his chest heaving.

As the captain's tread receded down the corridor, Top turned to Cole, who had come up the outside stairs and stood in the far doorway.

"You heard the captain. Cuff this piece of shit and get him over to the Air Cav unit. They'll have a place to stash him."

Whipping back around, he scowled at Bell, now up on one knee, arms clasped across his chest to hold onto the demons and keep them from racking his body. Top motioned to him.

"Bell, make out a guard roster—two hours each. Make sure he don't kill himself or some shit like that. You understand me?"

CHAPTER THIRTY-EIGHT
Why?

BELL TOOK THE 20 TO 2200 HOURS SHIFT outside a cement-covered bunker the Air Cav unit had converted into a cell, complete with a metal door and, on one side, a small square window with iron bars. Inside the cell, Hodge sat on a cot. The only other furnishing was a five-gallon bucket. At first, a few Air Cav soldiers came by, curious to know why someone from the MP compound was in the cell. By 2100 hours, the curious had been satisfied, and he was alone with Hodge, who had sat or lain quietly on the cot the entire time.

"Hodge, you doin' okay?" he asked, looking in through the window. "You need anything to eat?"

"I'm okay."

Bell leaned a shoulder against the cement side of Hodge's cell, his M-16 strap over his other shoulder, and stared up at the sky. There were only a few stars barely visible through the spotlights around the bunker. It was a hot, muggy night like every other night had been for weeks. He was beginning to doubt the monsoons even existed.

"They said you ratted on me, Bell," Hodge said in a low voice. "You ratted about my smoking dope on the roof."

"Fuck no!" Bell almost yelled, twisting around to look into the cell. "You know me better than that."

"Yeah, I didn't believe it. But still—"

"Who said that, man?" Bell pounded his fist on the window ledge in front of the bars. "What son of a bitch?"

"I don't know... Last week... Hayes told somebody and they told me."

"It's not true. It's—"

"Bell, how long you think they'll give me?" Hodge asked from his cot. He didn't wait for an answer. "Oh, shit. I - am - fucked. No wife... No nothing. God, what am I going to do? *What* am I going to do?"

"Why did you go after the C.O., Hodge?"

At first Hodge didn't answer. Then he said in a low voice, "Sergeant Hayes told me Captain Midnight didn't like us... us college boys. You know... rich white boys. Told me he was going to turn down my leave," his voice caught, "to go home... go see Glenda."

Hodge got up from the cot and came over to the window, grabbing the bars with both hands and pressing his forehead against them. "Cole said it, too. He said I was going to the field. Cambodia, or some fucking place like that. 'Cause... 'cause they think I'm a pothead.... Oh, God, what am I going to do, Bell?"

He started crying softly and twisting his head back and forth between his wrists and hands clenched on the bars.

"Good God almighty, what's going to happen to me?"

Bell didn't answer. He rubbed his bare arm below the rolled-up fatigue sleeve. The shaking had stopped. He just hoped it didn't start again when he woke up during the night.

Shifting the M-16 strap to the other shoulder, he leaned his back against the bunker and stared up at the sky. He squinted to see the few stars through the bright lights.

Tomorrow I have a day off. Then it's back on patrol.

CHAPTER THIRTY-NINE
Deconstruction

HE FOUND SANDERSON AND CHECKED his M-16 into the armory. Then they both trudged up the stairs to the club for a beer. Meyer was already there, at a table by himself, writing a letter and drinking a Coke. Cole, Dupre, and Moe Gilfillian, poker hands spread out in front of them, were arguing over a pile of MPCs. Ernie-the-cook, his hat on crooked and still dressed in his grease-stained kitchen whites, sat hunched over a table full of plastic cups, talking in a laconic drawl to the new mechanic, Gus Begay, who only nodded and stared into his drink. "Hey Jude" played on the Armed Forces Radio Network.

While Sanderson sidled over to the bar to order a beer, Bell stopped to count the holes in the ceiling. Eight, at least.

"Hey, Thuy," he called, starting for Meyer's table, "bring me a beer."

"You come bar, four eyes," Thuy called back. "I no wait tables."

He checked his stride and made a right turn to the bar.

Smiling sweetly at him, Thuy opened a Pabst Blue Ribbon, placed it on the counter, and waited for him to fish MPCs out of a pocket. Her heart-shaped face and smile gave her a look of seraphic innocence.

Bell took the beer and smiled back at her. "Thanks," he said.

"Have baby," Thuy said and turned to one side, pulling her hands across the front of the white silk pants to reveal a slight bulge. "Now you treat Thuy like honorable mother."

"Oh-h?" said Bell. "How long?"

"Four, five months."

"Congratulations. Maybe father come home soon."

Her smile disappeared, and she looked down. "I don't know. Far away. Maybe when war over." She looked up and smiled again.

"Then you go home. Everybody go home."

"I go home after a year in this place, but Vietnamese girl have to stay here forever. You never go real world."

He felt bad as soon as he said it. But it was true.

"I love Vietnam," she snapped, her smile gone. "This my country. This real world, too. Someday have peace. My baby not know war."

"I hope so. Maybe I come back and see you then."

Cole stumbled up to the bar and demanded a beer. Bell watched as Thuy opened it without smiling or looking at Cole.

Turning away as Cole smacked an MPC note down on the counter, he sauntered over to sit with Sanderson and Meyer.

"How's Hodge?" Sanderson asked as he pulled out a chair.

"Not good." Bell took a swallow of his beer. He was already beginning to wrap the afternoon's events in a tight shroud for burial deep within his mind. "You hear the captain say he'd signed orders for his leave?"

"That's what he said." Sanderson snorted. "Lot of good it'll do him."

"Well, Hodge told me, over at the airfield... he told me what set him off." Bell took another swallow of beer as the other two waited. "Foley and Hayes... those two bastards told *him* the C.O. had turned it down."

"Foley wouldn't know that," Meyer said. "I don't think he would." He leaned forward over the table. "Hayes might."

Bell shifted his beer can back and forth in front of him. "Except it wasn't true." He took another long pull from the PBR. "Hayes also told him he was going to the field."

"No shit?... Hayes?" Sanderson sputtered. He hit his fist on the table. "That lousy bastard."

"I wonder who else is on that list," Meyer said, "if there is a list."

"Ah, we happy few," Bell said. "We're the prime candidates." He lifted his beer. "To staying alive, bro's. Staying alive and staying out of the field."

He finished the beer and carefully placed the can on the table. Across from him, Gus was returning to his table carrying a fresh cup of ice and a 7-Up can in two huge hands that seemed out of proportion to his squat body.

By the time they pushed their chairs back, the empty cans on their own table were stacked high, and Thuy had gone home. The poker game had ended, and the players were outside on the deck, where Moe was pretending to lob grenades, throwing empty beer cans over the railing into a V-100 revetment. Ernie was dancing in a doorway, laughing and egging him on. Gus was gone.

As Meyer started to get up, Bell reached over and grabbed him by the arm.

"Remember the papa-san Hodge's crew brought in? The one shot in the head down on QL 4."

"I remember you guys talking about it." Meyer settled back into his chair. Sanderson hadn't moved.

"Engineers say they didn't do it.... One of 'em claims our people were out there. Going north, maybe coming back from Can Tho."

"Who was in Can Tho that day?" Meyer asked.

"We could check the trip tickets."

"What good would it do?" said Sanderson, staggering to his feet. "You can't prove a thing."

"I'd like to know," Bell said. They all stood now, and Bell leaned across the table, talking in a whisper. "I'm not so sure it was an accident."

Bowman came in to lock up and told them to leave. After disposing of their empty cans, they drifted out, leaving Bowman to contend with Moe, Cole, and Ernie out on the deck.

"You know," said Meyer, once Sanderson had gone off to his cloister downstairs, "you may think knowledge will set you free, but sometimes it's dangerous. You could end up going for a romp in the rice paddies."

He turned into his bay, leaving Bell standing alone. The inside lights were out. Somewhere in the dark, a tape recorder played a string version of "Moon River" to the accompaniment of intermittent artillery far across the canal.

Maybe surviving this place is just mental, Bell thought, leaning against the wall. *It doesn't ever go away, all the shit. It's all still there—like today. But if you can tune it out, let your mind go off into never-never land, it's as if you're somewhere else.*

Still, every day's different. Forget the one before when you start out on patrol the next. Drop a divider down and block it out so that yesterday doesn't taint the new day—the red sun rising in the mist from the river and hanging over the rice paddies like the prettiest picture you've ever seen. Each day a separate piece of life.

And each night, Bell marked another day off on his perpetual calendar—done, finito, past—before he wrapped himself in his poncho liner like a shroud to keep off the mosquitoes that gave Walker malaria. Usually he would sleep well, and sometimes he would dream— about Terri standing in front of the mirror, or about mowing the grass, or about hobbits and the Middle Earth from the paperbacks he had plucked out of the USO box.

CHAPTER FORTY
Interlude with Beadle

THE MONSOONS ARRIVED. In late morning or early afternoon, the clouds dragged in a large chunk of the South China Sea and dumped it on them, sometimes for a few minutes, other times for hours. Afterwards the sun reappeared, and they sweltered in an all-encompassing steam bath.

He awoke to a new Beatles tune, "Let It Be." Now that Poteet had gone, PFC Taylor, an FNG in the corner opposite Walker's empty bunk, had taken over the DJ role for the barracks. Taylor looked the way an MP should look: big, solid, and square-jawed, a lifer in the making.

Bell lay still, listening to the song and the soft whine of the fan rotating above his head. Finally sitting up, he grunted "morning" to Taylor, who informed him it was after 1300 hours and he had missed chow.

"I know, you dumb-fuck," he muttered under his breath.

Night patrol had lasted until dawn. All because some crazy Green Beret had decided to end an argument with the butt of an M-16. He said he didn't want to waste a bullet.

It had been another patrol with Sergeant Carter, but he'd been impressed with how Carter handled it all: trying to help the dying man, arresting the assailant, keeping the Air Cav contingent from killing him. He and Carter had even talked civilly. And there were no more dying cockroach or billy club sessions with prisoners.

Riding around the town—even before the fight at the airfield—Bell had grown comfortable enough with Carter to ask him something that had been bugging him ever since Hodge shot up the club.

"Where was Cole?" he asked. "You were up on the deck. But where was Cole?"

"Told that crazy fuck to stay below and cover me. Didn't want 'im up there." Carter grinned at him and shook his head. "Can't trust that clown. Not when he's waving a weapon."

"And Top? What happened to him? He didn't show up till it was over."

Carter shrugged. "Some've had all they can take—"

"Hayes told him the captain turned down his leave. Foley too."

"Told who?"

"Told Hodge. And he told me. When he was in the holding cell."

Carter was silent as the jeep rolled past the intersection to QL 4 and a half klick beyond before he replied: "Well, maybe that's what they believed."

Then Singleton had radioed and dispatched them to the airfield, ASAP.

***

Still sitting on his bunk, Bell swatted at a mosquito supping on his sweaty neck. The cloying heat and humidity permeated every corner of the barracks—morning and night—despite the rotating fans. Outside there was standing water in every depression, a standing invitation to mosquitoes that ascended in clouds when anyone went near. Even the soccer field across the road had turned into a lush green swamp ankle deep in water.

Once dressed and alert, his first stop was the supply room for new socks and underwear. No sooner had he crossed the threshold than Sergeant Sanchez waved him over to his desk and showed him a typed, two-page letter in Spanish.

"This will do it," the supply sergeant said, tapping on the pages with his finger. "A letter from the priest saying I need to come home. At once. My mother is dying." He chuckled. "All those damn hemorrhoids would get me was a trip to Saigon. But a dying mother? *Gracias a Dios*, a ticket on the big bird."

"Did you write that?" Bell asked, pointing to the letter.

"A friend, *amigo*, a friend." Sanchez looked at him for a moment, grinning. "The dear Padre is a true friend." He bobbed his head several times.

"Who's going to look after the supply room?" Jimmy Williams, Poteet's replacement, had lasted as supply clerk for only a week before Top moved him to the V-100 patrol to replace Hodge.

"Not my *problema*. Someone here will be the supply clerk, and they will bring in a new supply sergeant from Saigon."

"Come on, Sarge, why d'ya think this'll get you home?"

Sanchez's eyes grew wider at the question. He replied in rapid Spanish, then with a shrug, switched to perfect English. "Top feels bad about Hodge, and maybe they are a little scared, no?" He gave an exaggerated wink. "My mother, she lives in a small village in the mountains, a very remote village." Chortling, he affected a Spanish accent, "Weesh me luck, *amigo*."

"It'll never fucking work. They're not that stupid."

With a dismissive wave of his hand, Bell headed for the clothing shelves. Behind him, Sanchez, still chuckling, rattled the pages of the letter in the air.

Bell took a shower, shaved, and dressed in civilian clothes. After wrangling a ham sandwich from Ernie the cook, he moped around the club or sat outside on the deck, trying to read.

He was on the bench next to the railing, watching the clouds gather for the afternoon rains when Sergeant Beadle appeared with a can of Coke in one hand and a bag of chips in the other. He plunked down next to Bell, making the bench shudder.

"What are you reading?" Beadle asked. He shoved chips into his mouth and started crunching on them.

Bell told him and held up *The Return of the King* to show the cover. The motion brought a whiff of shaving powder and sweat-fused deodorant from Beadle.

Beadle nodded with a bemused smile and shifted his bulk, causing the bench to creak. Other than duty concerns, he hadn't said more than three sentences to Bell since they had arrived at the villa in the same deuce-and-a-half—nor Bell to him.

"You know, "Beadle said, "much of *The Lord of the Rings* was written during World War Two and undoubtedly was influenced by the war... but Tolkien debunks the connection." Between the clumps of chips, Beadle went on to paraphrase parts of the book's foreword, which Bell had read and recalled only vaguely. He was surprised Beadle even knew what the book was about, much less the author's commentary.

The man was no dummy. His pronunciation was more precise and erudite than Bell's own Southern drawl, though some of the effect was lost in the systematic destruction of the potato chips. Still, Bell couldn't shake the image Cole had given him—that of the big black sergeant with the Ex.O.'s skinny white driver.

He suppressed a shudder and forced the image out of his mind.

"Have you read much Tolkien?" Bell asked.

"Some." Beadle shrugged. "Years ago. He's not Shakespeare, but he tells a good tale." The sergeant downed a swallow of Coke and added, "I took some graduate courses at U. Mass. Ran out of money, so I joined the army. Still read a lot, take a few correspondence courses now and then, mostly history and literature."

Beadle was more of a mystery than ever. His uniform always looked rumpled, and he rolled from side-to-side when he walked due to his girth. He talked no more to the black soldiers than to the white ones, and he didn't favor one over the other. To everyone—even to Hayes and Foley—he was cordial, even pleasant, and his demeanor was open and honest, surely a useful attribute for a crook.

"I was in graduate school at UNC, English lit," Bell said. "I'm thinking of writing a paper on *The Lord of the Rings...* when I go back. Maybe something on the imagery." He shrugged and stared over the railing, thinking that he was a long way from going back.

"Try comparing it to 'Beowulf.'"

"You think so?" Raising his eyebrows, Bell looked back at Beadle.

Beadle nodded and took another swig of Coke.

"Yeah, anyway," Bell said. "If I'm able to go back to school. First I need to get out of this fucked-up place."

"What! You don't like the Nam—fighting to save the free world?" Beadle pulled his head back in mock horror. "Stop the V.C. before they reach San Francisco?" He chuckled and dredged some chips from the bottom of the bag.

Still depressed and irritated at having to clean up the mess caused by the Green Beret, Bell was in no mood to maintain a diplomatic silence.

"All this war's about is saving face for Nixon. We've got no business being here."

Beadle dumped the crumbs from the bag into one hand and tossed them into his mouth. He shook his head slowly. "I wouldn't spout off with that kind of stuff around here, if I were you." He turned to check the horizon. The wind had picked up, and the clouds were growing darker above them. "I don't disagree with you," he said, when he turned back, "but I do know that Ho and his bunch have done some pretty vicious things. And we made a commitment—"

"You need to cut your losses when you have a losing hand," Bell said. "We're not even fighting the real enemy. The Soviets are using this to bleed us dry. We spend billions, and they tie down a huge army with rubles."

A few drops of rain splashed on the deck in front of them, and Beadle crushed the Coke can between his large hands. "Captain appreciated what you did, trying to get the rifle away from Hodges." Beadle was smiling, nodding his head.

Now that was out of the blue. Bell stared at the sergeant a moment, then said what he had been thinking for the last weeks. "He sure didn't show it."

"He's got his own problems."

I bet, thought Bell, *with the local branch of the KKK out to lynch him—or get rid of him.* That made him think of Johnson.

"He won't forget..." Beadle was saying, but Bell interrupted him.

"You ever figure out anything about Sergeant Johnson, what happened? Why he got shot?"

Now it was Beadle's turn to be nonplussed. "No-o-o," he said slowly. "It could have been anybody, ARVN, American." He shrugged.

"I went down an alley with Cole." He had to say it. He had to tell Beadle. Like a confession. "Somebody jumped me and took a shot at Cole, at least that's what Cole says."

Beadle stared at him, tapping the empty can against the edge of the bench. "Why didn't you tell the Board of Inquiry?" he asked finally.

"No one asked me." *That didn't sound right,* thought Bell, so he added, "It was a different alley and quite a while before... uh, right after I got here."

Beadle wasn't saying anything, just giving him a hard look.

Bell sighed and added, "Cole talked to the board, and he knew what happened. I didn't. I only know what Cole told me."

"But you said somebody jumped you. Did they hit you or what?"

"Knocked me down... into a ditch... and ran."

Why do I feel like I'm lying? Bell wondered. *But that's how I remember it.* "Look, I was new on patrol, and Cole was the senior man. He told me not to put it in the report. And it was a long time before Johnson."

"What more can you tell me?"

"All I know it was an American. Civilian, military, I'm not sure." He thought a moment. "Only thing he said was something about 'fucking MPs.'"

"Somebody fired, though?"

"Yeah, Cole said they fired at him, but I'm..." Bell stopped and bit his lip, deciding not to say what he thought. "Cole said someone took a shot at him."

Beadle took a deep breath and let it out. There was a veil of rain descending from the clouds over the rice paddies beyond the canal.

"You ever think," Beadle said, "that sometimes *not* acting, *not* doing what you should do, can have consequences just as much as if you were the one pulling the trigger."

That pissed Bell off. He shook his head. "Reporting it wouldn't have changed a thing. Cole would've still gone down another alley, and Johnson, being Johnson, would go down there after him... and back him up."

And he really believed that. Or told himself he did.

"He was shot in the back," Beadle said.

"God, I... I heard," said Bell, feeling sick. "Anyone could've... down there.... I liked Johnson." He shook his head. "But Cole, I had no idea—"

Beadle reached over and patted his leg. "We never know the future. Just do the best we can while we're here. The best."

More drops were starting to splatter the deck and spot Beadle's fatigues and Bell's civilian clothes. A solid wall of rain obscured the rice paddies and the canal.

"We have to look after each other," Beadle said straightening up. "Make sure the guy next to you is okay... and try to help these people a little."

Bell gave Beadle a sideways glance. "We didn't do much good for Tony."

Beadle sighed. "No, we didn't. Sad, too." He looked sad with his big droopy jowls. "The boy was like a son to me. I was trying to teach him English."

He stood and stretched, pushing out his belly as he looked out at the rain moving toward them. "We have to keep trying. Stay dry, stay alive, and make the most of what we have. And look after your buddies."

"Yeah, I guess that's right." What else could he say?

As they walked inside the club together, Beadle put his hand on Bell's shoulder. "I wish you luck on going back to graduate school,

Specialist." He gave Bell's shoulder a slight squeeze. "Sure wish I had."

CHAPTER FORTY-ONE
The Corner Bunker

WHEN IT WASN'T RAINING, THEY SWEATED, and their clothes clung to their bodies unless they stayed in motion in an open jeep. Swarming hordes of mosquitoes rose from the ditches, fields, and canals and dominated the evenings and nights. For guard duty, he carried a green can of army-issued insect repellant and spent as much time swatting mosquitoes as looking out at the rice paddies beyond the canal.

Tonight he was on the corner bunker next to the road. ARVN intelligence had reported NVA regulars across the canal, so Sergeant Beadle added an extra guard, this one on top of the corner bunker. For protection, the guard hunkered down on a folding chair encircled by a chest-high parapet of sandbags. Covering him against the elements was a slanted tin roof, supported by four posts wedged between the sandbags. A suicide post, partly due to its location but mainly because it could collapse at any time.

He climbed the ladder after rattling it from below and calling to Keller in a whisper. He received no answer. When he reached the top, the unresponsive sentry roused with a start, grabbed his rifle, and jerked it around in a motion that almost launched Bell into space.

"Oh, Bell... it's you," Keller mumbled.

"Good thing it wasn't a sapper."

"He'd be dead."

"Don't think so."

"Ah, fuck you. Everything's quiet." Still muttering, Keller stumbled down the ladder and off toward the sleeping compound, flapping his sandals across the parking lot and past the ammunition bunker and the V-100 revetments.

0400 hours. He'd see the sun rise before he went off duty. Beadle had extended the watch to three hours since two men were posted on each shift, one here and one in the tower. The first guard in the corner, Moses Peoples, had brought out an M-60 machine gun and mounted it on top of the parapet.

He settled down as low as he could behind the sandbags, then sighted along the M-60 at the palm trees and gravel road illuminated by the spotlights on the fence line. The trees cast shadows toward the canal until the shadows were lost in the darkness. A chorus of frogs filled the night air and drowned out the artillery and everything else quieter than a chopper rotor or a machine gun burst across the canal.

He tried to see down the road, but he couldn't make out anything beyond the trees—not the canal, not the rice paddies, not even the flares that caused a faint glimmer in the sky over the trees. He heard a chopper circling and going into a dive, but he couldn't see it. He sighed and placed his M-16 across the sandbags, to one side of the M-60, and stared dumbly into the night. He soon became lost in his thoughts.

Kikki had died. Meyer had told him after one of Meyer's rare visits into town on his day off. Bell hadn't gone with Meyer and Dupre, who was back on patrol full time since Wesley Akers had taken over as courier—when Hayes didn't make the run himself.

That must be real convenient, Bell decided. *Fly up to Saigon and Long Binh. Move all over the Delta. Lots of business opportunities there for Hayes.*

Every day he had off, Bell went to the Convent, alone, to swim and to escape the noise, filth, and poverty of the war—to lose himself in an oasis of green gardens, white buildings, and muted voices of children playing. Dupre and Meyer, who didn't swim, had gone to Kikki's bar, but it was closed, although the metal gate across the front was unlocked and ajar. Meyer said he slipped inside to say hello and found Mai there with Sergeant Foley.

She had told Meyer about Kikki. The bar was closed in mourning, and Mai had come in only to put away some beer and liquor they had received. It wasn't hard to guess who had brought it, Meyer said. Foley placed his arm around Mai's waist and pulled her to him while she talked, and she responded mechanically, slipping her arm around Foley's waist.

Hearing a noise behind him, Bell jerked his head around. Moving slowly down the gravel road was a three-quarter-ton truck with its headlights off. It crept by the bunker and continued on toward the canal. In the perimeter floodlights, a large white American star was clearly visible on the door.

He studied the driver's profile—there was no one else in the cab—but he couldn't quite make out the face. *Hayes? Or maybe I'm just being paranoid, like Meyer says.*

The truck disappeared into the gloom, and the crunch of tires on gravel faded away. Holding his breath, he listened carefully, trying to hear above the babel of frogs in the ditches and flooded soccer field across the road.

From behind him came the sound of another vehicle. He swiveled around and saw a jeep approaching from QL 4. Only two narrow slits of light shone from its headlamps. Although it went by the bunker at a fast clip, he could make out ARVN markings on the hood and two occupants in the front seats.

Puzzled, he stared after it. A light flickered among the trees, far down the road. Followed by the faint putt-putt of a sampan, distinct during a brief pause in the frog serenade.

A truck, a jeep, a sampan—only one place they could go down there.

Why would Hayes, if it is Hayes, be going to a Vietnamese warehouse at five o'clock in the morning? And with these people, in an ARVN jeep and in a sampan? His mind was sluggish from want of sleep, but it wandered over the possibilities, none of them legitimate. He strained to hear more from the direction of the canal, but there were only the frogs, whose raucous performance had begun to abate with the waning of the night.

Some time passed, and then more noises came from the end of the road. A door slammed. An engine started, and before long, the jeep went back past the bunker, toward QL 4.

The three-quarter-ton truck soon followed, at a faster pace than before. It swung into the entrance to the compound and stopped at the closed gate. A figure emerged from the driver's side, but immediately stepped into the shadow of the bunker at the entrance.

Bell lifted the M-16 to his shoulder and sighted on the man as he moved toward the gate. *Too big for a Vietnamese. Probably Hayes... but what if I shot him?*

As the shadowy figure unlocked the gate, Bell lowered the rifle. *What lousy security we have,* Bell thought, watching. *Stuck out here, away from all the other Americans. Nothing but fucking bait.*

The gate swung open, and the man got back in the truck and drove through, stopping at the edge of a spotlight beyond the entrance. Leaving the truck's door open, he climbed out again, closed the gate, and then relocked it. Allowing Bell to see him clearly.

Taking a shallow breath, Bell gave a long, quiet sigh. *Son of a bitch comes and goes at will—anytime he wants.*

Hayes parked the truck between the gate and the corner bunker. Getting out, he closed the door softly and leaned against it, looking around.

Bell ducked his head below the sandbags. But not for long. Curious, he peered over the top.

Hayes was lighting a cigarette. With it cupped in one hand, he surveyed the compound and released a haze of smoke in the dim light. He seemed to be checking the building's entrance and the revetments in back, but not the corner bunker. He finished the cigarette, tamped it out on the asphalt with the toe of his boot, and then, taking his time, strolled to the rear of the villa and disappeared into the entrance to the motor pool.

Sitting up again, Bell stared into the dark interior of the compound. Hayes wouldn't know he was on the corner bunker.

Beadle had decided to man it late in the evening, most likely after Hayes left the compound. But who was in the tower?

Bell craned his neck to look up at the dark structure on the roof. Did the tower guard know what was going on? He couldn't see anyone up there.

Through the desultory croaking came the sound of a small motor, and he turned back toward the canal in time to see a light creeping past a gap in the trees, toward the town. Watching the empty gap lulled him into a hypnotic trance. Day was near. The sky was turning gray, and the clear shapes of more trees were beginning to appear beyond the ones illuminated by the spotlights in front of him. With the coming dawn, the frogs had subsided to near silence.

Startled, he sat up. A bicycle silently glided past on the road, going toward the warehouse. Silhouetted against the graying sky, a boy-san peddled it wearily, head down, baguettes of French bread, like raised fingers, sticking out of a wicker basket balanced over the rear wheel.

At 0700 hours he wrestled the M-60, his M-16, and the M-60 ammo down the ladder and trudged across the empty yard to check the weapons into the armory, which required finding Bowman since Sanderson was on R&R. The patrols were already out, and the mess hall was empty, except for Cole. He was bent over his plate, pushing scrambled eggs back and forth. His chin rested in his other hand.

After dredging eggs and bacon from the nearly empty serving pans and drawing a cup of turbid coffee, Bell searched for a place to sit, away from Cole. Finding no excuse to avoid him, he finally took a chair at the same table and, to break the silence, asked how he was doing.

"Just got off guard duty, the tower. Three fucking hours." Still staring at his eggs, Cole moved his hand from his chin to pull one side of his moustache.

"You see a truck come in, say five thirty or six?" Bell asked.

"0530?" Cole responded with a grimace. "Yeah, I saw it."

"That was Hayes."

"So what? Probably downtown. Spends a lot of time there... or out at the airfield." Cole finally stuffed a forkful of egg into his mouth.

"You *did* see him go down to the warehouse... and then come back here, didn't you? And there was an ARVN jeep.... It went down there not two minutes after he did."

"Don't pay no attention to shit like that," Cole said, chewing quickly and swallowing. "Gooks come and go down there all the time. What's the big deal?"

Bell chewed his own food slowly, thinking, *Cole is either dumber than I thought or he's covering for Hayes. But what if he tells Hayes I saw him?*

"Looks like Foley has your girlfriend now," Cole said.

"Who? Mai?... She's not my girlfriend."

"Well, Foley's humpin' her for sure. He was downtown last night, like Hayes." Cole smirked at him. "She must not've liked what you had to offer."

Bell dropped his fork and knife onto the plate with a clatter. "Maybe so, but just because something's for sale doesn't mean I'm buying." He felt himself flush with embarrassment. *Now that sounded dumb as hell. And mean to boot.*

Pushing back his chair, he stood without looking at Cole and hurried out, leaving the plate and cup for the mama-san to clear from the table.

CHAPTER FORTY-TWO
More Grenades

ONE AFTER ANOTHER, THE VETERANS LEFT FOR R&R, some in the fleshpots of Taipei, Bangkok, or Hong Kong, others in the more salubrious venues of Tokyo, Sydney, or Hawaii. Back in Nam, the routine continued: patrol, guard duty, ferry, a day off, and patrol again. Before they became too comfortable, something always happened to upset their equilibrium. The FNG Taylor ran over a girl-san crossing QL 4 and then *di di mau'd* as she was dying when a crowd of mama-sans began screaming and threatening him with sticks. Another night, they all scrambled to the bunkers after a mortar attack, this one again missing the compound, but closer than the ones before.

For Bell, it was just another day on patrol: the smell of lime and diesel fumes in the morning air; the deafening cacophony of scooters, *xich-lo*s, and three-wheeled Lambrettas; the exotic panorama of palm trees, banana trees, and rice paddies yellow-green in the early sun. His senses drifted aimlessly through a half sleep as Meyer drove the jeep toward town. *Tomorrow, and tomorrow, and tomorrow*, kept running through his thoughts.

Pulling the MP helmet liner lower over his glasses, he slumped farther down in the seat. He daydreamed, drifted back to the World, lying on the sand and rubbing lotion on a soft, warm body, the waves breaking on the beach with a roar—an ARVN deuce-and-a-half barreling past. He sat up.

"Meyer, you realize we've been here almost six months?"

"Five and a half and we have more than six to go," Meyer said.

"Fuck," said Bell. "They call you Eeyore back home?"

Meyer chuckled. "I'm a realist."

Bell was silent as the jeep slid by a white, two-story building with a curtain of red flowers draping the front walls. They were now on the road going around the town, the same route Johnson had taken their first days on patrol. With a feeling of something forever lost, Bell stared at the wide park and its green grass, ancient cannon, and ornate buildings and, farther on, the white-and-pastel-blue pagoda. Finally leaving this depressingly idyllic setting and approaching the seedier river docks, he perked up.

"I haven't seen Sandy lately."

"You didn't hear?" Meyer said.

"Hear what?"

"She drowned."

"You shittin' me," he said, twisting toward Meyer.

"No shit, bro. Heard it from Cole yesterday."

"What happened?"

"She went out on a Coast Guard tug, and the tug sank in the river. She was in the sack with a sailor. Cole said he actually talked with the guy." Meyer paused as he sped up to go around a Lambretta. "The sailor said he got her out of the tug, and he was trying to hold her up in the water. Then she tried to steal his watch. 'So he let the bitch go,' as Cole put it. She couldn't swim, and she drowned." Meyer turned onto the street leading to the station.

"Sweet Jesus, that's terrible," Bell said. He narrowed his eyes and stared at Meyer. "I don't believe it."

"She did drown, though. I saw the report. Of course, Cole wrote it up."

"The watch wasn't in the report, was it?"

"No," said Meyer. "Just she drowned, and the sailor tried to rescue her."

"How do you explain having one of Van Loc's leading ladies on board a goddamn tug, and it sank? Why'd it sink, anyway?"

"How should I know? Maybe it was sabotage. Look, I'm telling you what Cole said—and what he put in the report. Why are you so interested?"

"She was, well... unusual." And he had been attracted to her. "I still don't believe it."

His mood turned gloomy, steeped in sadness. He remembered seeing her on the docks—and in the room above the *Hoa Binh* bar.

What she looked like; what she said: nobody love Sandy, they only love body. Which was probably true. A beautiful body, a beautiful face, but a nasty disposition. Maybe she really was sick—sick in body, sick in mind. He looked out at the river, the waters dark and rippling, and the trees a dark smudge on the other side. He recalled a poem by John Milton, a pastoral elegy—something about a friend who drowned.

Syphilitic Sandy, weep no more.

Meyer turned down the street to the station and came to a stop behind a Quan Canh jeep parked in a parabola of sunlight angling through the eucalyptus trees. Bell was wide-awake now.

***

The morning was quiet—mostly. An engineers' jeep knocked over a *xich-lo*, bruising the passenger, a now-irate mama-san. By the time Bell and Meyer arrived, an equally irate crowd of her supporters had gathered, yelling epithets at the Americans and blocking their escape. The jeep's driver averted the storm only by handing over $20 MPC to the mama-san—at Meyer's wheedling suggestion. After this success at community relations, they toured the bars in town, drank free cups of Coke with the bar girls, and drove two intoxicated but docile warrant officers back to their barracks at the airfield.

The call came at 1445 hours—just when they thought they were safely through the day and they were leaving the station for their last run through town. Singleton stopped them on the porch. Someone had thrown a grenade into an empty ARVN jeep parked near a row of shops between the bakery and Madame Phoung's. While no one had been injured, there was a problem.

"QC's say they have the grenade throwers trapped in the bakery," Singleton said. "Chased them inside and blocked the exits, but they have hostages, maybe even a GI. You guys need to go see what's going on up there."

"Roger," said Meyer and headed down the steps to the jeep.

"Shit, shit, shit," said Bell, striding after him.

As soon as they entered Le Thai-to Street, they could see a column of black smoke rising high into the sky, but before they reached the source, a National Police roadblock stopped them. Beyond it and the intersection with QL 4, and just past the bakery, sat the remains of a jeep—front seats and top shredded, windscreen missing, spare tire blown off, sides of twisted metal—still giving off a thick cloud of black smoke.

Meyer stopped the MP jeep short of the roadblock. Getting out, the two wove their way through a gaggle of civilian onlookers and vehicles to the police jeeps parked across the road. Beyond the line of jeeps, QCs in their starched fatigues and civilian police in white shirts were scattered up and down the street, across from the bakery, and beside its front entrance. One of the QCs had climbed onto a second floor balcony above the sign that said "Boulangerie" and was trying to open a pair of shuttered French windows to get inside.

As they advanced on the smoldering jeep, another MP patrol pulled up to the roadblock and disgorged FNG Taylor, Cole, and Sergeant Carter—an unwelcome trio auguring nothing but trouble. Bell and Meyer halted across the street from the smoking jeep and waited for their superior to catch up with them. Farther up the street, Madame Phoung and a group of her girls, along with several of their patrons, lounged near the whorehouse gate, observing the scene from a safe distance. Also in that direction was someone else of interest.

"Goddamn!" Bell said to Meyer and pointed at an ARVN officer standing near a second roadblock beyond the bakery. "That's Major Binh."

The major was shaking his finger in the air while railing at Lt Nguyen of the Quan Canh. The lieutenant, his lips drawn in a tight line, was silent. The major motioned sharply toward the smoking jeep and then toward the bakery. Following the gesture, Bell spied a civilian policeman at the bakery door yelling to whoever was inside.

"Any of our people in there?" Sergeant Carter had arrived at Bell's elbow, Cole and Taylor close on his heels.

"Don't know," Bell said. I just got here."

"Let's go see," Carter said.

John Wayne to the rescue, thought Bell.

"You two," Carter pointed at Bell and then Cole, "you come with me. Meyer, you and Taylor... you stay here and give us cover if we need it. And don't trust the fucking gooks to do anything smart."

The others nodded, and Sergeant Carter started to turn, then stopped and looked at Cole. "Cole, don't pull that fucking .45 unless you damn well have to use it." He punctuated the end of each word. "And god-dam-it all, *only* if you need to protect one of us... or yourself."

Cole managed a smirk. "Sure thing, boss."

Carter gave him, then Bell, a severe look as if to make sure they understood, then started off at a trot up the sidewalk across from the bakery to where Lt Nguyen and Major Binh were standing on the far side. Cole quickly followed. Bell, keeping a wary eye on the bakery's entrance, brought up the rear.

Carter waited briefly for a break in the major's diatribe, but finding none, broke in, "What's going on, Lieutenant?"

The major gave an insulted curl of the lip at the interruption; then he pivoted on his heel and stalked off across the road, away from the bakery, and the smoking jeep.

Lt Nguyen grimaced. "Somebody throw grenade in major's jeep. He say two men in ARVN uniform." The lieutenant's voice was calm, but his English had lost its subtle polish. "They run in bakery, driver and white shirts chase them. Look crazy—drugs or something. I don't know. He want *my men* go in bakery."

"Anyone in there with them?" asked Carter.

"Yes. Man who own bakery, wife, children. Maybe customers."

"Any Americans?"

"I don't know." He shrugged. "Maybe, maybe not."

Shouts came from the front of the bakery, and a young girl appeared in the doorway beneath the balcony. Close behind her appeared a man in an olive drab ARVN uniform and cap, a red scarf covering the lower part of his face. He reached both arms across the girl's slight shoulders and held a grenade out in front of her.

The policemen grew quiet, and the girl's sobs rose above the low murmur of the nearby voices. Her arms were rigid by her side. She wore black pajama pants, a bright green-and-white blouse, and one sandal.

Breaking away from the MPs, Lt Nguyen started toward the man, addressing him in a low voice. The man shouted something in response; then he shoved the girl down on the sidewalk and jumped back into the shadows.

The lieutenant stopped less than ten yards away from the girl. Speaking rapidly, he gestured at the doorway. A high staccato of Vietnamese came from inside.

"He wants us to back off," Bell said to Carter. They were only a short distance behind the lieutenant with Cole next to them. "Let him and his friend go—or he's gonna throw the grenade... Kill the girl."

He was guessing, based on what little Vietnamese he'd learned. But he was sure he was right.

A second man loomed in the doorway—holding an older woman in front of him. His face was covered with green camouflage grease and red and white makeup like a grotesque clown. His one arm extended over the woman's shoulder, his hand clutching a grenade against her chest. His other hand held a .45, the barrel pressed to the woman's head.

He shifted to the left side of the door, and the first man with the scarf edged out past him, going around the girl on the sidewalk and holding the grenade above his head, a finger taut inside the pin. When he was several feet beyond the door, and moving along the wall toward the alley, he looked up. On the balcony right above him was a policeman, aiming a .45 down at him.

Screaming in Vietnamese, he lurched backward, under the balcony, and his hands separated. He held the grenade up in one hand, the pin in the other.

Everything seemed to happen in slow motion, but it only took seconds. The police scattered. The QC on the balcony fell backward against the shutters he had been trying to open. Lt Nguyen yelled, pointing at the woman, then at the girl on the ground.

Distracted, the clown-face man allowed the woman to break free. She lunged forward, grabbed the girl by the arm, and dragged her to her feet. Together they dashed across the street. As they ran, clown face pulled the pin on his grenade, as well.

There was a loud boom, next to Bell's right ear. Spinning around, he found Cole's .45 only a few feet from his face. He quickly glanced back in the direction the .45 pointed.

The bullet had hit the man with the red scarf in the stomach, knocking him backward, and he had half dropped and half lobbed his grenade. It made a short arc and landed on the ground near Lt Nguyen, bounced several times, then rolled past the lieutenant to where Bell, Carter, and Cole had been standing a moment before. They were already in motion—diving backward toward the line of jeeps, the lieutenant with them.

Seconds passed, then more seconds, and the grenade lying in the street did not explode.

But the other grenade did.

The clown-face man had made as if to retreat inside the bakery, but his partner, reeling from Cole's bullet, catapulted into him. He tried to stop his fall, while holding onto his weapons, but his grenade hand hit the doorjamb. The device popped out of his fingers and landed at his feet, sans lever.

He frantically kicked at it.

The grenade exploded between him and his friend, blowing pieces of flesh and fabric and globs of blood across the white stucco façade of the shop and into the street.

The first grenade still lay on the ground, free of its pin and lever, looking like it should explode at any moment, and everyone near it scrambled wildly to get farther away. Bell didn't stop until he was well beyond the line of parked jeeps and behind a stone wall across the opposite sidewalk.

Carter, Cole, and Lt Nguyen came over the wall after him. The four of them sat on the ground, panting—and waiting.

"Must be a dud," said Carter after several minutes. He took a deep breath, then reached over and grabbed Cole by the collar of his fatigue shirt. "You dumb fuck! I told you not to do that... Don't get out your .45, I said. I'm—"

"But Sarge, I nailed him." Cole twisted away from Carter's grip on his shirt. "Bastards were fucked up in the head. Damn gooks weren't doin' a—"

"Ah, shit! I'm gonna have your ass for this."

"Nobody got hurt but the bad guys."

"Dumb - fuckin' - luck. That grenade'd gone off, we'd all be dead. Or fucked up bad."

Carter stood and brushed off his fatigues. Cole remained sitting on the ground, his back to the low wall. Bell would've laughed and cheered Carter, if he hadn't had to clench his teeth and grip the stones with his hands to stop shaking.

"Lieutenant, can you get your demolition team to check out that grenade?" Carter was addressing Nguyen, who stood beside him. Then he added, "I'd put up some rope, keep people away from it."

Bell slowly got up on one knee behind Carter—and promptly gagged at the carnage in the entrance to the bakery. The mangled flesh showed no sign of life. The lower part of a naked leg and foot, a handle of red-streaked white bone extending out from it, lay on the ground several yards away from the bodies. On the other side of the street, the woman and girl who had run from the shop hugged each other and cried next to a green-and-white police jeep.

Bell felt himself shake as if he were cold instead of kneeling here in ninety-five-degree heat. He finished getting to his feet and stood staring down at his trembling hands.

Lt Nguyen had watched impassively while Carter berated Cole, and he didn't respond to Carter's questions about the grenade. Instead, he shouted orders to the QCs staring at the bodies in the bakery entrance, then hoisted himself over the wall and went to join them. Slipping out the doorway past him, two elderly Vietnamese, a man and a woman, skirted the contorted bodies and rushed across the street to the woman and girl. No one else came out.

Major Binh's jeep still smoldered in the street, but everything combustible in it had burned, and only thin wisps of black smoke rose from the tangled wreck. The major and his friends had disappeared. Madame Phoung and her entourage had also fled, retreating back inside the high walls, taking with them a capacity crowd of customers. Still more GIs waited outside the locked green gate.

Jogging in a wide circle behind the jeeps, and away from the grenade in the road, Taylor and Meyer joined Bell and Cole. Carter had followed the lieutenant a short way into the street, hesitated there for a moment, then came back to the wall. He stood apart, not saying anything to the others.

"You okay?" Meyer asked Bell.

"Guess so. Nothing hit us." He was still shivering. He glanced over at Cole, standing on the other side of the wall. Cole was checking his .45, popping out the magazine and clearing the chamber.

"What goes on in that fucker's mind?" whispered Bell, more to himself than to Meyer.

Lt Nguyen came striding back from inside the bakery and stopped in front of Carter. The lieutenant shook his head.

"No Americans." He surveyed the group of MPs. "We don't need your help," he said, addressing no one in particular. "Please go now."

CHAPTER FORTY-THREE
The Living Dead

HIS HANDS SHOOK. MEYER DROVE, and he sat hunched down in the passenger seat, gripping his elbows to control his hands. He could still see the grenade coming toward them and the blood and pieces of flesh splatter on the white stucco. *What was it?* His thoughts raced. *What was it? "Cowards die many times?"* He clutched his arms tighter into his gut and muttered to himself, "The valiant, the valiant... only once."

"You okay?" asked Meyer.

"Yeah, yeah. Just thinking."

"You should talk, you know. You'll feel better. That was quite a shock back there. Even from where Taylor and I were."

"I was thinking... about death. Something from Shakespeare."

"I know molecules and valances, but not Shakespeare."

Bell took a deep breath. "How the fuck did we end up in this... this bucket of shit?"

"We made a wrong turn on the road to success?"

"What do you mean 'we'? The US of fucking A made a wrong turn. We were minding our own damn business." He shivered. "And this fucking war ran the fuck over us." He raised both fists in the air and brought them down sharply in front of him. "Go-o-d-damn, how I hate this place!"

"Aren't you glad Nixon's going to get us out of here?" Meyer asked, looking over at him. "Just wish he had done it before they called my name."

"He's waiting on Godot."

"Who's Godot?"

"Nobody... imaginary figure in a play." He noticed his hands had stopped trembling. He stretched to release the tension in his body.

"Must've slept through that one," Meyer said, turning onto the gravel road leading to the compound. "Like the homeboys say, bro, it don't mean nuthin no how." He laughed and glanced over at Bell.

"Carter says he's going to write up the shooting," Bell said. "Have an inquiry. He's really pissed at Cole."

"So were the QCs." Driving past the gate bunker where a faceless FNG sat reading a book, Meyer added, "Maybe they'll send Cole out to shoot at Charlie—he likes it so much."

"Just hope they don't send us with him."

***

He shed his boots and duty shirt and slipped on a pair of new tire-soled Ho Chi Minh sandals, then, notepad and pen in one hand and a thin book of T.S. Eliot poems in the other, schlepped along the cement corridor to the club. First collecting a gin and tonic from Thuy, he headed outside to the deck and his usual spot by the railing, where he studied the dark clouds rolling in from the east and the fading light over the rice fields while he mulled over the day's horrors. Then taking a series of deep breaths, he studied the compound and mulled over Hodge's escapade with the M-16. He lit a cigar and watched the smoke drift away.

After reading a few poems, he placed the book on the bench and tried to write one of his own, about Sandy in her watery grave, an urchin begging life, begs no more. Only partially successful, he snuffed out the cigar and went inside to join Meyer and Landrieu at a table. Sanderson, just back from R&R, also ambled over.

"Rough day?" Sanderson asked after telling them a few tantalizing snippets about bedding two hookers at one time in Hong Kong. Bell's face must have shown he was only half listening.

"More excitement than I needed," Bell said. "You hear what happened?"

"Heard Cole fucked up."

Meyer filled in the details. Landrieu, drinking a beer, didn't say anything. He wasn't a regular with this group, but he wasn't unwelcome either. He had dropped out of a pre-med program at LSU and enlisted, he said, to get his bearings before trying again for medical school. He listened more than he talked, and when he did speak, it was usually to the point and often with a bite to it.

"You know what's strange," Bell said. He glanced around to make sure no one else could hear him above the strains of "Louie, Louie" on the radio. The only other Americans in the club were Bowman, Taylor, and two FNG's. Behind the bar, the old papa-san was talking softly with Thuy after depositing a case of beer on the floor.

"Every time some shit happens around here," Bell continued, "that fucking ARVN major shows up. Like Macavity the mystery cat."

"Who the fuck's Macavity the mystery cat?" Sanderson asked.

"Poem I was reading. Something bad happens and Ma-ca-vi-ty's not—"

"Poetry?" Landrieu said. "Stuff's not much good here."

Bell shrugged and gave him a dark look.

Sanderson started up again on the many amenities he'd discovered in Hong Kong, and Meyer left to go buy a Coke from Thuy. When he returned, Landrieu, who had been making wet circles on the table with his Schlitz can, looked up and addressed a question to Meyer unrelated to Sanderson's tale of sexual conquest.

"If this major's such a big muckety-muck, why did those guys throw a grenade into his jeep?"

"It's a Vietnamese thing," Meyer said as he dropped into his chair. "They do that stuff for fun—like frat initiations."

"From what little Carter got from Lt Nguyen," Bell said, scowling at Meyer, "those guys weren't VC. The major might even know who they were. He said they were crazy, on drugs or something." He shook his head. "Made no sense for 'em to come outside—"

"They were trapped... and desperate," Meyer said, becoming serious. "Fragging the jeep could have been a grudge thing, or a warning." He tapped the table with his finger. "No one was in it, and if there hadn't been QCs hanging around, they'd gotten away."

"It's still strange," said Bell, "really strange." The others nodded in agreement.

The rain had started, and they watched it through the open doors as it fell in billowing sheets and ran off the roof and the deck, roaring and splattering and turning the air inside the club cool and damp.

"You hear that Sanchez is going home?" Sanderson asked, giving a low chuckle. "His leave came through. Off to see his dying mother."

"I can't *fucking* believe it," Bell said, smacking the table with his hand. "That fucker goes home, and Hodge goes to jail. Where's the *fucking* justice in any of this shit?"

"It's all in how you play the game," said Meyer, pushing back in his chair.

They went to eat under the bright overhead lights in the mess hall—only an occasional flicker at the whim of the generator—while the rain continued its pounding deluge in the gloom outside. When the downpour finally stopped, the water that had been running off the roof in streams slowed to steady drips. Secure inside, away from the dense, humid darkness, they wandered back to the club for the evening cinema, settling onto a beat-up sofa and metal chairs, facing a collapsible screen in one corner, their backs to the deck and the smoldering war across the canal.

The evening's fare was *The Night of the Living Dead*, which Wes Akers had brought back from Long Binh in the afternoon. Behind them, the low rumble of artillery and sporadic flashes in the mist over the rice paddies gave a surreal context to the zombies attacking an isolated farmhouse. A flare lit the darkened room just as a dead arm rammed through a door panel on the screen—and the first sergeant bolted through the doorway to the club.

"Get dressed," he yelled. "Steel pots and flak jackets! M-16's! Fall in out front." He stood at the edge of the projector light, his waving arm making a giant shadow across the screen, obliterating zombies and humans with each swipe, while distorted images played across his face and sleeve.

"Move it! Move it! We have a riot at the airfield."

Singleton stopped the projector, leaving the group in the dark. A flare across the canal illuminated the room, and the audience started edging out of their seats, but not standing up.

"I said move it," Top bellowed again, his face as livid as one of the living dead in the dying glow of the flare. He flipped on the overhead lights. "Move your asses! Or you'll be out there," he jabbed his finger toward the canal.

CHAPTER FORTY-FOUR
The Riot

GRINDING THE GEARS, BEADLE DOWN SHIFTED to a halt by the Villa's front entrance. From the doorway, Top continued his harangue while the MPs, their M-16's in hand or over their shoulders, magazines locked in place, clambered into the back of the idling deuce-and-a-half.

Meyer barely had both feet in when Top raised the rear gate and snapped it shut. The truck leaped forward—then stopped dead, throwing Meyer forward over his compatriots' knees and against the cab.

It was Hayes in a jeep. The sergeant sped in front of the truck and out the gate—Cole perched in the passenger seat beside him.

Once on QL 4, the deuce-and-a-half fell in behind one of the night patrols, siren blaring. They raced past the intersection with Le Thai-to Street, past the scarred front of the bakery, past Madame Phoung's closed gate, and past the quiet drive to the Convent.

A riot? Bell doubted it. But he didn't know what was going on, nor did anyone else. But it didn't sound good. At least he wasn't shaking. Yet.

Waiting at the airfield gate were Sergeant Hayes and Cole. Hayes let the night patrol go by, then whipped in front of the truck. The second night patrol fell in behind, and they barreled down the airfield's empty streets between wooden barracks and Quonset huts.

Beadle swerved to a stop in the middle of the road between the Enlisted Men's Club and the dispensary to their rear, while the two patrol jeeps and Hayes jockeyed into position alongside the truck to blockade the street. Piling out in full war gear—flak jackets, steel pots, and M-16's—the MPs collected in front of the vehicles and faced toward a group of thirty or forty men, half a football field away.

The group surged in waves back and forth across the road, shouting and shaking their fists at a smaller clutch of soldiers gathered around the EM club's entrance. An occasional object, a bottle or rock or can, sailed between the groups. In the road, the group was all black, at the club all white.

A race riot. Bell grimaced and gripped his weapon tighter. *I'm caught in the middle of a fucking race riot.*

The scene was lit up like a bizarre movie set by a pair of bright spotlights at the club's entrance. Those lights, along with the streetlights and dim bulbs over the doors to the Quonset huts lining the road, made sparkling starburst halos in the dust and moisture on his glasses.

"Line up—two ranks," yelled Beadle. "Crowd-control formation."

Bell was where he'd vowed never to be: in the exposed front row of a formation, with Sanderson and Dupre on one side and, to his dismay, Cole on the other. A second row of MPs and other conscripts from the compound lined up behind them—Meyer just to Bell's rear. As they formed ranks, M-16's angled up across their chests, Bell glanced over at Dupre, who had been on night patrol.

"What happened?" he asked.

"Big fight at the EM club," Dupre said. "When we got here, they had two white fuckers in the dispensary." His eyes shifted to Sanderson, then back to Bell. "The brothers are really pissed. Couple of 'em followed a white dude inside, pounded on him right there on the table."

"Must've had some reason," said Sanderson, lowering his rifle.

"We managed to push 'em outside, but there was a crowd, so we went back to the gate to meet you guys."

The now-formed ranks stood ready: fifteen bodies, eight in front, seven behind. The damp air clung to them. Bell's hands were sweating, his fatigue shirt was wet with sweat. Sweat ran down his forehead and streaked his glasses. But he wasn't shaking.

"Move out," Beadle screeched, and Bell felt a sudden surge of adrenaline. "When you reach that group in the street, go into lock step and move them away from the club."

The two ranks of MPs double-timed up the road, then slowed to a walk less than ten yards short of the black soldiers, who turned and began yelling and shaking their fists at them. Beadle lumbered behind his troops, driving his heavy form forward as quickly as they advanced.

Beside them, rolling slowly along the edge of the street, was a jeep with Hayes in it. Between the jeep and Bell was Cole, advancing in line with the others, but with his M-16 angled far forward of the rest.

As they closed the last few yards, the shouts, catcalls, and names hurled at them reached a crescendo. "Go back to your hole, pig! Kill the pig! Honky bastards! Fucking Uncle Tom! Motherfuckin' Oreo!"

Bell saw only angry faces and fists in front of him and broken glass littering the ground under his feet. His senses of light, sound, how the M-16 felt in his hands, the perspiration on his body, were heightened, but his emotions were deadened. He had to do this, even if he didn't want to do it, hated doing it.

The MPs continued moving forward, crowd-control formation, rifles angled across their chests, magazines fixed and loaded with 5.56mm bullets, lock step, left foot forward, drag, stomp, feet together, push the crowd back. They moved in formation across the shards of glass and broken asphalt and through puddles of muddy water left by the evening rain.

Bell, Sanderson, Dupre, Cole, and the others in the front rank made contact with the mass of black soldiers, who shoved against them and gave ground grudgingly. Hayes stopped his jeep and stood up on the seat.

"Push 'em back!" Bell heard him yell. "Keep going! Keep on going!"

The black soldier in front of Bell shoved at his rifle, and Bell tried to talk to him, "Man, go home. Don't do this." He saw that the soldier was wild-eyed, almost stumbling drunk, and his eyes didn't seem to focus on Bell's.

From behind came Beadle's shrill voice, "Left foot—forward, drag. Push them back. Don't stop! Stay together, men, shoulder-to-shoulder. One - step - at - a - time."

Sanderson was also talking to the black soldier in front of him. "Hey, bro. Cool it... You're gonna get hurt. We're all gonna get hurt."

The soldier was Meyer's erstwhile friend Stick from the engineers.

"You fucking Uncle Tom, you fucking Oreo," Stick said through clenched teeth. "You ain't nuthin but one of them."

From beside the first rank, Hayes was yelling, "Use your gun butts, goddamn you. Hit 'em! Hit 'em! Hit 'em in the balls!"

They were past the EM club now, and the white soldiers had disappeared from view. Down the street, Bell saw two black soldiers come out of a barracks. They each looked to be carrying an M-16. The two started running toward the conjoined mass of MPs and angry blacks.

Hayes' voice hit a fever pitch, "Hit the bastards with your gun butts."

The mob tightened and congealed into a single dam, and the MP advance ground to a halt. In front of Bell, the mass of soldiers was three deep, pushing against his raised M-16, pressing it into his chest. An M-16 was pushing against his back and Meyer was yelling in his ear, urging him forward.

Hayes started screaming, "Shoot 'em! Shoot the motherfuckers! Shoot the fucking niggers! Do it! Do it!"

Bell glanced at Cole. "Don't fucking do it, Cole," he yelled. "Goddamn you, don't listen to him!"

Beadle, close behind the second rank of MPs, turned on Hayes. "Shut up! Shut up, you idiot! What the hell are you doing? Shut the fuck up!" To the MPs he yelled, "Ignore him. Stay together. Keep moving forward."

Suddenly, the volume of voices in front of them dropped, and Bell heard another voice yelling from behind Hayes on his right.

"Stop it! Stop it! Get those MPs outta here! Pull 'em back!"

"Company, halt," screeched Beadle.

They did. A tall, white-haired man in pressed fatigues with a colonel's eagle on his cap took long strides between the front rank of MPs and the black soldiers facing them, sweeping the two sides apart like Moses at the Red Sea.

"Get those MPs out of here," the colonel yelled at Beadle. "This is my airfield. I don't need military police. I'll handle this." He glared down the front row of MPs, then at Hayes. "And that son of a bitch," he yelled, pointing at Hayes, "get that drunk bastard down from there and off my base! Now!"

Beadle stood at attention. "Yes sir," he said and saluted the colonel. Then to the MPs he yelled, "Fall back! Return to your vehicles. Cole! Get Hayes and drive him back to the compound."

As the MPs edged backward, the colonel turned to the group of black soldiers. "You men, go on to your barracks. If you have grievances, I'll meet with three of your representatives tomorrow."

There were a few shouts: "Don't believe it" and "the honkys started it," but mostly silence.

"Anyone who doesn't disperse right now will end up in the brig." The colonel paused and looked along the line of faces in front of him. "I intend to get to the bottom of what happened. Everyone will receive a fair hearing."

The MPs backed down the road. With an incoherent mutter of voices, their opponents also began to fall back, breaking into small groups and drifting toward the barracks.

Turning to Beadle, who stood watching his men retreat, the colonel said loudly enough for them to hear, "You MPs just make things worse. If I want you, I'll call you." Almost as an afterthought, he returned Beadle's salute, then wheeled around and strode off toward the EM club and the jeering white contingent that had reappeared out front.

As soon as they reached the compound and turned in their weapons, Bell headed upstairs to the club. Most of those not on duty were back in front of the movie screen waiting for Singleton to restart the second reel of *The Night of the Living Dead*. Top was nowhere in sight. While Bell waited for Thuy to get him a beer, he listened to the drone of the movie behind him and stared out the open doors toward the canal.

Sanderson stood by himself on the deck, leaning on the railing with both hands. Instead of going to watch the movie, Bell took his beer outside and sidled over to the railing, next to Sanderson. Without speaking, he stared out past the perimeter lights and palm trees into the starless night. Flares burst one after the other far off over the rice fields and floated to the ground in small circles of light.

Bell took a long swallow from his beer. "Some night, huh?" he said after the last of the flares winked out.

Sanderson remained silent for a long time, then pounded on the railing with his fist. "How do you think that makes me feel? Facing all the brothers... and then that motherfucker yelling to hit 'em, shoot 'em." He turned and looked at Bell. His cheeks glistened in the light from the club. "Like they were animals. Nothing but animals. How do you think I feel?"

"I guess... I don't really know," Bell said.

"Ain't nobody here I don't get along with. Even Foley. But I'm sick of it. Brothers call me an Oreo and Uncle Tom 'cause I hang out with you guys. And you, my honky homeboys, you get on me about jive'n with the brothers." He gave a low growl deep in his throat. "Hayes out there on that jeep, drunk as shit, yelling those things."

"Nobody listened to him." Bell hesitated, and then added, "The airfield commander did the right thing."

"Mighty damn lucky somebody did."

They watched a chopper drop a flare and circle over the rice paddies, near the canal, shining its spotlight in broad sweeps. The bright light reflected off the standing water in the paddies.

"You know what Muhammad Ali said," Sanderson turned his face toward Bell's, "Cassius Clay for you white boys."

"I know damn well who Muhammad Ali is."

"Well... when they were trying to draft him, he said, 'I ain't got no quarrel with the Viet Cong. They never called me nigger.'" He shook his head. "Black people need to stick together, not fight each other for the white massas."

That irritated Bell. "So where was your black captain tonight?"

"Up in Long Binh... front of some sort of board. 'Cause of that damn Hodge."

Shit! He thinks the captain's being made a scapegoat. "Look," Bell said, "we all know black people have had it bad, slavery and segregation and all. The South, the whites... just have to be dragged—"

"You never had people hate you, treat you like shit, just because of the color of your skin."

"I only know the South." He paused and watched a Lambretta rattling down the road past the compound. "It won't be easy, but most whites will change," he hesitated, with second thoughts. "If their leaders set an example."

"Wallace? Nixon? They don't say 'nigger' anymore, but they say shit that means the same damn thing. Talking about 'those people' and 'law and order.'"

Bell was silent as the Lambretta's lights disappeared at the canal.

Sanderson glanced around as if to make sure no one else was on the deck, then raised his voice, "Don't you see, Bell? Problem is, those people *won't* change. We been fucked over too many times by whitey, and we're tired of waiting for him to change and let us in the front door."

Inhaling the dank air, Bell stared at him a moment, then gave a long sigh. "The Panthers don't have the answer. They provoke a bunch of shit—"

"I don't know anything anymore," said Sanderson. "I - just - don't - fucking - know." He leaned over the railing, his head down. "Here I am, the fucking armorer, sleeping with all them fucking M-16's, and I don't even like guns." He turned and punched Bell's arm. "Come on, let's go get drunk."

CHAPTER FORTY-FIVE
Gus

EIGHT HOURS ON THE GATE. The dullest, most useless job in the compound. Well, maybe not the most useless. The VC, if they attacked, might just try to come in this way. Certainly easier than climbing the fence or tunneling in and having to get past the rolls of concertina wire. Just come in the front-damn-gate, like everybody else.

All that stood between the VC and those inside—the off-duty MPs, Sanderson in the armory, the cooks in the kitchen, the motor pool mechanics, Top and the HQ staff, and the old papa-san and the mama-sans—was Bell with his M-16 and trusty .45, with which he couldn't hit "See Rock City" on a Wilkes County barn.

Woe is us if they ever try to come in through here: the only clear thought he'd ever had about being gate guard. So he stuffed the final volume of The Lord of the Rings into his pocket and went to get his weapons, thinking as he trudged down the hall, here we are in a fucking war zone, and nobody has a clue what the fuck we're doing.

In the days since the grenade attack on Major Binh's jeep and the riot at the airfield, Cole had been relieved of duty and Hayes had been relegated to overseeing the work detail, full time, which still didn't stop his comings and goings. First Lieutenant Floyd had returned from a temporary assignment in Can Tho to make his nagging presence felt on everyone, while the C.O. seemed more detached than ever and the lower ranks strove only to continue their same routines unmolested by their masters.

Yet an uncomfortable change was in the air.

His unease was what had moved Bell to go poking around. He still wanted to know who shot the old papa-san on the road to Can Tho. Yesterday at the station, he had reviewed the incident report and jotted down the date, time, and location, to the extent the V-100 patrol had described it. Then turning in his .45 after duty, he'd persuaded Sanderson to pull the armory records and show him who had checked out M-16s that day: Akers, Hayes, Foley, and several others not on regular patrols. At least it wasn't Cole. He and Cole had been on town patrol together when the old man was shot.

This morning, while Foley was at breakfast, he'd stopped by the motor pool and cajoled Gus Begay into letting him go through the trip log. The only trip tickets issued the day the papa-san was shot, and for days before, were all for patrol jeeps.

"Why you want to know who took a jeep out way back then?" Gus asked.

Bell hesitated. Gus didn't say much to anyone. He was built like a water buffalo, with black hair and skin almost black from the Arizona sun. But he was always smiling in a bemused way, as if he were puzzled at how he had ended up here with all these palefaces—and a few black faces—none of whom seemed to know what to make of him. Or that's what Sanderson said.

Odd thing was that Ernie the cook had latched onto Gus. Then again, Gus was a customer. He bought a little weed every other week, Ernie said, and smoked it up on the roof, by himself. Ernie had heard him up there singing some Indian thing or other. And Gus had a big knife he carried when he went into town, carried it in a leather sheath under his shirt. Called it his scalping knife. All this Ernie had told Bell and Meyer over a beer in the club.

That's when Bell decided he'd never trust Ernie to keep his mouth shut about anything—except who his supplier was. Ernie and his Tennessee drawl and idiot laugh, dirty kitchen whites and hat cocked to one side. Ernie the court jester.

Unlike Ernie, Gus wouldn't spill anything he told him. And he liked Gus. Not only because Gus had a pleasant face and sage reserve, but mainly because Gus's eyes smiled when he looked at you.

So he'd told Gus the whole story: about the papa-san riding a bicycle on the old Can Tho road being shot by someone from the new road, and that the engineers had seen an MP jeep—that shouldn't have been there—going up the new road about the same time.

Gus shook his head. "I wasn't here, so I don't know. Patrols have trip tickets. Akers always gets a trip ticket—lieutenant makes him. NCOs maybe or maybe not."

"All the NCOs?" Bell asked. "Beadle? Hayes? Any particular ones, more than others?"

"Sergeant Beadle makes sure he cover his ass. But Foley and Hayes, they never have trip tickets when they go out. Especially motor pool jeep."

And neither of them would hesitate to shoot a gook if they could get away with it.

He thanked Gus and asked him not to tell anyone he'd been asking. Then he went to get his M-16 and .45 for the gate, on the way thinking, where does any of this get me? What good does it do?

He settled onto the metal folding chair inside the gate bunker and stood his M-16 against the bunker wall. Sliding his MP helmet liner onto the plywood window ledge, he stared past it, out the chicken-wire-covered window, at the pocked-marked, rust-streaked white building beyond the open gate. An attractive young woman—conical lan, black pajama pants, and a fresh-looking white camisole—emerged through a narrow opening in the building's metal-gate and padded barefoot across the gravel approach to the compound, on across the road, and turned to go toward the canal. A small child clung to her neck, and another trailed arm's length behind her.

The window framed a tranquil scene: the mottled white building, the little barefoot family, the swamp-grass soccer field, and the blue sky with its high white clouds—crisscrossed with black hatch marks. He focused first on the scene then on the wire window, shifting back and forth, measuring his world far and near.

Despite a profound feeling of malaise, he resolved not to worry about what he couldn't control. He concentrated on leaching all anxiety from his mind, squeezing what few drops of pleasure he could from the beautiful morning.

Those sparse drops soon exhausted, he leaned back in the chair and, with a prolonged sigh, took out his book. Giving one more cursory glance out the window, he bent the pages open and started to read, at once becoming lost in Frodo's struggles in the land of Mordor. So much for the VC and NVA.

While he read—book in lap, chair tilted back, looking up only at the sound of a vehicle—a patrol went out, then Hayes and Foley in the three-quarter ton, and after them the C.O., by himself, without a driver. Five minutes later, Lt Floyd, pasty-faced, lower lip in a pout, eyes straight ahead, whisked past in a jeep driven by Wesley Akers, not bothering to slow down or even acknowledge the existence of a gate guard, much less show him their trip ticket.

The sun rose higher behind the bunker, and with it the temperature inside. His eyes drooped, and he stalled on a sentence about Sam and the ring. Before his two worlds could merge, he was brought back to the real one by the dull sputter of a jeep and the rattle of rocks as wheels left the parking lot's asphalt and rolled onto the gravel of the exit.

Across from the wire-covered window, Gus the mechanic coasted to a stop in a headquarters jeep. He flashed a broad grin and leaned across the empty passenger seat to wave a trip ticket in Bell's direction.

"Where ya goin', Gus?" He called through the crosshatched screen.

Gus replied in a sentence that contained "airfield" and "drive," but he only half listened since he knew the mechanic was probably taking the jeep for a test run—and to the airfield PX in the process.

"Fine, fine," he answered and motioned Gus to go on, using the hand not holding his place in the paperback. As Gus shifted into second and disappeared out the gate, he resumed reading.

The gate bunker grew hotter. After a break provided by an FNG on detail, he moved the metal chair outside into the shade next to the bunker entrance where he could receive the benefit of an occasional breeze. A mid-morning somnolence had settled over the compound. From inside the villa came a few muffled voices, the old mama-san and her consort and staff calling to each other as they cleaned and did their chores. Dupre and the two FNGs on work detail had retired to the mess hall or the club for their morning break, which, in the absence of Hayes and the attention of Top, would stretch out for at least an hour. Even the sounds of artillery and choppers coming and going at the airfield had assumed a lazy rhythm that lulled him into a dreamlike trance.

Finishing a chapter and feeling almost content, he parked the book open, face-down on his leg, and passed the time watching a grasshopper climb into the sun atop a long feathery stem in a clump of grass at the corner of the bunker. Once on its perch, it began chirring, transporting him to the field behind his house on a summer's day. Shifting his gaze, he stared vacantly at a phalanx of high white clouds with dark undersides billowing up beyond the soccer field and town.

A pair of Vietnamese soldiers crossed his line of vision, walking up the other side of the road, holding hands. He tried to put himself into their heads.

What are they thinking? What do they think about me, about all these strange foreigners who live in this old villa, in what must be luxury to them?

A noisy rattle of gravel roused him from his daydream as jeeps on the road made the short approach to the compound.

Lieutenant Floyd's jeep sped past the gate bunker, then an unmarked jeep with Landrieu driving, and behind it the MP patrol jeep with Sergeant Carter at the wheel. Now alert, Bell spied the first hint of trouble. In the back of Lt Floyd's jeep was Gus, hunched forward, head down almost to his knees.

No sooner had the lieutenant's jeep halted then the lieutenant was out of it and charging toward the gate bunker. Slowly rising, Bell slipped the book into a side pocket and drifted a few steps forward in the dust cloud left by the vehicles.

The lieutenant's yelling was incoherent, except for epithets like "you dumb fuck" and "that drunk goddamn Indian."

Bell looked around and arrived at the obvious conclusion. He's talking to me. But why's he so pissed?

As Floyd approached, the first thing Bell noticed—aside from the ominous blimp bearing down on him with its moon face and skinned head—was a dark red welt on the lieutenant's pasty cheek. The eye above it had swollen into a purple circle surrounded by almost translucent skin.

"Oh shit," Bell thought, glancing at Gus, who Sergeant Carter was helping out of the back of the jeep. It didn't take a genius to work out what had happened. Gus was handcuffed, his hands down in front of him. Carter was almost gentle in the way he pulled the squat, hunchbacked figure out of the jeep, holding him by one arm above the elbow and, once his prisoner had stumbled onto the asphalt, steering him toward the entrance to the villa.

Hoping to get Sergeant Carter's attention, to find out what had happened, Bell stared past Lieutenant Floyd, now directly in front of him, hands on hips, persisting in his tirade. But Carter's eyes stayed on Gus.

"You hear me, Specialist?" came through the haze. "I said, I'm relieving you of duty."

"But I didn't—"

"Shut up!"

"He had—"

"I said shut up!" Floyd turned and motioned to Landrieu, watching them from where he stood beside the patrol jeep.

"Landry," Floyd shouted, getting the name wrong. "Get your ass over here. Cover the gate til I can get somebody to finish this fuckup's shift."

With Bell dispatched to his apparent satisfaction, Floyd tacked around and lumbered toward the villa entrance, where Wes Akers was waiting for him, holding the door. Bell could see a smirk on Akers' lips, directed at him.

Approaching the bunker, Landrieu shrugged and gave a tight grimace. "Slugged the lieutenant." He nodded vaguely toward the entrance through which Gus had disappeared with Carter and Akers was now going in Lt Floyd's wake. The screen door slammed shut.

"Down in front of Madame Phoung's," Landrieu added, going past Bell. "Those two had to call us to subdue the fucker." He chuckled, shaking his head. "Man, oh man, he sure got in a few good licks on the ol' fat boy."

"Oh, shit," was all Bell could say. "Shit!"

He grabbed his M-16 from where it was leaning against the side of the bunker and stumbled away, toward the villa's entrance.

CHAPTER FORTY-SIX
Nor Any Drop to Drink

INSIDE AND FREE OF HIS MP GEAR, he lay down on his bunk and sorted through what had happened—over and over.

Gus works in the motor pool. He had a trip ticket. He seemed okay when he went out, just Gus, not saying much, sort of sleepy eyed like he always is. And he had a trip ticket; he waved it at me. He's always taking out jeeps to test and going where he wants. They all do in the motor pool. I should've looked at the paper. But I did. Well, not to read it. Trip tickets don't mean anything anyway. Gus could get an old one and change it to suit him. Or forge Foley's name on one.

Shit, shit, shit! How could I have screwed up like this? What were the odds Gus'd go out and get drunk at ten in the morning, and then take a swing at that fat fuck Floyd? I've never seen Gus drunk. Well, maybe once or twice, like most everybody here. Except Meyer. Get anyone drunk in this place and they're an unguided missile, and who knows where they'll end up.

Madame Phoung's is a likely spot. And Gus drunk? But never violent, not to anybody.

Oh, shit, Bell thought, and started the cycle over again.

Finally, driven by hunger tightening the knots in his stomach, he decided to go face the gang in the mess hall. Looking at his watch, he discovered it was almost 1400 hours. Most would've eaten and gone, a small reprieve but little consolation to his overwhelming sense of shame and chagrin.

When he got downstairs, he found only Meyer and Taylor, who had come off patrol for chow—and they were about to leave. Taylor said hello as if Bell had the plague, then left a little too quickly, telling Meyer he'd meet him outside.

"We heard what happened," said Meyer, giving Bell a beatific smile as Bell sat down at the table across from him.

"Shit, you probably know more'n I do." He sawed off a piece of gravy-covered meat and examined it on the end of his fork before stuffing it into his mouth. Chewing, he mumbled, "All I know is Gus was out raising hell, mixed it up with the fat looey—and yours truly gets blamed."

"Close." Meyer pushed away his plate, empty except for a smear of white gravy, and polished off the remains of a glass of milk as Bell waited for him to continue. "What we heard, both on the radio and from Wesley Akers, is that Gus stopped at Madame Phoung's. He had been drinking. A lot. And when they wouldn't let him inside, he got rowdy."

"Too early for business?"

"No. He was abusing the baby-san at the gate, calling her names or something. Lt Floyd happened to be riding by with the wiseacre and stopped to see why Gus was there. Akers claims our resident Navaho was mad because Vietnamese girls don't like Indians—or somebody told him that—and he was going to show them."

"Drunk, huh?" Bell muttered from behind a mouthful of gravy-coated green beans. "He wasn't when he left here."

"When Floyd tried to haul him in, good old Gus took a swing or two—and connected." Meyer chuckled. "Even Akers was laughing, telling us Floyd landed on his fat butt. They radioed the station, got Carter and Landrieu to 'come help 'em 'round up the wild Injun,' as Akers put it." Meyer paused, his face serious now. "The other thing, he was carrying a knife the size of a bayonet."

"A knife! Fuck! But he had a trip ticket. He takes jeeps out all the time."

"Hey, you don't have to tell me."

"Somebody revved him up." Bell swallowed and glanced at the door, then looked back at Meyer. "He's *never* been like this before, and he's *never* had any problem with the Vietnamese. Even has a girlfriend, so Ernie told me. Somebody's been feeding him a line, and

I bet I can guess who."

"You think Foley..." Meyer broke off as Ernie came out of the kitchen in his duty apparel—white apron, sweat-stained t-shirt, and crumpled white cook's hat. He sauntered over to the table.

"Hey, hey, heard about crazy ol' Gus deckin' that doughboy. Ha, ha, would've loved to seen that." Grinning and looking from Bell to Meyer, he took out a cigarette and lit it, exhaling smoke over the table.

"You have to do that, Ernie? I'm tryin' to eat," Bell held up a lump of meat on his fork, "whatever this crap is."

"Oh, sorry, bro. Not thinkin'." Ernie snuffed out the cigarette in the gravy on Meyer's plate. "Chicken-fried steak," he said, releasing a last stream of smoke. "Guess you got in a shit-load of trouble, huh?"

"Why'd Gus do it?" Bell asked, still glaring at Ernie. "You know him better'n I do. Better'n any of us." He waved his fork at Meyer.

"Man, you don't know the kinda shit Gus's been takin' off Foley. Him and Hayes, too. Raggin' him all the damn time. Like ta drove the chief nuts."

"He's never been like that before." Bell sighed and looked down at the plate, studying the swirls of gravy and flattened mash potatoes.

Meyer stood to leave, plucking his helmet liner out of an empty chair. He paused to adjust the .45 and billy club on the belt around his rotund waist.

What an awkward looking guy, Bell thought, staring at him. *Wouldn't hurt a fly. How could I... how could anyone, not help but like him? And I don't look any better than he does in that getup.*

"Bell," Meyer said, glancing at Ernie then back at Bell. "You'll be okay. My Aunt Golda always says the righteous shall prevail."

"You think anything's gonna keep me from getting fucked over in this place? I may end up in LBJ with Hodge."

Meyer held his fist up in a salute. "Hang tough, bro, hang tough." He headed out the door.

"Ah, don't worry," Ernie said. "Been busted twice, and I'm still the cook. Heh, heh, heh." His husky chuckle rattled through his sunken chest.

***

Bowman roused him from a troubled sleep. His book had slipped off his chest onto the poncho liner, and at the clerk's call, he knocked it onto the floor.

"Bell! You've got two slots on guard duty tonight." Bowman was leaning over him from between the bunks. "Lieutenant Floyd says you have to pull both the first and last shift in the tower."

"Aw, fuck! That's not fair. He can't do that."

"Hell he can't." Bowman hesitated, looked around, and sat down on the empty bunk opposite Bell's. "He's really pissed," Bowman said, shaking his head.

"Fucker wouldn't even listen to what happened," Bell said. *Not that I had the presence of mind to tell him.*

He sat up, facing Bowman across the narrow space. The sun, now low in the sky, peeked from beneath the rain clouds, and the sleeping bay briefly became brighter.

Bell shook his head at Bowman. "Look, man, Gus was okay when he left here. He must've gotten drunk downtown."

"That's not what Foley says. He said Gus was drunk this morning... in the motor pool. He sent him back to bed, but Gus left for the airfield."

"I saw him when Foley was at breakfast, and he wasn't drunk then."

Bowman shrugged. "So he got drunk after that. Sergeant Carter actually stood up for you." Wrinkling his forehead, Bowman exhibited a thin smile. "They had a big argument about it."

"They what? Who had an argument?" Bell straightened up to focus better on Bowman's face, clean-shaven with rosy cheeks like a cherub in a Renaissance painting. He was dressed in clean starched fatigues, his hair regulation length, even though he was leaving the next week.

"Carter and Floyd came in to see the captain," Bowman said. "He wasn't there, but they had a big discussion in his office. Heard it all."

Bowman took a breath and let it out slowly like he was trying to decide whether to tell Bell all this. He continued when Bell didn't say anything.

"Foley came back from the airfield, and he and the first sergeant went in then. They left the door open—no one else around, but me. To hear Floyd tell it... to the first sergeant, you were just as much at fault as Gus. And Foley kept saying Gus was drunk before he took the jeep out. Then Carter pipes up and says he 'don't believe it.'... You know how he talks. He didn't come right out and say it, not to Floyd, but I think he'd seen Gus earlier. Anyway, Sergeant Carter said they couldn't blame you."

"He did? Sergeant Carter?"

"He said they should ship Gus out and leave you alone." Bowman shook his head and grimaced, an unnatural expression on his smooth face. "Afraid that's not good enough for the lieutenant. He's really steamed, and Foley was pouring it on. Oh, yeah, Hayes was there, too. Didn't say much, but you could tell he was sort of prodding Foley along—"

"Fuck, fuck, fuck!" Bell slumped down, his elbows on his knees, head in his hands. "What did I do to deserve this?"

"Carter got kind of heated, and the lieutenant told him to stay out of it." Bowman reached over and lightly patted his knee. "Don't forget guard duty."

He stood and started to leave, then stopped. "Hodge is on his way back. Captain Templeton's bringing him."

"Huh?" said Bell. "That can't—"

"Oh, but it is. Captain called after chow. He didn't say much— you know how *he* is. The board dropped everything, and they're dismissing the charges against Hodge. Well, I'm preparing papers for an Article 15, and he'll be busted in rank and lose pay."

"But he won't go to jail?"

"Like the shooting business never happened. Just insubordination and disrespect to a superior officer or something like that—after they figure it out."

"That's great!" Bell's mood lifted slightly. *It is great.*

"Helps to be C. Hamilton the fourth and have the third to back you up." Bowman pivoted around and, square shouldered and erect, strode out of the bay.

Watching him leave, Bell felt a sudden rush of fear, and panic. *Oh God, what can I do? Run. Hide. Like Top under the stairs.*

Stop it! Anger, along with the bile of hate, quells the panic.

I'd like to kill that son-of-a-bitch Floyd. Go after him like Hodge did the captain. And what a fucking mess that was. What good did it do Hodge or anybody?

What about Gus? He caused this mess. But God, is he in deep shit. I'd hate to be in his shoes. And Carter? I can't believe that dumb fuck defended me. Maybe he's not such a dumb fuck.

Hayes? Right now, he fears Hayes more than hates him—or do the two emotions serve in tandem? Does Hayes hate him or only view him as a nuisance, to be squashed like a bug if he gets in the way? And like Captain Midnight, he *has* gotten in the way.

The briefcase exchange in My Tho, Markovic with Avery's jeep in the motor pool, the prisoners in the mess hall, it all starts to make sense. Then I saw Hayes coming back from the warehouse, and Cole must've told him. Goddamn that Cole.

Does Hayes know about my visit with Gus and my investigating the killing of the papa-san? Did Hayes and Foley ignite the fuse to Gus's insecurities. But why? Surely, not just to get at me.

Hodge is coming back—despite Hayes and the others who misled him, despite his shooting venture in the club. He's coming back—like an albatross around the C.O.'s neck.

There has to be a way out of this mess.

CHAPTER FORTY-SEVEN
Funny Numbers

WITH THE SUN OBNOXIOUSLY PROCLAIMING A NEW DAY, he plodded down the outside corridor toward the stairs. Nerves already stretched to the limit, he was exhausted from his two guard shifts and lack of sleep between them.

The orderly room door swung open behind him, and Sergeant Carter's call broke the early morning silence. "Hey, Bell, get your ass in here. I have something I need you to do."

He turned slowly, trying to look as weary as he felt, and stumbled back toward Carter. "I'm beat, Sarge. Can't it wait?"

Ignoring the plea, Carter ushered him inside. "You're helping Sanchez today. C.O. wants an arms and equipment inventory. You're a college boy; you should be able to count real good."

"Look, Sarge, I've been up since five, and I didn't get much sleep before that. Can't I catch some *zz*'s first?"

"Bell, your ass is in a sling already," Carter said with a wheeze, "and you'd best get with the fuckin' program. Things are changin' fast. Captain Midnight's outta here. Turnover to the new C.O.'s next week."

He paused for this to sink in, and Bell rewarded him with a startled look. *So Hayes and the NCOs had won.*

"And somethin' big's comin' down," Carter said. "Scuttlebutt has it we're movin' out. Least half the company. You wanna be on that list? 'Specially with your fuck-up yesterday."

"That *wasn't* my fault, Sarge."

"Maybe so, but that ain't gonna do you no good. None at all." Carter eyed him in a way, with his brow furrowed, that almost exhibited concern. "Any-damn-how, you shouldn'a let that redskin outta here without a trip ticket."

"He had one."

"We didn't see no sign'a one."

"Look, just ask Gus."

"Gus? Gus is on his way to LBJ. And it don't matter what Gus says. Foley says the Injun'd been drinkin' all night. Stumblin' drunk when he kicked him out of the motor pool and sent him upstairs."

"I tell you he wasn't drunk, Sarge. I saw him when he left."

Carter stared at him thoughtfully a second. "Well, even if *I* believed ya, it won't do you a bit of good. It's what fatso believes that counts. Ya wanna stay here, better start showin' you're some use to somebody."

"You know I love it here," Bell said, slumping with one shoulder against the wall. "I wouldn't want to abandon all my friends—like you and Sergeant Hayes."

As soon as he said it, he knew he had made a mistake. Whatever sympathy Carter had for him disappeared in the angry reddening of the sergeant's already florid cheeks.

"Don't ya smart off at me!" Carter stuck his face close to Bell's. "You may think you're some sorta hotshot college boy, but in this man's army, you ain't nuthin but another piece of shit. You're goddamn lucky I didn't bring charges the time you cussed me out down at the station."

"I'm sorry. I thought—"

"You're not here to think, dickhead. Just go do what you're told." He stepped back.

"Yes sir!" Bell snapped to attention and saluted.

"Don't start that shit with me! Get the hell outta here—go see Sanchez." Opening the door to the orderly room, he added in a softer tone, "I'll tell him to let you go after chow." But he closed the door with a growl, "if I don't find somethin' better for ya to do."

When he reached the supply room, he found Sergeant Sanchez standing in front of the waist-high counter, busily leafing through a notebook and pulling out old forms and inserting new ones.

Dispensing with his usual jovial greeting, Sanchez assigned Bell to do a physical inventory of the items listed in the stack of loose forms he had dropped on the counter. His imminent departure, he exclaimed with exasperation, depended on him giving the C.O. *complete* records, accurate or not, by the end of the day.

Bell spent the first hour of his assignment counting boxes of ammo in the ammunition bunker and rifles in the armory. He found two boxes of M26 grenades that were not listed on the forms but failed to find a number of other items that were: a dozen M-16s, two M-60 machine guns, and one V-100 twin machine gun replacement. Another inventory sheet enumerated eight jeeps, a quarter-ton, and two deuce-and-a-half's. There was only one of the larger trucks in the compound; and when he ticked off the M151A jeeps on his fingers, he came up with seven.

"Hey, Enrique, the numbers on these fucking forms don't match," he said, coming back inside from the ammunition bunker. He let the screen door slam shut behind him.

"Don't worry about it." Sanchez was back at his desk, writing what looked like a letter. He pointed to the vacant supply clerk's desk and typewriter. "Type up a new form and put in the right frigging numbers. This is an inventory, not a frigging IG inspection."

"Why do we have all these bad numbers? Don't you make a record to reduce the inventory when you turn something in?"

He knew that the correct procedure was to turn in worn-out or damaged equipment at the depot in Can Tho and obtain a receipt, which was kept in the supply room records and cross-referenced on the revised inventory form. Knowing Poteet, and Sanchez, the stuff to be turned in had probably ended up in a canal somewhere. Of course, there was always the possibility that some of the missing items had been traded with ARVN units or sold on the black market.

"Look, my friend," Sanchez said, shaking his pen at him, "these forms were here when I came eight months ago. They weren't worth a shit then, and they're not worth a shit now." He grinned, nodding his head, and lowered the pen. "You know, *amigo*, that phony Indian Poteet never took the time to update shit, and since he left, I haven't had time to do anything but try and get the stuff we need here." At Bell's skeptical look, Sanchez added, "Hey, sometimes things get lost, they get damaged, they get used up. No frigging body ever pays any mind to records 'round here."

"Lost? How the hell can you lose a two-and-one-half ton truck?"

"I think Hayes sent the deuce-and-a-half down to Can Tho. It's been gone a while."

"What about the jeep? The records say we should have eight jeeps, and I only know of seven. And Avery's jeep was replaced."

"Must be the one Biggers' wrecked last year. It probably went for salvage."

"Sarge, didn't you—or someone—get a turn-in sheet to show the vehicle's disposition, something to make a record of what happened to it?" He narrowed his eyes, cocking his head to one side. "Was Biggers' jeep replaced?"

"Jesus Christ, Bell, this is a frigging war zone. Things get blown away all the goddamn time—mines, mortars, who knows what?" Sanchez shrugged. "Some of it," his mouth turned down at the corners and his head bobbed side to side, "maybe stolen. You know how the gooks are. They'll steal anything." He chuckled. "Mama-sans even stole all the forks out of the mess hall, until we started counting them every night."

"I'll type the inventory, but it's your baby to sign."

"That's fine by me, *amigo*. In a week, I'll be far away in the sack with my honey." Sanchez pointed to the gold-framed picture. "She says I look like—"

"I know, I know, Desi Arnez. Thought you were going to see your dying mother."

Sanchez patted his full head of black hair and grinned at Bell.

"Tell me the truth, Enrique, what's going on here?"

"Going on? Going on? *Amigo*, we are fighting a war to save

freedom and democracy for the white man's world, no?"

"Don't shit me, man. You're going home. I'm going to be here... well, maybe I'll be here, another six months." He took a breath. "Like with Sergeant Hayes. What's his game?"

Looking around, Sanchez came from behind his desk, over to the counter, and motioned for Bell to step nearer, as if the room were bugged. He leaned across the counter and spoke close to Bell's ear.

"*Amigo*, the less you know, the better. Hayes moves stuff. He makes things happen. And he makes beaucoup *dinero*." He rubbed his thumb and fingers together under Bell's nose.

"Okay... if you say so." Bell pulled his face back. "Who does he... you know, work with here, in the compound? Foley? Sergeant Beadle?"

"Beadle? Hah!" Sanchez gave a raucous laugh, smacking his hand on the counter. Then he shrugged. "*No sé, amigo.*" Reaching across the counter, he tapped an index finger on Bell's chest. "Mind your own business. You got enough troubles."

Bell considered this a moment, then tried another tact. "Who's Hayes' contact in town? Major Binh?"

"Ah, Major Binh! The one whose jeep blew up? Now *that* was a piece of work." He grinned.

"So what exactly does Binh do? I mean, I thought he was in the district office, but he's military, not civilian."

Sanchez shifted on the balls of his feet, eyeing Bell across the counter. "Whatever you are thinking, *señor*—don't." He smiled slightly, fixing Bell with his small dark eyes. "You know why the C.O. is leaving?... No? Hayes wanted him gone." He gave a derisive snort. "Hayes maybe sent your friend Hodges to go after the black *hombre*. If Hodges did *not* get him, *no hay problema*. HQ would not leave him down here—not after that."

"That sounds—"

He waved his finger at Bell. "All very simple. Captain Midnight was sniffing around. You sniff around, maybe same-same happen to you. Maybe you should think about why you have your little *problema*." He reached across the counter and patted Bell on the shoulder. "You look tired, *amigo*. Go ahead, take a break."

Numbed by Sanchez's warning, Bell spun around and strode out the exit to the tarmac, where he wandered between the V-100 revetments and the perimeter, and then around to the gate bunker, and back. Removing a cigarette from an almost-full pack, he lit it and took a few long draws, thinking about how cynical—and threatening—the dapper little supply sergeant had been. Staring back at the supply room, he wondered, *what does Sanchez have to do with all the crap that goes on here?*

He flipped the cigarette into the concertina wire by the fence. *That's it for those things*, he decided. It was the last cigarette he'd ever smoke. The hot sun and the sweat soaking his t-shirt drove him back inside. He wanted to ask more questions, but Sanchez waved him off and set him to typing new inventory lists with numbers that he, Sanchez, provided. No need to count anything at all.

Before he finished typing the final lists, Bowman arrived with a summons to the C.O.'s office.

CHAPTER FORTY-EIGHT
Better a Court Martial

HE SUSPECTED THE REASON FOR HIS SUMMONS, but the somber company clerk declined to enlighten him further. Slinking past the first sergeant, who silently glowered at him over a freshly-typed form, Bell stopped at the C.O.'s open door and looked in. There, instead of Captain Templeton, sat First Lieutenant Floyd, overflowing the captain's chair, chubby elbows resting on the chair arms, rocking impatiently back and forth.

The lieutenant motioned for him to enter and gave a gruff order to close the door behind him. Coming forward, he stopped in front of the desk and stood at attention, erect, head up. No command came to stand at ease.

The lieutenant glared, lips pressed tight, one pasty jowl pink from sun or anger and the other one lividly bruised from where Gus had slugged him. Above it, a wide circle of purple enclosed the eye, making him look like Petey, the mutt from *The Little Rascals*, except Petey never looked so disagreeable.

Addressing Bell by his full name and rank, the lieutenant recited from a paper he held up in front of him, his puffy white hands resting on the gray metal of the desk: Specialist Justin Darrell Bell had allowed Specialist Augustus Begay to leave the compound, driving an M151A vehicle while under the influence of alcohol and without authorization for the vehicle, *et cetera, et cetera, et cetera*. Therefore, Specialist Bell was charged with negligence and dereliction of duty.

Specialist Bell tried to interrupt, but the lieutenant told him to shut up and listen until he finished reading the document.

In a growling monotone, he continued. He was offering Specialist Bell a non-judicial disciplinary action, an Article 15, in lieu of a court martial, if he agreed and accepted the punishment: reduction of one grade in rank and loss of $100 pay over two months.

"Well, specialist, are you ready to accept your punishment and move on?" the lieutenant asked, looking up at Bell through squinting eyes, the left one almost shut.

"But sir, he wasn't drunk when—"

"Don't lie to me, Bell. Sergeant Foley told me how the man had been drinking, and how he looked when Foley got to the motor pool. Not more than an hour before *you* let him out the gate with a vehicle. Without authorization."

"He had a trip ticket."

"Goddamn it, Bell, he did not," yelled the lieutenant, his cheeks, where the one was not already purple, turning bright red. "My driver searched the jeep... and Gus. There was no goddamn trip ticket."

"I saw one. At least, a form that was filled out."

"Bullshit. You lie to me again, I'll tear *this* form up and bust you two grades. And confine you to quarters." He spun the document across the table toward Bell and slammed a fist on the metal desk. "You going to accept this or not? I've got better things to do than waste my time with the likes of you."

Bell's mind raced. He picked up the paper and pretended to read it, seeing only the words "Article 15, reduced in grade, and $100." That meant a lot of money to him. Not to mention the humiliation and injustice of it all. But if he refused, he would be court-martialed, and he could end up even worse off, even in Long Binh Jail. His chances of ever getting another college degree, or even a decent job, ruined.

What am I going to do, what I am going to do, kept running through his mind, his panic deepening. He tried to remember what the Uniform Code of Military Justice said about Article 15s and courts-martial.

"Well, Specialist?" Lt Floyd tilted back in the chair, making it squeak in protest.

They'll have to prove I neglected duty, that I was negligent. They will have to show Gus was drunk when he took the jeep out. But he wasn't. And he had a trip ticket. I should've read it. But people go out without trip tickets all the time—Gus told me that. And Gus was a mechanic, taking jeeps out to test-drive them. Then another thought. *I might be able to expose some of the crap going on...*

"Okay, okay, you've read it now. Are you going to accept this *non-judicial* action—or do you want to take the risk of going to jail?"

The lieutenant's chin lay in folds against his neck as he rocked back in the chair and squinted up at Bell.

"Respectfully, sir, I refuse it," Bell blurted out, not sure where he was going with this. He took a breath. "I request a court-martial. I want a full hearing."

The red flush spread across Floyd's entire face, but reddest of all were the small ears that poked out from the shaved sides of his round head. His fingers drummed on the desk, followed by a sharp rap of his knuckles.

"All right. Okay. Fine. If that's the way you want it." He glared at Bell, the corners of his mouth turning down and pulling his lower lip into a pout.

"Whatever happened today doesn't hold a candle to what Hayes—"

"Di-s-s-missed," barked Floyd in two long sneering syllables. He rocked forward in the chair and hit the desk with his fist. "Get out of my sight!"

Bell pivoted heel and toe and marched to the door, shoved it open, and exited, staring straight ahead. He continued on through the orderly room without acknowledging Top or Bowman, who were silent as he strode defiantly, head up and shoulders squared, through the outer door.

I'm right, he was thinking. *It was the right decision. But fuck-it-all, if I lose the court martial, I'm ruined, my whole life is ruined. Fuck, fuck, fuck!*

Maybe I should go back in there.

Fuck no! I won't go down without a fight. I'll blow this corrupt place apart, expose Hayes and his black market operation, make 'em investigate who killed Tony, who shot the old papa-san, Avery's jeep, and all the other shit here.

But what if they won't let me bring any of that up? I'm not Perry Mason, but I know courts only consider what's relevant, material.

Maybe I should go to CID.

Fuck! I don't really know anything, only what I suspect.

Maybe I can go to Major Dobbs' friend. If I can find him, if he's still in country.

Fuck!

There in the captain's office, facing that prick lieutenant, I wasn't afraid of him, just mad as hell. I didn't tremble or break out in a sweat. I was rational in rejecting the Article 15.

Or was I? Was it just my anger talking? Fuck! I could end up in LBJ.

Bullshit! Not likely. But there's the possibility. Oh, shit! I could end up in a grunt unit. Where they send the fuck-up MPs.

He remembered what the lieutenant said about Foley, what Foley had said about Gus being drunk. And Hayes was there, when they picked up Gus at Madame Phoung's.

Is this all a set up? Like Hodge and Captain Midnight?

The court martial could be rigged. Where there's money, things get done, as Sanchez so blithely reminded me. Things get done the way the money says they need to get done to keep the money coming.

Ah shit, shit, shit! What the fuck am I going to do?

CHAPTER FORTY-NINE
The Best Laid Plans

AFTER A SOLITARY MEAL OF CHOCOLATE CHIP COOKIES and a Coke consumed in a sliver of shade at the rear of the deck, he retired to his bunk. He tried to sleep, gave it up, and pulled out his last Tolkien book. The bay was quiet, hot, and still—except for the oscillating fan on the trunk at the end of his bunk. Not even the mosquitoes exhibited much energy in the heat.

Unable to read, he removed the fan from the footlocker and rummaged through the jumble of letters, books, and newspapers in the tray until he found a notepad. He needed to write down the questions buzzing in his head.

How could he redeem himself and avoid a court-martial? Or win it? Could he expose Hayes and his dealings in the black market, or was he only fantasizing?

How did it all fit together? Hayes, Major Binh, Beadle, the C.O.? The missing inventory and screwed-up records? Did Roberts' suicide, if that's what it was, have anything to do with all this? Avery's accident? Gus? Phan waving a pistol under his nose? He'd only asked something about Binh. Or was it Roberts?

Phan wasn't just an errand boy, like the dead boy-san.

Poor Tony. He still had the note from Tony's boot. He looked through his footlocker again and found it. Mai said there was a reference to the warehouse. And to Binh. And tires.

Tires sold well downtown. He tried to remember. Had he seen an inventory of tires in the supply room?

He stood above the fan and held out his arms to cool off. Sweat ran down his neck and stained the front and armpits of his olive-drab T-shirt.

Taylor came in, went to his wall locker with only a nod and a grunt, then gave him a strange look on the way out.

Standing there in front of the fan, Bell kept mulling over his questions, and coming back to two that puzzled him more and more: What was in the warehouse and why had Hayes gone down there at five in the morning? Maybe if he could find out, he could... do what?

He needed someone to talk to.

Sanderson would laugh it off, make a joke of it. And Hodge— even if he were back, he had zoned out to never-never land long before this thing with Glenda: with all the Scotch, the tokes with Ernie, the side-business of selling gas out of the V-100.

But Meyer would listen, maybe even understand. Maybe help him with his budding plan. He looked at his watch. Three o'clock. Meyer would be off duty soon.

He found Meyer in the mess hall, sitting by himself at a table and still dressed in baggy duty fatigues and MP gear, one leg propped up in the seat of a chair catty-corner to him. He was eating cling peaches out of a can.

Bell took a Coke from the cooler and sat down across from him. "You can't do any better than that?" he asked, pointing at the can.

"I like peaches. Just wish I had some ice cream."

Bell looked around to make sure that none of the cooks were near. The only other person in the room was the subaltern mama-san, intent on cleaning off the tables and setting out salt and pepper shakers and metal holders filled with paper napkins. From outside, beyond the corridor next to the mess hall, came the thump of a basketball and shouts of a two-on-two game.

"Floyd offered me an Article 15," he said.

"No! You're kidding?" Meyer's eyes widened and the spoon paused above the can. "What for? Gus wasn't your fault."

"The fat lieutenant says it was."

Bell recounted his meeting with Floyd. While he talked, a housefly buzzed the table, then landed and wandered onto a red square next to his hand. Cupping his palm, he swept it up, shook it vigorously in his fist, and hurled it against the concrete floor.

Meyer, cutting a peach with his spoon, scrunched up his face as Bell squashed the stunned fly with the toe of his boot.

"Thanks," Meyer said. "I like entertainment while I'm eating."

Bell looked up from his handiwork. "Ira, if I *am* gonna get out of this, I need to find out what's going on here."

"It's called a war."

"It *ain't* the war." Bell slowly shook his head. "It's all the other shit."

"And what might that 'shit' be, bro?"

"Goddamn it!" Bell leaned forward over the table. "They're stealing shit—here, the airfield, selling it on the black market, lining their fucking pockets, while guys just like us are out there dying." He pointed outside, where a series of whoops signaled a basket. "Maybe to protect their little racket, they even arrange for shit to happen right here."

"Shit to happen?" The spoon clinked against the inside of the can. "What have you—"

"Like Avery's accident. Or Hodge going after the captain. Or Tony." He tapped the table top with his finger. "Or this thing with Gus and me."

Meyer raised a shaggy black eyebrow. "And so, my friend," he said, swallowing a bite of peaches, "who might these people be? The evil ones doing this to you?"

"Hayes. Maybe Foley. And others."

"So, what are they covering up?" Meyer said, dropping his foot to the floor and sitting up. "Whatever they're doing, they're no different than all the other jerks making money off this stupid war." He waved his empty spoon over the table. "Like I've told you, bro, you're being paranoid."

"But don't you see—"

"You worry about things you can do nothing about. Take the Article 15." Meyer bobbed his head emphatically. "And stay out of this *mess*."

"Sanchez *admitted* to me that Hayes is running a black market operation, and not just a measly little one... the vortex for the whole fucking Delta. Right fucking here."

He started recounting his conversation with the supply sergeant, but Meyer interrupted him. "Why are you telling me this? You're the one who said your only goal here was to avoid the fighting and go home alive." Meyer nodded as if agreeing and angled the can to fish out another peach.

"Just look at this." Bell shoved his list of questions across the table.

"What?" Meyer gave him a puzzled look, but he picked up the paper and studied it. Then shaking his head, he dropped it on the table as if it were toxic.

"So where did you learn to write?"

Leaving the list where it was, Bell ticked off the questions on the fingers of his left hand. "First, what's Hayes' racket? How does it work? Does he get tires and shit from here and sell 'em downtown? If he does, who's helping him, supplying him? Foley, maybe? Second, what's his connection to the locals—like this Major Binh we run into all over the place? Third, why did those jokers blow up the major's jeep? Certainly not to kill him. Shake him down, maybe? Fourth, why did Phan pull a pistol on me when I asked about Binh and Roberts? Fifth, why do people who could threaten Hayes's business just go away... like the captain? Or get eliminated? That advisor, Dobbs, he told me Avery was working with MACV on something here—*here* in the compound. Then he has an accident." He stopped and waited for this to sink in.

Meyer shrugged and popped another peach into his mouth.

"So maybe it wasn't an accident," Bell said, releasing his fingers. "There was something odd about the steering rod on his jeep, a funny weld, Markovic told me. Then Markovic gets transferred." He paused, tight lipped, before adding, "Ain't it possible this thing with

Gus is a way to get rid of me or... I don't know," he waved his hand in the air, "keep me from interfering?" He trailed off, waiting for Meyer to say something.

But Meyer didn't. Staring into the peach can, he clanked the spoon around the bottom in an effort to dredge up the last of the syrup. The basketball game outside had disbanded, and it was quiet except for the kitchen noises.

"Look, the list goes on," Bell said. "Why is that warehouse on the canal such a popular place? Hayes wasn't out for a drive the other night because he couldn't sleep." He paused, hoping for a reaction, but Meyer's eyes remained focused on the peach can. So he continued, "Bet it was Binh or his people who went down there after Hayes."

Again he waited for Meyer to respond. When he didn't, Bell smacked his Coke can down on the table.

"Dammit, Meyer, what do you think?"

"I don't know." Meyer shrugged. "Could be. But why do you care?" He carefully placed the empty can on the table and rested his hand beside it. "We keep going over this. How does anything on that," he motioned to the list, "solve your problem—if you should find the answers? We're peons. Nobody pays any attention to Spec. 4 draftees."

"Do you remember how Tony looked? His hands had been tied. He was executed, close range—probably an M-16." Bell pressed his index finger to his forehead, just above his glasses. "Right here," he said, tapping his finger against his skull. He inhaled sharply and held out the note from Tranh's boot.

"He had this on him." He waved the note over the table, offering it to Meyer. "Mai told me it has directions to the warehouse—right down there," he pointed out the door, "and a list of stuff, including tires."

"So you told me, about a hundred times."

"It has names on it. Look at it, just look at it, will you."

Meyer took the thin rice paper and examined it while Bell watched.

"Makes no sense to me," Meyer said after a few seconds and deposited the note on the table, beside Bell's list. "It's all Vietnamese." He stared at Bell. "But you think this name here," he tapped his finger on the page, "is Major Binh?"

"That's right. Then there was the civilian who killed himself. I didn't know enough at the time—back when Hodge and I were in the pagoda—but I swear Hayes or the other guy said something," he shook his head in frustration, "that linked Roberts to Binh, 'gook major' or something. And the schedule of some sort in his room, with Binh's name—"

He stopped talking as Ernie walked out of the kitchen, said "hello," and lit a cigarette on his way past them into the corridor. When he was gone, Bell leaned forward and said, "I've had it, Ira. I need a way out of this. It may be my only chance in a court martial."

"I don't see how any of this helps you."

"If I could find out what's goin' on here, what's in that fucking warehouse—"

"So you find something. What are you going to do? Call the police?" Meyer chuckled, but Bell ignored it. He leaned farther across the table.

"I can write it up," he said, talking fast, trying to work out how he would handle it. "Like a statement, or official report, and you can witness—"

"What! Me witness? And we do what with this—"

"Contact CID, or someone in HQ. We can give it to them. Dobbs mentioned a name."

"That's just it. You don't even know the person. We don't know anyone... no one we can trust." Meyer shifted his empty peach can back and forth on the table and stared up at the ceiling, then back at Bell. "Even if we find out... whatever it is, we can't go to anyone here." He shook his head and grimaced. "The lifers are probably all in on *whatever* it is—or they've shut their eyes. They're not going to hang themselves," his head bobbed, "screw up their retirement. They just want to get by and go home, like the rest of us. And you, Mister Bell," the head motion was now side to side, hands waving in the air, "I really don't see how this, this *evidence* or whatever it is, helps you. You're already in trouble, and you just told me about all of the bad stuff *you think* happened to the others who poked around."

"I've got to do something. Hayes is in deep shit after what he did, you know, during the riot. And Captain Templeton might believe me if I have some evidence. He'd understand that this thing with Gus was all a set up."

"The old 'I been framed' routine. Yeah, right." Meyer gave a snort. "The captain is leaving, and then who are you going to appeal to?"

"I can go to brigade. With enough facts—"

"Do you have a camera?"

"Only a little Brownie."

"Bell, they're getting a personnel draw to go into Cambodia, and the two of us may be on it."

"How do you—"

"If we aren't, we sure will be if we mess around with Hayes."

"How do you know they're getting people for Cambodia?"

"Heard the captain tell Top. I had to take a package to the orderly room, and they were in the captain's office. He'd just come back from Saigon, and they didn't hear me come in. We're supposed to give brigade ten bodies, he said, some from here, some from other locations. They may shut down the compound in My Tho."

Bell sat pensively, chewing on his lower lip. Finally he said, "Sergeant Carter mentioned something this morning—people 'moving out.' More like, he threatened. He didn't say anything specific, but Cambodia's a possibility."

"Now's not the time to get noticed, not any more than you have already."

"Look, will you go down there with me?" Bell asked.

"Down where?"

"Down to the warehouse."

"Oh, for God's sake, Bell!"

Bell sat back in his chair. "I'm desperate. I need something on these bastards." He paused, but Meyer only stared at him. He took a deep breath. "You told me one time you could open any lock made."

Meyer sighed and, shaking his head slowly, pressed his forehead against the back of a raised hand. After a few seconds, though, he began nodding in the affirmative. He looked up. "I can. Learned it from my cousin, at the hardware store."

"You can get us in." Bell came forward again, placing his elbows on the table. "If there's anyone there, we'll just watch from the trees."

"Don't you think they'll have a guard?"

"Maybe, but I doubt it. I've driven down there a couple of times, and I've never seen one."

Meyer looked at him for a long moment, then shrugged and gave in with a faint smile. "Okay, what the hey? But if you call anyone in Long Binh, leave my name out of it."

He picked up the empty peach can and tossed it into the garbage bin behind him. As he turned back to the table and opened his mouth to add something, Cole and Landrieu strolled into the mess hall. They were carrying their MP helmets and wearing their patrol gear.

Cole gave them a broad display of white teeth under his thin moustache, followed by a sniggering laugh. "You boys always spend your afternoons making out in the mess hall?"

Quickly snatching up his list and Tranh's note, Bell said, "Hey, Cole, I thought you were *off* MP duty."

"They need me." Cole raised his free hand in the air, fist clenched, and nodded in Landrieu's direction. "Taylor went on sick call, so I took his place."

"Good God," said Meyer, standing up. "None of us are safe now."

Cole slapped his holster like he was about to draw his .45 and pointed his index finger with his thumb up at Meyer. "Watch it, buster."

Rolling his eyes toward the ceiling, Landrieu walked past them to the kitchen. While he was asking the mama-san for sandwiches to take on patrol, Meyer and Bell slipped by Cole and hurried out the door.

CHAPTER FIFTY
The Warehouse

A PELTING RAIN ARRIVED LATE IN THE DAY and continued well past nightfall, tapering off to a fine mist by the time Bell and Meyer, unlit flashlights in hand, set off down the gravel road. Hordes of mosquitoes rose up to greet them, and a din of frogs filled the air. Peering through the fence, Bell had spied only a few Vietnamese gigging frogs in the ditches along the road. He managed a soft chuckle at the perverted justice of it all, being at the bottom of the food chain. The Vietnamese ate the frogs, the frogs ate the mosquitoes, and the mosquitoes sucked pints of blood out of him and Meyer.

For defense, he carried a half-empty can of army-issued insect repellant in the side pocket of his fatigues. Neither of them carried any other weapon. Not being on duty, they couldn't very well ask Sanderson to open up the armory for them, not for this.

The motor pool, though, was wide open, and Bell had sauntered out with a stray pair of bolt cutters, just in case Meyer wasn't as expert as he claimed. Tucked down one trousers' leg and covered by his fatigue shirt, the eighteen-inch tool forced him to walk stiff legged, almost like a zombie from the movie.

Meyer had volunteered his camera, a slightly superior model to Bell's Brownie, though he wouldn't promise the pictures would turn out since the flash worked only half the time.

A Filipino band was playing for Sanchez's party in the club. A female singer in a shimmery silver halter-top and tight black pants, exposing a flat brown stomach and teardrop navel, gyrated under strobe lights the band had set up around the stage. Although the party was not really Sanchez's going-away bash—it was an emergency leave after all—he'd let it be known *he* was the one who had hired the band. Having achieved victory, he wasn't about to leave without a celebration.

As Bell and Meyer strolled out the gate, they waved to Landrieu and Cole coming in to pick up Thuy to take her home. No one had asked any questions about where they were going or why they were leaving the villa at this hour. Indeed, the stars had aligned to support their expedition. The post on the corner bunker was empty, Sanderson was in the tower from ten until midnight, and Hodge was keeping vigil for their return.

For Hodge was back. Coming into the sleeping bay after twisting Meyer's arm in the mess hall, Bell almost collided with Hodge and Sanderson exiting into the outside corridor. Before he could say anything, Hodge grabbed him in a one-armed embrace.

"God, am I sorry, Bell. I am so fucking sorry." He was shaking his head, his face contorted, eyes brimming with tears.

Bell pulled away and gripped Hodge by the arm.

"No sweat, man. Hey, hey, no sweat. Forget it." He stared at him, feeling chagrin at the pain in Hodge's face. Besides, he didn't want an apology.

"You okay?" he asked. "They treat you okay up there?"

Hodge wiped his eyes with the back of his hand. He looked years older. His cheeks were paler, thinner—no more surfer good looks. Even his hair had lost its sun-bleached streaking. And he seemed far less cocky.

"Hardest part was calling home," he said. "Telling my folks."

Bell narrowed his eyes. *And asking them to save you from the fucking dungeon.*

Hodge must have noticed Bell's look and understood what he was thinking. He shrugged and gave him a taut smile.

"Have to give the captain credit," Hodge said, shaking his head, this time not in any demonstration of agony. "He's the same to me as everybody else, even after what happened—like a fucking piece of granite."

"Heard he got reamed out," Sanderson said from one side. "Letting you go crazy like that, bro."

"I don't know what happened. They released me into his custody and sent me back down here. I'm confined to the building." Hodge took a deep breath and let it out slowly. "He told me to stay sober, behave myself, or he'd see I was gone for good. About the only thing he said the whole way back."

Bell wanted to know what had happened with Glenda and the leave, but he didn't want to ask. It couldn't be good.

"So where are you two going?" he asked instead, gesturing to Sanderson. Sanderson's direction of travel was clearly toward the club.

"Gonna get a beer to celebrate the man's return," Sanderson said, bouncing up and down on the balls of his feet. "Happy hour!"

"Only one," Hodge said, looking off down the corridor.

So Bell followed them into the club, where he convinced Hodge over his one beer that he, Hodge, could be their lookout without violating his parole. He didn't trust Sanderson to stay sober until midnight, even in the tower. All he asked of Sanderson was to snag a key to the front gate from Bowman and give it to Hodge. Then Hodge was to watch from the roof and let Meyer and him back inside—if they were still gone after the last patrol rolled in.

Safely outside the gate, Bell and Meyer crossed the road and hurried along the ditch beside the flooded soccer field—well away from the direct beam of the perimeter lights. Once past the fence line, Bell pulled the bolt cutters out from his pants' leg, and they scurried back across the road, then skulked beneath the canopy of banana and palm trees stretching from the perimeter to the warehouse.

Faint lights shone in the windows of the huts beyond the soccer field and along the canal toward town. On the villa's side of the road, there were only a few hooches farther back under the trees. The windows in those were dark.

"Hope no one saw us," Meyer said. "They might wonder why

we're going in the wrong direction." Meaning away from town.

"Everyone's inside the club or too drunk to care," Bell said, swinging the bolt cutters to one side like a battle ax. He glanced over his shoulder at the compound and the tower jutting above it like the keep of a castle. "Jesus, I shouldn't've had that last beer," he said, then veered off the road toward a tree.

"Hurry up!" Meyer hissed. "This is s-s-spooky as all get-out."

Bell surveyed the underbrush in front of him. They were still a hundred yards short of the warehouse. As he buttoned his fatigue pants, a series of flares shot high into the air over the rice paddies. Then a line of tracers arced across the sky parallel to the canal. Several bursts of rifle fire and an explosion followed.

"Oh, shit," he muttered and grabbed the bolt cutters from where he'd propped them against a tree. He ran back to the road—and collided with Meyer, down on one knee, staring toward the canal. He clasped Meyer's shoulder.

"Rangers must've set up an ambush." His voice would have harmonized with the croaking frogs, had they not fallen silent.

The alert siren at the MP compound wailed behind them. In front, across the canal, the sporadic rifle fire and burr of the machine gun continued.

"Get down!" Meyer grabbed his arm. "Rangers don't shoot us, our guys might. We're nothing but shadows."

"Over there," Bell said, pointing, and with Meyer following, he scrambled toward some low palms. As the firefight across the canal continued, they flattened themselves in a patch of grass. Water soaked through Bell's fatigues, overwhelming the dampness he already felt from the misting rain.

"How are we going to get back inside?" Meyer asked in a hoarse whisper. "If they stay on alert—"

"Bide our time. Sanderson knows we're out here, and he isn't going to open up on us." He took a deep breath. "God, I hope he's not got a bottle up there." He shifted his weight and rested his chin in his hands. "Let's see how bad it gets before we decide what to do."

Meyer didn't answer.

But there were no more flares and no more rifle fire or explosions. A Cobra circled over the rice paddy, then swung across the canal and illuminated the palms near where they were lying in the grass. After an eternity, which Bell's watch showed to be closer to ten minutes, the chopper eased away and off down the canal. The "all clear" sounded at the compound.

"Ever tell you how much I hate being wet?" Meyer said as he got up on his knees and brushed mud and grass off the front of his fatigues.

"Training, my man. Out in the boonies, you'll be a lot wetter'n this."

"Thanks." Standing, Meyer tugged his wet fatigue shirt and trousers away from his body. "Shouldn't we go back?" he said, more a statement than a question.

"No way. We've got plenty of time. And Hodge will wait for us."

"Yeah, you hope. Your show, Inspector Clouseau."

They slunk along the edge of the road until they came to the gravel parking area at the warehouse. From deep in the shadows under a low palm, Bell surveyed the clearing. A single light cast a dull halo in the mist, illuminating little more than a metal door at the nearest corner.

Surprising how dim the light looks, Bell thought, *when it seems so bright from the tower.*

The palm fronds rustled above their heads. There were no sounds beyond the usual ones belonging to the night, and no other lights or movement nearby.

Bell trotted across the parking area, aiming for the door. When he tried to stop, his foot skidded in a mud puddle, and both legs flew out from under him, throwing him backward and sending the bolt cutters flying.

He hit the ground at Meyer's feet.

"You okay?" Meyer asked, leaning down.

"Yeah, fuck!"

He rolled onto his side, then pushed up, out of the muddy water, and struggled to his feet. Limping in a wide circle, he rubbed his hip, then his elbow.

"Just a bruise, I think. Ah-h-h! Hurts like hell." He raked wet sand off his trousers' leg and his arm, then bent down to retrieve the bolt cutters.

"Have to hurry," Meyer said from near the door. "Give me some light."

Bell switched on his flashlight, and shielding it with his body, played the beam over the entrance. Extending all the way across the door was a flat metal bar held in place by a heavy bolt on the left side, an L-shaped anchor in the middle, and another L-shaped anchor on the right doorjamb. Connecting the bar with the right doorjamb anchor was a padlock.

Meyer tugged at the lock and, after examining it for a moment, removed a small leather case from his pocket. He unsnapped the case to reveal a set of picklocks. One after another, he slipped the picklocks into the lock and jiggled them against the tumblers.

"Hurry up!" Bell said. "Thought I heard a sampan."

"Hold the light steady!" Meyer hit his arm, then resumed testing the lock. It gave a click and popped open. "Voila!" Slipping the lock out of the anchor, he stood aside for Bell to see.

"Fan-fucking-tastic!" Bell stepped past him and, hitching the bolt cutters in his belt so that they dangled against his leg, lifted the bar. He wedged it up, at an angle, against the warped door panel. "Now we shall see," he said and pulled the door open a few inches.

Moving his flashlight up and down then back and forth, all he could make out in the dark interior was the shadowy front of a truck and objects along the wall beyond and behind it.

"Nobody here." Not that he expected anyone. He opened the door a bit wider and eased through the narrow opening.

What was that strange smell? A musty old house—with a dozen cats?

Meyer followed him, but only after Bell's urgent beckoning.

Once they were both through the door, Bell turned and said in a whisper, "We can't leave this open," then he jerked the door shut.

From outside came an ominous clank.

"Oh fuck," groaned Meyer. He held up the padlock in Bell's light.

"Fuck, fuck, fuck!" Bell rattled the door. It wouldn't budge more than a quarter inch against the bar.

"So what do we do?" Meyer asked in a loud whisper. He stepped closer to the door and gave it a shove.

"Dunno." Bell felt the sweat pop out on his face and back, warmer than the damp from his wet fatigues. He rattled the door again, harder this time.

"Why didn't you fix the bar?" With a click, Meyer's light flashed on. "So it wouldn't come back down?"

Both lights shone on the door now. Except for a handle to pull it closed, it was a blank surface.

"You came in behind me," Bell said, his voice echoing in the dark. "If you'd put the fucking lock back, the bar wouldn't've gone down."

"You raised the bar; you shut the door," Meyer said, still whispering. "Lot of good four years of college did you."

"Five, and I didn't study breaking and entering." Bell played the light along the doorjamb. He could see a small opening between the door and the jamb, and the outline of the bar on the other side.

"If we had a thin piece of metal, we could slip it through here, lift the bar..." He trailed off in a sigh and rattled the door again. No change in result. "Maybe there's another way out."

"God, I hope so." Meyer was breathing heavily next to Bell's shoulder, his flashlight wavering over the crack. "This is not good, Bell. This is definitely *not* good."

CHAPTER FIFTY-ONE
In the Dark

BELL SWUNG HIS FLASHLIGHT AROUND. Except for their two small circles of light, the warehouse was dark.

"Gotta be a light somewhere," he said. He ran his hand, illuminated by his flashlight, down the wall next to the door.

There it was. A light switch. He flipped it up. Two rows of lights flashed on above them, along with the roar of a fan.

Meyer reached past him and slapped the switch off with his hand.

"You'll wake the dead," he said. With the lights out, the fan roar subsided.

"Doubt anyone can hear it," Bell said. "You ever hear anything down here, when you're in the tower?"

"No. Just sampans. Or vehicles. But somebody in the hooches or on the road might hear it."

"Shit!" Bell paused to think. Then he flipped on the switch again. Lights and fan came back on.

"Just for a minute," he said.

"Wait, don't—"

"To get our bearings."

"We could—" Instead of finishing, Meyer let out a low groan as Bell surveyed the interior and started rapidly cataloguing what he saw—like the competent cop he'd never wanted to be.

A three-quarter-ton truck was parked just past the center of the concrete floor, its bed enclosed in a canvas tarp, its hood pointed toward double garage doors next to the entrance where they stood. Half empty pallets of beer and soda lined the wall beyond the front of the truck. Behind it and all about the rear of the building were boxes, dozens of boxes, boxes of different sizes and shapes, boxes stacked in irregular rows and in stacks of differing heights as if hurriedly deposited on the floor. To the right of this haphazard array of boxes were at least a dozen large wooden crates, like those used to ship appliances or furniture or oversized television consoles and stereo sets back in the World.

In the back corner, to the right of the wooden crates, were rows of tires, standing in head-high columns like huge Oreo cookies. Jeep, truck, maybe civilian, Bell couldn't tell for certain. Next to them, dwarfed by the tires, were two small wooden crates that didn't seem to fit with the commercial merchandise; they looked military.

Above, four bare metal rafters stretched from the front of the warehouse to the back beneath a low-pitched roof. The two outside rafters rested on metal supports braced by diagonal struts. On the two middle rafters were a series of overhead lights, three on each rafter, mounted in reflective covers similar to street lamps. The lights brightly illuminated only the space immediately below them and left large areas of the building in shadows, especially beyond the ¾ ton truck and the boxes at the back.

The noisy fan vent was in the front wall, above the double garage doors through which the truck had been backed in.

There were no windows and no other obvious exits. Between where they stood at the entrance and the front of the truck, the floor of the warehouse was empty.

Bell switched off the lights and the fan. Not much more than a minute had passed.

"Okay," he said, no longer whispering. "We just stay calm."

"Speak for yourself," said Meyer.

"Has to be something here to use on the door, to pry it open." He waved his flashlight in a wide arch across the front of the building. "Maybe we can get those big doors open." He took a deep breath." Don't worry."

"I worry." Meyer was already heading for the garage doors. "I only hope no one else wanders in."

Together they examined the doors, moving their lights over every fissure and seam. The doors opened on hinges, out to the sides—and they were secured on the outside.

After mutual exclamations of disgust, Bell swung his flashlight beam around to the body of the truck. There were no markings, and it looked like it had been repainted. He followed the light to the driver's side, opened the door, and started to climb in. The bolt cutters caught on the metal frame and sent him sprawling against the steering wheel.

Damn good thing, I didn't hit the horn, he thought—then remembered no one outside should be able to hear them. He hoped. But it would've scared Meyer shitless. He grunted, almost a chuckle. *Yeah, me, too.*

He removed the bolt cutters from his belt and leaned them against the running board. Then he began bouncing the flashlight beam around the cab.

No identifying documents. The package compartment was empty. All he found were a couple of cigarette butts on the floorboard and some candy wrappers with Vietnamese writing.

He slid out of the seat and, retrieving his bolt cutters, closed the door softly. Hitching the bolt cutters back in his belt, he circled the truck to the back.

Meyer, who had been examining the pallets of soft drinks and beer along the wall in front of the truck, was now poking around among the stacks of boxes behind it, calling out his findings in a low voice: ivory soap, Sony tape recorders, Nabisco crackers, Vienna sausage. The boxes contained almost every kind of nonperishable good GIs could buy at the airfield PX: toiletries of all kinds, canned fruits and meat, radios, tape players, cartons of cigarettes—especially cartons of cigarettes.

While Meyer did his inventory, Bell ran his hand along the truck bumper and bent close to it with his light. Under the fresh paint, there was the faint outline of "ENG." Engineers.

So this is where their missing ¾ ton truck ended up.

He stood and leaned over the gate and into the back. Nothing but a few boxes up toward the front, next to the cab. He glanced at the boxes stacked high behind him. The glow of a flashlight shone above a row farther back where Meyer was bent down reading labels aloud: toothpaste, chewing gum, Bayer Aspirin, a box of condoms, Chesterfield Kings—and a big box of toilet paper.

Had someone been unloading the truck? Or were they starting to load it?

Bell began wending his way among the stacks, reading the labels: shirts-civilian, sunglasses, Winston Kings, flip-flops, foot powder, socks, boots, underwear. A few on top were wide open with the flaps up and almost empty, like the contents had been removed piecemeal.

And distributed retail to the local consumers?

It wasn't only PX goods. There was just about everything they had in their own supply room—or in any U.S. Army supply room. And on top of one stack, there was a small box marked RX: Tetracycline.

There was as exclamation off to his left: "Ha, look at this!"

Bell came out from behind a row of boxes and shifted his light in that direction. Meyer was standing over a low stack of wooden crates lining the wall beyond the rear of the ¾ ton truck. He was shining his flashlight down into an open crate.

"Scotch," he said, "Ballantine's." He swung his light down the line of crates. "Chivas Regal in that one. Think it's the remains of Beadle's heist?"

"Not much left if it is," Bell said.

Meyer placed his flashlight on top of an adjacent crate and pried off the top of one labeled Chivas Regal. From inside, he pulled out a fifth and held it up in Bell's light.

"Want a snort? I don't drink—not Scotch."

"I'll grab a bottle on the way out," Bell said. He paused, holding his light on the Chivas Regal. "Or maybe you'll learn to like it and help me pass the time."

"Not here I won't," Meyer said and dropped the bottle back in place with a clink of glass on glass. He picked up his flashlight and edged forward, toward the front of the truck.

"Half a pallet of Schlitz—up there." He pointed his flashlight to drink cases stacked eight and nine high on the wall between the truck and the large garage doors at the front of the building. The passing beam revealed two smaller, double doors nestled between the crates of Scotch and pallets of beer, doors that the truck had hidden from their view when Bell turned on the overhead lights.

They rushed to try their new find, but these doors, too, were barred and padlocked on the outside.

"Fuck!" said Bell, rattling the doors.

Meyer grabbed his arm. "Watch it!" he said. "There could—"

"I doubt it. There's only a dock out there, and it's still early for sampans." Bell looked at his watch. "Not even midnight yet."

"But you don't know when they'll come get this stuff. This is a regular distribution center—"

"For shit stolen from the PX," Bell said, finishing the sentence. "Why don't you take some pictures?"

"We need more light." Now back at the rear of the truck, Meyer was angling his flashlight beam over the irregular rows of boxes, toward the tires in the far corner. "Let's go see what's back there," he said.

Leading the way, Meyer wove among the boxes. At the tires, he ran his flashlight beam up and down the columns, then stood on his toes to peer over them. Bell went past him to the pair of small wooden crates by the wall.

"No markings," Meyer said from behind him. "Could be ours—"

"What the hell!" Bell called out, his voice echoing in the rafters. He held up an object he had removed from one of the wooden crates. They both lit it up with their flashlights.

A grenade. Holding it out at arm's length like it was trying to bite him, Bell canted his light to the side of the wooden crate. "M26," he said. "Like the ones in the ammo bunker, 'cept the lot numbers are sanded off."

"What were you—"

"Inventory for Sanchez." He swept his light along the wall behind the tires. "What the fuck!"

Carefully replacing the grenade in its nest, he slid into a narrow opening between the tires and the wall. Meyer followed.

There were a dozen or more M-16s leaning cheek by jowl against the wall. Several had magazines in them. Bell picked up the closest one—one with a magazine—and examined the side under their flashlights.

"Has a serial number," he said, hefting the M-16 in one hand. "We can take it, get Sanderson to check the number."

"Why?" said Meyer. His light bounced from a shrug. "What does it matter? No one cares."

Bell didn't answer. Placing his flashlight on the floor, he released the magazine and checked the chamber, then shoved the magazine back home. "This could prove useful," he said. He started to chamber a round, then thought better of it. Not yet. Not while they were stumbling around in the dark.

"We need to get out of here," Meyer said. Pointing his flashlight past Bell, he illuminated the space between the wall and the columns of tires, then beyond. "I think there's a door over there."

"But I didn't see—"

Meyer was already backing out of the narrow opening, so he followed, still carrying the M-16.

There was a door—with a real door knob.

"Back door?" Bell said, puzzled.

"Don't think so." Meyer moved his light up the wall, revealing a black void where the wall ended and the rafters extended into darkness. The wall was really nothing but a plywood partition.

The doorknob turned easily and Bell shoved the door open. The dancing beams of their flashlights showed a small office—gray metal desk and gray metal file cabinet, swivel chair behind the desk and a couple of chairs facing it. Next to the file cabinet was a small floor safe, like the ones in old black-and-white gangster movies.

The inside wall to the left of this setup held another closed door.

Shining his light upward, Bell could see that the office, like the main part of the building, had no ceiling below the rafters. The shaft of light gleamed on a shiny metal roof more than six feet above the top of the inside partition. But to the left side, there appeared to be something flat resting on the rafters.

Meyer was halfway to the other door, when Bell, lingering at the entrance, froze. Had he heard tires on gravel?

"Shine your light here," Meyer said, his voice a normal tone.

Bell listened. There was only silence, except for scratching noises coming from Meyer.

"Bell?" Meyer said. "Can you help me here?"

Bell shrugged. "Must be getting jumpy," he said.

Stepping gingerly past the chairs, he directed his flashlight toward Meyer, crouched by the second door, using his picklocks to try to open it.

"More light," Meyer said. Meyer's flashlight was on the floor, tilted up against his foot.

"That doesn't go outside," Bell said, coming up behind Meyer.

"You have a better idea? Here hold this... and keep the light steady." He handed Bell the leather case with the other picklocks.

Bell propped the M-16 against the wall, took the leather case, and reached his flashlight past Meyer's arm to shine on the lock. The lock clicked, and Meyer shoved the door open.

They found themselves inside another room, longer and darker than the office behind them. To the left of the door, stacked in a pyramid against the plywood partition separating them from the main part of the warehouse, was a row of lumpy burlap sacks. The pyramid ended in stair steps almost to the top of the wall. A foot or so above the last row showed the edge of a large partition, like those making up the wall, lying across the exposed beams. The loose partition extended out over the warehouse floor, as if stored across the rafters to be out of the way.

The room was empty except for the burlap sacks—and a few rats. A long, naked tail disappeared into a small crevice among the sacks. There was no other way out for anything larger.

Meyer slipped inside the long room and swept his flashlight around the interior. Bell was about to follow, when, again, he thought he heard something, this time a muffled sound from the front of the warehouse.

"Someone's outside," he said, *sotto voce.*

Whipping around, he lunged back across the office—and stumbled over a chair in front of the desk. The chair fell. As he grabbed for it, the handle of the bolt cutters in his belt caught under one of its arms. But to his relief, he avoided a resounding crash. He righted the chair and listened. Outside there were voices—raised voices—near the front entrance. Vietnamese voices.

From the office doorway, he stared out across the warehouse floor, first shining his light toward the canvas top of the truck, then at the wide array of boxes between him and the front door and finally at the columns of tires in the back corner. Where could he hide? Where could they both hide?

"Meyer, Meyer," he called in a too-loud whisper.

Someone rattled the entrance door they had left closed, and barred, without the padlock—now in Meyer's fatigue pocket.

CHAPTER FIFTY-TWO
Hide and Seek

SWITCHING OFF HIS FLASHLIGHT, Bell stuffed it into a side pocket and started back into the office, toward the shadows cast by Meyer's light. Then Meyer's light blinked out.

He froze. He wanted to join Meyer—and reach the M-16, but now he couldn't see his hand in front of his face.

The front door clanged open. A male voice rang out, and lights came on, along with the roar of the exhaust fan. The down-directed lamps leaked only a dim glow over the top of the partition and through the open door into the office.

He had to decide which way to go—back in the office for the M-16 and into the storeroom with Meyer, or out among the boxes. They couldn't see him back here—not yet. But he had to move fast.

With three long strides, he was away from the office and inside the maze of cardboard boxes and wooden crates. Better they split up—maybe one of them could escape. And he'd have a better chance in the main part of the building, where all the exits were. The fan would cover his movements. He hoped.

The Vietnamese were conversing in high-pitched agitation that carried above the noise of the fan. *Ah, fuck*, Bell thought, *because there's no lock on the door.* He made out three voices, one of them a raspy female's.

Bent low and wending his way among the hodgepodge of boxes, Bell found a place in the shadows near the ¾ ton truck where he could see the front of the warehouse. Just inside the entrance stood three people he didn't want to meet here, or anywhere: Madame Phoung, the ubiquitous Major Binh, and Phan, the frog-faced civilian cop who'd pulled his service revolver on him.

The major and the madame were bickering loudly in Vietnamese.

As he watched, Phan broke off from the other two and headed across the open warehouse floor, directly toward him. At the same time, a whisper of cool air kissed his neck. Twisting around, he saw Meyer crouched behind him, at an opening in the maze not far from the office door. He was waving frantically for Bell to come.

Bell shook his head and jabbed his finger at Meyer to go back. What he wanted was for Meyer to hide in the storeroom, and get the M-16.

A loud ripping noise came from close in front of Bell, and Meyer disappeared. Bell snapped his head around.

Through a gap between the boxes, he spied Phan's uniformed legs not more than two rows in front of him. The white shirt seemed to be fumbling in a box. After a couple of minutes, the legs pivoted away, and Bell saw Phan go past another gap in the boxes. He was peeling the wrapper off a candy bar—and he was headed toward the office door.

Bell dropped to his knees and scooted into a cave-like opening between two large appliance crates. The bolt cutters dug into his side. Sliding them out from his belt, he carefully placed them on the cement floor next to his knees.

Another light came on at the rear of the building, shining over the partition for the office. *Oh shit!* Bell thought. *Meyer. The M-16.* His heart wasn't just racing; it was pounding like a hammer on an anvil.

He strained to hear what Phan was doing. There were no shouts, so Meyer hadn't been discovered. The major and the madame were still arguing, but in lowered voices, at the front of the building.

Then an excited stream of Vietnamese rattled out not more than ten yards from where he was huddled between the boxes. Phan.

Major Binh and Madame Phoung ceased their argument, and the three voices quickly came together in the open area not far from the office door.

Had Phan discovered the rifle? Were they going to search in there? Search in here?

Bell looked frantically about. As the voices continued in a staccato echo over the noise of the exhaust fan, he decided his only route of escape was to the front, away from the office, to where there was a way out.

Crawling on hands and knees, he was half out of his hidey-hole, when he remembered the bolt cutters. He reached behind him and grabbed them by the handle, making a scraping noise on the cement floor that sounded like chalk on a blackboard. He froze, listened a moment to the voices—unchanged—then scrambled around the end of the row of boxes, away from the office door and the voices, and past another two rows and the crates of scotch along the wall.

Madame Phoung's voice rose in a singsong harangue that, along with the exhaust fan, drowned out the other two and, he hoped, any sound that came from him or from Meyer.

He slipped past the rear gate of the ¾ ton truck, to its far side next to the canal, where he was in deep shadows, away from the overhead lights. Breathless, he leaned against the truck's side slats, near the rear wheel. Trying to control his heart rate and his breathing, he stared up at the rafters.

What he saw made his jaw drop. A bare arm reached out from the overhead partition they had seen lying across the rafters above the sacks in the storeroom and extending out over the main part of the warehouse.

The hand waved to him.

That fucking Meyer. That crazy fucking Meyer.

He must've climbed the stack of burlap sacks and edged out onto the partition. There he would be hidden from anyone entering the storeroom and, above the lights, in a dark recess safe from the view of anyone at the front of the building.

Then Bell saw the thin wooden partition sag.

It was held in place only by the steel beams spanning the building. The hand above him disappeared, and the sagging shifted more toward one side, over a beam. There was a protesting creak he could hear even above the fan. It almost sent him running for the front door.

Instead, he held his breath and listened.

Though less distinct, the voices continued unabated, unchanged by the creaking partition. Madame Phoung was still berating somebody or something. It sounded like they were moving around in the office. Or were they in the storeroom?

Above him, the partition sagged a bit more and gave another sharp creak.

Shit! Keep still, he wanted to yell. Meyer outweighed him by a good thirty pounds.

It should've been him up there.

To his front, there was a soft "whump" muffled by the fan. A gust of air swept past his trousers from under the truck. Above, the partition creaked again.

The front door of the warehouse clanged shut like the ringing of a bell, clear and distinct from the roar of the fan.

"Hey, what are you people doin'?" came a yell from the entrance. "I don't have all the fucking night,"

Hayes.

Bell dropped to his knees and peered around the rear bumper of the truck.

Beyond the rows of boxes, Major Binh and Phan were hurrying across the open floor to the front of the warehouse, Binh carrying Bell's abandoned M-16 and Phan toting a burlap sack. The major waved the M-16, upright and not threatening, at Hayes, who continued walking toward him.

"Lock gone," said Binh, loud enough for Bell to hear him clearly. "This in there," he gestured back toward the office. "You here before?"

"Hell no. I just got away. Damn warrant officers were probably screwing around."

"I no like."

"Doesn't matter..." Hayes' voice dropped as he and Binh met in the middle of the open floor, and the two began conversing in low, intense tones. Phan went on past them, carrying his burlap sack toward the exit. Not long after Phan moved out of Bell's view, Madame Phoung shuffled into it. She remained silent, off to one side. If any of them had heard the creaking partition, it was forgotten.

Phan soon returned, without the sack, and as he hustled toward the back of the warehouse, the major handed him the M-16. Then Hayes and Binh, still talking and gesturing at each other, drifted after him, away from the truck, toward the back corner and the columns of tires. Madame Phoung shuffled along behind them until they were all out of sight, but not out of hearing. The Madame joined the conversation, and the volume rose in a mix of Vietnamese and Pidgin English.

"She worthless fucking whore," yelled Major Binh in the first words Bell could understand. The major hove into sight, advancing toward the rear of the truck, Madame Phoung not far behind him, her voice shrieking at his back in Vietnamese.

Bell looked around. Where could he go? To the front? Under the truck? At least he was shielded from the lights here, and in dark shadows.

Not more than ten yards from the far side of the truck, the major pivoted and appeared to speak past Madame Phoung as she wagged a finger in his face. Hayes came into view. His leathery face was impassive, his eyes under his field marshal's cap fixed on Binh.

Binh was ignoring the madame and talking to Hayes in a subdued growl. All Bell could make out was "jeep" and "grenade."

Sweat was streaming down his sides from his armpits. The collar and back of his fatigue shirt felt like a sopping wet dishrag.

Madame Phoung fell silent, then she turned and quickly shuffled her sandals around behind Hayes. Bell was struck by the thought: *she's afraid of Binh.*

When Hayes finally responded to Binh, he gestured toward the truck and said in a loud, sneering hiss that overrode the fan noise, "Take what the fuck you want. I'm done with this fucking place; I'm done with all of you fucking people."

"You no talk..." Binh began, taking a step toward Hayes, but Hayes stopped him with a raised hand.

"You shouldn't have offed the boy-san," Hayes said. "That was—"

"He rat on me," shouted Binh.

"Never happen," yelled Madame Phoung from behind Hayes.

Hayes shook his head. "That was dumb as hell." He jabbed a finger at Binh, then swept his arm in a wide arc toward the boxes and the columns of tires. "Fucking QCs'll be here at dawn—maybe before—and they'll clean all this out. And they're after your ass for sure now. Do what the fuck you want with this shit."

"No sweat," Binh said, backing away. He was close enough now that Bell could hear him clearly, even talking in a normal voice. "We load truck. Sampans come, maybe one hour. Everything else we blow to heavens." He threw both hands high up over his head in a comical gesture and yelled, "Boom!"

Uh-oh, Bell thought. He couldn't see the major's face, but he could imagine the malevolent grin. Hayes looked back over his shoulder, toward the columns of tires in the corner. "Yeah, I see your boy."

"Use claymores and—"

"That fucking clown'll blow us all up," Hayes said.

"Hah! First we take what we want."

"Well, I want some of that scotch." Without waiting for Binh to reply, Hayes marched past him, toward the back of the truck.

At the word "scotch," and before Hayes completed his first two steps, Bell leaped sideways, like a cat, and slid under the bed of the ¾ ton and behind the rear wheel. No longer frozen in fear, he held the bolt cutters tightly to his chest to keep them from hitting the floor or the metal of the chassis.

Craning his neck—his heart pounding, his breath coming in

quick, shallow gasps—he watched Hayes' boots pass behind the rear of the truck, not more than five feet away from him.

There was a grunt. The sound of Hayes lifting one of the crates?

Could they see him? As quietly as he could, Bell scrunched up against the rear wheel, near where Hayes was walking back past him. He just hoped that Madame Phoung's and Major Binh's eyes were on Hayes and not focused on the floor under the truck.

Watching Hayes' jungle boots, he saw them go to where Madame Phoung's sandals were still planted. There was no sign of Major Binh.

"Here, take the booze," Hayes said. "Out to the jeep."

"I want my—" Madame Phoung.

"No! No! Hurry, *di di*! You go with me." Then lower. "Before that shit decides to even the score."

Leaning on one shoulder, his head almost touching the cement floor, Bell could see Madame Phoung's short frame sag under the weight of the case of scotch that Hayes must have dropped into her arms. She staggered off toward the front entrance, bent forward with her burden and swaying side-to-side, sandals slapping the floor. Hayes followed her to the front, but he was soon back. Ignoring Binh and Phan, wherever they were, Hayes retraced his steps to the wall, where he picked up a second case of scotch. This time he went around the front of the truck. Bell heard a door open and slam shut.

Hayes returned twice more for additional cases, but Madame Phoung failed to reappear. After his third trip for the scotch, Hayes returned once more, but this time he crossed the floor well away from the truck and made for the back of the building. As his boots disappeared from sight, he yelled out, "Hope the fuck you know what you're doin'."

Bell felt a cold shiver run down his spine. *Was he talking to Binh? Or to Phan? What were they doing back there?* With no one in view, he edged out from under the truck and crouched beside the rear wheel. Kneeling low to the floor and edging forward a bit, he could see all the way across the warehouse to the column of tires. Binh and Phan were both there.

Hayes reappeared close to the truck, blocking his view and moving far more quickly than before. In one hand, he carried a briefcase, a courier's case like the one he'd received from the Green Beret in My Tho. With the other hand, he half carried, half dragged a loosely packed duffle bag. He wasn't looking in Bell's direction, but back toward the far corner.

"Happy trails, pardner," he called out. "Fun while it lasted." Snapping his head straight ahead, he gave a snorting laugh and added, "Fucking amateurs."

He disappeared toward the front entrance. In a moment, Bell heard the front door clang shut.

His arm and hand holding the bolt cutters had grown numb; his hip throbbed from where he had fallen at the entrance; his knees ached from the cement floor. Grabbing onto the side slats of the truck, he pulled himself upright and leaned against it. From above him came a low rasping sound. He looked up. Meyer's partition was sagging even more. Only an inch or so extended over one of the rafters. All that was saving them from detection was the roar of the fan—and their adversaries' distractions at the back.

They're going to blow this place up, raced through Bell's mind. *That's what Binh said.* He bit his lip, trying to figure out how much time they had.

The QCs are coming—when? At dawn? After Binh finishes taking what he wants, and driving the truck out, loaded with boxes. Or maybe in sampans. Had Binh had a warning from someone with the QCs?

He glanced behind him, at the doors leading to the dock, then checked his watch—not midnight yet. But the sampans could come anytime now and open those doors.

Meyer would be okay, hidden up there. But what the fuck would *he* do when they started loading the truck? When the sampans and

Binh's minions showed up? What the fuck was he going to do? And he had to pee again.

New noises came from the rear of the warehouse.

Edging forward along the side of the truck, he reached the front and peered over the hood. Major Binh and Phan were opening boxes and talking, the major's voice taking the form of commands. Then he bent down and hefted a box in both hands. After readjusting his grip, he headed for the truck.

Phan quickly followed him with a second box.

Bell ducked down below the hood and prayed that the two were only going to load the back—and not coming up to the cab.

He heard the rear gate drop, and the truck gave a slight shudder. He more felt than heard someone, probably Phan, climb in the back and slide first one then the other box across the bed of the truck and up against the cab.

For the next ten minutes, the process was repeated, one box after another. Kneeling on one knee, his head down, looking under the truck, Bell watched the feet—a pair of boots and a pair of polished policeman's shoes—coming and going at the rear. When at last there was a long pause, and no feet in view, he peeked over the hood.

The two were struggling with a large appliance crate, lifting it, carrying it a few feet, then dropping it again. When they finally succeeded in lugging it forward across the warehouse floor, he ducked down again.

The truck shook and visibly dipped as they shoved the crate into the back.

Three more of the large wooden crates followed the first.

He thought he heard something behind him, outside on the dock. Binh's sampan moving crew? If they came through the double doors, where could he go? Under the truck? Eventually someone would notice him. Or the truck would drive out of the building, leaving him in its wake like a pile of water buffalo shit lying on the floor. Even if the lights were out and they didn't see him, they'd lock the place up.

Or maybe not. Just blow it sky high—with him and Meyer inside.

Phan and Binh hadn't been back for a few minutes. Their voices—at a different pitch from the fan—drifted to him from across the warehouse, along with the smell of cigarette smoke. Bell raised his head and looked past the hood.

There was a substantial dent in the haphazard rows of boxes. Phan and Binh stood in the newly cleared area, apparently resting from the exertion of carrying the appliance crates. Phan was holding a lit cigarette.

Major Binh gestured toward the column of tires in the far corner and appeared to give an order. Dropping his cigarette to the floor, Phan ground it out under the toe of his shoe, then grabbed the M-16 from where it leaned against a low stack of boxes and slung it over one shoulder. He proceeded to the corner, but not to the tires.

Going down on one knee, he lifted the top off one of the small wooden boxes there. The top of the second box was already lying beside it on the floor.

Then Bell saw what they had been doing, and why Hayes had been in a hurry to leave.

Near the boxes there was a spool of thin wire and what looked like pliers or wire cutters. Lined up next to the wall beyond them were the contents of the already open crate: M26 grenades, several of them with long strands of wire swirled in coils beside them. One end of each coil was looped several times through the pin of the grenade, booby traps in the making.

Phan grabbed the second wooden crate by its rope handles and carried it closer to the stacks of tires. Dropping it to the floor—hard enough to make Bell cringe—the white-shirt cop unslung the M-16 and leaned it against the wall.

Then he turned and hurried in the direction of the ¾ ton truck, and Bell.

Bell slid down and under the front of the truck, almost hitting his head on the bumper. But Phan veered off—toward the entrance. Bell lay on his side, the bolt cutters wedged painfully under his thigh, and stared past the front wheel.

The major was nowhere to be seen. In the office? Outside? No, he would have seen him go past.

After a couple of minutes, the white shirt returned, his legs and polished shoes moving briskly across the open floor. From under the truck, Bell could see the bottom of a jerry can—sloshing with liquid? Next to the far leg was what looked like an army first aid kit with a large red cross on its cover.

"Shit, shit!" Bell said under his breath. His heart quickened its already fast pace. "What the fuck's he doing?"

He low crawled from under the truck, the bolt cutters in the crook of his arms like a rifle, then stood and peered over the hood. Maybe he could slug Phan, if he came near. Or perhaps sneak along the outside wall to get closer.

But that still left the major and his .45.

Phan was down on one knee next to the crate of grenades he had opened near the tires. He was measuring out lengths of white cord from a spool.

Bell's memory flashed back to Tony, in the high grass by the road. The white cord around his ankles. *But why? He ratted to the QCs? Was that it?*

Phan cut several lengths of cord, then opened the first aid kit and took out a role of medical tape. Removing several of the grenades from the crate, he wrapped one with white tape, twice around. The lever secured, he pulled the pin and threaded a yard-long piece of cord through the space under the lever.

Bell swiveled his neck, trying to see Meyer on top of the partition. No sign of him.

How were they going to avoid getting blown up? Announce themselves to Major Binh? "Hey, wait. It's us. We were just having a look around. Bye now."

Bang, you're dead. Or boom.

Major Binh appeared next to Phan. Was he coming from the office? He proceeded to inspect his minion's handiwork—two grenades with white bands of tape around them, linked by a strand of white rope. As Binh, and Bell, watched, Phan spliced another grenade to the strand, about six inches from the last one. Then another. Except this one had no tape around it. Phan looped the cord through the grenade's pin and tied it.

The major made a comment, and Phan responded by pointing to the column of tires and then to the jerry can of liquid beside him. An animated discussion ensued but stopped dead at a loud clang and a sudden whoosh of air. Both men pivoted toward the entrance.

Bell twisted around as someone yelled, "What the hell's goin' on here?"

Bell couldn't see him, but he recognized the voice. *Cole.*

"Where's Bell? Where's Meyer?" It was Landrieu.

Bell started to jump out from behind the truck and yell, "Here I am!" But he stopped when he saw Phan grab the M-16 from against the wall—and chamber a round.

CHAPTER FIFTY-THREE
Saved or Damned?

COLE CAME INTO VIEW, THEN LANDRIEU, several yards behind him and nearer the truck. They were edging forward across the empty floor between the truck and the entrance.

Bell ducked down in the shadows behind the truck's hood. *Why'd they barge in like that? Surely, they cased the place, saw that the front door was the only way in, the only way that wasn't barred. And they must've seen the major's jeep.*

"Where are they?" Landrieu repeated, his voice lower but still audible to Bell, no more than a first down away. How could he get Landrieu's attention—without exposing himself?

Neither MP had drawn his .45, though Bell could see Cole, who had fallen behind Landrieu, caressing the butt of his. Both were eyeing Phan. The M-16 was across Phan's chest, not pointed at them.

"What you want?" Major Binh was doing the yelling now. "Why you here?" He jerked his .45 out of the holster and waved it at the MPs. "This Vietnamese place," he yelled, this time almost a scream, and began advancing toward Landrieu, as if to force him back out the door. "You no belong here."

Phan was slinking along to one side and slightly behind Binh, in the direction of the truck. Away from the tires—and the grenades lying on the floor. The M-16 was angled up, but Phan's finger was inside the trigger guard. He could drop the barrel at any second and fire.

The major, still advancing, leveled his .45 at Landrieu, swung it around at Cole, then brought it back to Landrieu.

"You leave," Binh shouted, jerking the .45 toward the entrance. "You go now!"

Both Landrieu and Cole raised their hands, chest high in front of them. They had come to a dead stop and seemed to be wavering on backing up.

"Okay," said Landrieu. "But you haven't seen our guys?"

"Nobody here," Binh shouted. "No Americans. You go away."

Bell's heart raced. What could he do? Binh might shoot Landrieu—and Cole—at any second. Or he might just chase them out, leaving him and Meyer stranded in here until... until what?

He had to do something.

He stared down at the bolt cutters in his hands. His only other weapons were the flashlight and the can of insect repellant. Maybe he could use those to distract Binh long enough for Landrieu and Cole to get their weapons out.

Landrieu was still trying to argue with Major Binh. But he had begun backing up, toward the entrance—and away from Bell.

"We were told two of our people were down here," Landrieu said, loud enough for Bell to hear him clearly above the fan. "You no see them?"

"Not here! Not here!" Binh shouted, waving his .45 and still advancing. "No Americans here!"

The two MPs must have seen all the PX goods, so how could Binh let them out of here alive? Not unless they were already privy to this business.

Cole maybe, Bell decided, *but not Landrieu.*

They were all four in his line of vision now. He could see that Landrieu's eyes were fixed on Binh, and Binh's .45. Cole, though, was shifting more toward the front of the truck, his hands held out to his sides like a West Texas gunfighter, eyeing his adversary, Phan, who was gliding like a snake from the end of one row of boxes to the next, toward the rear of the truck.

Why was Phan going there?

Cole glanced from Phan to the front of the truck and his eyes met Bell's. Cole's only reaction was a slight lift of one black eyebrow before he returned to watching Phan.

Cole knows we're here, so they can leave and go get help. But can they get back before Binh clears out—and blows this place up? Then Bell had another thought. *Maybe Cole won't tell Landrieu or anyone else? He despises me—and Meyer.*

Binh will never let them leave. They know too much. I've got to do something, and I've got to do it now.

Binh had stopped, but he was still shouting and waving his .45. Then he dipped his head to one side.

Checking on Phan's progress?

When the white shirt reached the truck, he'd have cover to fire at both Landrieu and Cole, and quick-draw Cole would never get his .45 out in time, not to shoot a man with a rifle at the ready. A rifle that could fire multiple bursts in several directions in seconds—or on fully automatic, seventeen rounds in a heartbeat.

What could he do? Throw the can of insect spray or the flashlight to distract Phan and Binh? He had a good throwing arm, could throw a strike nine times out of ten—well, maybe five out of ten.

Maybe he could hit Phan with the flashlight. Or the bolt cutters? That left Binh with a drawn .45, and a nasty disposition toward Americans.

For the first time, he realized that the flashlight was gone. He'd lost it.

He still had the bolt cutters. Not easy to throw, but he could poleax Phan with it—if Phan came close enough. And didn't see him first.

If only Cole would look at him again, he'd show him the bolt cutters, let him know what he was thinking. But Cole was focused on Phan.

Bell slipped past the right headlight and down the side of the truck, past the passenger door and the canvas-covered bed. Stopping by the rear bumper, he crouched down to watch Phan moving toward him.

Take a run at Phan now? Too far. The M-16 would cut him down in a flash. Throw the can of insect spray, yell to distract the white shirt, so that Landrieu and Cole can get out their weapons? Too risky.

From above came a scraping noise, and he looked up to see the partition sway and shudder. He swore under his breath. "Keep still, damn it, Meyer."

Phan glanced up, as well, but it didn't seem to dawn on him that there was someone above him. He continued toward the back of the truck, moving as if he and Cole near the front were engaged in a slow pantomime dance.

There was a loud rasping sound above, and Bell jerked his head up.

The front of the partition suddenly broke free of its mooring, and Meyer appeared, hurtling feet first toward the floor. Meyer grabbed for the nearest beam, caught it, and pulled himself up—but couldn't hold on. The partition slammed against a diagonal support behind Phan and canted to one side, breaking Meyer's fall and becoming a slide that propelled him downward at a forty-five degree angle.

Even as Meyer began his descent, Bell leaped from behind the truck and ran at Phan—who was concentrating on Meyer, and tracking his fall with the barrel of the M-16.

At the first sound of the partition slipping from the rafter, Binh had spun around to point his pistol at the falling objects. After a moment's hesitation, Landrieu started forward, pulling his own .45 from the holster.

Then Phan brought the M16 back around.

Bell swung the bolt cutters like a baseball bat. They caught the shorter white shirt a glancing blow in his arm and shoulder—and the M-16 erupted in one long burst, emptying the magazine as its barrel arced upward.

Bringing the bolt cutters back to strike again, Bell saw it all. The rifle burst cutting Major Binh down like a giant sword, the bullets slashing off the top of his head, the huge bloody gash in his chest and shoulder.

Binh's body pirouetted and fell backward and to one side—flesh, blood, and bone flying in every direction as the loud bur-r-r of the rifle echoed through the warehouse and the spent bullets ricocheted off the walls.

A large section of brain, almost the entire right hemisphere, fell with a liquid plop in a red-tinged, white mass less than a yard from Bell's feet.

As Bell stood dazed and deafened, bolt cutters raised over Phan's head, Phan flew backward like he'd been hit with a cannon ball.

Bell felt the concussion from the discharge of the .45 as much as he heard it. Swiveling his head like an automaton, he stared at Cole, crouched a few yards away, his .45 extended at eye level in both hands.

"Killed the motherfucker," Cole yelled and leaped up, throwing his hands in the air. "Killed him deader'n shit!"

"You could've hit Bell," yelled Meyer, now on his feet and hobbling around.

Landrieu, who had checked his forward motion when the rifle fired and dropped to the floor, slowly got up on his hands and knees.

"You guys okay?" he yelled, looking around wide-eyed at the carnage. Blood and bits of flesh had sprayed across his left arm and speckled his face.

Lying directly in front of Landrieu, face up on the floor, was Major Binh. Except there wasn't a face, or not much of one above the jaw and mouth.

"Holy shit!" Cole said. His .45 up in both hands, he was edging forward, gawking at the bloody torso and mutilated head.

"No one else hit?" Landrieu yelled again, his voice dropping a notch.

"I'm okay," Meyer shouted over the fan. "Better check on Bell."

Bell's legs wouldn't support him. He dropped the bolt cutters and sank to the floor, his eyes fixed on the slimy red-and-white convolutions in Major Binh's brain.

"I feel sick," he moaned.

As Landrieu and Meyer reached him, he bent forward and vomited, then fell over on his side, bathed in sweat and shaking against the cold that pierced him to the core, cold that was unrelated to the stifling heat inside the warehouse.

Landrieu turned to face Cole. "Goddamn it, Cole." He wiped his face on his rolled-up shirtsleeve. "Did you have to shoot the motherfucker? He'd emptied the rifle already."

Cole stared at him, wide-eyed with excitement. "You see what the '16 did to that gook? Fuck-ing amazing. Just fucking amazing."

"Get us out of here," sputtered Meyer. "Quit *dick*-ing around."

Bell lay on his side, shivering. Meyer reached down and grabbed him by the arm, pulling him up. As he rose to one knee, Bell finally released his grip on the bolt cutters, and they clattered to the floor.

Landrieu, still glaring at his partner, absentmindedly lifted the bottom of his fatigue shirt to his face and began swabbing flecks of foreign matter off his nose and cheek. Awakening to what he was doing, he dropped the shirttail, then ordered Cole to cover the corpses—"to keep the flies off," he said—and went to help drag Bell outside.

***

With Bell settled in the front passenger's seat of the patrol jeep, Meyer asked Landrieu from the back, "Why did you come down here?"

"When we got in, Hodge was at the gate waiting for you two. Must've been shortly after midnight, maybe half past. He said you'd gone down here and asked us to check on you. We saw the ARVN jeep..." He shook his head. "Sorry fuck went on in."

"But why didn't you have your .45's out?" asked Bell. "Those two—"

"Top told Cole to keep it in unless I told him... after that last fuck-up." He shrugged. "No reason to pull 'em, and Cole just went on in."

"You see all that stuff?" Bell asked. He had put on a poncho and stopped shivering. He ached all over, but now, away from the sight of Major Binh's brain, he was feeling better.

"Yeah, but I'm not sure what *that stuff* has to do with you two."

So they told him about Hayes and what had happened, pausing only to answer Landrieu's few questions. When they had finished, Landrieu made no comment, except, "Okay," and picked up the radio handset next to Meyer.

"Let's call for a Medevac to come get the dead gooks."

After he completed the call, he walked back inside to confer with Cole. Meyer and Bell, now drained of speech, waited in the jeep.

When he returned, Landrieu got into the driver's side. "We need to go back to the compound so that I can get a camera. You two can write up your statements. Cole can stay the fuck here... make sure nothing disappears." He started the ignition. "Just so you know, I'm in Criminal Investigation."

"No shit?" Bell said, sitting up in the seat. "You're CID?"

"No shit," said Landrieu. "I'll let the C.O. and first sergeant know about this, but it's my investigation now, and I report directly to brigade. We've been looking into the black market down here for months." He pulled the jeep onto the gravel road. "HQ sent me down after Beadle got settled in good."

"Is Beadle CID?" asked Meyer.

Landrieu gave a tepid laugh. "Not hardly. More like a magnet when it comes to things disappearing. Only no one can pin anything on him."

"Macavity, the mystery cat," Bell said, pulling the poncho closer around him. "You know anything about a raid on that place? QCs in the morning."

"Fuck no." He braked the jeep to a stop, and turned around in the seat. "Where did you hear that?"

***

At Landrieu's repeated knocks, Top stumbled out of his quarters wearing only his fatigue pants. His chest was a pale pink and surprisingly hairless between sagging tits. A ragged scar snaked down the left side of his gut and into his trousers.

Glowering at his three subordinates, he drifted first to one side, then the other, nodding his head and muttering in rambling sentences. After a couple of minutes of this, Landrieu set off to find the C. O. Left alone with Meyer and Bell, Top stared bleary eyed at them, then told them they were sorry excuses for soldiers. He wobbled off to his room, slamming the door behind him.

"If I didn't feel so bad, that would be funny," Bell said. He had removed the poncho and sat at a desk in his still-damp fatigues, trying to write a statement with hands that were almost under control. The clock over Bowman's desk said 2:20am.

At Captain Templeton's swift entrance, they jumped to their feet. Fully dressed in pressed fatigues, and looking fresh and alert, the C.O. strode briskly past them.

"At ease," he said, stopping at Top's desk. His stony eyes looked the two up and down, taking in their damp, rumpled condition.

Landrieu, a few steps behind the captain, tacked over to a file cabinet and retrieved a camera from the bottom drawer. First checking it for film, he headed to the door.

"I need to get back down there and document the crime scene before they take the bodies," he said over his shoulder to the captain. As he grabbed the doorknob, he added to Bell and Meyer, "I told him what happened."

Once Landrieu had gone, the C.O. pulled out the chair behind the first sergeant's desk and sat down. Meyer and Bell stood, hands behind their backs, feet apart, facing him.

"What were you fellows up to?" the captain asked, staring at them, his head cocked to one side. "Sergeant Landrieu told me some of it, but I want to hear it from you." So Landrieu was really a noncom.

Bell talked in fast sentences, with short pauses to catch his breath.

Realizing his explanation was disjointed and seeing a confused look in Captain Templeton's eyes, he tried to summarize, "Hayes and Major Binh are—well, they were—the main players in a black market operation. Tires, booze, PX stuff, currency... even weapons."

"And marijuana," Meyer interjected. Bell looked over at him, and Meyer shrugged. "The sacks in the storeroom."

"They were cleaning out the warehouse," Bell said, turning back to the captain, "disposing of the evidence. They didn't know we were there, but we would've been—"

"And you two private dickheads," the captain, glaring at them, broke in for the first time, "thought you could snoop around and be heroes, like a couple of cartoon characters—Scooby Doo or Deputy Dawg or some shit like that. Instead, you almost got killed. To boot, I end up with a dead gook major I have to explain to brigade," he paused, "or somebody does." He rapped his knuckles on the desk and rocked back and forth in the chair, a line of perspiration on his forehead gleaming in the fluorescent lights.

"That kind of crap is *not* your job. People like Landrieu do the snooping." His lips pursed, he shook his head slowly. "I should throw the book at you shits for almost fucking up his investigation."

"But, sir..." Bell started.

"Don't interrupt me," the captain snapped, raising his voice. The room was quiet as he drilled into them with dark, unyielding eyes, while they shifted uncomfortably on their feet.

"I'm not gonna do a goddamn thing with you," he finally continued, tapping his fingers on the desktop. "I'm leaving this shit hole... going to Germany. So you bunch of fuck-ups aren't my problem. Not anymore." He stopped, still staring at them without blinking or smiling.

They remained standing stiffly as before—supposedly at ease, feet apart, hands behind them. They both had figured out that it was useless to protest, to argue their good intentions.

The captain shook his head again and gave them a grim smile.

"And you'll probably end up in Cambodia in a few days." He slapped the top of the desk and rolled the chair back. "Finish your goddamn statements and get the hell outta here."

"Yes sir," Meyer and Bell answered at the same time and snapped to attention. The captain swung the swivel chair around and got up. Without another glance at them, he strode out of the orderly room.

Meyer looked over at Bell. "Nice guy." He threw the pencil he was holding down on Top's desk. "See what you got us into."

CHAPTER FIFTY-FOUR
Cambodia Bound

THEY DIDN'T REACH THEIR BUNKS UNTIL after 0330 hours, and Bell awoke at 0630 to Carter's heavy tread through the barracks and booming voice, "Get out of bed, you lazy shits." Followed by names: "Robert Cole, Hamilton Hodges, John Henry Dupre, Ernest Earnhardt," and two FNG's who had arrived the week before. "Pack your gear and check out a rifle. You're movin' out. Have your asses out front at 1300 hours with everything you got, and wear your flak jacket and steel pot." He paused for a breath. "You'll be joining the My Tho squad north of the ferry. From there it's westward ho for all you cowboys."

As he went past, Carter grabbed Bell's foot and gave it a rough jerk. "Specialist Bell, you report to the first sergeant, 1100 hours."

The clumping of Carter's boots continued into the corridor and over to the adjacent bay where he called the name of another FNG and told him to pack up and report outside with the others at 1300. As Carter thudded back into the corridor, he yelled at Meyer and told him to go see the first sergeant at 1130.

Bell groaned and turned over. Through the fog of exhaustion, he felt a wave of relief that Carter hadn't told him to pack and be outside with the others. *But maybe that means I'm going somewhere else— like a grunt unit. Or to Long Binh for a court-martial?* He shoved that thought out of his mind and tried to sleep, but couldn't. Around him, he heard those whose names had been called talking in low, nervous voices as they dressed and started the first rituals of packing.

They'd need him, he decided—now that the others were leaving—so maybe he was safe. Then back to the same old routine? He felt bad for Hodge. Poor bastard might go crazy over his wife. Again. But what could anyone do?

He tossed and became more worried about the meeting with Top. Maybe they really didn't need him. Was he going to be court-martialed, then sent to Cambodia with another group? Shipped off to a grunt unit in the Central Highlands?

He finally got up and started for the showers, stopping on the way to commiserate with Hodge, who was down on one knee, fumbling through the footlocker at the end of his bunk. He had just returned from seeing Top, he said in a hollow voice. He'd turned him down for a leave. Lots of divorces, Top said, wives having babies—probably not even his. Jody's got your girl and gone, he said. Hodge emitted a low sob and put his face down in his hands.

Feeling helpless, Bell uttered platitudes: he'd only be out there a few weeks; he could get R&R soon, maybe even a compassionate leave at his next unit. But Bell was thinking, *at least you're not in jail, you dumb fuck.*

Hodge's response of "no, no, it won't work out," had the sound of rising desperation. Giving up, Bell hurried off to the showers. He was afraid for Hodge, of what Hodge might do.

At breakfast, Bell found Hodge, Meyer, and Sanderson together at a table in the mess hall. Hodge toyed with his eggs, speaking only once to Sanderson to ask him to make sure that a package and a letter he was writing to his wife went out with the next courier run. Bell and Meyer were also subdued, since they had no idea what awaited them with the first sergeant. For a diversion, they told the other two about the previous evening, avoiding a full description of the end of Major Binh, at least while they ate their scrambled eggs and bacon.

"Hah," said Sanderson after they completed their story. "Hayes is a regular fucking gangster, like in the movies."

"He and the major both," Meyer added.

"The major was, but is no more," Bell said. Remembering the brain, its white convolutions and red mucous. Good thing he was starving.

Hodge said nothing, deep in his own thoughts.

"It appears that Madame Phoung is in business...," Bell corrected himself, "*was* in business with Hayes and Major Binh. But all was not sweetness and light. That grenade in the major's jeep—compliments of the dear madame."

"Why would they meet at the warehouse?" asked Sanderson. "Why not at Madame Phoung's or a bar somewhere?"

"They were divvying up the loot," Meyer said.

Bell waved his fork in the air. "Some of the goods had already been taken out of there. The sampans at night, they were ferrying shit into town." He took a bite of egg and swallowed it almost immediately. "Tony was shot by those bastards. Binh or Phan. Hayes said it... accused Binh..." He looked out the door and shook his head. "And the rope Phan was using to rig the grenades was exactly like what we saw next to Tony's body."

"Jesus fucking Christ! Sanderson said. "Why would they shoot him? Especially like that?" He shook his head, slowly. "He was just a boy."

"He was eighteen," Bell said. "Old enough to be drafted. Old enough to be running errands for Major Binh. Almost as old as Markovic."

"Goddamn shitty," Sanderson muttered, pushing his plate away. "Kid was fucking harmless."

"The *kid* got crosswise with Binh, ratted on him or something." Bell stopped and looked around. "Maybe he was working with the QCs. Or helping Madame Phoung double cross Binh. Or helping Hayes."

"Ar-r-gh, it's all crazy," said Sanderson. "Gives me the creeps."

It gave Bell the creeps, too, and he wondered what was going to happen to Hayes, now that they had exposed his racket. And where did that leave him and Meyer?

"What I don't understand," Sanderson said, leaning back in his chair, "is why they didn't take all that Mary Jane you said was down there."

"I don't think it was all marijuana," Meyer said. "Sacks on top felt different from the ones lower down."

"Yeah, Phan made off with only one of 'em, but they still had the rest of the night." Bell chewed on that thought, and then shrugged. "Maybe Sergeant Landrieu will figure it out."

"*Sergeant* Landrieu," Sanderson said, shaking his head. "Now there's a kicker. Never would've guessed it."

Meyer shoved his chair back, preparing to leave. "So, Bell," he said, "what was the connection with your suicide victim, what's his name?"

"Roberts."

"You kept trying to tie him into Binh and that group."

"I don't know." Bell shook his head. "There may be a connection, but I don't know what it is. Maybe he got in too deep, or someone was onto him. Maybe he just didn't want to live in this fucking place anymore and going home wasn't an option. I just don't fucking know."

During the remainder of the morning, the men shipping out packed their gear, filled small boxes with personal items they wanted to send home, and wrote letters to wives, mothers, and girlfriends. Bell and Hodge sat close to each other on Hodge's bunk and talked in funereal tones while Hodge packed old letters to send back to Glenda. Most of the conversation was about her, and why he had been picked to go, and what he would tell her in the letter he was writing since he couldn't call her.

Finally leaving Hodge to his letter, Bell wandered back to his bunk, where he escaped into the last chapters of *The Return of the King*. At 1055 hours, he roused from his fantasy world to go see the first sergeant.

In the orderly room, he found Spec. 4 Bowman in his usual place, looking straight ahead at his typewriter and filling in blanks on an army form, like the day Bell had arrived months before. Since Bowman was scheduled to go home in seven days, his solemn rosy-cheek countenance seemed to grow more cheerful by the hour. He nodded and smiled pleasantly at Bell.

"Top's not here. Just went to get his sixth cup of coffee." Bowman chuckled. "C.O. got him up at 0600."

Bell sank down on a folding chair that sagged to one side and waited silently for Top's return. Two large boxes with six brand new chairs had arrived the week before, but they were nowhere around. *Gone downtown*, he thought.

Bowman typed monotonously on, pulling out one form and replacing it with another: orders for those leaving. *Nothing but paper,* Bell thought, watching Bowman type, *and it changes lives forever. Like an M-16.*

At 1115 the first sergeant appeared, balancing a full cup of dark liquid in front of him and looking much steadier than he had in the wee hours of the morning. He waved for Bell to follow him into the C.O.'s empty office and, once inside, ordered him to close the door. Setting his cup on the bare desk, the first sergeant dropped into a low-backed chair behind it.

Bell stood in front, hands by his side, but not at attention, and waited.

"Bell, do you know why you're here?" A rasping growl.

"No, First Sergeant."

"You're here 'cause someone up there is lookin' out for your sorry ass." He stopped, eyeing Bell's nervous shifting from one foot to the other.

"You goddamn college shits deserve to go with the other fuck-ups, but the C.O.," he rolled his eyes, "took your name off the list. That fucking Meyer, too. And he's dropping the Article 15. Overrode Floyd." Top almost chuckled, but swallowed it in a grimace. "Fat little turd's already headed off to brigade, gonna be some Colonel's adjutant... But I don't know why the fuck the captain did it—especially after your shenanigans."

He stared at Bell as if he expected a response. Bell remained silent, absorbing the news. It felt like winning the lottery, or not being drafted. But not quite.

The first sergeant took a long swallow from his cup, placed it in front of him on the bare metal surface, and continued talking as he ran his fingers along the edge of the desk.

"He may be withdrawing the Article 15, but I'm not having you two *pink-os* pulling MP duty in my outfit." Glowering at Bell, he was silent for a moment, then took another sip from the cup, after which he fell into a coughing fit that ended with a hacking: "Had enough of your shit."

Scrunching down and pulling out a handkerchief from a side pocket, he wiped his mouth and nose, and then leaned forward over the desk.

"Bell, you're the new supply clerk." He paused, his head tilted to one side, watching him. "Think you can handle that, soldier—without fucking it up?"

"Yes, First Sergeant."

Bell suppressed a grin and stared without blinking at the gaunt, red-faced man in the chair. The close-set eyes that stared back at him, also unblinking, showed watery red edges.

"We're gonna have an I.G. inspection," Top said, shifting the coffee cup around in front of him. "I want the fucking inventories straightened out. *Ex-act-ly* what we have *right* now. Nothing more, nothing less. You understand?"

Bell understood. Inspector General meant trouble for Top. The records had to match up with the reality of what was there.

Not waiting for an answer, Top leaned back in the chair and rapped the surface of the desk with his knuckles.

"That Sanchez didn't do jack shit. The new supply sergeant from the hundred-and-first will be here next week." He squinted up at Bell and sighed. "Right before the I.G. Try to give him a clean slate, will you?"

"Yes, First Sergeant." Bell hesitated, and then veered off into uncharted waters. "Top, can't you do something to keep Hodge here? He's not like Cole and the others you're sending..."

Bell trailed off as the first sergeant's face froze, and then flushed a bright red.

"He... Hodges is a good man, and his wife is, you know," Bell plunged ahead, despite the deepening red hue of Top's face. "But he's not a soldier. He's... I don't know... he pretends to be tough, but he doesn't belong here. He's just a draftee who wants to go home, raise a family. He's really upset about his wife. He's stopped drinking." (*Well, maybe that one was a bit of a stretch.*) "He... he's just gonna get hurt if—"

"Goddamn it, Bell!" Top recovered his voice. "What the fuck do you think this is? Boy scout camp?" The watery eyes glared at him. "What do you think all these other men want?" Throwing a hand up in the air, he brought his fist down hard on the metal desk. "Why should you bunch of college pricks," he wheezed in his anger, "the few of you sorry fucks who actually got caught, have it any better than the rest of us? Why should you get rear echelon jobs and let the real men do all the fighting?"

He pounded the desk with his fist, as if he wanted it to be Bell's head, causing the cup to jump and slosh brown liquid down one side and onto the desk.

"First Sergeant," Bell said quietly, uncowed but shaking with anger, "we didn't ask for this. We didn't volunteer... and most of us don't believe in it. We're glad to let the real men go fight—if that's what you like. But there are millions of rich—"

"Don't give me that shit!" He slapped the desk with the palm of his hand, spilling more liquid from the cup. "We're doing our job, and you and Hodges *will do yours.* Like me and Carter... and... and all the other lifers here."

"Send me," Bell said.

The words came out almost as soon as the thought crossed his mind. Forced out by anger and pathos, by nihilistic feelings for himself and sorrow for Hodge. He could take it; he had no ties; no one depended on him.

Oh shit! My mother! The thought came to him in a flash.

"What did you say?" Top stared at him in disbelief.

"Send me... instead of Hodge."

Years later, when he thought back on this moment, it occurred to him that a person is defined not by what goes on in his mind, but by what he does, the choices he makes, and by what he says that others hear. And heed. A voice crying in the wilderness is no better than silence.

He had gone too far to turn back. He had volunteered, taken a stand for something. He didn't really want to go to Cambodia. But he had to do it. For Hodge. For himself. To prove that he could.

Without speaking, the first sergeant picked up a pen and moved it down a list of names on the top paper in a stack in front of him on the desk. He tapped the point by a name, and then looked up at Bell with squinting eyes, a look filled with suspicion.

"The orders have been cut," he said.

"But, Top—"

"Goddam you, you're stayin' here!" He hit the desk again with his palm. "Enough of this crap!"

"But—"

"Shut the fuck up!"

In the silence that followed, the first sergeant scowled morosely at Bell. Then he continued in a quiet, measured voice. "The new C.O.'s over in his quarters with Captain Templeton. After they finish, you *will* drive Captain Templeton to the airfield. Do you understand, trooper?" He paused, glaring at Bell through bloodshot eyes.

"I understand, First Sergeant." He sucked air in through his nose, and then let it out slowly through clenched teeth.

"Bell," the tone was almost pleading, "don't fuck this up." Top looked down at his hands resting on the desk. When he looked back up, his eyes seemed to focus on a point far in the distance. "A bunch of my guys got messed up during Tet. Watched a couple of 'em die." He paused, as if remembering. "There was a draftee... good man, but a pain in the ass—like you and your buddies. It hurt me. Hurt me a lot."

Top hit his chest with his fist. "You may not like me, *and* you may think I hate your college-boy guts." He stopped and screwed up his face, then nodded slowly. "And I guess I do—but goddammit all, you're still one of my people! And I'm gonna look after you, whether you like it or not." His face took on a weary, sad expression. "You boys are my family... only one I got. And if *I* tell you to do something, goddamn it, it's for your own goddamn good."

Bell thought, *my own good, my ass*, but he didn't say anything.

"Don't pull anymore tricks like last night. Just stick to your job."

Top drained his cup. Taking out his soiled handkerchief again, he wiped off the C.O.s desk with it. "Now get your ass outta here," he said, waving his hand toward the door.

"Yes sir, Top, sir." Bell, now calm—and even feeling a little sympathy for the man—still wanted to show him he wasn't defeated.

The first sergeant glared at him without responding. *Is the glare a little softer*, Bell wondered, *or is the man just weary?*

"Go on," Top said, his thin lips pressed in a grim smile. "Get moving. And tell that kike buddy of yours to come on in here."

Bell came to attention and made a sharp military about face. Then he ambled, like a civilian, to the door and out past Meyer, now the one sitting dejectedly in the tilted folding chair. Grinning, Bell gave a thumbs-up, and then jerked his thumb back toward the office where Top sat waiting for the next member of his family.

CHAPTER FIFTY-FIVE
Fire and Smoke

WAITING TO TAKE THE C.O. TO THE AIRFIELD, Bell loitered next to a jeep with a canvas top and a long antennae curving above it. Meyer stood beside him in the shade of the building, and together they watched the group leaving for Cambodia pile their gear into the back of a deuce-and-a-half.

Top had informed Meyer, so Meyer said with a laugh, that he was "a clown and a fuck-up" and no good as a cop and, like Bell, was being removed from MP duty. He'd be the new company clerk, replacing Bowman.

Tonight, the two fuck-ups had patrol one last time. They had agreed to celebrate their good fortune afterwards, but for now, they shared a deepening sadness as they watched the forlorn soldiers prepare to leave. Ernie and the FNG's climbed in the back of the truck first, then Dupre and Cole, and finally—Hodge. Only Cole seemed to move with any purpose, with anything more than a dazed lassitude.

Hodge threw his duffel bag and a small suitcase onto the truck bed and stood his M-16 against the side bench as he climbed in. Watching him, Bell shook his head, amazed they would let Hodge anywhere near a rifle. *They must really need warm bodies for this one.*

Glancing back at them from under the shadow of his steel helmet, Hodge exhibited the face of a condemned man on the gallows. He dropped heavily onto the seat, removed his helmet, and turned to stare down at his jungle boots.

Behind Bell, the screen door opened and slammed shut. Sergeant Hayes trudged past, giving Bell an eerie *deja vue* moment. The sergeant was half carrying, half dragging a large, over-stuffed duffel bag with his left hand. His right hand held the familiar briefcase, clamped tight against his leg. He said nothing to Bell and Meyer; he didn't even look at them.

"I'll be damned," said Bell. "What's he doing here? Fucker should be in the brig."

Hayes heaved his duffel bag into the back of the truck, between the feet of the exiles lined up along the sides, and disappeared around the passenger side of the cab without looking back at the building. He had no rifle or battle gear, just his tailored and starched fatigues and his field marshal's cap low over his eyes.

Meyer shook his head. "Makes you wonder."

From around the corner of the villa appeared Sergeant Beadle, folding a trip ticket with his thick fingers. Since his gear was already in the back, he strolled casually to the driver's side and opened the door. As usual, his fatigues were rumpled, loose around his legs and chest, and tight across his stomach and buttocks. Pausing, he turned, more like a ship listing to one side, and with one arm hooked through the open window, raised his right hand, palm forward. The gesture was followed by a wide grin.

Bell looked around and, finding no one else there, realized that Beadle was waving to him and Meyer. Hesitantly, he raised his own hand and returned the wave—and the grin—with a confused mix of feelings.

Beadle hoisted his bulky form onto the driver's seat. As the truck's door slammed shut, the screen door behind Bell swung open, and Landrieu sidled out. He made his way through the barrels and stopped beside Bell.

"Top said you'd give me a lift to the airfield. I'm done here, and I have to go to Saigon, to give my report."

"Okay." Bell paused long enough to clear his throat, and then asked, "What happened with Hayes? Why's he leaving," he pointed to the truck, "with them?"

"We were after the other one, Beadle... but we never got a thing on him." Landrieu stuck his hands in his pockets and looked away.

"And we don't have enough on Hayes to take him in."

"Ah, man, he was in it up to his neck," Meyer said.

"Your word against his." Landrieu turned to stare straight at Bell. "An eighteen-year veteran with a good record—and you've made it mighty damn clear you don't like lifers." He shook his head. "He was nowhere around when I got down there last night."

"Jesus Christ, Landrieu," Bell said, not believing what he was hearing, "you've been here for two goddamn months. You saw all that shit *down there*. The grenades came from here. Probably the tires, too."

"Maybe," said Landrieu. "I took a statement from Sergeant Hayes this morning, and he denies everything. He suggested you might be the ones in league with the ARVN major. Suggested I look into when *you* showed up *down there*."

"Bullshit," said Bell, clenching his fists. "Bull-fucking-shit. Why would we have been hiding? Did you check his briefcase? We told you about that."

"I haven't seen a briefcase, and I don't have any reason to check it. Brigade will get all of the statements and decide what they want to do. If we need to find Hayes, we know where he is." He paused and gave a taut smile to Bell then Meyer. "We know where the both of you are, too."

"You could go check the briefcase now," Meyer said quietly. "He has it in the truck."

Landrieu looked at Meyer for a few long seconds, then turned and strode back past the sandbags and through the door into the villa.

"Shit," Meyer said in a whisper.

Beadle had started the truck engine and was backing up from the fence to head out the front gate. Cole, Dupre, Hodge, Ernie the cook, and the FNG's stared out the back, duffel bags and suitcases piled at their feet, rifles propped against their knees. They all wore flak jackets and held their steel pots on their knees, except for Cole who wore his helmet at a jaunty angle.

Before the screen door could close behind Landrieu, Top caught it and bounded outside. In one hand, he carried a clipboard raised to eye level.

"Yo! Hold up," he yelled, as the truck coasted toward the gate bunker. At the yell, Beadle's eyes appeared in the side-view mirror, and he braked the truck to a stop.

Waving his clipboard, Top lurched across the parking area and up to the deuce-and-a-half's tailgate.

"Cole, get your ass outta there," he said, his voice lower, but loud enough for Bell and Meyer to hear. "You ain't goin' nowhere." He hit the tailgate with his clipboard. "We gotta keep some real men here—somebody who can fight."

***

On the way to the airfield, the captain and Landrieu said little to each other or to Bell. But before the captain appeared with his bags, Bell did managed to pry out of Landrieu that Hayes had volunteered for the Cambodia mission, which, Bell surmised, must've dampened brigade's interest in pursuing an investigation. They needed bodies, or perhaps Hayes' connections worked for him again.

Bell also learned that Sergeant Beadle had gladly accepted a new logistics assignment. He'd be handling supplies for the MPs in Cambodia—*a great opportunity for a shrewd businessman,* Bell thought as he drove past Madame Phoung's. In front of the green gate stood a gaggle of American soldiers, waiting for it to open and admit them to the madame's pleasures. Business was good there, too.

At the airfield, Bell carried the C.O.'s duffel bag through the entrance of the makeshift terminal and to the door leading to the flight line, where the captain and Landrieu would board a C-123 for Saigon. Lugging the heavy bag across the open cement floor, he considered thanking the captain for dropping the Article 15 and removing him from the list for Cambodia—and perhaps mention Hodge. He thought better of it when they stopped at the door and he confronted the captain's set, unsmiling face.

He saluted instead and said, "Good luck, sir."

Barely glancing at him, the captain returned the salute and handed his valise to a soldier loading a baggage cart. The captain's face looked lined, less like the smooth black marble that Bell remembered from when he first arrived. The short black hair had sprinkles of salt all across it.

Captain Templeton was almost through the door when he stopped. He turned slightly to look back—and nodded at Bell. "Good luck, Specialist." He hesitated, his lips pressed together, then added, "You need to thank Sergeant Carter."

With that, he hurried out to the plane. Following a few steps behind, Landrieu gave a perfunctory wave and disappeared through the door. Outside, the plane's engines were rising to a thrumming roar.

Safely rid of his charges, Bell sauntered across the open terminal, his hands in his pockets, toward the daylight of the exit. Turning over the captain's final words in his mind—thinking about Sergeant Carter and trying to understand why he should thank Carter and knowing he wouldn't. Then he started to worry about why the captain had wished him luck.

Meyer's right, he told himself. *I need to stop obsessing about things I don't understand and can't change. Just deal with reality.* Shoving aside his anxieties, he took in the bustle of soldiers coming and going around him, catching snatches of their ribald, macho conversation, and enjoying it. He was in no hurry to get back to the compound and night patrol. He felt almost free.

While the fresh passengers boarded, the ones from the newly arrived C-123 from Saigon were straggling into the terminal after picking up their bags on the tarmac. Bell had almost reached the open exit to the parking area when a voice called out behind him.

"Hey, ding-a-ling, how about a lift?"

Bell turned and saw a thin, pale figure that looked familiar.

"Walker, that you?"

"In the flesh," the soldier replied, "but mostly bones."

Walker was many pounds lighter and almost as gaunt as an old papa-san, his fatigues hanging on his limbs like a scarecrow, his gaunt face making him look less like Napoleon than a pale asylum imitation.

As Walker dropped his bag on the concrete floor, Bell reached out and gripped a bony hand. Walker's other arm stretched across Bell's shoulder, and Walker gave him a hug as light and brief as a passing breeze.

"They sent you back here?" Bell asked. "Why didn't you go home?"

"Malaria's not enough for a ticket home. Docs say I'm better." Walker sighed in a weary voice. "For a while, I get reduced duty, then I serve out my time. Like everybody else."

"You need to talk to Sergeant Sanchez."

Walker didn't respond, but instead looked around like he was searching for someone. "All I got's this bag," he said, holding up the small satchel and patting Bell on the shoulder. "You saved me from having to call for a ride."

On the way outside, Walker asked about Kikki, and Bell told him. Walker hadn't heard from her in weeks, and no one had let him know that she had died. Now, he gave no reaction—no sound, no movement of the head and shoulders, nothing. He just continued walking straight ahead. He was silent as he tossed his bag into the back of the jeep and fell into the passenger's seat. As the jeep jerked onto the airfield's main boulevard, he reached up and rubbed his forehead, then wiped his eyes with a skeletal hand.

"Life's a bitch," he said. And that was it. He reached over and placed his hand on Bell's shoulder. "Hey, let's go out the engineers' gate." He pointed toward a side road. "It's quicker, and you don't go through town."

Bell knew the route, but he didn't often use it because it went around the airfield perimeter instead of through the areas they patrolled—and he knew it wasn't quicker. It just avoided the town.

He swung the jeep around the corner and started down the

perimeter road. A line of choppers taking off from the Air Cav muster area flew low over the road, buffeting the jeep and deafening its occupants, before banking toward the west. The sun reflecting off the windshield of one of the Hueys briefly blinded him as he stared up at the green-clad figures in the open side doors.

Driving slowly, he watched the dark line, like a perforated dragon's tail, move across a patch of bright blue sky and then under a mass of white clouds high above the green paddies beyond the perimeter. Soon the roar of the rotors faded to a low hum.

In the distance, to the left of the choppers, a wispy column of black smoke rose from an area near the edge of the base.

"What's that over there?" Bell asked and pointed at the smoke.

"Shit detail. They burn buckets of shit from the latrines out there." Walker chuckled, a rasping sound deep in his chest. "Didn't you know that? Long as you've been here? Horrible damn job."

"Yeah, I knew that." Remembering Hayes at My Tho, telling the FNGs that the black smoke over Fire Base Schroeder was shit burning, and he had been wrong.

"Never paid much attention to it before," Bell said. Then he added as an afterthought, "Guess burning shit's not as bad as being out in the boonies."

"Yeah, well, them poor bastards get both. Get sucked right down into it, one big burning vat of shit."

As they drew closer, he could smell the smoke, now thicker and darker, and see three figures lugging cut-in-half metal drums from a deuce-and-a-half over to where several other half barrels had flames and smoke rising out of them. A gust caught the entwined columns of smoke and shifted them down over the jeep. The stench was gagging, rancid, far worse than the smell along the canals and ditches in town.

"Ah, the aroma," said Walker, holding his nose. He flung a hand out toward the burning drums. "An offering to the gods of war."

"Yeah, incense in the temple of Nam."

One of the three soldiers, a tall black man who looked like

Meyer's friend Stick, sloshed a dark liquid, diesel fuel, into a half barrel a short distance from the two already aflame. A shirtless white soldier threw a match into the fresh barrel while a second black soldier, his torso glistening in the hot sun, watched from a few feet away. As Walker and Bell went past, flames shot out from the barrel, and the three soldiers leaped back, scrambling to escape a jagged tongue of fire.

ABOUT THE AUTHOR

MUCH OF THE MATERIAL FOR *QL 4* COMES FROM JIM GARRISON'S EXPERIENCES WITH THE U.S. ARMY MILITARY POLICE IN THE MEKONG DELTA IN 1969–70. He travelled from a blue-collar, small-town life to his first year in Duke Law School to Vietnam as an army MP in far less time than it took him to write *QL 4*. The endemic violence, corruption, and poverty, as well as the daily challenges of being a military cop in a war zone, left a lasting impression that reached well beyond his years of practicing law.

Garrison returned to Duke Law School following Vietnam and during his legal career wrote reams of briefs and other legal folderol. He began writing *QL 4* after his son asked, "What did you do in the war, Dad?" and then challenged him to write about it.

The novel is shaped by Garrison's belief that life is determined by choices made, even when those choices must be made in the middle of the Vietnam War in the Mekong Delta.

Garrison's law career came to a close when he was paid to go away in a corporate merger. To his wife's chagrin, he decided to stay home for the kids, one living in Germany, the other in Delaware (just in case they called) and to pursue his first loves, reading good literature and writing. That's when he started *QL 4*, which he'd been mulling over for years. Garrison is represented by Loiacono Literary Agency.